RECKLESS

RECKLESS

ANDREW GROSS

Don't Look Twice
The Dark Tide
The Blue Zone

NOVELS BY ANDREW GROSS
AND JAMES PATTERSON

Judge & Jury
Lifeguard
3rd Degree
The Jester
2nd Chance

RECKLESS

ANDREW GROSS

**Doubleday Large Print
Home Library Edition**

wm
WILLIAM MORROW
An Imprint of HarperCollinsPublishers

FIRST EDITION

ISBN 978-1-61664-261-7

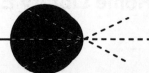

**This Large Print Book carries the
Seal of Approval of N.A.V.H.**

To the memory of Eleanor Zorman—a devoted fan, but an even better mother-in-law

RECKLESS

London.

Beep, beep! Beep, beep!"

Amir, "Marty" al-Bashir's six-year-old son, raced his motorized Formula One model around the dining room table, almost crashing it into Anna, the Lebanese housemaid, as she brought out their Sunday lunch of flatbread and spiced lamb.

"Amir, watch out!" his mom, Sheera, yelled. "You'll run Anna over. Marty, is it not possible for you to tell your son to stop?"

"Amir, listen to your mother," Marty called from the den, distracted. He and his older son, Ghassan—they called him Gary—were crouched in front of the wide-screen TV in the midst of a crucial football match. Manchester United versus Chelsea. The match was scoreless with only seconds remaining in the first half, and Man U was his son's favorite team—they had just acquired Antonio Valencia, his favorite winger and the hottest foot in the game.

"Oh, no, look!" Gary shouted as Marty focused back on the screen. A Chelsea attacker had curled a thirty-meter beauty just inside the left post, an inch beyond the Manchester goalie's outstretched dive.

"Damn, now look what you've made me miss, Sheera," Marty groaned, deflated, "a goal!"

"A goal, big deal. Your son is driving that thing around the house like Jenson Button. Amir, *listen* . . ." Sheera's voice grew firm. "If you don't stop this instant, you can forget about going to Universal Studios when we are in L.A. *Do you hear?*"

As if on autopilot, the model race car came to a stop. From the floor, Amir caught his father's amused gaze and grinned sheepishly. "Yes, I hear, Mama."

"Come on, boys, your mom's gone to a lot of trouble for us. Let's eat." Marty rose and the family drew chairs around the sleek van der Rohe table in the stylishly decorated town house.

Outside, the view from the wide third-floor window of their fashionable Mayfair Georgian was over Hyde Park, among the most desirable views in town. The home cost close to six million pounds, but as the chief investment officer of the Royal Saudi Partnership, a sovereign fund of Marty's native Saudi Arabia, it was hardly more than a rounding error on the daily tallies of one of the largest troves of investment capital in the world.

"Marty," which al-Bashir had been called for years, was simply an Americanized form of Mashhur, his birth name, given to him in his undergraduate days when he had studied under Whiting and McComb at the University of Chicago and followed up with stints in portfolio strategy at Goldman and Reynolds Reid, and in private equity at Blackstone in New York.

It was only back home in his native country that Marty was called anything else.

Now he oversaw a giant fund with interests that stretched to every point on the globe and every conceivable type of asset.

Stocks. Mezzanine capital. Currencies. CDOs. Complex derivatives. They also had vast real estate holdings—in New York's Rockefeller Center and London's own Trafalgar Square. When the price of oil rocketed, they bought up ethanol-producing sugarcane fields in Brazil. When the commodity fell, they bought up offshore U.S. development leases and massive tankers. Royal Saudi's holdings were more than a trillion dollars. Their hands were in everything. In times of crisis, they had even been called on to prop up many national treasuries around the world.

He and Sheera had met in the U.S. while he was at Reynolds and she, a daughter of a prominent law professor from Beirut, was studying economics at Columbia. They'd been married for twelve years. The job had given him ease—most would say luxury—and over time, they had acquired many Western ways. They had a flat on the Côte d'Azur, a penthouse in the Trump Tower on Fifth Avenue in New York; they took the family skiing at Gstaad and Aspen; Gary and Amir were enrolled in the finest schools. His only regret was that, to appease the royal family's wishes, his wife had had to give up her own career to raise her family. Sometimes he wished that despite his rise to the top of the financial world and the important responsibilities that had been bestowed on him, if she could handle the investments and he could manage the kids, both their home *and* the Saudi royal portfolio would be in better hands.

Sunday was their traditional family meal. Afterward, they might head a few blocks away to Hyde Park and kick the football around a bit. On the way back, they might stroll along Shepherd Market window-shopping the fine antiques and new fashions. These days, with teleconferencing and the financial network set up here, he jetted home barely twice a year, mostly to see his folks. He had been away from Riyadh for so many years, distanced himself from their customs, that Marty pretty much thought of the royals as clients now rather than brethren. And he knew, because of the results he produced, his overseers looked the other way.

"Okay, who wants first?" Marty picked up a plate and looked around. "The *cook!*" he said proudly, and spooned some of the stewed lamb over the yogurt and bread and handed it to his wife, serving her first in the Western way. If his parents ever saw him, they'd be horrified.

The trill of his cell phone sounded from somewhere in the house. His office.

Sheera shook her head and groaned. "Now on Sundays too?"

"I'll make it short. Promise." Marty got up. "You just make sure you save me some of that lamb." He winked a warning at Amir, whose appetite seemed to never end.

With the vast amount of activity Royal Saudi controlled there was no such thing as boundaries when it came to nights or weekends. Their interests ran every day, 24/7, across the globe. Though the aroma of lamb and fresh baked bread made ignoring the call momentarily tempting.

Marty followed the ring to his office and shut the door, stepping over the cables to the Wii video game attached to the TV. Gary's Christmas gift—another Western concession! The BlackBerry was vibrating on the coffee table and Marty sank himself onto the couch, tightrope-walking over the brightly colored Lego Transformer that had been left on the floor; this one was Amir's.

Never ends, he sighed.

He expected it to be Len Whiteman, his second at the firm, but Marty's mood shifted when he checked the digital read-out and saw "Private Caller." His stomach clenched. Cautiously, he drew the phone to his ear. "Hello?"

"I hope this call finds you well, Mashhur al-Bashir."

The use of Marty's Saudi name jolted him. He knew immediately who it was. The first call had come six months ago, preparing him. He had just been hoping against hope, as time marched on, as their lives grew and prospered and became more acclimated, that the real call would never come.

"I am well," Marty replied, his throat dry, returning the greeting in Arabic.

"Our sons and daughters around the world require your service, Mashhur al-Bashir. Are you prepared to do what is asked of you?"

Marty thought to himself that it had been so long. His views, passions, had all been so different then. Never religious, or even political. It was simply more about pride in his culture. The dismissive manner in which his nation had been treated by the West. They had given him his start, his education. Now he had lived among them for years and had changed.

Six months ago the first call had come. Reminding him of his duty. What he was expected to do. In a flash, all the prosperity in his life and the good fortune he had earned seemed a universe away. There was no turning away from this. He realized he owed them everything. All his good fortune. He had made his bed a long time ago.

"Yes," Marty al-Bashir answered dutifully.

"Good. The tide of events is evolving," the caller said, "don't you agree? Global opportunities have shifted. We, here, are not happy with certain signs. We feel it is time for a change in direction. In strategy. Do you understand?"

"I have a new plan already drawn up," Marty replied. He knew the ramifications that would result from it and he closed his eyes.

"Then begin it," the caller said, "starting tomorrow. Execute your job, Mashhur al-Bashir. The rest is already set." The caller paused a second. "Shall we say, the planes are in the air."

They hung up, the sounds of his family, laughing, returning from outside. Marty remained on the couch for a while.

All he knew and had grown used to was about to change.

He got up and stepped over to the window, accidentally kicking over his son's Transformer, the Lego pieces flying about. *"Damn."*

Tomorrow, the world would wake up, go to school, to work, laugh, love, eat with their family, everything seeming the same. But by day's end there would be a change like the world had never seen.

He bent down and picked up his son's broken Transformer, the brightly colored pieces all around.

"God, help us all," Marty al-Bashir muttered in perfect English.

PART I

PART I

CHAPTER ONE

They entered the house through the sliding glass doors in the basement, which Becca, their fifteen-year-old, sometimes left ajar to sneak in friends at night.

Upstairs, April Glassman stirred in her bed. She always had an ear for noises late at night. The curse of having a teenager. Marc could go on snoozing forever, through fire alarms, she would joke, but April had a built-in antenna for the sounds of Becca tiptoeing in past curfew or Amos, their goldendoodle, on guard at the living room window, scratching at the glass over a late-night deer or squirrel.

The house was a large, red-brick Georgian at the end of a private drive off Cat Rock Road in backcountry Greenwich. Every bend in the wood seemed to magnify at night. She opened her eyes and checked the time on the TV cable box. Two thirteen A.M. She lay there for a few seconds, listening. She definitely heard something—creaks on the floorboards, muffled voices—in the foyer or on the stairs.

Suddenly Amos started barking.

"Marc . . ." She nudged her husband.

"Honey, *what*?" Marc Glassman groaned, mashing his pillow into a ball and rolling over.

She leaned over and shook his arm. "I heard something."

"Probably just Amos. Maybe he spotted a deer. You know those bastards never decide to come out before two A.M."

"No," she said, alarmed. "I heard voices."

"Okay, okay . . ." Marc exhaled, giving in. He opened his eyes and took a peek at the clock. *"Grrr* . . . I'm sure it's just Becca . . ."

Their daughter now had a boyfriend at the high school, a junior on the wrestling team, who drove, introducing a whole new set of complications to their lives. Lately she'd been sneaking out after the two of them had gone to sleep, or on weekends, sneaking in her friends at all hours of the night.

"No. It's a Sunday, Marc," April replied, recalling how she had kissed her daughter good night hours ago and left her curled up in bed with Facebook going strong and a chemistry textbook on her lap.

"Not anymore . . ." Groggily, he sat up, rubbing a hand across his face, flicking on the light. "I was just gonna get up and check out the overnights anyway."

As the chief equities trader at Wertheimer Grant, one of Wall Street's oldest firms, it had been months since he slept a whole night through. Singapore opened at midnight, Australia an hour later. Europe and Russia got going at four. Six months ago he might've made it undisturbed till morning. But that seemed like a lifetime ago. Now the bottom had fallen out of the market. The whole subprime mess, Fannie and Freddie reeling, AIG. The banks teetering. Not to mention the company's stock: a year ago it was over eighty and he and April could have gone off and planted tomatoes somewhere for the rest of their lives. Last

Friday it had closed at twelve! It would take him another decade to recoup. Immediately flashing to his positions, his stomach wound into its usual two A.M. knot.

Now April was hearing voices . . .

"I'll go take a look."

In the last months, April had watched as her husband dropped ten pounds from the stress. She knew that something was wrong. She knew the firm was hurting and how much they were relying on him. How much he was expected to produce. Marc never shared much about his positions anymore. The pressure on him was crazy.

She leaned over and put her hand on his shoulder. "Honey, will this ever go back to normal?"

He threw off the covers and grabbed his robe. "This is the new normal."

That's when they both heard another noise.

A creak on the stairs. Marc put a finger to his lips for her to keep quiet.

Then another. Closer. A knife slicing through them.

Someone was coming up the stairs.

"*Marc . . .*" April caught his eyes. Her

look was laden with worry. "Amos stopped barking . . ."

He nodded, feeling the same thing inside. "I know."

The next creak seemed to come right from the upstairs landing. April's heart skipped a beat. Her husband's gaze was unmistakable.

Someone was in the house.

"Just stay there," he said, nodding to the bed, raising a hand for her to stay silent.

They all knew about the recent rash of home break-ins going on in the backcountry. They were all just talking about it last Saturday night with the Rudenbachs at Mediterraneo. Marc listened closely at the door. They never put on the alarm. What the hell did they even have the damned thing for, he'd asked himself a hundred times. Just wasting all that stupid money. Truth was, he couldn't even remember the damn code—or even where the panic button was.

"Marc . . ."

He turned. He stared at April's freckled face, her soft, round eyes, hair raised in a nighttime ponytail. Except now, he saw only fear in it. And helplessness. *"Becca, Evan . . . ,"* she whispered.

Their rooms were just down the hall.

He nodded firmly. "I'll go check it out."

He took a step, and suddenly the bedroom door flew open. Two men, wearing ski masks and plain blue work uniforms, pushed their way into their room.

April let out a scream.

"What the hell is going on? What are you doing in here?" Marc stepped up to them.

The first one in the overalls suddenly knocked him with a fist to his face back onto the bed.

"Marc!" April reached out to him.

Her husband removed his hand and stared at his fingers. There was blood on them.

"What the hell do you want?" he demanded.

"Shut up," the first one said. The man was large, his voice husky. A tuft of red hair peeked out from behind his mask. He had a gun, accounting for the blood in Marc's mouth. "Just shut the fuck up and you might just live."

"Oh, God, Marc, please . . . ," April murmured, her heartbeat now accelerating

wildly. Her thoughts flashed to her children sleeping down the hall. *Just keep them away.*

The second man shut the bedroom door behind him. The one with the gun came over and pulled April off the bed. "Get up. Put your hands behind your back." His accomplice took out a roll of duct tape from his uniform and twisted April's wrists behind her back, binding them tightly. She looked at her husband with fear in her eyes as he ran a second piece of tape across her mouth.

"What do you want with us?" Marc pleaded, helpless, watching his wife being bound. "Listen, I've got a safe downstairs. We've got some money . . ." He shot April a steadying look, as if he was trying to say, *Hang in there, honey. It'll be okay. That's why they're here. For the money.*

This isn't the first one. No one's been hurt so far.

"*Where?*" the one with the gun demanded.

"Downstairs. In the study. I'll show you. Look, we haven't seen your faces. We don't know who you are. Just take what you want and let us go, okay?"

"Show me." The man with the gun grabbed him by the arm and pulled him up.

That was when, to both their horror, the bedroom door opened again and their daughter, Becca, half-asleep, wearing a baby-blue Greenwich High sweatshirt and rubbing her eyes, wandered in. "What's going on, guys . . . ?"

Before she could even let out a scream, the second intruder grabbed her and covered her mouth.

"Please don't hurt her!" Marc begged, seeing his daughter's face turn white with alarm. "She's just a kid . . ."

Eyes wide, April struggled against her binds, trying to go to her. *Oh, baby, no, no . . .*

Becca tore the man's hand away. *"Mom!"*

They watched, unable to do a thing, as the second intruder wrapped the tape around Becca's mouth and roughly bound her hands. Her uncomprehending eyes were round with fear.

"Throw 'em in there," the man with the gun directed his accomplice, pointing to the master closet. Becca, who had always had a fear of small spaces, twisted her

head back and forth, trying to resist. Un-
heeding, the accomplice shoved the two
of them in. April fell to the floor, twisting
against her binds. *Don't do anything foolish,* she tried to say to Marc, desperation
in her eyes. *Just give them what they want.
Please . . .*

They shut off the lights in the closet and
closed the door.

Her daughter let out muffled screams,
writhing against April in the dark. All April
could do was huddle as close as she
could, trying to convey with all her strength
that everything would be okay. *Just stay
calm, baby. They're only here for money.
They're going to leave and this will all be
okay. Daddy will come get us. I promise,
honey, please . . .*

Tears glistened in her teenage daughter's eyes. April put her head against hers,
trying to transfer all her conviction and
strength, and she began to think, *Her hair
is so soft and she smells so pure, my little
girl . . . Now she'll remember this the rest
of her life. You bastards. You've stolen the
innocence from her. Her trust.* Her thoughts
flashed to Marc downstairs—*Marc, please,
just give them anything! Don't do anything*

heroic. Just let them go—and then to Evan, only seven, sleeping down the hall, her sweet little baby. *Just sleep, honey, through it all. It's going to be okay . . . Please, Evan, please. It's*—

That was when she heard the sound: two far-off pops, coming from downstairs.

April and Becca looked at each other. She'd heard it too. April's heart began to leap with fear.

Marc.

Panicked, tears started to run down her cheeks. *What did you do, Marc? What did you fucking do?*

Suddenly, there were footsteps. Heavy ones, pounding back up the stairs. Becca squealed, her large eyes doubling in size. The whole house seemed to shake.

What did you do?

Desperately, April fought against her binds. She looked at her daughter. All she could do was simply press herself into her as tightly as she could, panic building in her daughter's eyes.

My babies . . . April started to cry, her thoughts flashing to Evan as the approaching thuds entered the room. *Oh my God, what's going to happen to him, my poor little sleeping boy? Do whatever you have to do to me, but please, not him. Not to Becca.*

The closet door flung open. Light burst into their eyes.

Not my babies, April tried to scream. She threw herself in front of Becca. *Not them, not them . . .* She stared back at the hooded faces with eyes that were both begging and defiant.

Please . . .

CHAPTER TWO

Remind me again," Annie Fletcher asked, wiggling out of her navy U of Michigan T-shirt. "Why is it they always call it *blue* Monday?"

"No idea," Hauck gasped, his breaths quickening, gulping in air.

She rocked above him, hands balanced against the rattling headboard, swaying in perfect rhythm to the thrust of his thighs. Annie's body was small and light, but her breasts were full, and her short, dark hair fell over her face, still messy from sleep.

In the background, the newscaster

on the early morning show announced brightly that it was going to be a clear and sunny day.

"Never gonna think that way again," she said, starting to really heat up. Because of the demands of her restaurant and Hauck's new job—not to mention her son, Jared, moving east with her and boarding five days a week at a nearby school for kids with special needs—they only got to see each other a couple of days a week, and so things tended to be very physical between them.

"Me either," Hauck huffed, cupping her thighs, the rush of climax coming on.

They had been together for six months now—on and off, mostly on—Annie's responsibilities at the restaurant clashing a bit with Hauck's commitment to the new job. She didn't push for more. He didn't offer. Annie was trusting and open. It wasn't so much a relationship as it was a loose, easy friendship—*with benefits*—what time would allow.

Their rhythm grew faster and faster. Sweat coated their skin. "Thought you had to get to the market . . . ," he said to her, feeling her breaths beginning to deepen and knowing she was only a few accelerating tremors from letting out.

"Damn arctic char are just gonna have to wait . . ."

The voice from the TV said stock futures were trending down again for the fourth day in a row.

But Hauck and Annie weren't listening. Their IRAs could have been in total free fall and right now neither of them would have given a damn.

Finally, with a last gasp, Annie arched, stiffening, then fell back onto him, joyfully spent of breath, draping her satisfied body over his, her chest feeling about a thousand degrees. "Damn." She sighed from her head all the way down to her little toes. "Now that's the way to start the workweek. That was a good one."

"That was *three*." Hauck flung back his arms in mock exhaustion. "I'm an old guy. You're killing me."

"*Three?*" She rested her chin on his chest. "Two, I think."

"*Two* since they talked about the transit fares going up," he told her. "One more since traffic and weather."

"Oh, yeah, *three*," she purred content-edly, releasing a long, slow sigh. "Math was never my strong suit."

Hauck turned and focused in on the digital clock. "Damn. Look at the time! I've got to scoot."

Annie restrained him as he tried to wrestle free, digging in her chin more sharply. "You know, I'm happy, Ty . . ." She smiled, a kind of coy, amused grin, being purposefully annoying. "Are you happy? You don't always look so. I know you're sort of a tough nut to crack."

"Apparently *not*," he said, chuckling at the lame joke. "And yeah, sure, I'm happy . . ." He tried to roll her off. "I'll be happy if I can get you off of me and hop into the shower."

"Oh, right," Annie chortled, "like this wasn't exactly what you had in mind when you snuggled over to me before the alarm went off . . ."

"Alright, maybe," Hauck admitted a little guiltily. *"One . . ."*

"You're just a glass-half-empty kind of dude, aren't you? Never show too much of yourself. Never trust the moment."

"I'm not half-empty at all." Hauck finally

spun her off and faced her sideways. "I'm actually completely half-full. It's just that it's buried. *Very, very* deep."

"Right; if it were any deeper, you'd find oil in it," Annie said, and deciding it was funny, twisted his nose.

"Laugh-out-loud," Hauck said, screwing up his face. But then he laughed too.

That was because, truth be said, he *was* happy. The lines etched in his face might not have shown it, but Annie had brought things out in him he had never let surface before. The uncomplicated will to just enjoy life. To relax, stay in the moment. For the first time, it seemed things that had weighed heavily on him for so long—the deaths of his daughter, eight years before; his brother, only last year; and Freddy Munoz, his protégé on the force—all seemed to have been pushed back into some closed, time-locked vault he no longer felt compelled to open and to which he had momentarily lost the key.

Not to mention the fact that he had suddenly left the force and gone into the private sector. After fifteen years.

Now he traded up to a jacket and tie every day and had spiffy new digs in an office park on the water. Earning three times what he had before. He had colleagues in Europe and Asia on his speed dial. He even glanced through the *Wall Street Journal* every morning, pretending he was keeping abreast of business news, after he checked the sports scores on ESPN.com, of course. He had opened himself up to a new feeling, the arc of his new life seeming to work out. He was, like Annie pushed him to do, trusting the moment. Okay, maybe like he'd said, it *was* somewhere down deep, somewhere that didn't come up to the surface very often. But it had been a long time since he felt this way. Boundaryless. Free of regret.

"Really, I gotta get up," he said. He lifted her off. "I'll do the coffee."

Annie fell back against the pillows, groaning loudly, "Alright . . ."

The news anchor came back on. "And now, back to our lead from the top of the hour . . ."

The congestion on the Merritt Parkway had given way to something far more serious.

"In Connecticut, the town of Greenwich is waking this morning to a horrifying triple murder. An equities trader at a prestigious Wall Street firm was brutally shot to death during the night along with his wife and daughter in their expansive home in back-country Greenwich. Cindy Marquez is on the scene . . ."

Hauck sat up, his years as head of detectives taking over, as the attractive reporter, bundled against the cold, stood in front of two large stone pillars leading to a typical Greenwich home.

"Kate, the local police believe that the motive behind this family's tragic end was simply a robbery gone bad. A string of break-ins up here has rocked this affluent community for months. But until now, none had ever turned so violent.

"Marc Glassman"—a photo flashed on the screen—"who was forty-one and worked as a lead equities trader for troubled Wall Street giant Wertheimer Grant, was found shot downstairs in their posh five-bedroom home off of Cat Rock Road . . ."

Hauck sat up. A tremor knifed through him.

"Hold it a second," he said, disentangling

from Annie's legs. He stared, his heart rate accelerating, as he edged closer to the screen.

"The bodies of his wife, April, who was well known in local charities and schools, and their teenage daughter, Rebecca, were found in an upstairs closet. A younger son . . ."

Hauck fixed again on the photo. A shot of the family in happy times. His mind raced as the reporter described the grisly scene; he fixed on the husband—slightly receding hair, in a fleece pullover and sunglasses, one arm around his daughter, who was wearing an oversize college sweatshirt and had long brown hair, and the other arm around another child, a son, younger, a mop of yellow hair and smiles.

Then he focused in on the wife.

Pretty. Happy looking. In a green baseball cap, her light-brown hair, in a ponytail, peeking through the vent. A beautiful smile that was both proud and tragic at the same time.

"*Oh, God . . .*" Hauck groaned, sucking in a fortifying breath.

"I know, it's horrible," Annie said. She

came up behind him and rested her chin on his shoulder, staring past him at the screen. "Are you okay?"

He nodded silently, not an answer as much as it was all he could do. A heavy weight fell inside him.

"I knew her," he said.

CHAPTER THREE

The gleaming white Dassault Falcon touched down gracefully at Westchester County Airport, only a stone's throw from the Greenwich town line.

The sleek six-passenger jet taxied off the runway to the NetJets private hangar. When the engines cut off, the door opened, and the attached stairway lowered down. An attractive couple stepped off—a stylish woman in her forties, blond hair flowing from underneath her cowboy hat, a fur draped around her shoulders; and her companion, dark complexioned, sunglasses, a little younger, in a navy cashmere blazer and jeans. The woman stopped at the top of the steps and said a word of thanks to the pilot, complimenting him on the landing.

"Always perfect, Mike."

"Always a pleasure, Mrs. Simons. We'll wait to hear from you on the Anguilla trip."

"I'll have Pam be in touch as soon as I know. You have a nice week."

As they stepped down to the tarmac, both wore the tan of a week of spring skiing in Aspen.

Merrill Simons was forty-four and a household name around the charity circuit in Greenwich. Over the years she had chaired dozens of balls, served on a thousand committees, pretty much knew everyone. That went hand in hand with being married for twenty-three years to Peter Simons, chairman of Wall Street's Reynolds Reid.

But that was all ancient history now. Their divorce had been finalized a year ago, six months after he had moved in with Erskina Menshikova, the Victoria's Secret lingerie model, granting Merrill the house on Dublin Hill, the place in Palm Beach, and the penthouse overlooking the park on Fifth

Avenue, not to mention continued use of the private jet.

The very same six months before the divorce was final, Merrill acknowledged, with a certain degree of relish, Reynolds Reid's stock had begun to collapse, due to the firm's heavy exposure in the mortgage crisis and the resulting wave of global sell-offs. She'd always suspected Peter didn't know shit about dealing with a balance sheet, any more than he knew about being a father or keeping a marriage together.

She'd gotten that one right!

Now she enjoyed the thought that he was probably sweating bullets with a net worth about a quarter of what it was at the time of their settlement and was probably no longer able to get it up with his silky-thighed, golden-haired trophy catch. Which was only a matter of time anyway, she knew firsthand—regardless of Reynolds's stock plunge.

Merrill had found her own "new chapter to write" as well, as Pete had aptly phrased it the day he told her he wanted to leave. Dani Thibault was handsome and successful in his own right. He had business interests throughout Europe—hotels and commercial office deals—partially financed by his ties to the Belgian royal family. He was a breeder on the polo circuit. Wind-surfed. Skied like he'd been born on them. He didn't seem to need her money, and he seemed to love how he had awakened her forty-four-year-old body from its long slumber. He did things to her that her hus-band hadn't done since he was a trainee back in the bond department. Actually, had *never* done, if she was truthful! Dani seemed to know the world—he could line up fabulous evenings at private clubs in London, could get a table at El Bulli near Barcelona or Robuchon in Paris. Even her kids—Louisa was in L.A. working at a pro-duction company, and Jason was still a junior at GW—were taken with him too and loved the fact that their mom had pulled herself up and transitioned to a new and happier life. *That she was getting laid.* Mer-rill's girlfriends in town, mired in their own tired, unfulfilling marriages, were ogling her in jealousy.

It was just that a few details that con-cerned her had recently come up. Regard-ing Dani.

She hadn't shared them with him. She'd

been keeping them to herself the entire trip. Things were getting deeper between them, and she'd begun to realize just how little she actually knew about him. About the man she was falling in love with.

And a little of what he had told her just wasn't adding up.

As they deplaned, two cars were waiting on the tarmac. One, a black, chauffeured Mercedes C 63 AMG, was Dani's. His familiar driver opened the door. The other was Merrill's own silver Audi wagon.

"I have to head into the city," Dani said in his hard-to-pin-down but definitely sexy European accent. She had guessed German; he said Dutch, with a touch of French in it, maybe, from Brussels. "I have meetings until five. Then we have this thing at the library tonight, right? I'll change at the apartment, if that's okay."

"Of course. I'll have Louis bring me in."

"Look smashing." He grinned, his hand sliding underneath her fur jacket and giving her butt a squeeze. "I'll walk around until I spot the sexiest woman there."

"Better be on time then," Merrill said, winking coyly. "Someone else may have the same idea."

"It's been lovely sharing the slopes with you, Ms. Simons." Dani clasped her fingers in his. "Let's do it again."

"And you, Sven." She giggled, using the ski-instructor fantasy name she had given him after two bottles of champagne. "Please feel free to come off the trail whenever you're in town."

He smiled, drawing her to him to give her a kiss. Merrill put her palm against his shirt and held him off just slightly, brushing her lips across his cheek. "I'll see you there."

His BlackBerry rang. He sighed when he saw the caller. "I have to take this," he said. He motioned to the driver and climbed into the backseat of the Merc. He waved to her. "Until tonight."

The black doors shut and the darkened window rose, slowly obliterating Dani's face.

Merrill's houseman, Louis, packed her bags in the Audi. He opened the door and she got in.

Yes, everything is perfect, she reflected. The Audi passed through the wire gate of the private terminal and wound onto the access road leading from the airport.

Everyone loved Dani. He was charming, affable, and successful, and he made her feel twenty years younger in bed. She'd be a fool to let something get in the way.

She didn't like the sensation of distrust gnawing inside her.

There was just this one thing.

"Back to the house, Ms. Simons?" Louis turned around and asked.

"Yes. I have to change. I have an appointment in town."

CHAPTER FOUR

They didn't talk about it much. Over their coffee. The grisly scene on TV.

Only that it was someone Hauck had known from around town, Annie lamenting how these break-ins were getting crazy and how lots of people were buzzing about it, even at the restaurant. She shook her head, bewildered. "And what kind of person could have done that to such a beautiful family? *For what?* Money?"

Hauck shook his head in dismay. He didn't know.

He chewed on seven-grain toast, quiet, leafing through the papers, until Annie realized he was still affected by it. There was something there that didn't seem to be going away.

"I know you feel you have to do something about this." She came around the counter and put her arms around him from behind, stroked her knuckles softly against his face. "But that's over now. You're a businessman now, right?"

He nodded halfheartedly.

She winked and pinched his nose. "So, go biz."

Hauck had been working for the Talon Group for six months now. He still felt a little awkward with the transition, being an executive for the first time in his life after being a cop for so long. Dressing up in a suit and tie, doing meet-and-greets at Fortune 500 companies, trying to close deals for data protection and internal forensics with corporate controllers and heads of company security who sometimes recognized his name from the prominent cases he had worked.

Part of him still felt like a fish out of water. Even when he deposited his paycheck and saw about three times what he'd been earning before.

Hauck showered and shaved, his short dark hair barely needing to be brushed. He still looked trim and fit in his towel, despite being on the other side of forty. He dressed, choosing an oxford shirt and a salmon-colored tie to go with his blazer. Annie hopped in as he was getting out. It was a visiting day at her son's school. Afterward she'd trade her dress for jeans and head to the restaurant.

In her towel and with wet hair, she straightened Hauck's knot when he came in to say good-bye. She centered his jacket across his shoulders and smiled, pleased. "You look nice."

"So do you," he said, his finger tracing along the edge of her towel. "We should pick up on that thought later."

"Sorry. *Later* I've got two turns for dinner and about two dozen lobster and jicama spring rolls to make. Rain check though."

"Deal. Anyway, say hi to Jared for me. You remind him I want to see him at practice Wednesday." Hauck had begun coaching a twelve-and-under hockey team and he was teaching Jared, Annie's son, who was nine and had Down syndrome, how to skate. The other kids seemed to like having him around and all picked up on his positive attitude. Jared seemed to enjoy it too.

"I will. And you sure you're okay, babe? I know how you can't do anything about that poor family now and how that makes you feel."

"I'm okay," he said, patting her butt. "Promise."

Annie smiled and pushed him to get out. "Like you would even tell me if you weren't . . ."

Downstairs, Hauck tossed the newspaper and his briefcase into the front seat of his new, white BMW 550i—the one change he'd allowed in his life since accepting the job with Talon, having traded in his ten-year-old, gas-guzzling Bronco—and pulled out of the garage.

He drove down to Greenwich on the Post Road, which ran parallel to the highway. Greenwich was different now. Even here, downturn had hit hard. For the first time in years, you could find vacancies along the avenue. Whole floors were now empty in the red-brick office complexes where once-inviolable hedge funds had reigned supreme. Word was that half the gated homes along North Street were privately for sale.

For years, the joke was that "white-gloved" cops directed the traffic on Green-wich Avenue, past Saks and Polo.

Now the cops were gone—no need anymore.

Stopping at a light, Hauck went over his day. He'd been trying to track down this mortgage "thief" who had closed on three multimillion-dollar refinancings on the same property on the same day—the county clerk's office having taken several months to catch up with the high volume in mort-gage recordings—and was now, surprise to no one, nowhere to be found. He also had a one o'clock with Tom Foley, his boss, who wanted him to meet someone.

At every light, the image of the murdered Glassman family kept edging into his mind.

C'mon, he urged himself, flicking on the radio. Like Annie said, *that chapter of your life is over now.* He had to accept there was nothing he could do. He turned to the all-sports channel and wove onto Bruce Park toward the bottom of Greenwich Avenue, past the station where he used to work, minutes from his new, fancy office on

Steamboat. He listened vacantly to the sports jockeys rambling on about the free-agent baseball signings, basketball play-offs, all the while his blood continuing to heat like a backed-up furnace and throbbing with a familiar ardor.

Are you okay? Ty . . . ?

No, he wasn't okay. He sat at the light with this pent-up feeling in his chest, fingers wrapped tightly around the wheel.

Until he couldn't take it anymore.

Hell with the new chapter.

As the light changed, he jerked the Beemer into a sharp left onto Mason, barely avoiding a turning bakery truck, its horn blaring. He sped back up the hill and onto the Post Road, swinging a left onto Stanwich, his heart racing with the same familiar rush he'd felt for twenty years.

CHAPTER FIVE

About two miles down, Hauck hung a right at Cat Rock Road, the fancy houses thinning on each side. A mile down, he ran into a police barricade, the winding road narrowing to one lane. A blue and white police car was set up blocking the road, waving only local traffic through. Hauck downshifted. A chain of news vans had pulled up on the side of the road like a caravan.

Lowering his window as he approached, Hauck saw a patrolman he recognized, Rob Feretti.

"Lieutenant!" the cop exclaimed, peer-

ing in the window, instinctually addressing Hauck with his old rank. "Nice wheels . . . What brings *you* out here?"

"Steve Chrisafoulis up there?" There were lots of flashing lights up near the house.

"He is, sir." Feretti nodded.

"You mind if I go through?"

"Thought you gave all this up?" The patrolman grinned. "The house is just up there on the left. It's a bad scene in there."

"I bet it is, Rob. Thanks."

He was waved forward, around a short bend where there were two more blue-and-whites stationed, lights flashing, blocking the entrance to a drive. Feretti had radioed ahead and Hauck was let through. Just a few months ago he was in charge of these men. No way the fact that he was a civilian would change that now.

He drove between the stone pillars and down a long, curving driveway leading up to the large house. It was an impressive red-brick Georgian. Hauck parked at the far end of the circular drive. There was a heavy congestion of police vehicles and medical vans in front. In the months since he had left, he'd been back to the office

only a couple times—once for the opening of the new first responders wing, and
once for a retirement party for Ray Reiger,
one of the old-timers on his staff.

A couple dozen police and crime-scene
techs were crowded around the entrance.
Hauck said hi to a few of them, who instinc-
tively waved back with surprise. *"Hey, lieutenant!"* No one stopped him. He stepped
past a uniformed officer stationed at the
door. Inside, there was a large, two-story
foyer with a round marble table and a winding staircase leading to the second floor.

A small crowd was gathered in a room
off the entrance hall. Hauck stepped in. It
looked like someone's office, probably Marc
Glassman's. Built-in shelves filled with
books and photos. Signed baseballs. The
actual bodies were gone, but the blue outline drawn on the floor by the desk next to
a large bloodstain was marked "1." Marc
Glassman had been shot downstairs,
Hauck recalled. He took a look around and
saw a wall safe open and the desk drawers removed and overturned on the floor.
*Police believe that the motive behind this
family's tragic end was simply a robbery
gone bad . . .*

Across the room, Hauck spotted Steve Chrisafoulis, who had taken over his job as head of detectives, talking to Ed Sinclair, one of his crew.

Steve gave him a look between confusion and surprise. "Whasamatter, new job not keeping you busy, Ty?"

"First big case . . ." Hauck shrugged to Steve, waving hi to Ed. "Couldn't stay away."

"Pretty morbid, if you ask me." He and Steve shook hands. Hauck liked the man, who'd put in fifteen years in the city before he moved up to Greenwich. In fact, Hauck had pushed for him to take his place after Freddy Munoz was killed. The detective had been devoted to him. *Follow you into hell with gas tanks on,* he had once joked. Chrisafoulis shrugged apologetically. "Listen, Ty, I don't mean to be short, but you can see there's a lot going on . . ."

"I know that. I was wondering if I might look around."

"Look around?"

"April Glassman," Hauck said. He glanced at the blue-taped outline of her husband on the floor. "We worked on a few projects together over at the Teen Center."

His stomach shifted at the bald-faced lie.

The new head of detectives scratched at his mustache. "Look, Ty, I don't know . . . Fitz could show up anytime . . ." Fitz was Vern Fitzpatrick, Greenwich's chief of police, Hauck's old boss. Hauck had left the force after they'd had a parting on his last big case, no longer certain where the chief's loyalties were.

Instead, Hauck said, "You're pretty sure this paints up as a robbery?"

Chrisafoulis shrugged. "Safe's open. Whatever was in there's gone. Drawers rifled through. The fourth such break-in in six weeks out in the backcountry . . . Same upstairs, next to the wife and daughter. Call me crazy . . ."

Hauck nodded grudgingly. "I heard there was a boy as well?"

Steve nodded. "In fact, it was the kid who called it in. Seven. Woke up with the whole thing happening. He hid out in a hall closet."

"Unharmed?"

"Unharmed," Steve confirmed. "Pretty resourceful bugger too. He snapped off a few shots on his sister's cell phone as the perps took off."

"Anything come back?"

"Two of them. Wearing ski masks, work uniforms. The lab is working them over now." He grinned good-naturedly. "Maybe I ought to leave something for that press conference, huh, LT?"

A call came in scratchily over the detective's handheld radio. Brenda, the department's secretary, who used to be Hauck's secretary too. "Chief wanted you to know, they scheduled a press conference at eleven thirty, lieutenant . . ."

Chrisafoulis responded, "Tell him I'll be there." He clicked off the radio and snorted back a laugh. "Must be a little strange to hear, huh?"

"You mean 'lieutenant'?" Hauck shrugged it off. "Listen, I knew what I was doing, Steve."

"You know, *today,* you're welcome to have it back if you want to rethink it," the detective said, gloomily looking around. "You assured me it was just a walk in the park out here in the burbs."

Someone called for him from outside the room. Steve waved, bobbed the radio in his palm like a heavy weight.

"Those other jobs," Hauck said, "if I

remember right, one time the perps came in and found the family at home?"

"The Nelson place." Steve nodded. "Out on Riversville."

Hauck looked him in the eye. "So how'd that one go?"

"I know where you're heading . . . They shoved them into the pantry at gunpoint and took whatever they could and ran."

"What I thought, Steve."

The head of detectives looked at him and exhaled, then backed away. "The wife and daughter were in the bedroom upstairs. Lemme know if you find anything." He winked. "Can always use the help. Take a minute, before you go."

CHAPTER SIX

The bedroom had a few techs and detectives Hauck knew well milling around and he said hi, fielding a few questions about how things were going and what he was doing there.

He looked around the room—shades of yellow and green, colorful and warm. Hauck felt he could see April's personality in it, the floral curtains and painted vines on the wall. The bed was still tousled from last night. A Jodi Picoult novel lay on her nightstand. A few framed pictures of her family and the dog.

Even her familiar scent—fresh, like

daisies—returned to him after all these years.

He made his way over to the master closet and waited until the last CSI tech left.

Two body outlines were next to each other, almost overlapping. Hauck envisioned April shielding her daughter, their mouths taped, wrists bound, terror leaping wildly in her heart. She must've heard them. The gunmen coming back upstairs; the door opening, light bursting in. Her daughter's frantic, muffled screams. The vast depth of fear subsumed in a greater sadness.

That must have been horrible for her.

He had seen it so many times. Always left him numb in his heart. People he had loved.

Why did it always feel as if it was the first?

They had been kept in here while her husband was led down to the safe. What the hell had gone wrong? Had one of them seen one of their faces and the bastards had to cover their tracks? Had Marc tried to fight back? The dresser drawers were open, clothes, photographs, papers strewn over the floor. On top of the console, an enameled jewelry box was rifled through.

Robbery.

Hauck kneeled and pressed his palm in the center of the first blue outline. For a second, it was as if he felt her warm heart still beating there. After all these years. A fist of nausea rolled up in his gut. The past rushing back, a driverless train out of control.

He had seen this so many times, he thought he could just put it aside.

But he couldn't. Everything always came back.

In the clash between memory and forgetting, memories always won.

"Ty . . . ?"

He recognized her as soon as he turned. After all these years.

At the back of the line behind him at the dry cleaner's on Putnam. The soft green luminous eyes, the midwestern drawl bringing him instantly back. The pleased surprise so radiant in her smile.

"April?"

"Oh my God, Ty . . ." He stepped out

of the line and she hugged him. "God, it's been years . . . Four?"

"Maybe five!" he said, drinking in the sight of her. "How are you?"

However many years had passed, she looked the same. Better. Years had blossomed on her. Confidence shone in her face. With her honey-brown hair and freckles still dotting her cheeks, you could have mistaken her for a fairer Julianne Moore. She had on patched jeans and a long, gray sweater under a large down parka. Looking quite the country girl. There was something that sparkled in her.

"I'm fine, Ty. We're fine. I heard you were in town here. On the force. You don't know how many times I meant to come in and say hi."

"So, hi," *Hauck said, grinning.*

She giggled back. "Hi!"

It was like when you see someone you haven't seen in years and you've forgotten just how much that person once meant to you. And then it rushes back, all at once. He took her hands and studied every line on her pretty face.

She said, "You know, I think about

you a lot. I ran into Doctor Paul last month. Believe or not, we bumped into each other at the movies in Stamford. Sorta like we are now . . . Some art film. You ever see him anymore?"

"No. Not in years." He shook his head. "Not since . . ." They moved away from the line. "So tell me how you are."

"I'm fine. Really," she said as if he needed convincing. *"I am. We all are, actually. Marc's still at Wertheimer. Doing great. Becca's twelve now. She's into ballet. She's actually pretty good. She's trying out for* The Nutcracker *at SUNY Purchase."*

He grinned. April had danced as a kid. "Why am I not surprised?"

She smiled at him. "Always the good guy to have around . . . So what about you?"

"Well, I'm here. Two years now. I'm living in Stamford. I'm head of the Violent Crimes Unit on the force."

"And your wife? It was Beth, right?" He nodded. "Did things ever work out?"

"No." He shrugged resignedly. "We never got back together. Split up for good around three years back."

"I'm so sorry, Ty."

"It's okay. Jessie's getting big now herself. She's ten. A bit more into soccer than ballet."

"Who would've ever guessed that?" April smiled knowingly.

There was a lull. Hauck realized he still had her hands in his. Finally, without drawing his eyes to them, he let them go.

"You look good, Ty. All that stuff seems like such a long time ago. Another life. We both turned corners, didn't we? We made it through. That's what he always said."

"We did." Hauck nodded. Her face brought so much back to him. "We did."

April glanced at her watch. "Ugh. Becca's probably waiting for me at school. Doing the high-class chauffeur thing. We ought to get together. I'd really like that, Ty."

"Yeah, we should." Hauck knew it was one of those things that would probably never occur.

"I should go." Then suddenly her eyes brightened. "Hey, c'mon, out here . . . There's someone I want you to meet."

She looped an arm through his and took him outside. A silver Mercedes SUV was parked in front of the store. She led him around and unlocked the rear passenger door. There was a boy in back. Four, maybe five. A mop of straw-colored hair. Eyes as lively and moss-green as his mom's. Maybe it was the sunlight that shone off his face, or the light that fell on April's, radiating from her, as if she was showing him a snapshot of her own heart.

"This is Evan, Ty . . ."

Hauck stood up, his gimpy knees emitting a crack. A pressure built up in his stomach, the sweats coming over him. He pressed back against a sensation of tightly coiled anger and the feeling of being sick.

Memories always won.

A young CSI tech he had met once or twice named Avila came up behind him, startling him. "Bad scene, huh, lieutenant?" The kid blew his cheeks out like some twenty-year veteran who had seen this a hundred grisly times.

"It's not 'lieutenant' anymore. I'm no longer on the force."

"Still, it's hard to put it away, isn't it, sir? I guess it stays in the blood."

"What stays in the blood, son?" Hauck looked at him.

"I don't know." Avila shrugged. "What we do."

He looked back at the kid with his black crime kit, barely six months into his career. He gave him a wizened smile. "No, you can't," Hauck said. He patted the kid on the shoulder and left.

You can't put it away.

You can't put what's inside behind you.

No matter what corner you turn.

CHAPTER SEVEN

The Talon Group, Hauck's new employer, was a worldwide security company doing business in thirty countries.

Most of their revenue came from the corporate division. Background screening for key employees and directors. Forensic accounting. Data recovery. Protections against internal theft. Another division handled crisis management—PR, media training. And there was another side of the company, GTM, Global Threat Management, that specialized in providing protection for diplomats and contractors in the Middle East and on dangerous posts abroad, and acted as a consultant to various foreign governments.

Hauck had joined the company as a partner in the firm's new office in Greenwich.

Leaving police work was a big shift in his life. He'd been in law enforcement for twenty years, rising rapidly out of college through the NYPD's detective ranks and ending up in their Office of Information. Then, after his younger daughter was killed and his marriage fell apart, he eventually found his way back near the place he had been brought up, in the drab, working-class section of Byram on the Greenwich–Port Chester border. Slowly, he built his life back up, taking over the Violent Crime division in town, graduating to head of detectives. Solving two high-profile murder-conspiracies got him on the TV crime shows and made him a bit of a celebrity around town. Put him in line for chief when Vern Fitzpatrick retired.

But rubbing up against that same established power base, he knew he could never fully be happy there.

Now he had a corner office with a fancy view of the sound. A pretty secretary out front. Access to important executives. Right off the bat he had brought in two new pieces of business: High Ridge Capital, a hedge fund—he coached one of the partners' kids—and the town of New Canaan, which was looking into security screening on new applicants. A lot of the work had been pretty mundane. Compliance issues. His bright spot was the mortgage thief.

That afternoon, around one thirty, Hauck's boss, Tom Foley, senior managing director of the firm, knocked on Hauck's door. "Ty, there's someone I'd like you to meet."

Foley was tall, Princeton-educated, wore suspenders over his pinstripe shirt, and he came in with a stylish, blond-haired woman Hauck pegged as being in her midforties. She wore a white cable-knit sweater over crisp beige slacks, her hair pulled back into a refined ponytail. Pastel-pink lipstick. She also wore one of those fashionable white Chanel watches on her wrist.

Foley said, "Ty, say hello to Merrill Simons."

Hauck stood up and came from around his desk. Merrill Simons looked like she could've been on the cover of *Greenwich*

Magazine, hosting a garden tour at her *Town and Country*–style twenty-million-dollar estate. He shook her hand and motioned to the couch. "Why don't we sit over here?"

Hauck's office was spacious and bright, with a comfortable sitting area—a couch, two chairs, and a walnut coffee table. Above them was some kind of contemporary oil painting Hauck couldn't figure out but that had come with the office. The windows looked out over Greenwich harbor.

"Ty's our newest partner," Foley explained to Merrill. "He's heading up our Greenwich operation for us. For years, he ran the local detective unit in town and worked on some pretty high-profile cases. He likes to play it all down, but we're lucky to have him here."

"Tom just has a fascination with cops," Hauck said. They all sat down. Hauck's secretary, Brooke, stuck her head in and asked if Merrill might like a soft drink or a coffee. Merrill said she would take a tea. She appeared slightly nervous at first, uncomfortable at being there, and to Hauck, she seemed the type who was *never* nervous or uncomfortable, used to being in the company of important people no matter what the setting.

"Simons," Hauck said, thinking aloud. "Any relation to *Peter* Simons?" Peter Simons was a big financial guy in town. Credit Suisse, Lehman, or something. To Hauck, they all seemed to merge. What he did recall was that the Simonses had some monster *Architectural Digest* spread up on Dublin Hill, threw lavish parties, and were influential on the charity circuit and the cultural boards in Greenwich. They were like royalty in town.

"Used to be." Merrill shrugged, almost guiltily. "We were divorced a year ago."

"I'm sorry," Hauck said. "I've actually been up at your house. You threw a party for the French president and his new wife a couple of years back. I oversaw some of the town security."

"I remember you." Merrill brightened. "You're the lieutenant from town, right?"

"Was," Hauck said, smiling. "Change of uniform. And I think I may have once taken one of your boys on a tour of the station. He was part of a group from Brunswick.

Tall, inquisitive kid. Shaggy blond hair. If I recall, he wanted to see where we locked up the first-time drug offenders . . ."

"That's Jason." Merrill laughed. "That kind of inquisitiveness we could certainly do without. Probably hoping to say hello to a few of his school chums. I hope you cured him."

"I did my best," Hauck said. "But as I recall, you raised a pretty determined guy."

Merrill's tea came. She took it and thanked Brooke. She took a sip and seemed to feel more at ease.

"So, Ty," Tom Foley started in, arms on his knees, "you're probably wondering just why Merrill's here. I'll let her tell you, but suffice it to say it's a very private matter, one that could easily find its way into the local papers, and I assured her we'd handle it with complete discretion."

"Of course. Goes without saying," Hauck assured her. "That's why we're here."

Merrill nodded, gearing herself up. She opened her large crocodile-leather bag and took out a manila envelope. "For the past year, I've been seeing someone . . . ," she began to explain. She removed a black and white photo and laid it, tentatively, on the table.

Hauck picked it up.

It was of a man of about thirty-five or forty. Handsome. Dark, European features. A rugged chin. Short, wiry, dark hair. "His name is Dieter Thibault. He goes by Dani. He's Dutch. His mother was Belgian, I think. At least that's what he's led me to believe. Things have moved along quite quickly. I suppose you could say we've fallen in love."

Hauck waited while she took another sip of tea and faced her, putting down the photo. "Go ahead."

"This is a little difficult for me . . . ," Merrill said, glancing at Foley.

He nodded her on.

"You're doing a bit of due diligence, perhaps? In case things get on to the next level," Hauck inferred.

Merrill gave him a slight nod. "I should stress that Dani is quite successful in his own right. He's built hotels, done some Internet deals in Eastern Europe. Some members of the Belgian royal family are investors with him. Photos of him with them are very prominent in his office in New York. He's never needed my money. In fact, it's his lifestyle I've sort of fallen into. It's just that . . ."

Hauck waited for a moment while Merrill moistened her lips. She seemed to hesitate.

"It's just that what, Ms. Simons?"

"It's just that some of these things . . . I've had my people looking into them. Informally, of course. Some of the transactions he's made, his personal background . . . family, university degrees. Sources of income. I'm not exactly sure how to say this. But all of a sudden, I'm not sure they're adding up."

"Adding up?" The unease was etched deeply into Merrill Simons's face. Hauck moved closer.

"It's as if anything that goes more than a few years back is a complete blank." Merrill looked up and faced him. "I'm not sure Dani is who he says he is, Mr. Hauck. And before this gets deeper, I want to know who the man I'm supposed to be falling in love with really is."

CHAPTER EIGHT

Roger Cantwell stared at his Bloomberg screen in dismay.

High above Park Avenue, on the forty-eighth floor of the sleek glass tower that bore his company's iconic name, the managing director of Wertheimer Grant read the banner headline flashing across CNBC: MURDERED TRADER WAS WERTHEIMER'S INVESTMENT STAR.

His stomach knotted. He took a breath the way his personal trainer had instructed him to do to ramp down the stress. But no simple cleansing breath could wash this mess away.

It was awful.

The days since Marc Glassman's murder had thrown the once-shining firm into a maelstrom. *A frigging roach motel of rumor and distortion,* Cantwell thought with dread. He himself had gone through a mix of emotions and worries he had never experienced before. First, the shock. The disbelief, imagining the horror of it. Cantwell had known the trader well. Though it was his rule to leave the investment responsibilities to his senior staff, as head of the firm, and as someone who had never lost his love for the trenches, he'd been in dozens of strategy sessions with Glassman over the years, not to mention sales conferences, golf outings, charitable events. *My God,* Cantwell thought, *we were all together just a few days ago at the firm's winter opera event at the Met.*

But soon the grief started to morph into worry. CNBC's headline was correct. Marc *was* Wertheimer's brightest shining star. In the midst of this year from hell—with the mortgage crisis eviscerating the firm's balance sheet, their earnings dropping like a weight, their stock price tanking in the midst of the global sell-off, rumors flying—

Glassman was one of the rare people actually making money for the firm. Some might even say the only thing propping it up.

Now that was gone.

Now there were just these headlines.

Cantwell turned around and gazed gloomily out his office window. He could see the skyline of lower Manhattan to the south, the East River. To the west, the skating pond in Central Park. He liked this view. He wanted to keep it for a while. He wanted to keep the company jet too.

Along with sponsoring Phil Mickelson and hobnobbing with world movers and shakers at places like Davos and the Aspen Institute, not to mention the appearances on Fox and CNBC, where attractive reporters sought out whatever he said.

He just didn't know how much longer he'd be able to keep any of it.

The board was growing weary. The firm had a ton of toxic mortgage exposure. Christ, they'd been packaging that shit all the way up, right from the start. Now no one knew what anything out there was worth. "Mark to market," it would kill them! Not to mention the stock price. Some big-name hedge fund asshole was out there shorting the shit out of it. The market cap had already plummeted from one hundred and ten billion down to fourteen. Not to mention their dwindling cash reserves. And their overnight borrowing on the repo market drying up, all these whispers . . . If the true picture ever got out, if there was ever a run on the accounts—Cantwell swallowed—they'd be toast.

He looked at the wall of photographs of him with leaders and celebrities that had been taken over the years. Yes, he'd been paid millions over that span. Yes, he had the cushy duplex on the park and the compound at Lyford Cay in the Bahamas, not to mention the place on the beach in East Hampton. But most of what he had was still tied up in company stock. And he'd been buying it all the way down. He had to show faith, didn't he? Now, having borrowed against a substantial part of it, he had to wait it out. At their current value, his holdings were only worth maybe double what he owed.

And now Marc. Cantwell turned away from the screen. He had barely been able to sleep the past two nights. There was pressure from everywhere. The board. The investor community. Even the Fed. Now the fucking press . . . People were saying they might have to merge. Cantwell responded with defiance. *Wertheimer Grant doesn't merge.* The firm had been around for ninety-five years. It was an American icon. Wertheimer Grant *acquires* firms. Maybe it stumbles; maybe it loses its way for a while. But it doesn't fall.

Wertheimer Grant is Wall Street.

Cantwell's stomach tightened as he watched the stock tick down to a new yearly low. Eight and a quarter. Just two months ago it had been fifty! "Murder of prominent trader creates market unrest . . . Redemptions reportedly high. Wall Street speculating on whether the firm can remain independent . . ."

They didn't need this kind of exposure now.

"Mr. Cantwell . . ." His secretary Mary's voice buzzed in. *"Mr. Biondi and Ms. Pearlstein are here to see you."*

"Sure, yes," Cantwell answered. He got up and turned away from the screen. "Send them in."

Stan Biondi was his senior investment

manager who oversaw all trading at the firm. He was Marc Glassman's senior boss. Brenda Pearlstein was their corporate counsel in charge of compliance issues. They'd buzzed him a while ago to see if they could come on up. What the devil could the two of them be up to?

"We have to stem this fallout over Marc," Cantwell said, stepping over to the conference table as they came in.

Biondi shut the door behind them. He and Brenda came over to the table. Biondi's face looked like the Dow had just nosedived eight hundred points. "Roger, we need to talk."

Brenda, always tough to read, wasn't providing any more cheer.

"Here, sit down." Cantwell pulled out a chair. But as he did, Biondi pointed to his desk. "No, over at the screen."

The head of trading went around Cantwell's large architect's desk. He bent over his monitor and punched in a request. At the prompt, he added his security code.

Cantwell tried to read their faces. "What's going on, guys?"

"It's about Marc."

"I know. A complete nightmare." Cantwell sighed. "I don't know how we're ever going to replace . . ." He was about to say *him,* but, in fact, what Cantwell knew he meant was the trader's *earnings.*

"Roger," Biondi said, "I don't give a shit about replacing him. Come around."

An unsettling feeling rose up in Cantwell's gut as his manager steered the computer screen around. Several columns appeared on the screen. Cantwell immediately saw it was Marc Glassman's trading positions. They would be current as of today, and Cantwell saw many of the numbers were highlighted in green, representing profits.

He exhaled. "We're actually lucky to have all that now, Stan, considering . . ."

"Considering *what*?" Biondi clicked to the summary page, known as the Recap. It listed the cost and current value of all of Glassman's positions. *"Look,"* he said to Cantwell, and fixed his eyes on him, his face ashen.

He ran the cursor to "Total Outstanding Position." It showed Glassman had open positions of $4.9 billion. Cantwell looked at his head of trading, puzzled. That couldn't be right. No individual had that kind of limit. The firm's exposure could be fatal. Even a senior trader like Marc had maybe three, three and a half as his max.

"What's going on here, Stan?"

"Okay, Roger, *I-look . . .*" Biondi always spoke in a rapid cadence, but now he was almost stammering. "I admit, I may have let some of this go on . . . We needed earnings. You know that. Marc always delivered. I realize how this looks. It didn't all happen in one swing. It was gradual, over time. I know I'm on the line here . . ."

"Let *what* happen, Stan?" Cantwell went to advance the screen. "The guy's more than a billion dollars overdrawn. What kind of effing controls do we have here, anyway?"

Sheet-white, Biondi grabbed his arm. "Roger, there's more."

Cantwell looked up, his eyes no longer just on Stan but on Brenda as well, the compliance lawyer, wondering what she was doing here, a deepening worry building in his chest. *"How much more?"*

Biondi wet his lips. He typed in another account on the screen. A second ledger of stocks and open positions came up.

Glassman's.

Another trading account.

Roger Cantwell's eyes stretched wide. The dread in his chest wormed straight to his bowels. "Stan, tell me what the hell is going on here, *now . . .*"

This new account held over $3.7 billion. That made over eight total. "It's out of the Singapore office," the head of trading said. "Roger, I don't even know how this got set up. I know I once signed some letter of authorization that he could trade the Pac markets out of there . . . But a lot of this is just murky. Papered over. I still don't understand—he's been shifting funds between accounts, all over the globe, covering his trades . . ."

Now a tremor of panic ran through Cantwell. This was all they needed. He put his fingers to his temples. "Are there more?"

Sweat had come out on Biondi's brow and he hesitated, glancing at Brenda.

"Don't screw with me, Stan!" Cantwell's glare bore right through him. *"Are there more?"*

"One," Biondi said, swallowing. He brought up a last screen.

The Recap read $2.8 billion. *Two-point-eight billion.* Dizzily, Cantwell started doing the math, but Brenda Pearlstein beat him to it. "It's over eleven billion dollars, Roger."

Eleven billion dollars. Cantwell felt his legs buckle. He sank back down. Biondi could be fired for this.

He could be fired.

"How long has this been going on?"

"A while." Biondi fell into the leather chair across from him. "Look, you know the numbers, Roger. We needed earnings. Marc's always been driving them. I just let it go on. But, Roger, listen, there's—"

Cantwell leaned forward and clicked back to the three Recap pages again. Most of the positions were in green. Gains. Each account showed Glassman well ahead. Up almost 7 percent. Close to eight hundred million. *Thank God.* An exhalation of relief poured out of him.

"At least the little prick knew what the hell he was doing." Cantwell blew out his cheeks, feeling a second wind, sitting back down. The bastard had done it again! *This might actually help them.*

"Tell him," Brenda said, her eyes trained on Biondi.

The head of trading nodded, gulping.

"Tell him," Brenda said again, "or I will."

"Tell me what?" The iciness of her expression didn't suggest she was buying Cantwell's image of a happy ending. "Tell me fucking *what,* Stan," he turned back to Biondi, "before I throw you off the forty-eighth floor!"

"It's a disaster," the trading manager said, spitting it all out. "Worse than a disaster, Roger. All these gains . . ." He pointed to the screen, the columns of green. *"Here,* and here . . . They're merely paper trades. Made up. To cover his losses. They never took place, Roger." Biondi's face was white. "They're all completely false."

"False . . ."

Cantwell's jaws parted as he stared at the screen, the full enormity of what Biondi was telling him slowly, impossibly, settling in. Their reserves were already shredded. The market would drop six hundred points tomorrow on the news. Their stock would open up at two.

This could sink the firm.

"How much are we in for?" Cantwell uttered.

One word fell off the head of trading's lips. *"Billions."*

CHAPTER NINE

Over the next days, Hauck began digging into the background of Dani Thibault.

Merrill had given him some things to work with, Thibault's Dutch passport number and the name of two businesses he supposedly owned: Christiana Capital Partners, of which his business card listed him as managing director and founder, and Trois Croix Investments, Limited, out of Luxembourg (which Merrill suggested was supposedly named after the street in Brussels where Thibault had been born). She also indicated he had served in the Dutch army. "Dani said he was in Kosovo. Part of the peacekeeping forces there." That was one of the things that initially had set off her doubts. Her lawyer had been unable to find a record of any military service.

That first visit, after Tom Foley had walked her to the door, he came back to Hauck's office. "Impressive woman, huh, Ty?"

"What's going on?" Hauck asked him. "I thought we don't normally handle this kind of thing. It's pretty routine PI work."

"Normally we don't." His boss stepped over to the door. "But this time we do. You may have had a chance to look over the client list here, Ty." Of course Hauck had. Talon had a worldwide contract with Reynolds Reid, Merrill Simons's ex-husband's firm. "Keep me up to date," he said, patting Hauck on the back, telling him what a great job he was doing, backing down the hall.

So Hauck started in. He began with the same steps Merrill Simons's own attorneys had taken. Thibault was a Dutch citizen. But his background was supposedly Belgian. He purported to have ties to the royal family there, the source of his network of contacts and income. He also claimed to have a degree from the London School of Economics.

Hauck began with a criminal history. He put in for it in the U.S. and internationally with Interpol too. He Googled "Thibault." A trail of gossip references popped up. Linked with Merrill in the society pages. Galas they had attended. Charitable foundation dinners. Prior to that he was seen in the presence of a couple Bollywood actresses and a British female race car driver. The article was headlined 2007'S GLAMOUR COUPLES.

Thibault played in the big leagues.

There was also a series of references and articles in business publications. Thibault's firm Trois Croix had been negotiating for a small Caribbean resort chain along with a large Spanish retailer. Trois Croix was described as an investment firm based out of Luxembourg and Thibault as a "well-connected Dutch financier." One article mentioned a series of companies Hauck had never heard of that were part of his holdings: I-Mrkt; Havesham Property Holdings in London; a boutique hotel on Mustique. He was said to have been a board member of several large firms and a former investment manager at Bank AGRO in the Netherlands. Apache Partners, a prominent New York private equity firm, was mentioned as a financial adviser on the acquisition.

An article dated four months later, in something called *Caribbean Business News,* described how the hotel-chain purchase had not gone through and that the company was now seeking another option.

At the end of Merrill Simons's visit, as she stood up to leave, Hauck had said discreetly, "I don't mean to trouble you, Ms. Simons, but it would help if I could have one or two additional things."

She took out her car keys from her purse. "I'm listening . . ."

"I could use a current cell phone number for Mr. Thibault. And his e-mail account, if you're okay with that. Banking information . . ."

"I don't know . . . ," Merrill said, appearing a bit concerned.

"It would make things easier," Hauck said. "I promise, he won't know."

"I'm sure you know how hard this is for

me," she said, hesitating. "I have deep feelings for Dani. I'm actually hoping this all is just a small waste of your time . . ." She went to the door. "Why don't we just see how this initial pass-through goes?"

Hauck nodded, walked her over to Foley, and handed her his card. He didn't like what he was doing either. Ripping up the floorboards of someone's life. Digging into his affairs. On the job, he had done it a million times. But this was different.

Dani Thibault wasn't under suspicion for committing any crime.

After Merrill had left, Hauck typed in what she had given him, creating a data file.

This time we do, Tom Foley had said. Take on the PI case. As well as what Hauck saw, with Peter Simons's ex involved, as an obvious conflict of interest.

He picked up the phone and buzzed Brooke outside. "See if you can get me Richard Snell at our office in London."

CHAPTER TEN

At the same time, Hauck did his best to keep his hand in the Glassman murders as well.

He couldn't put away the image of April. It dogged him—the sweet, bright eyes that shone back from the photographs of her. The light touch of her hand on his when they had last bumped into each other in town.

It's been what, Ty—she beamed, happily—*four years . . . ??*

Five.

They had met in a support group Hauck had gone to for a while after Norah was killed. He couldn't escape the dreams that made him constantly relive it. Grief that wouldn't go away. Blame unwilling to soften. By then, Beth and he had given up. September 11 had brought with it a whole new scrapbook of faces and lives he had been unable to save. Names of the unaccounted for he was charged with following up on. Frantic loved ones calling in. Not knowing. It was as if he was trying to find a glimpse of Norah, his dead daughter, in every face, every call he fielded.

Only two out of two hundred he followed up on ended up being found alive.

It just got to him. For the first time in his life what was constraining him was greater than what he could do. One day he put in his notice. Out of nowhere, he walked into the office of the assistant chief of the NYPD and told him he couldn't do it anymore. Their shining star. He had made detective, got fast-tracked into management, faster than anyone before. His career had arced upward in a steady, unflagging line.

As part of the settlement he agreed to talk it out with someone. A police shrink. The doctor urged him to come to the group. Just to show he didn't need it, he went.

Hauck didn't think about those years much anymore. The Dark Ages, he liked to call them. Depression. Maybe it was a chemical thing, lurking in his brain for years. Maybe it was like the towers, the well-built wall he had erected around himself— sports hero, Colby grad, the pretty wife, the picture-book family, his career—all brought down. Leaving ashes behind.

Whatever it was, he had built himself back up. He had moved away, to Greenwich. Found a new home. Slowly found new people to love. Rebuilt his career. Clearly, his life was moving upward once again.

The Dark Ages.

The memories were back again.

He remembered watching her from across the circle of twelve patients. She was both pretty and at the same time quiet, hurt. Their eyes met with a brief smile. Both of them saying, in the way everyone there seemed to say, *I really don't belong here, you know.*

"April," Dr. Paul Rose said, "we have a few new people here. Would you give us a little about yourself and tell us why you're here?"

"Sure," she said, shrugging diffidently. "I'm, uh, *Frasier* got canceled on Thursday nights, so I was free . . ." There were a few polite laughs. "Sorry," she said, flattening her lips. A delicate light shone on her face.

Then she told everyone about her darkness.

The Glassman murders received a lot of attention. Marc Glassman's notoriety and position made all the cable news shows and the front page of the *Wall Street Journal*. The FBI was involved. Along with the SEC. It seemed unbelievable that Marc Glassman had turned out to be some kind of rogue trader. That he had cost Wertheimer Grant billions of dollars. What kinds of controls were there? Now the firm hung on the verge of collapse. Rumors were everywhere. THE MURDER THAT MAY SINK ONE OF WALL STREET'S MOST RESPECTED FIRMS, the *New York Times* headline read.

All sprung from a local crime spree that had gotten out of control.

Finally Hauck knew the right thing was just to stay out. He made his decision. Let the right people back at Havemeyer Place handle it. He walked away. He had Annie.

April, could you tell us why you're here . . . ?

Hauck recalled that most mornings Steve Chrisafoulis dropped off his daughter at the high school before heading into work. A few days after the story broke he waited for him, until he saw the blue Chrysler minivan pull up and Emily jump out and shut the door, merging with a group of kids on the sidewalk. She waved. "Bye, Daddy . . ."

Steve waved back. "See you tonight, hon . . ."

Hauck stepped up just as he was rolling up the window.

"Funny, I didn't know you had kids in the school here." The detective smirked with a roll of his cynical eyes.

Hauck shrugged. "Can't help myself. Sometimes I still hang around here, just to make sure everything's okay."

"You better watch yourself. Someone may get the wrong idea and you'll get yourself arrested, Ty."

"Look, I know it's awkward to talk to me on this, Steve."

"It's not awkward," the detective said. "It's more like inappropriate. You're not wearing a badge now."

"You don't find it just a shade peculiar how this break-in seemed to bust the Wertheimer thing wide open?"

"*Peculiar?* I also think it's peculiar how the safe in the house was emptied and the drawers were rifled through, Ty."

"Any thoughts on what they might have been looking for?"

Now it was Steve who shrugged. "Money, jewelry. Call me crazy . . . Look, I really gotta get on to the office now."

"How's the boy? How's he doing?"

"Spooked." Chrisafoulis nodded. "Like anyone might be. He's with his grandparents up in Darien. One day he's gonna have to come to terms with what he saw in there. The rest of his family murdered. How's your kid doing, Ty?"

"Jessie? She's doing great, thanks. Starting high school this year. You said the kid had taken some pictures . . . Anything ever pan out?"

"Ty, you're asking something I can't divulge. You know that. This is the second time you've pumped me for what's going on. Want to let me in on the story, dude?"

Hauck bent down at the window. He met the new head of detectives face-to-face.

"You remember that career night we did at the high school a year or two back?"

"Yeah."

"April Glassman set it up. We just got friendly."

"Friendly . . . ?"

"Not that kind of friendly, Steve. We just had a cup of coffee. Bumped into each other once or twice. Started talking. You know how it is; sometimes you just find a person you can open up to. Stuff comes out."

"Pretty gal." Chrisafoulis's mustache twitched, amused. "Look . . ." He reached across to the passenger seat and unfastened his case. He lifted out a large white envelope. "Fitz finds this out, I'm gonna have you barred from the office Christmas party, you understand?" He grinned. "I know how tough it is to find someone you can open up to."

"Got it." Hauck smiled and met his eyes. "Thanks."

"We blew up the shots." Steve lifted out a series of eight-by-ten photos. "He snapped them off from the upstairs window overlooking the drive."

The first was a shot of the backs of two men, wearing masks and what seemed to be dark work uniforms, one carrying a black trash bag, heading away from the house. The second shot showed them climbing into a black SUV at the end of what Hauck recalled was the Glassmans' long driveway. "A Chevy Suburban," Steve said. "Too bad the plates were obscured. Would have made things easy. Amazing what these little buggers will do, huh?"

Hauck flipped through the photos and the last ones were tight blowups of the first. Magnified around fifty times. The two men hurrying off. The first just had the side of one of their faces; he had taken off his mask. White. Thirties. Looking away from the camera. Not much there.

The last one did have something distinguishing. It was a close-up of the perp's neck. He was white as well. A knot of hair, braided up like in a small ponytail, peeking out from under the mask.

And something on the back of his neck.

"We thought it was a birthmark or something," Chrisafoulis said, seeing Hauck pause. "But the lab was able to enhance it. Turned out to be a tattoo."

"Like a dragon's tail?" Hauck asked, squinting.

"Or the tip of an arrow. Hard to tell. You know the only reason I'd even show you these is what you did for me. This stays between us, right? You got your own job now. You left. This one's mine."

Hauck handed him back the photos. "Not much of a getaway bag for all that loot," he said skeptically.

Chrisafoulis looked at him. Steve might have been new to the rank and all the crap it brought with it, but he'd been a detective in the city for fifteen years, knew his work as well as anyone and exactly where Hauck was heading. "Okay, there was something I might not have mentioned . . . Upstairs. By the wife and daughter. We did find something unusual, now that I think of it."

"What?"

"You know how the drawers were all rifled through, stuff thrown about? But right on the dresser we found a jewelry case. Rings, bracelets. Some pretty juicy stuff left in it."

Hauck winked. "They must've been in quite a rush."

"Yeah." The head of detectives nodded. "Quite a rush."

Hauck tapped on the edge of the

window and stood up. "Thanks. Pretty resourceful kid, that boy, wouldn't you say?"

"Yeah, *very.*" The head of detectives
bore in on him as he turned the ignition
and put the car in gear. "I feel a little
strange saying this, Ty, but try not to do
anything that might tick you off if *you* still
had this job."

CHAPTER ELEVEN

Within days, the first responses on Thibault began to arrive.

A search of his criminal history came up empty, both in the States and with Interpol. His photograph hadn't matched any that caused alarm. An asset check showed no liens or judgments against him. His personal bills were paid in full and on time.

Thursday, Hauck was at his desk with a coffee, going over an immigration search on the guy who had perpetrated that mortgage fraud, when Richard Snell from London called back. "I've got an update on that subject you had me looking into."

"Thibault," Hauck confirmed. He grabbed a pen. He had never met Snell, but the Brit was ex-Goldman, ex-Kroll, and had a reputation in the firm as a top-notch manager. "Go ahead."

"First, as you suggested, I checked his name against the alumni roll of the LSE. There is no record of anyone named Dieter Thibault having been there, which I know is to no one's surprise. There was a Simone Thibault, who received a degree in 1979. You're certain you have the correct school?"

"I'm only going on what I was told," Hauck replied. It only confirmed what Merrill Simons had already said.

"You also stated you did a criminal and Interpol check," Snell continued. "No reason to be redundant then. I did a quick search into the two investment companies you supplied. Christiana Capital Partners and Trois Croix. Both companies are basically investment shells. For a network of individual funds that are hard to track. They've been mentioned a couple of times in the business press here as among the bidders trying to buy up various real estate and Internet properties. Combined, they do list assets under management as over one hundred million euros. No one really has a sense of where the cash originates from. You mentioned some kind of connection to the Belgian royal family . . ."

"Supposedly there are photos of them in his New York office."

"Haven't been able to confirm that one yet. These families tend to go on and on, of course. More minor royals running around Europe than the rest of us. But no one I've run Thibault's name by has ever heard of him in those circles, Ty. I'll keep at it. But I did raise some peculiar issues though . . ."

"Fire away."

"Thibault's own CV lists stints at various banks. The KronenBank in Lichtenstein is one. It's a bank that has been under some scrutiny in the past, coinciding with the time Thibault was there. It's known as a loose place for people who would like to transfer assets quietly and without detection. They set up instruments known as *stiftungs* . . . Heard of them?"

"Remind me."

"*Stiftungs* are, in effect, trusts," the Brit explained, "protected from most outside scrutiny, perfectly legal, but where the identity of the benefiting recipient can be a bit murky, shall we say. By intention. These assets can then move about from bank to bank across the globe, not so easy to trace."

Hauck had had some experience with money transferred through these vehicles into offshore accounts in the race to locate Charles Friedman in the Grand Central bombing case. Very difficult to trace without a subpoena from Interpol, which was almost impossible to get.

"KronenBank is a small, restricted private bank," Snell went on. "Thibault was listed as a *Vermogensverwalter,* the equivalent of an investment manager. The bank was also in the news some years back for something they call 'doubling up.' Taking commissions from both the client *and* the financial broker where they placed their money—say, a U.S. hedge fund. It all could be perfectly legitimate, of course, but in this particular case, there are reasons I'm slightly skeptical."

"Why is that?" Hauck asked.

"I don't know . . . Thibault's company lists Simpston Mews, Limited, as one of the real estate transactions they have been a

part of. It's a big development along the
Thames. Along with the Kai Shek Waterfront Project in Shanghai."

"Uh-huh."

"I asked our people who would know
here. No one's ever heard of Christiana or
Trois Croix in this arena. Not to mention
something else . . ."

Hauck flicked his pen. "What's that?"

"Thibault also lists the AMV Bank in Belgium as a place he once worked. I contacted the head of personnel there. A man
named Gruens. He confirmed that a Dieter
Thibault did, in fact, hold a position there.
Between the years of 1992 and 1994. His
title was key account-holder manager.
Looked after VIP depositors, I assume.
Very efficient, Gruen remembered. Well
regarded. Good marks from his clients as
well. In 1994, he moved on."

"To Bank AGRO. In Amsterdam," Hauck
concluded, checking Thibault's history.

"No. To manage some investment fund
in Switzerland, as Gruen recalled," the Brit
corrected him. "It's been almost fifteen
years. The records are boxed away in
some warehouse somewhere."

"*Switzerland?* I don't see that in Thibault's

background anywhere," Hauck said, flip-
ping through his papers.

"No," Snell confirmed, "you won't." The
Brit seemed to be hesitating, as if he was
holding something back. "Gruen asked
me why I was interested in Thibault after
all these years. Not to divulge anything, I
said he had a cash bequeath set aside for
him, that he'd been named in a will. Which
seemed to generate no small surprise . . ."

"Why?"

"Because Herr Gruen, as it happens,
seemed to recall that the Dieter Thibault
who worked at their bank went missing
while on a business trip to France and was
never seen again. A year or two after he
left."

Hauck stopped writing. "That would be
1994 or '95?" he said, surprised.

"He said that one of Thibault's clients
had read about it somewhere and passed
it along to the bank. As I said, fifteen years
ago. I went so far as to wire him a photo of
your Thibault, from the Internet."

"And?"

"And the Thibault who worked there was
apparently short and already starting to go
bald," Snell said flatly.

"Oh," Hauck grunted, his mind flashing to Merrill Simons, sinking back in his leather chair.

Thibault had falsified his past. More than that, he had taken over someone's identity. A likely dead person's. If that was false, everything about him could be false. Who did that—except a person with a great deal to hide? Hauck thought of Merrill. The awkward smile, the hopeful expression on her face when she talked about how she hoped things would turn out. *I suppose you could say we've fallen in love.*

"It would be of help if you could find me a set of fingerprints," Snell said. "Or better yet, a sample of his DNA. Soon as you give me the go-ahead, we'll track down just who this bugger really is."

CHAPTER TWELVE

Wednesday and Saturday nights Hauck coached a team of twelve-and-under kids in a local youth hockey league. The dad of his second-line winger was the sponsor: the Trident-Allen Value Fund Bruins.

Hauck had played peewee and Catholic league hockey since his early days in town, when he was more of a football star. When he moved back, he'd played defenseman in an over-forty league until a bullet from the Grand Central bombing case (coupled with another to his abdomen) put an end to his playing days.

Now he took some joy in teaching the

kids a few of the basic skills and how to come together as a team. Not to mention twice a week he got to lace up the skates—though a few of the kids could outrace him end-to-end without even busting, and he could barely spray up any ice these days.

Wednesdays, they practiced at the Dorothy Hamill rink in town. That night, he picked Jared up at Annie's place. He had taught the boy how to skate and Jared liked being on the ice in makeshift pads and a helmet with a stick in his hands. Hauck thought it was good for him to be with the regular kids. And Annie agreed. There was always a shoot-around net set off in one of the corners and Jared would try to steer pucks into it, never quite able to lift them off the ice. Every once in a while he'd call out to Hauck in an elated voice. "Look, Ty, er, coach, *I scored a goal!*"

That night, practice was getting a little spirited. They were playing a team from Long Island that weekend that was supposed to be really strong and nothing seemed to be working. Jeremy Purdo, the goalie, was stopping everything that got to him, daring the offense to get one by.

By the time Annie showed up after nine to take Jared back, tempers were flaring. He didn't want to leave until the team did. Hauck said it was okay for her to let him stay.

The frustration on the offense grew. "Schuer, you're supposed to be over here!" Tony Telco, the first-line center, shouted. Another kid yelled, slamming his stick, "Balzon, are you even awake, dude?"

Maybe Hauck let it go on a bit too long.

Near the end, a shot from the point came in and there was a scrum in front of the net. One of the attackers went down as the forwards tried to jam the puck in the net. Jared skated close by.

"Hey!" Hauck blew the whistle loudly, trying to settle everyone down.

For a second, no one stopped. A lot of pushing and shoving. The pile moved closer to Jared. Hauck grew a little worried. He skated in Jared's direction and blew the whistle three times. *"Alright, that's enough, now!"*

The players finally stopped and the puck squirted out of the pileup in front of the goal. With everyone standing around, Jared slowly wove his way in and pushed out his stick, lifting a neat chip shot past Purdo, the sprawled goalie, who shot out his stick to try to stop it as the puck went by.

"Goal!" Jared shouted, raising his stick into the air.

For a second everyone just stood around, Jared's call echoing through the rink. Then the buzzer went off and the rest of the attacking squad shot their sticks up. *"It's in!"*

Jared gleefully looked around. *"Goal, coach! Goal!"*

"It's a goal!" Hauck confirmed, signaling with a point toward the ice that it was in.

The members of the power play all skated over, smirking at the goalie, patting Jared on the helmet. Even Purdo came up and tapped his stick against Jared's pads. "Sweet one, dude!"

Jared made his way along the boards to where Annie was seated, bundled in a knit cap and muffler. "I scored a goal, Mom!"

"I saw! I saw! Yes, you did, babe."

Hauck skated over. He affectionately patted Jared on the back. "So whaddaya think, you ready to take a regular shift?"

"I don't know, Ty. Maybe it was a little lucky." He had a smile as wide as the Long Island Sound.

And so did Annie, beaming, except there was a hint of tears in it.

CHAPTER THIRTEEN

In the stylish dining room of her Normandy on Dublin Hill Road, Merrill Simons sat around the dinner table with her guests.

On her left was Ralph Tamerin, founding partner of Tamerin Capital, a large hedge fund in town, and his wife, Kitty; Tom Erkin, a wealthy investor in biotechs; Ace Klein, the flamboyant president of U-Direct! who had his own cable show; and George and Sally Ravinowich, wealthy investors whose famous yacht was one of the largest schooners in the world.

Dani was holding court as well.

Merrill had assembled the evening for him; he was hoping to stir up a little interest for the buyout of an auto-parts company in the Baltic he was trying to put together. She watched how he worked the table. Charming and worldly, he created confidence by painting a picture of prior deals he had done over there, along with their dazzling returns.

Deals, Merrill was now realizing, she had never quite seen.

She'd decided not to confront him with any of her suspicions just yet. She'd asked about certain things, and for each question Dani always had a glib reply. She decided to wait until something firm from Talon came back.

And for now, everyone seemed suitably dazzled. Except for George, who was even more dazzled by the Del Dotto cabernet.

"Merrill, this is first-rate juice," he said, tipping over the third empty bottle. Dani had made sure the wine steadily flowed.

"I bet there's another one or two down there," Merrill replied. Wine was always Peter's thing, not hers, and his cellar, from which they used to entertain a who's who of industry, was one of the perks of the divorce. She smiled impishly at Sally and Kitty. "I'm sure Peter wouldn't mind."

Normally, she would have asked Louis, who handled things like that, to bring it up, but he was overseeing the desserts in the kitchen, so she headed out of the dining room to the door leading down to the basement.

On the way she caught a glimpse of herself in a mirror. She knew she looked good for forty-four. She'd had a little work done, like most of her friends. Eyes smoothed, tummy tucked, a little Botox, of course. But she still looked perfectly natural. She worked out regularly and had her own private yoga instructor. She smoothed out her ruffled, white off-the-shoulder blouse and headed down.

One thing you could definitely say was that Merrill Simons knew how to entertain.

In the basement, she passed through the gym, the yoga studio, the private surround-sound theater with fifteen seats. The accumulated toys of her twenty-two years with Peter. While he was growing in the firm, they were able to share each other's rise into means and importance. They were invited to lavish parties, traveled to exotic places. Had the kids in prestigious schools. They had science wings and squash centers named after them.

But once Peter reached the top, everything seemed to change. He grew to think he was the most important man in the universe, and the people he surrounded himself with usually verified that fancy. He no longer seemed to recall that she knew him as an insecure bond trader who couldn't even decide what tie to wear. He became a fixture on CNBC and took calls from finance ministers from around the globe. He traveled with knockout Ivy League assistants. First it was the kids, then it was the stress and demands of the job. He stopped touching her. Then it was the long-legged lingerie model with the hard-to-pronounce name.

Now, Merrill mused, how the "powers that be" had swung.

He had the dwindling stock price and the impossible-to-get-rid-of-at-any-price apartment.

She had the hundred-million-dollar settlement!

She went to the wine room and opened

the ornate Lalique etched doors. It was a giant space, Peter's showcase, packed with prestigious first growths and cult wines from California only a Wall Street CEO could afford. She went over to the far wall, remembering from where they had pulled the Del Dotto. She took out the last two bottles of the case. She heard the door reopen behind her and spun around.

Dani came in.

"You scared me," she said, her heart skipping a beat. "What are you doing down here?"

"I needed a break," he said, a sly look on his face. He shut the door.

He went up and took the bottles from her and placed them on the table. In the chill of the cellar, she realized her nipples were showing through.

Dani smiled. "A proper hostess never serves her own wine."

"Emily Post, I suppose?" she asked, brushing past him.

"No. Dani Thibault." He grinned. He moved his hand along her slim body and drew her to him. "You smell intoxicating, darling . . ."

"Dani, please. Everyone's waiting. Not here . . ."

"Everyone's talking about interest rates and how Obama is screwing them." He shifted her around so that his pelvis pressed against her rear and she felt him all hard. "Trust me, they don't even know we're gone."

"You're crazy," Merrill said, trying to pull away. "Besides, Louis may come down any second."

"Louis's got his dick in the crème anglaise . . ." He kissed her neck, running his tongue along the curve of her exposed shoulders. "And I've got mine in . . ."

He cupped a hand over one of her breasts and with the other pulled the blouse out of Merrill's jeans, deftly pinning her hips against the table. It sent sparks of excitement mixed with uncertainty traveling down her spine. *"Dani, please . . ."*

She felt the warmth of his lips brush along her neck and almost involuntarily felt herself shifting against the hardness pressing against her.

"It's the fucking wine cellar," she said, her blood heating, and at the same time wondered what the group around the dinner table, two of whom were in her garden and book clubs, would say.

"Exactly." Dani grinned, mischief in his eyes.

With one hand he unbuckled her gold chain belt and flicked open the snap of her jeans. Merrill felt a flame of desire dance through her. With the other, he ripped at his own belt and zipper and slid his trousers down. This was rougher than he usually was, more forceful, and she thought, for a brief second, that it was as if it was almost in answer to her own doubts and fears. He slid her red panties down.

"Goddamnit, Dani, please . . ."

Merrill wanted to pull herself away, end this, but before the words made it to her lips, he had lifted her up against his pelvis and pushed inside. She gasped at the first feeling of the size of him filling her. He rocked, pinning her by the thighs, and her blood surged with the secrecy of what they were doing, holding off the forces of weakness and shame. She begged herself to say *Stop, stop,* but all she heard was her own trembling breaths, everything intensifying. Her skin started to heat, and

Dani's animal grunts became louder and more excited.

The banter at the dinner table was a million miles away.

They both came within a minute, shivers of satisfaction relaxing Merrill's spine. She shut her eyes, feeling both as alive as she ever had and angry at her own weakness at the same time. She felt used—used in many ways tonight.

"Who are you?" Merrill whispered as he pulled out of her, leaning against him.

"I'm the man who makes you feel alive again," he said, releasing his hand from her waist. "What more do you need to know?"

Dani lifted away. He rebuckled his pants. He took the two bottles. "I'll take these up," he said. "You may want to get yourself together."

Merrill rose, readjusting her blouse and jeans. She didn't turn around, even after he had left. Instead she closed her eyes.

I meant, really, who are you, Dani?

CHAPTER FOURTEEN

Later, after everyone had left, Merrill took off her earrings in the bedroom while Dani took a shower.

Up until tonight, deep down, she had always really trusted him. She'd been sure that whatever might come out would only confirm the feelings she had for him.

But tonight she sensed something completely different in him. A side she'd never seen before. She'd watched him operate, and a ripple of suspicion had wormed through her that he might, in fact, be using her to gain access to people. She observed him artfully describing his deals, the opportunities that the Baltic and Eastern Europe were now presenting, in that polished, sexy accent of his. The network of contacts she had never quite met. The history of past deals she saw no evidence of.

She had never really seen them, had she?

For the first time, she saw him as someone trying to weave a kind of spell. As an operator. And then there was the way he had taken her in the wine cellar. An animal side of him she had never felt before. Rougher than he had ever been. Almost as if he had sensed some suspicion in her. And was telling her something.

I'm the man who makes you feel alive.

She felt his arms wrap around her again. Coming at her from behind. The exhilaration that both thrilled her and repulsed her. *C'mon, Merrill,* she said, composing herself. *Your mind is getting away from you. This is crazy. This is not your style.*

She placed a bracelet in the jewelry box on her dresser and pulled off her ruffled blouse. She spotted Dani's wallet on the night table.

She had to know. But something suppressed her urge to look inside.

If he wanted to keep part of his past life secret, that was his business, not hers. He had never harmed her, never asked for anything. He made her feel youthful and vibrant and wanted again. The rest . . .

Why are you giving yourself over to doubt?

But gradually the urge to know him more deeply took hold of her. She went over to the nightstand in her bra and panties, hesitating, the temptation fighting her better instincts. She opened the billfold, listening for confirmation that Dani was in the shower.

It was a billfold he had bought at Harrods in London. Dani always walked around with wads of cash. Euros and dollars. He was like a walking cash machine.

Where did it all come from?

Merrill slipped it open. In the card folder, there were several credit cards: Amex, one personal, one from the business; Visa; a Eurocard; and several bank cards, from here and in London. All made out to Daniel Thibault or D. Thibault. Or Christiana Partners. These she had seen many times before.

Behind the see-through window, there was an international driver's license. His

face. Dieter Franz Thibault. The address
was the apartment Dani maintained in
London. Behind it, there was another local
Dutch license as well.

A tremor of shame traveled through her.
This was silly. Suspicion was not a space
she felt comfortable being in. What was
she even looking for? Dani was a charming and generous man. He had proved it
countless times to her. It wasn't about what
was in a person's wallet. She could see
into his heart. She wasn't some schoolgirl
carried away by her feelings . . .

Feeling guilty and foolish, Merrill quickly
scanned the remaining cards. There was
the University Club in New York. He must've
gone to the LSE, like he said, to be a member there. Some other private clubs in the
city. One Alfred Place in London. Various
other membership cards in places like Paris
and Madrid.

She quickly fanned out some business
cards. A private banker at ABN AMRO in
Amsterdam. A contact from Cerberus Capital, one of the largest private equity firms
in the U.S. Everything was normal. No secrets.

See. There's no scary man in the attic,

Merrill. Dani is who he says he is. She shoved the contents of his wallet back inside, starting to feel like a fool.

The shower stopped. Merrill heard Dani climb out.

"I'll be out in a minute," he called. She could hear him toweling off.

"I'm just taking my jewelry off."

"Along with everything else, I hope," he called.

She went to put the wallet back when, fumbling, her heart quickening, some photographs fell out of the inside flap. "Oh, damn . . ."

The first was of the two of them. Sailing off the Dalmatian coast last August. Dani could handle a skiff like the snap of a bra. She hadn't felt so swept off her feet since she was a young girl. They had anchored and made love on the deck in a rocky cove. It filled her with biting shame to even be questioning those memories.

She was about to fold the wallet back up when the second photo came out. It had been stuck to the first.

Something made her look more closely.

The photo was of two women. One was young, in her thirties, her hair pulled back in a bun. The second woman was older, maybe in her seventies, hardened lines across her drawn, unpampered face. They stood in front of a streetcar. It looked like any undetermined European city.

Merrill was struck by the faces.

There was something remarkably familiar in them.

It was Dani. In both of them. Merrill stared wide-eyed. The resemblance was clear as day.

One could be his twin, definitely. But he had never mentioned one. The older woman, Merrill thought, bringing the photo into the light, the older woman could be his . . .

It gave her a start. The feeling of doubt reflexively springing back up. *Can't be . . .*

Dani had told her many times his parents were dead. Since his university days. His father had died in an automobile accident, his mother from cancer. He said that he had no sisters. No family. They had been in Europe several times together. He'd never said anything about any relatives.

But the similarity was unmistakable.

This had to be his mother. And his sister. Maybe even a twin.

Merrill searched for the signs of age on the photo. Maybe it was from long ago. But the edges were still remarkably firm. And what she saw next sent her head spinning even more.

In the background, on the streetcar, behind the two women, was an advertisement. It was for a film. Partially blocked by the two women in front of it.

They died when he was at university, Merrill told herself, but the image she was looking at was the same in any language.

The film was *The Dark Knight.* Heath Ledger starring as the Joker.

You had to have been in a cave somewhere the past year not to have been aware of it.

The Dark Knight had come out only last year.

CHAPTER FIFTEEN

It was after eleven, that same night, when Kevin Mitman turned his BMW X5 onto John Street, the kids finally dozing in the back.

Timmy had only calmed down about the game a few minutes ago. The Rangers coming back from two goals down in the third against the Devils and winning in overtime. Petr Prucha, Melissa's favorite player, had tipped in the winning goal. The crowd went crazy. When Prucha had skated out for his star-of-the-game ovation, Tim stood on his chair and cheered, fists in the air. As they left the Garden, they even bought Melissa his number 25 jersey.

In the front passenger seat, Kevin's wife, Rosemary, stirred.

"We're home!" Kevin said.

"Mmmm." Ro opened her eyes. "How're you doing, honey?"

"Not bad. Everyone's asleep."

"No, we're not!" Tim suddenly chimed in.

Ro glanced at the clock and groaned. "Well, you will be soon, mister."

They were supposed to have left the night before. Up to Mount Snow for a few days of skiing on their spring break. But then some business things came up and Kevin figured they might as well go to the game, as opposed to giving the seats away, though Ro, who thought hockey duller than listening to the business channel, had to be dragged.

"I'll get the kids in bed," she said. "You take out the recycling."

"Uh, yeah, okay," he said with a sigh. The driveway was fifty yards long and it was twenty degrees. *Doesn't driving count for anything?*

He wound the SUV down toward their

home, a large ranch on two backcountry acres, which they'd bought when Kevin had taken over the family's printing company. It was pretty remote—a twelve-minute drive from town and the nearest market. *You don't want to forget the milk,* he always joked. But they liked it. They had deer and even coyote, and in the spring, the same geese always on their pond.

Kevin was about to turn in. "We're here, gang . . ."

Suddenly something didn't seem right. Instead of turning, he slowed at the gate.

There was an empty black van parked on the side of the road—unusual, because no one ever parked out here. The nearest house to them was hundreds of yards away. Everyone had driveways and garages large enough to hold a dozen cars.

He noticed something else too.

"Ro, did you leave the lights on in the house?"

"No," she said, staring down the driveway. They were always strict on that one. Thousand-dollar electric bills and Kev's business was soft. "Just in the foyer," she said. "Like we always do."

From the street, they could see lights on throughout the house.

"Shit!" Kevin pulled up on the darkened street, keeping out of sight.

In the back, Timmy leaned forward. "What's going on, Dad?"

"I don't know."

Melissa woke up. "Why aren't we turning? What's happening?"

Kevin turned to Rosemary. They'd all heard about the string of burglaries in the backcountry. The local papers had had it all over. They were supposed to be in Vermont. He flashed through the possibilities. *Who would have known? The newspaper delivery people. The mailman. The gardeners . . .*

He passed the house and pulled up to a stop about a hundred yards down. "What do we do, Ro?"

"There's no way we're going in there, Kev." His wife shook her head, fear in her eyes.

He nodded. He bit his lower lip and punched in 911 on the Bluetooth. A female duty officer answered on the second ring.

"Greenwich Emergency."

"This is Kevin Mitman. I live at 2019 John

Street," he said, meeting his wife's eyes. "We just came back from a hockey game. I'm outside in the car." He took a breath and grabbed his wife's hand. "I think some-one's broken into our house."

CHAPTER SIXTEEN

It wasn't them.

The two stunned burglars, clad in athletic sweatshirts and jeans, were descended upon by the Greenwich police—lights flashing and guns drawn—carrying a plasma TV up the Mitmans' driveway, heading back to their van.

The two robbers were barely adults. Yemeni kids from Norwalk. One was twenty-two, the other nineteen. They were shaking in their boots. An hour's interrogation back at the station had them giving up who they had felt up in the fifth grade. They owned up to several of the break-ins. The McLains.

The Polashes. The St. Angelos. They gave up the whereabouts of a basement apartment where the police still could find much of the stolen cache.

It wasn't them.

They got their prospective locations through another cousin who delivered the local paper each morning. That's how they knew when homeowners planned to be away. Neither of them had much of a record. The older one had been pinched for shoplifting. The nineteen-year-old was actually enrolled in Norwalk Community College and this was his first arrest. The older one had a gun on him, an old, passed-down Beretta .22 that he'd bought on the streets. More for show than any real effect.

No match for the Heckler and Koch nine-millimeter that had been used on the Glassman family.

When they were confronted with the murders, everything started coming out of them. They even had an alibi for that night. The younger one's cousin was having a betrothal celebration in Passaic, New Jersey. He had spent the night at the cousin's house.

The older one had spent the night at a

bar in White Plains. Until two A.M. Closing time.

They were stupid and out of their league, and it was good to finally shut their little operation down.

It just wasn't them. Hauck knew. It wasn't the two who murdered Marc and April Glassman.

That morning, he caught Chrisafoulis on the phone as he was scrambling between news briefings. "You got one minute," the head of detectives snapped. "You see what's happening out there, don't you?"

Hauck said, "Yeah, I see it."

What he was talking about were the ten news vans that were backed up like cattle cars onto Mason Street outside the station. CNN, Fox, the local Connecticut stations. Reporters surrounding anyone who came out who looked like they might have some connection to the case. The Glassman murders were page-one news—the grisly scene, the rich suburban family murdered in their secluded home, the calm of Greenwich shattered. And it had brought down a Wall Street icon too.

"It wasn't them, was it?" Hauck pressed.

He doubted the motive was robbery from the start.

"Ty, you know I can't keep doing this. I only have so much room."

"*Steve...*" His voice was insistent. "Were they the ones who did the job?"

"They admitted to *several* jobs," the detective said evasively. "The two out on North Ridge and Willow. They told us where some of the loot was stashed. How they staked out the homes . . ."

"You said that one of the Glassman perps had long reddish hair. You said he had some kind of tattoo on his neck." Hauck knew he was going further than he should. "You said they wore work uniforms. You found tire tread marks on the street. The gun that killed the Glassmans was an H and K nine-millimeter. C'mon, Steve, you know damn well what job I'm talking about."

He waited a beat before Chrisafoulis replied. And when he did, it was short and under his breath. "No. They copped to the other break-ins. But not the Glassmans. One of them is nineteen, the other twenty-two. The guns didn't match up, or the tire tread. Or the descriptions. You should've seen them; shit came out of their pants—"

"Are you buying?"

"They said they set up the jobs through a friend who handled the local paper route. That's how they knew who was away. The Glassmans—they didn't even get the *Greenwich Times*. These guys also had solid alibis for the night of March sixth. We're getting confirmation, but there was a gas receipt in the car that already put one of them on the Jersey Turnpike around that time . . ."

"Yeah, I'm buying." Chrisafoulis sighed resignedly.

Hauck let out a grunt of disappointment. But not surprise. He never thought this fit the pattern of a burglary. It may just have all been a diversion. The safe left open, the drawers rifled through. It may have all been to mask what they were really there for.

Who would have wanted Marc Glassman dead?

"You know where this is leading, don't you, Steve?"

"You're driving around in a BMW now, Ty. You don't have business of your own to spend your time on?"

"Glassman sank the firm. I don't know who would've had anything to gain, but I know what the result of all this is, and it's sitting there on the front page of the *Wall Street Journal* today."

The detective paused. Maybe he was thinking it over. "You never used to read the *Journal,* Ty. You never made it past the sports."

"I guess things change."

"No, they don't," the detective said. Hauck wasn't sure what he was talking about. But he didn't think it was the paper. "They don't."

They hung up. Hauck stared at the bold headline of the *Wall Street Journal* on his desk: FED WEIGHING BAILOUT ON WERTHEIMER; HUNDRED-YEAR-OLD FIRM COULD LEARN FATE TODAY.

Marc's still at Wertheimer. Doing great, April had said.

He balled his fists and dropped them against his desk in frustration. *Who had something to gain?*

His line rang again and Hauck waited before picking up, lost in that question. When he did, on the fourth loud ring, the caller surprised him.

"Mr. Hauck, it's Merrill Simons."

"Ms. Simons . . ." Hauck hadn't contacted her yet with what he knew. He didn't want to cause her any real hurt until he had put it all together. "So far I haven't heard back on much yet. What can I do for you?"

"The last time we spoke . . . ," she said, hesitating. Then she cleared her throat. "I have those other things on Dani you asked me for."

CHAPTER SEVENTEEN

Roger Cantwell stared out at the dark Manhattan sky. The illuminated spire of the Chrysler building shone brightly a few blocks south. It had been a week since the initial disclosures on Marc Glassman. A week of hell. Sleeves rolled up, tie loosened, Cantwell had poured himself a tall Springbank single-malt, his favorite. It had been poured many a time to toast a successful deal or an acquisition.

He couldn't believe it had come to this.

Wertheimer Grant was one of the most respected names on Wall Street. It had weathered *twenty* financial downturns. Led

the recoveries on the way back up. The
firm's commercials—*"Your future is our
future"*—were broadcast during the Super
Bowl. Just a year ago they had a market
cap of a hundred billion.

How could no one be coming to their
rescue? How could there be no fix?

It was insane.

He had made a final pitch to Tom Keat-
ing at Treasury. Christ, they had known
each other for thirty years, used to get
hammered together to celebrate their deals.
Both of them had started as bond salesmen. Wertheimer was far too important to
ever fail. Yes, Cantwell realized, life would
clearly change for him. The cushy bonuses
were gone. And the plane. His legacy would
forever be scarred by the company's having to accept public money. He didn't look
forward to how it would play—in the papers or at his golf club. He wasn't a hundred percent sure if he'd be able to even
stay on.

Still, they had to keep themselves in
business.

**They were Wertheimer Grant, for
God's sake.**

He threw back another hard swig.

The scotch, smooth as it was, burned, and that felt good on the way down. *Frigging Glassman . . .* That little prick had brought down the whole firm. Whatever their fate, the market was going to tank six hundred points tomorrow!

No, Cantwell thought, gazing out at the city he was once such a commanding force in; if he was honest, the bastard had only been the last indefensible boot that had pushed them over the edge. It had been years of the belief that nothing could stop them. More arrogance than greed. The end came so suddenly it hit them like a truck. No one had seen it coming. Not the risk managers, not the rating agencies, not the press. A giant with muscles, as someone had described it once, stuffing itself with cake.

That's what they were. Accountable to no one.

Well, now the giant was about to take a mighty fall.

Cantwell rolled the scotch around his tongue, his mind drifting to a time years before when he was just starting out, wet behind the ears. They had this bond issue from Texas from a basically bankrupt town no one could sell. He was twenty-six, thrust into a job he had no training for, with a boss, Charlie McAfee, a real bastard, Cantwell recalled, who was happy to throw him to the wolves.

"Sink or swim up here," the fat fuck said, grinning, puffing on a cigar. "You know how to swim, Roger?"

Asshole didn't know who he was dealing with. Roger Cantwell chuckled.

He swam. With the goddamn dolphins, he swam! He sold it. He got it done. Every last share. Damn thing ended up over-subscribed. He took it across the country, to pension funds and small brokerage houses. He wrapped the purchase into a twofer with solid triple-A's. Three hundred and fifty million dollars. That night, he had a feeling of self-importance he would never forget. He'd puffed on his first Cuban cigar. Screwed a hot waitress at Doubles like he was some kind of porno star.

Six months later he had the old fart's job.

Cantwell drained the last of his drink. *Funny,* he thought now, *two years later the bond defaulted.* They all knew it would. Blamed it all on Charlie.

It had made his damn career.

There was a knock at his door. Cantwell turned. Ronald Wu, his CFO, with Brenda Pearlstein. They'd just been finishing up with Treasury and had come to give him the painful news.

"Come on in," Cantwell called, resigned. He came away from the window and sat on the long walnut conference table. "So what are the terms?" he inquired. "Just how much flesh do those vultures want us to give up?"

Wu was a brilliant financial mind and over the years had negotiated many tough acquisitions. But this time he was somber.

"*Terms?* There are no terms, Roger. They passed." He came up and collapsed in a chair at the end of the conference table. "No more discussions. I've alerted the attorneys. *We're done.*"

CHAPTER EIGHTEEN

THE WALL STREET JOURNAL

Once-Mighty Wertheimer Collapses as Treasury Department Declines Bailout; Wall Street Stunned

Once one of Wall Street's most historic companies, Wertheimer Grant was forced to shut its doors as last-minute options for the troubled firm, including a prospective bailout by the United States Treasury, failed in the wake of the damage done by a rogue equities trader recently murdered in his Greenwich home. The beleaguered firm was also the victim of a balance sheet weighted down by questionable mortgage-backed assets.

Wertheimer, whose shares last summer traded at over a hundred dollars, sold off in heavy after-hours trading last night for under fifty cents a share.

The once-defiant CEO, Roger Cantwell, who is said to have spent the night in constant talks with potential partners from around the globe, was unavailable for comment. Ronald Wu, Wertheimer's CFO, released a short statement saying the firm "is committed to protecting the interests of its loyal account holders and investor base and right now is studying all available options, including selling off its assets."

Employees of the hundred-year-old firm came to its forty-eight-story glass headquarters on New York's Park Avenue in shock, let in to collect their personal belongings by security personnel. Secretaries and analysts huddled on the street in disbelief.

"The ship sank," one veteran hedge fund manager said. "Since the news of that trader, there's been a weeklong run on the accounts. They no longer had the reserves to fight it off."

The firm succumbed to a balance sheet eroded by heavy investments in toxic subprime mortgages and hurt further by the recent admission that one of their most highly regarded traders had lost as much as twelve billion dollars through unauthorized activity. These latest losses only came to light in the wake of the Glassman family shooting deaths, thought to be a robbery at his spacious Greenwich, CT, home, but now questions have arisen as to whether it was indeed part of a recent home break-in spree there.

"They were too big, too brash," one Wall Street insider said. "They didn't see the oncoming train. How fitting that it was being driven by their own star."

For the fifth straight day, the stock market was expected to tumble to new lows, dragging the financial sector farther down. Shocking revelations of losses and malfeasance have become part of daily life on Wall Street, and the biggest concern, given the loss of reserves and the increasingly questionable value of all mortgage-related securities, is no longer whether Wertheimer Grant will survive, but which "unsinkable" Wall Street icon will be next.

CHAPTER NINETEEN

In her cluttered, windowless office, in the basement of a drab gray building a block from the Treasury Department in Washington, DC, Naomi Blum was trying to put it all together too.

Everyone was buzzing about it. Wertheimer Grant going under. Years of believing they were the right hand of God had dragged them to the edge. Not to mention huge bets on the subprime mess and leveraging up thirty to one.

All it took was a single rogue money manager to push them over.

But what was adding to the trouble was

the new news feed on her computer: MUR-
DERED TRADER NOT LINKED TO LOCAL BREAK-INS.

Not linked . . .

Naomi sucked on a kiwi-mango smoothie,
her lunch. On her desk was a slim blue
folder labeled SECRET AND CONFIDENTIAL. She
had been copied on it by a liaison over at
the FBI. The file contained a series of tran-
scripts picked up from the cell phone of a
wealthy Bahraini businessman long suspected of being a financial go-between with
people in the region who might want to do
the U.S. harm. Probably why the transcript
had landed on her desk in the first place.
She put on her glasses and browsed
through the last, cryptic entry, dated February 8.

What did it mean?

As the lead investigator for the newly
formed Financial Crime and Terrorism Task
Force, a unit of eight under the Department
of the Treasury, her job was to identify and
interrupt wide-scale financial fraud and
conspiracies that might have national-
security or market-impact implications.

They were the first responders, so to
speak, in potential economic attacks
against the United States. They followed

money around the world, charted patterns of deposits in nonconforming banks, monitored the real work of certain questionable "charities," and pretty much "chalkboarded" various potential security threats to the financial landscape here.

It all sounded very important—at least that's what Naomi's mother always told her.

Still, Treasury wasn't exactly the glamour posting these days.

In her two years on the job, they had laid open giant health care schemes aimed at bilking hundreds of millions of subscribers with underpaid claims. They'd prosecuted two prominent hedge fund principals who had diverted billions in duped investors' assets—one who was apprehended trying to fake his own death in an attempt to flee the country, the other presently serving a twenty-year RICO charge at the federal correctional facility in Jesup, Georgia.

Of course, by the time it all got to an arrest, Treasury was no longer running the show. It would be turned over to the financial terrorism section of the FBI. Or the AG's office.

Still, Naomi didn't mind. She sort of liked

being the behind-the-scenes investigator. Like CSI. The *real* CSI, not the TV glamour guys who took the bad guys down and, guns out, were first through the door.

Not that she couldn't handle herself in that way if she had to.

Naomi was five foot three, fit as any field agent, wore stylish black glasses, and kept her dark hair short, Mika Brzezinski–style. She had what guys might call a sort of "bookish" look, like a library rat, despite, behind her frames, her brilliant gray eyes.

She hadn't set out to be in this role. She had actually started out studying music theory at Princeton. Under Amos Kershorn. Her big claim to fame was being first cello in the Anne Arundel County High School Orchestra outside of Baltimore. Along with being an all-Ivy striker on the women's field hockey team.

After 9/11, her twin brother, Jeremy, a lacrosse player at UVA, had dropped out and enlisted. All he said was it was something he just had to do. Growing up, the two of them couldn't have been less alike and still come from the same womb. Jeremy was six foot two, wide shouldered, charismatic, solid as a rock. Cocky as all hell.

Only started cracking the books the night before a test.

She was a foot shorter, quiet, to this day actually kept her driver's license hidden behind her library card. She'd gotten the brains, they always joked, and Jer got whatever was leftover. After a tour in Iraq, he was sent to Fort Benning in Georgia as part of Airborne Ranger training, but in his second week there, the copter he was flying in crashed. He survived but lost both his legs. When she went to see him in the hospital—this big, brave, brawny guy, first-team all-ACC—he turned away. Empty. A shell of what he once was. Even a blind person could have seen the disappointment written on his face.

Two days later, she left Princeton and signed up herself.

She had never really been into the military or overly patriotic before. Her dad was a newspaper editor in Baltimore. She just felt inside that it was something she had to do. In the steps of her big brother. She even pushed for Jim's old regiment, but the army took a look at the fancy school she'd come from and those impressive test results and placed her into an intelligence unit. Naomi spent two years in Iraq as a junior member on the army's internal investigative team. One of her assignments was to look into the bloodbath that occurred at Nisoor Square in Baghdad, where a handful of private security guards, claiming they were provoked, fired wildly into a crowded square, leaving seventeen Iraqis dead. Naomi pushed hard in her search, sure that an unprovoked and criminal act had been committed. She urged her superiors to detain the participants, but by that time the agency had secretly whisked the guilty contractors "out of country," and the government seemed intent on papering everything over and letting them go.

Years later, it still burned her.

Naomi realized that the accountability went much higher, but by that point the result was merely a whitewash, a PR exercise, though in the wake of press exposure from her findings, the security outfit was forever banned from Iraq.

After her second tour—she saw action on a couple of hairy convoys—she opted out and went back to school. Changed her major to economics. A degree in music no longer carried the same weight in her

new way of thinking of the world. She figured she'd go to law school, maybe Wall
Street, do the sixteen-hour-days-until-you-
make-partner thing, but when she was
recommended to Treasury by a superior
she had worked with in the field, and he
told the department they would never find
anyone smarter or more dogged on a case,
something just clicked.

What clicked was the chance to finally
feel she was making a difference.

She'd always been on the small side
physically, and private. Part of her had always needed to prove that she was tough
enough. It went back to the way she played
attack on the field—hide on the flank, spot
the opening, worm her way in among the
bigger girls. Use her speed and guile and
knowledge of the game.

Then hammer it home.

It was what she was still doing. At Treasury. She just happened to be the only one
doing it with the five-note opening progres-
sion of Glass's "Music in the Shape of a
Square" tattooed on her butt.

Naomi looked again at the FBI security
transcript. She sipped her smoothie. She
didn't know the caller, but she damn well

knew the person he was caught speaking to.

And it wasn't making a whole lot of sense.

The conversation had taken place about a month ago. Since then the world financial markets had fallen apart. The Dow was down 20 percent. One of the largest institutions brought down by a rogue trader.

And here was one of the most influential financial managers in the world, who oversaw one of the largest pools of investment capital anywhere, in contact with a suspected terrorist money mover.

And the cryptic words uttered in Arabic that had been passed along to her. That scared her. That left her wondering what this was all about.

The planes are in the air.

CHAPTER TWENTY

Monday afternoon, Hauck sat in his car across the street from the Lake Avenue Lower School in Greenwich.

Three weeks had passed since the Glassman murders. Still no link to their killers had been found.

At a little after two forty in the afternoon, a stream of kids began to emerge from the gray concrete building. Moms, in capri pants and yoga outfits, chatting with other moms or on their cells, pulling up their SUVs. Some of the kids carted stuff from school, brightly colored presentation boards or artwork, knapsacks slung over their shoulders. Others carried baseball gloves or lacrosse sticks, shouting excitedly about the Rangers' playoff game tonight or *American Idol*. The cars pulled up; the kids climbed in; the moms waved good-bye to one another and drove away.

The entrance quieted down.

A couple of minutes later, Hauck saw the small, sandy-haired boy in jeans and a Derek Jeter jersey come out, holding on to the hand of an older man. His grandfather. He carried a piece of paper all rolled up, a red knapsack slung over on his back.

Hauck remembered him as he saw him three or four years ago. In April's car.

Evan.

It was his first day back at school after the incident. The local papers had picked it up. A couple of school officials came out and watched as he and his granddad made their way to the parking lot, making sure there were no reporters badgering them.

Hauck wanted to make sure too.

The boy had done well. He had snapped a couple of photos that might one day be used as evidence. He was a chip off the old block. His mom would have been proud.

Hauck didn't know what had made him

come here. Other than it made him feel close. Still attached. Mindful of his promise. He hadn't forgotten. He wouldn't.

See, I wasn't just passing through, he said.

The boy climbed into a silver Volvo wagon and his granddad drove away.

Hauck had an urge to follow him. But he just put the car in gear and remained there.

CHAPTER TWENTY-ONE

It took some time for the picture of Dani Thibault to begin to come together.

Merrill had hoped it might all just be a big waste of his time. A bit of overcaution on her part that would calm a few fears but ultimately lead nowhere.

It wasn't.

Hauck tapped on the office phone, deciding whether to call her.

Thibault had lied about where he had gone to school. He had lied about having served in the Dutch army, assigned to a peacekeeping mission in Kosovo. He had lied about his connection to the Belgian

royal family too. The truth was he had
dated a party-happy cousin of the queen
for a couple of weeks and maybe attended
a family outing or two with her where the
photos that hung on his office walls were
taken. The relationship fizzled out, except
for the requisite gossip-column snapshots
of the two of them in posh clubs that Richard Snell had located on the Internet.

For the most part Thibault's career con-
sisted of a few progressively more senior
positions in various shady banks, managing
wealthy clients' money and setting up hard-
to-pierce financial trusts. He had taken his
name and part of his background from a
man who had been killed fifteen years ago
in France.

Who does that, Hauck wondered, *but a
person with something very important to
hide?*

These last two weeks, Hauck had
learned everything he could about
Thibault's personal affairs. He knew where
he got his suits in London—at Kilgour on
Savile Row. He knew where he stayed
while in Dubai—at the Burj, seven stars.
He knew what restaurants he frequented
when he was in New York—Veritas, Daniel,

Spartina. He paid his bills. There were no liens or judgments against him. His e-mail traffic showed a variety of normal business and personal contacts. Nothing out of the ordinary. Maybe a bit of a kinky side when it came to Merrill. He didn't even seem to have anyone else on the side.

And he hadn't committed any crimes.

All Hauck found was a shadowy past that surely covered up something that the man had gone to great lengths to conceal. Even from Merrill. Why was it up to Hauck to destroy him? He wasn't with the police any longer.

We don't do this kind of work, he had said to Foley. Mess with people's lives.

This time we do.

He opened a thick folder filled with photos he had compiled of Dani. Some were from *Greenwich Magazine* at charity events. He and Merrill. A few were from the Shiny Sheet in Palm Beach. The Garden Club Ball. Page Six in the *New York Post.* He didn't exactly shy away from publicity.

He thumbed through a few contact sheets a friend of his who worked for *Fairfield Style* had sent over. A gathering for the state's attorney general on Ron

Tillerson's yacht. "Merrill Simon and financier Dani Thibault." Saturday polo matches at Conyers Farm. Thibault had some horses. The two of them looked happy, in love. Holding hands.

It was her choice, what to do with what they had found. Her call.

This wasn't exactly the kind of work he had signed up for when he changed careers.

He picked up the phone and dialed Tom Foley to let him know what information they had. Let his boss decide how to take it to Merrill. Her ex-husband was still a very important account. It was still a new job for Hauck, and the whole thing was a bit uncomfortably politically charged. The receptionist at Talon's New York office put him on hold.

He opened the folder and slid the photos back in.

One, near the bottom, caught his eye.

It was at the Conyers Farm polo gathering. A Patrons of Greenwich Library literacy thing. A bunch of the usual types Hauck had dealt with over the years: men in blazers and green pants, the women in expensive sundresses and large hats.

Thibault, wearing a white linen blazer and open white shirt, was caught in conversation with someone who seemed slightly familiar, behind dark sunglasses, his back turned to the camera but his profile clearly visible. It was an outtake, cropped from a larger shot. The two of them never even knew it was being snapped.

Hauck was about to stuff it back in the file when it hit him with a jolt just who the man Thibault was talking to was.

He put down the phone.

It made the next step with Thibault no longer Merrill Simons's call.

It was a face Hauck had seen in the papers and on TV. Very much in the news. He flipped it over, his antennae buzzing like crazy, looked for the date. *June, last year.*

It would have been meaningless back then, the two of them talking.

But *now,* with the Dow dropping a couple of thousand points, with one of Wall Street's biggest firms toppled, a close friend from his past brutally killed, Hauck fixed numbly on the forgotten photo, his blood on fire.

The man caught with Dani Thibault, looking away, was April Glassman's husband, Marc.

PART II

CHAPTER TWENTY-TWO

It was two in the morning and James Donovan was scared.

For weeks, he'd shut his eyes this time of night and listened to his wife's steady breathing. He'd looked in on Zachy, his four-year-old, asleep in his room. He'd gone online, checked his positions. The Alt-A's collapsing. Volumes drying up. Until he couldn't take it anymore. Felt like he was about to explode.

Then he'd leashed up the dog and gone downstairs in the dead of night for some air.

He'd done something terribly wrong.
Now he didn't know how to take it back.

Tonight, the sharp breeze off the East
River blew right through his parka. Remi,
his white bichon, looked up at him as if she
wanted to head back inside. James wasn't
ready yet.

He didn't know what to do.

The first check he'd taken had been for
1.6 million dollars. Deposited into an account in the Cayman Islands he opened in
his son's name. He'd waited until the funds
were in his hands. The next one was for
2.3. Life-changing money. Given what was
going on in the markets, money he'd never
have been able to duplicate. Not with the
mortgage securities markets gone to hell.
With the firm talking about no bonuses this
year. Or next. With the stock slid all the way
to six.

*They were prepared to give him five
million!* How could he turn that kind of security away?

At first, it had been easy. Like with all
sure things, it was easy to lure yourself in,
justify it. Hard to pull yourself out.

It had made sense. For his family. Buddies of his, people he had gone to B-school with, they made that in a crappy year. Lapping up homes in the Hamptons. Shares in private jets. Renting villas in the Caribbean. Fancy wine cellars.

Why not him?

Besides, the firm was basically tapioca now. Tanking. He was just part of the picture.

But then everything changed. That guy from Wertheimer, in Greenwich. That changed the whole effing thing. Every time James thought of him he broke out in a clammy sweat.

They killed the guy's whole family.

He led Remi farther up the block on the leash. He noticed the black SUV parked up the street from his building. The windows were blacked out, but still he thought he saw a face, the same face, one he'd seen before, watching.

Was he going crazy? Hadn't he seen the same vehicle yesterday? As he came home from the office. The same man behind the glass. Hadn't he been there the day before, when he and Leslie had snuck out for a bite? He'd asked the doorman.

Hadn't noticed it before. Manny just laughed and said, "Probably driving some big shot in 225 over there, Mr. Donovan."

Yeah, some big shot, Manny. James wondered if the guy from Wertheimer had ever felt someone tracking him.

Or he could just have been making it all up. Driving himself nuts. He tugged on the dog. *C'mon, do your thing.* He felt like he was running on amphetamines. Like his brain was about to explode.

James knew, really knew, it was too late. Too late to undo everything. *You've made your bed, Jimbo. You wanted it both ways.* Now he just had to see it through.

If he came clean, he'd be fired on the spot. Probably prosecuted. Serve jail time. At the very least, he'd be banned from the business for life. What else did he know how to do? Christ, he was just thirty-two.

No, the better option was to simply see it through. Take the rest of the money. This thing with Marc Glassman just had him spooked.

He glanced at the parked SUV again.

James dragged Remi into the lobby. Carlos, the overnight attendant, waved, mop-ping the floor. Third time he had seen him this week. *He must be wondering . . .*

Upstairs, James unleashed the dog, took off his parka, flicked on Bloomberg. He took a glimpse at the overnights from Asia. Downward pressure again. The spread was like a spike driven into his heart. He grabbed a Dove bar out of the freezer and went back down the hall. Looked in on Zach sleeping. It was after three now. In two hours he had to get up and cover his trades.

How had he let his life fall apart?

In the bedroom, the light was now on. His wife, Leslie, sat up in bed and watched him come in. She'd noticed changes in him for weeks. Clamming up. Shutting her out. Not wanting to play with Zach.

James was sweating. His face was empty. He could no longer hold the tide back. He sat down, and she crawled up beside him worriedly and took his hand. He didn't know what else to do except clasp on tight to hers.

Could he tell her?

Could he ever admit what he'd done?

"What's going on with you, Jimmy?"

CHAPTER TWENTY-THREE

Thanks for coming in, Ty."

Hauck sat across from Tom Foley at San Pietro, a block from Talon's Fifty-fifth Street headquarters. Foley had ordered a Belvedere vodka on the rocks with olives, and Hauck, who never drank during the day, asked for a beer. He had brought with him the file he'd assembled on Thibault and needed an okay before proceeding. Foley suggested lunch. The leather booth in the back gave them some privacy from the lunchtime crowd.

"Cheers." Foley tilted his glass. "Here's to staying afloat in the storm. Funny"—the

Talon director chuckled—"some of the guys and I were just tossing out a few ideas, Ty, where we think you can be useful to the firm."

"I'd love to hear about that"—Hauck took a sip of beer—"but I wanted to bring you up-to-date on Merrill Simons. You asked me to keep you informed."

"Oh, right, of course . . ." Foley nodded, seeming almost distracted. He took a second sip of his vodka. "Shoot."

"I know she's a friend of yours," Hauck said. He opened his satchel. Leaning forward, he told him what he and Richard Snell had put together. Thibault's falsified background. His phony degrees, military service. His overstated claims about the Belgian royal family that bordered on fraud. The dead man's identity he had stolen. Which brought up deeper things. "The guy's a fraud, Tom. Maybe a whole lot worse. I'm sorry."

Foley put on his glasses and paged through the file. He winced at some things and shook his head. "The prick. Knew it was too goddamn good to be true. Have you told her?"

"No. I thought I'd run it by you first."

"She's going to be crushed," Foley said. He went to take a drink. "Maybe it's best if—"

"*Tom.*" Hauck put his hand on Foley's wrist. "There's more." He took out the photograph he had found of Thibault with Marc Glassman in Greenwich and slipped it on top of the file. "You see who that is?"

Foley squinted above his glasses, and when it registered, the composed Yankee demeanor almost cracked. "*Sonova effing bitch!*" He rubbed his hand across his mouth. "Where was this taken?"

"In Greenwich. At Conyers Farm. At a charity polo event, last summer. Listen, Tom . . ." Foley seemed to be trying to calculate just what this meant. "Alone it doesn't prove anything. It could've occurred in a hundred ways. They may have been talking about what to feed the goddamn horse. But I checked around a bit. Glassman didn't have any connections to Greenwich Polo and I can't imagine he was part of Dani's regular crowd."

Foley nodded, pursing his thin lips in concern. "Anything else that ties the two of them together?"

"Not that I've found. Yet."

"What about anything criminal in Thibault's past?"

"Criminal," Hauck asked, "or suspicious?"

"Something firm, Ty."

Hauck shook his head. "Other than raising a substantial sum of money on an overstated relationship to the Belgian royal family and falsifying his identity . . . But I think this is something the FBI or Interpol might well show an interest in too."

Foley placed the photo back on the pile. "Doesn't prove anything, you know?"

"No." Hauck nodded. "Not in itself. But there's still an unsolved homicide in France. And I think maybe all those folks whose money he's representing might want to know who he is."

Foley gulped down the rest of his vodka and motioned to the waiter for another. Hauck shook his head. "I'm fine."

"Have one," Foley said, raising two fingers. He rested his forearms on the table, gold cufflinks showing through his sleeves. "Listen, Ty, I'd rather, if you can see it our way on this, that none of this had to come out."

Hauck fixed his eyes on him, surprised.

Foley shrugged. "I mean, it's clear Merrill

should know her boyfriend's a piece of re-fuse. But the rest . . ." He tapped the photo. "This other thing . . ."

"This other thing what, Tom? Marc Glassman brought down a Wall Street bank. His family's murder is still an open homicide. Thibault's got a murky past, is deep in certain financial circles, and is seen together with the victim. To me it's a bit more than '*this other thing.*'"

Foley took in a breath and nodded. He rubbed his palms together in front of his face. "I want you to listen to me, Ty. We didn't put you on here, give you all this money, so you could continue thinking like a cop. You're not representing the town of Greenwich anymore. You're representing us. Wertheimer's gone. The Treasury's carving up whatever meat is left on the bone and selling it off. Other than that fancy building, their only real asset is their retail brokerage operation. It's still second only to Merrill Lynch. You have any idea who's in line for that?"

Hauck stared at Foley. Now he did.

"Reynolds Reid. That's who. Who also happens to be, other than the United States government, our largest account! See how it's all fitting in, Ty? And our job is to protect the interests of our accounts now, not the people. Not investigate wrongdoing. That's the government's job." His boss stared at him directly. "Now I know I asked you to check out this guy—for a friend—and you did. You did it well. But that's it now. That's as far as it goes. You've got no proof he's done anything wrong. So he's caught talking to a guy at a public venue whose luck happened to go the other way. You going to look into everyone Marc Glassman might have talked to? I bet if you checked out where these pictures are from, they've got him yapping to twenty people like Thibault that same day."

"Tom, this is a guy who's gone to great lengths to camouflage his past. Only people who do that are people with something to hide. At the very least, we have to look into who he is."

"No." Foley shook his head with a frozen stare. "No. At the very least, we do what we can to make sure our client sees through a very important deal. If rumors start to fly that this trader dude was dirty or compromised in some way, if people start looking into this Wertheimer thing and then it gets

mixed back up with Merrill, the CEO's ex-wife, or *us* . . ." The second round of drinks came and Foley winked at the pretty bartender who brought them over, then looked back to Hauck, his gaze tight. "You're a partner here now. Not a cop, so I don't expect you to act like one. So your priorities are ours. After the sale goes through, maybe then, in a couple of weeks . . . a month. Then you can rattle the cage a little harder. We'll look at it again. How's that?"

"And what about Merrill?'

Foley inhaled a deep, conflicted sort of breath, then shrugged. "This isn't something she has to know about right now. Trust me. A month. String it along. We'll see then. You see what I mean?"

Hauck wet his lips, a bitter taste in his mouth. It felt uncomfortable, soiled, even rolling over what Foley had proposed. In his past life . . .

But maybe things *had* changed. Accepting the job and the money. Maybe he had to get used to that. New priorities. After all, nothing had been proven. Hauck felt himself nodding, fighting the urge that he was going against everything he was made of inside.

"Good." Foley smiled and gave a pat to Hauck's shoulder. "A couple of weeks, a month." He lifted his new glass, the color coming back to his complexion. "Now if that's all done maybe we can shift the subject to you, Ty . . . and how we see you fitting into this organization."

CHAPTER TWENTY-FOUR

The idea that Talon might use him as a kind of spokesperson appealed to Hauck, against his better nature, on the drive home.

Maybe it was helped along by a couple of beers.

His boss had talked about taking advantage of Hauck's reputation for independence, uncovering money launderers and even a corrupt senior state senator, and thought that would go well with some of the government contracts they were after. While Hauck had shied away from any publicity after his last big case—the killing of a

federal prosecutor from up in Hartford—
the story had become front-page news
and had brought an end to the career of
one of the state's most powerful politicians
as well as put a stain on the legacy of one
of its wealthiest tycoons.

He drove onto the Major Deegan Expressway, past Yankee Stadium, trying to
push the questions about Dani Thibault
and Marc Glassman out of his head.

He punched in Annie's cell. She was at
work, and he'd promised to let her know
how the meeting went. But as soon as it
began to ring, something made him think
twice and, not sure why, he clicked the line
off.

The truth was that nowhere in Hauck's
soul was there a single, isolated place
where Foley's response on how to handle
Thibault sat peacefully in him, nowhere
in the back-and-forth of his conscience
that the option of just doing nothing, letting
it sit—*what's right for our accounts, that's
your priority now*—made sense.

Instead, as he swung the Beemer
onto the parkway heading to Connecticut,
twenty minutes from home, there was Merrill. The doubts he saw deep in her eyes.

She didn't want to put it aside. *I want to know who the man I'm supposed to be falling in love with really is.*

You're not representing the town of Greenwich anymore . . .

Instead, there was Thibault. A cipher. A con man. Or much, much worse. Deals that didn't happen. Relationships that didn't exist. What kind of man did all that? What was it he had to hide?

You know who's bidding on Wert-heimer's retail business, Ty? Foley had patted him on the shoulder.

He was feeling played.

Instead, there were headlines about the once-mighty Wall Street firm in ruins. Jobs lost. The Dow in freefall. Fortunes deci-mated. Marc Glassman and April and their beautiful daughter dead.

Now if that's all done maybe we can shift the subject to you, Ty . . .

What is it, he thought as he lost himself in the rhythm of the drive, *that's really be-ing protected here?* Just because he had made this shift in his life, just because his company ID now said Talon, not the Greenwich police, he couldn't just put it behind him. The unrest in his blood was the same, the same he'd always felt.

How do you put away something that is as true to you as the beating of your own heart?

How do you put the truth behind you?

"Well, the first thing you should know"—April smiled, taking a sip of coffee—**"is you're not going crazy. Insanity is inherited, you know." She bit her lower lip. "You get it from your kids."**

He laughed, taking a sip of his latte too. "I always thought it was the other way around."

"Popular misconception," she said. "Forgiven. Everyone makes that mistake at first."

"Thanks for initiating me."

After his third time there, their eyes bumping into each other a few times, they had happened to leave the building together and talked for a second on the sidewalk. There was a Starbucks on the corner and she asked him if he liked mocha lattes.

"I'm more of a black, no sugar man. But I'm aching to have my horizons expanded."

"Then my treat."

They had walked over to a couch. She ordered for him. "I'm sorry to hear about what happened," she said, stirring her coffee. There was something immediately open and trusting about her, and since the accident, since Hauck's marriage had dissolved and he had walked away from the force, he hadn't shared much with anyone. So it was nice just to sit down with someone. And she was pretty. And kind. "Losing a child."

"Look," he said, "things have a way of getting a bit gloomy upstairs, so we don't have to talk about this if you don't want. But thanks."

"It's not your fault, you know." She shrugged. Her eyes were a soft moss green. "I know you don't believe that now, but it isn't."

All he said was "I know."

April's smile widened. "No one would believe that you do, you know. Know that."

He was in a state he had never felt before. Nothing had ever come easily to him. He had to work at everything— school, sports. Those rushing records in high school, they took every ounce of sweat and determination he had. Getting himself into Colby. His brother had talked his way into law school; for Hauck, it just seemed right to go a different direction. Onto the force. And he rose. Made detective before he was thirty. His fancy degree got him recruited to One Police Plaza. Department of Information. Under the eye of the assistant chief. His marriage thrived. Two adorable girls. Back then, the arc of his life seemed unlimited. Forever rising. For just a moment, a fleeting instant, he had let all that focus and dedication relax. Taken his eye off it.

You could never take your eye off it. Then . . .

"I may not be crazy," he said, smiling back, "but I've sure done some crazy things. Recently . . ."

"Tell me."

"I don't know, all seems kinda stupid now. After the thing with Norah, I sat outside a D'Agostino in Elmhurst for three hours in the middle of the night until I took a brick and flung it through the storefront window."

"Oh? They give you a roast chicken past the sell date?"

"No." He shook his head with a bit of a smile. "That's where I was headed when I let the car back down the drive-way . . . When . . ."

Even the way she looked at him made him feel better. Like there was an end to this. Like one day, someone would find him interesting again. "Seems stupid now. My precinct head had to intercede. Anyway, that's how I got here."

"I drove my daughter to ballet on a combination of OxyContin and antide-pressants. I ended up in Bucks County, Pennsylvania."

"What was in Pennsylvania?" he asked.

April smiled. "Don't know. The Amish. I just mean to say, you've got no mo-nopoly on letting the walls fall down. Your daughter was killed. You felt responsible. Sometimes we all just have to do crazy things. Who threw that brick? You?"

"I don't know." Hauck shrugged. "Maybe someone inside me."

"What does Dr. Paul say? Doctor-patient confidentiality aside, of course."

"He said it would be good to find out who that person is."

"Look . . ." She touched his arm, leaning closer. "Those people upstairs . . . Some of them have been coming to this group for over ten years. The honest-to-God truth is, there are two types—the ones whose brain chemistry has been out of whack since they were kids. Whose every day is a fight to keep things in balance. Then there's the people for whom the walls that kept everything together have just temporarily come down. Like your walls. Whether you like it or not." She cupped her hands around her mug. "Those are the ones just passing through." There was a twinkle in her eyes. "Sorry, mister, that's you."

"Thanks," he said. He felt almost embarrassed. **He looked up and saw her staring at him, not suggestive in any way. But he was sure he saw a little sadness in her too.**

"So which type are you?"

By the time Hauck hit the Merritt Parkway, the unrest had grown into something that he had felt many times before and wouldn't easily go away.

Just passing through. She was right. He had gone to the group for eight sessions. That inner person, he knew damn well who it was now.

It was the person who was about to do *this.*

He reached for his cell and punched in a number off the speed dial. After a couple rings, a familiar voice picked up. "Collucci," the person answered.

Vito Collucci was an ex–Stamford detective who had his own successful investigative agency now. Sometimes it had helped to have a source for these kinds of things outside of the force, and he had helped Hauck many times.

"Ty," Vito said, sounding pleased, "I'm

surprised a big shot like you has time to remember the little fish like me. You got my e-mail?"

"Yeah, Vito, that was nice of you. Thanks. You mentioned if you could help out in any way . . ."

"Jeez, that was only a figure of speech, my friend. But the hell with it, if you're serious, shoot."

"I need you to pull me a cell phone history." Hauck reached over and opened his case. Holding the wheel, he pulled out the profile and read Vito the number. "The subject's name is Thibault." He spelled it for him. "First name Dieter. Or Dani. D-A-N-I. I know this isn't particularly glamorous, guy."

"Yeah, and I can't even charge you for it," the private detective replied. "But I'm a little confused. Don't you have people in that high-profile firm who do this kind of thing routinely?"

Hauck paused, exiting the parkway at Long Ridge Road. *Just a small step,* he cautioned himself. *A toe in the water.*

But that's how everything always got started.

"If it's okay, I was thinking we might keep this separate from my high-profile firm, Vito. Alright by you?"

The Stamford investigator laughed. "That didn't take long, Ty."

CHAPTER TWENTY-FIVE

His daughter Jessie came up for the weekend. Now that she was fourteen, she took the train up from Grand Central. Every once in a while they drove up to Butternut in Western Massachusetts and went skiing or saw her cousins up near Hartford. Sometimes they just hung at the house and watched a bunch of movies. She was reaching for her independence now full-throttle, and Hauck realized it was getting harder and harder to lure her up there. Something was always popping up—a basketball game at school, Amanda's party, a Rooney concert. More and more, she spent her time with him with her legs hanging over the couch, on Facebook or on her cell gabbing.

This time, he caved and agreed to take her to see *Knocked Up,* despite the R rating. Which he regretted from the opening credits.

"Jeez, Dad," Jessie said afterward as Hauck checked uncomfortably for the sign of some other kids her age, "it's not like it's stuff I've never seen."

When the hell had Nemo morphed into Seth Rogen?

That Sunday, he got up early and stole some time on the computer. He took a jog around Hope Cove, and the April morning air was salty and starting to warm. Another month and it would be time to take out the boat. It was anyone's guess if Jessie would be up for that anymore.

Later, he made pancakes for her when she came out at nine thirty, wiping sleep out of her eyes. He watched her, as he sipped his coffee, in her sweatshirt and pajama bottoms, wondering if there was anything quite as hopeful or beautiful in the world. He missed Norah—he thought of her scrunched-up nose and singsong laughter every day. Eventually Jessie caught him staring blankly. "What, Dad?"

"Nothing," he said.

After breakfast, he put his face in the sun on the deck overlooking the sound and took out the Sunday *New York Times.*

Jessie was already on the phone on the couch, watching Comedy Central. He started with the sports section. Tiger and Phil were gearing up for a showdown at the Masters. The Yanks lost to the Red Sox on opening day.

As he threw the sports aside and searched for business, a headline on the front page of the metro section grabbed him.

Suicide Victim in High-Rise Is Second Wall Street Trader

The body found hanging yesterday morning in the office of a superintendent of a midtown apartment building was identified as that of James Donovan, a mortgage bond trader at Wall Street firm Beeston Holloway. Mr. Donovan was a resident of the building.

The death is being considered a suicide, and Donovan is the second high-profile Wall Street trader in the past month to meet a sudden end. Mark Glassman, a securities trader at the recently collapsed Wertheimer Grant, was fatally shot along with his family in what was thought to be a break-in at his home in Greenwich, CT, on March 6. The resulting scandal of losses and trading mismanagement helped to take down the firm.

Donovan, 32, was a high rider, recently described by friends and coworkers as having appeared "bothered" and "preoccupied" of late, perhaps resulting from the precipitous turnaround in the mortgage bond market. Staff at the upscale building where he lived with his wife and son said he was often seen in the middle of the night walking his dog, and seemed to have some arrangement that allowed him access to the superintendent's office, where his body was discovered early Friday morning as the building's super, Luis Verga, arrived for work. Mr. Verga would not comment other than to say he knew Mr. Donovan and that "he was a good guy," but one building staffer said Mr. Donovan often used the office to take late calls because "it was a twenty-four-hour-a-day job and he didn't want to bother his wife at late hours. He was on the board. At Christmas, he made it worthwhile."

Friends and coworkers described the successful trader as changed in the past few weeks, "kind of withdrawn and edgy." "He felt under a lot of pressure," one coworker said. Susan Fine, spokesperson for Beeston Holloway, said, "Jim was an excellent young man and an adept trader. His future was on the rise."

Speculation that Donovan's suicide was related to a pattern of financial mismanagement that helped bring down the once-mighty Wertheimer Grant began to circulate as soon as the news of the trader's suicide hit the streets. "Such speculation is completely unfounded and untrue," Fine said when asked to comment. "Beeston has tight operational controls." She added that the firm, despite its own dramatic stock slide over the past weeks and rumors of impending write-downs against its balance sheet, "is on sound financial footing."

Donovan, who is originally from Sayville, Long Island, and received an MBA from NYU, leaves behind his wife, Leslie, and a son, Zachary, four.

Hauck put the article down. He stared, doubt swarming in him, at the placid sound.

He didn't really believe in coincidences, and like every cop, he lived by the rule "Where there's smoke, there's fire."

A second Wall Street trader suspiciously dead was now a fire.

CHAPTER TWENTY-SIX

At 6:40 that Monday morning, Naomi came in from her early run along the Potomac. She threw her shell top on the chair in her two-level apartment in Alexandria, her gray Bon Jovi T-shirt and tight black leggings soaked through with sweat. She took a water bottle out of the fridge and placed the cool plastic against her forehead, exhaling. That felt good.

Six miles.

She had done it in a little under thirty-two minutes. She was building up for next year's Marine Corp marathon. Pushing for an under-three-twenty time.

Next week she'd push herself up to eight.

She peeled off her shirt, down to her sports bra, and got ready to head into the shower. She checked her government e-mail.

This second dead Wall Street trader was on her radar. She was taught to look for patterns, and for this one she didn't have to look very far. By seven, a staff assistant would forward her links to any news story that might be of interest, and over the *Post,* coffee, and the *Financial Times* Naomi would scroll through them to bring herself up to speed for the day. Yesterday, news came out on James Donovan, who had died under unusual circumstances. From Beeston Holloway. Hung himself. Couldn't stand the pressure. These young guys had come out of college, made more their first year than Naomi had to her name. They'd only seen the market go one way—up!— their entire lives.

At least that's how it was being portrayed in the press. She'd already brought it to Rob Whyte, her boss at Treasury. It didn't smell right. No matter how it was being portrayed. "You watch," she told him, "something's not right on this. I should go check it out." She scrolled through her in-box, looking for whatever had been posted on the trader's suicide.

There was a new item flashing. Along with the red message light on her Black-Berry.

It was a text from Rob. Naomi saw that he'd posted a link.

The subject was "Second Trader Dead." The only thing it said was "Need to talk on this TODAY!"

Something else had happened.

Putting her yogurt down, she clicked on the link, which turned out to be an update of the earlier story, on Bloomberg, dated only an hour ago.

DEAD BEESTON TRADER IMPLICATED IN SECOND INVESTOR SCANDAL. BILLIONS UNACCOUNTED FOR. COMPANY CALLS DAMAGE "MATERIAL AND PERVASIVE." AUDIT UNDER WAY.

STOCK REELING IN OVERSEAS TRADING.

She knew it! She turned on the TV. CNBC was on it. Their angle was an out-of-control Wall Street unable to cope with the downturn. First Wertheimer, now Beeston.

No, she now felt sure—that wasn't what was going on. *Not at all.*

She was taught to look for patterns. Patterns that could be woven into puzzles. Threats.

This one was right in front of her.

Naomi grabbed her BlackBerry and texted her boss. "Already on it," she said.

CHAPTER TWENTY-SEVEN

The second investment manager to die under suspicious circumstances quickly became front-page news.

The media paraded it as a sign of Wall Street "on 'roids!" No controls. All oversight shattered. Donovan became a tragic case of the life-altering pressures of highly remunerated "dice rollers" unable to cope with their evaporating positions. The post-boom world.

First it was the subprime debacle, Wertheimer going belly-up. Then it was Fannie and Freddie teetering, AIG coughing up blood. Now it was Beeston. Portfolio managers having to double down on their bets to make up their widening losses, taking their firms down with them. Over the edge. These people weren't programmed for anything but success.

James Donovan had only known life one way. Up.

He just couldn't handle it.

Hauck opened the door to the Seventeenth Precinct station house. He'd left work early that afternoon and driven to the city. Monday was the night he usually had Annie over and cooked dinner, but tonight, this new development was on his mind.

On the way in, he'd caught the news. Beeston said it was engaged in heated talks to save the company. They were now admitting Donovan had cost them billions. Pundits were speculating that he had started to panic when the scandal at Wertheimer hit, knowing he could no longer keep the lid on his own giant losses. Now the only momentum on the Street was toward outright panic. Wertheimer was history. Beeston Holloway could be next. The whole financial sector had zero support.

Hauck winced. The Dow had tumbled to its worst level in eight years yesterday.

The precinct station was on East Fifty-first. Hauck went upstairs and asked a woman sitting behind the duty desk for Detective Campbell.

The woman pointed toward a portly, red-haired man at a desk against the window in a V-neck sweater who was on the phone. "Over there."

Hauck walked over and waited for the detective to finish up. Campbell was scribbling notes on a pad, his foot up on an open drawer. "Gimme a second," he said, signaling Hauck with a look that told him to wait. His desk was piled high with open files and paperwork; against the wall he had two framed pictures of his kids. There was a wooden chair next to his desk and a couple of books stacked on it. Hauck took note of one: *The Idiot's Guide to Understanding Wall Street.*

He chuckled.

When the detective finally got off, he wheeled around in his chair to face Hauck and crossed his legs. "Shep Campbell, sorry . . ."

"My name's Hauck." Hauck draped his sport jacket across his arm. "I used to be in homicide with the one fourteen in

Queens, and later at the DOI, under Chief Burns."

Campbell nodded, jabbing his finger in recognition. "Yeah, I know you, don't I? Didn't you get your face on the tube for some big case you had up there? The Grand Central bombing, right? That guy who wasn't dead . . . You're Hauck."

"That's it." Hauck took out a card and handed it to him. The detective pursed his lips and blew out a frowning chirp. Cops who jumped ship to the private sector generally weren't esteemed by those who had stuck around, worked out their time on a city salary. They came across a bit like sellouts.

Campbell took note of Hauck's firm and put the card down. "Went over the wall, huh? Can't exactly blame you. You found your ticket. Kids gotta go to school." He cleared the books off the chair next to his desk and motioned for Hauck to sit down. "Bet yours are in some fancy academy up there now, right? What brings you back down?"

"The Donovan thing." Hauck ignored the rest. "I was hoping I might ask you a few questions."

Campbell sighed loudly. "Topic of the day."

"I'm trying to figure out if there are any links to that other thing that took place up in Greenwich. That trader who was killed with his family."

The detective nodded, grabbing a bag of pistachios, not offering one to Hauck. "I see. That thing was connected to a home break-in ring up there, wasn't it?"

Hauck shrugged. "That's what it was deemed at first."

"Then I'm sure you read that this one was deemed to be a suicide." He split a nut and tossed the shell into his trash bin. "What sort of similarities are you looking for?"

"Two money managers dead under suspicious circumstances? I was wondering if you had a chance to look over the victim's phone records yet."

"Phone records?"

"Or maybe at the building's security cameras. I assume they have them."

"For what?"

"For anyone who might've entered close to the time of death."

"Security cameras . . ." The detective

popped the nut into his mouth and looked at Hauck's card again. "Hauck, right? *Talon* . . . Heard of it. Big firm. This says you're a partner up there. I know it's hard to turn down these kinds of opportunities. Maybe if something came my way . . . We all have to make a choice. You mind telling me just what is your particular point of interest here?"

A pushy ex-cop from out of town. A well-paid one at that. Coming around and sticking his nose into an active case. No particular jurisdiction. Hauck expected the response. "I knew a member of the Glassman family who was killed up there. I'm just following up to see if there's any link between these two cases. Two rogue traders. Lots of losses. Two Wall Street firms driven over the edge. You heard the news today?"

"Yeah, it's all here on page one oh six, right in my trusty bible." Campbell picked up the Wall Street manual, smirking. "I assume you're not buying into the home-invasion angle?"

Hauck shrugged. "All I'm buying is just to follow up. For a friend."

Campbell nodded again, mock-sympathetically, but his gaze stayed on Hauck, then shifted again to his card. "Hmmph, you know, maybe this is *my* ticket out." He snorted. "I'm not exactly Warren effing Buffett, y'know . . . Not much ever came my way. Listen, Mr. *Hauck*"—he made the name sound like "cancer"—"I know you've got some time in. You seem to have a personal interest here, and I don't want to be nosy. I also know what it's like when you leave the force."

"Sorry?"

"You know, you leave early, miss the action. You probably deal with a lot of corporate stuff up there. White-collar clients. Like to keep your hands on the tiller."

Hauck didn't respond. The suffering-cop routine was starting to wear thin.

"But the facts are, Mr. Hauck, Mr. Donovan left his apartment in the night around three fifteen A.M. Like he was prone to doing lately. His wife woke up and took note of the time. Fell back to sleep. He had a key to the super's office in the building, which is likely to get the poor sucker canned in this environment. The fingerprints on the door handle to the office were *his* and his alone. He used electrical wire the super kept in the storage closet there, which he slung over the ceiling pipes. The guy had a recent history of being upset. Not sleeping. He was on mood stabilizers. People at work said he was wired like a fuse. Not exactly a big surprise when someone's lost the equivalent of the GNP of Belarus." Campbell chuckled. "You notice how nothing less than a billion even makes the news today? Even his wife suggested the man was acting a little off lately. Forgot birthdays. Walking the dog at three A.M. You don't have to be Sigmund Freud to see the guy was depressed. Even his firm's not pushing that anything was screwy on this. So why would we need to check his phone records? Or any video? Just who should we be looking for?"

Hauck could have answered, *Maybe for a connection to Dani Thibault, or for the man April Glassman's son had taken a shot of, with the braided red-brown hair, tattoo on his neck.* But he didn't want to bring up Thibault as a topic until he had something more to go on. Or until Foley gave him the green light.

And this guy was just trying to clear cases. And this one didn't require much work.

"Like I said, just following up for a friend," Hauck said, taking his jacket off his arm.

"You said you knew him, huh?"

"Knew whom?" Hauck wrinkled his brow, not sure who the guy meant.

"Donovan," the detective said. "The vic."

"I didn't say I knew him. I said I knew one of the persons killed in Greenwich. A minute ago you didn't seem to imply he was a vic."

"No dealings with him at all?" the detective asked, removing another pistachio from the bag.

"No dealings." Hauck looked at him quizzically. "Why?"

"No reason. Just trying to get things straight. That's all." He held up Hauck's card. "Talon, huh? Mind if I keep this? May need some advice someday, if my ticket ever comes in."

Hauck stood up and folded his jacket back over his arm. "Be my guest."

"You know, maybe I will," Campbell said, standing up as well; his gut was round and he was five inches shorter than Hauck.

"Check out those phone records after all. Like you said. You never know what might turn up. If I did, you have a name I should be looking for?"

"You'll let me know when you do," Hauck replied, "and I'll see if one comes to mind."

CHAPTER TWENTY-EIGHT

On the way home, Hauck took a chance and stopped on East Fifty-third Street, at the building where Donovan had lived.

He was met by the doorman at the entrance and asked to speak with Donovan's wife. The man, who'd clearly been alerted to keep the press and any interested outsiders at bay, looked over Hauck's card as if there was a secret code in the paper stock. Hauck convinced him to call upstairs. "He says he was a policeman from Greenwich," the doorman said into the phone, "that he's following up on some things pertaining to some other case up there.

He said it would only take a minute, Ms. Donovan. You want me to let him up?"

The answer was apparently yes, and, eventually, the doorman directed him to an elevator bank on the far end of the lobby. The lobby was a full walk-through with a rear entrance that led onto Fifty-second. Hauck spotted a security camera perched on the wall above the rear door.

As he passed, it occurred to him he'd like to have a shot at checking out that film.

When the elevator opened on fifteen, he was met by a dark-haired woman with a pained demeanor in a black dress, her hair tied back in a bun. She introduced herself as Deena Wolf, Leslie Donovan's sister. "We just buried my brother-in-law yesterday," she said, as if to dissuade him. "My sister's already spoken several times with the police . . ."

"I'll only take a second," Hauck promised. "It's important."

The woman nodded, looking harried. *"Please . . ."*

Inside, about a dozen people were gathered in the foyer and small kitchen. Sounds of laughter and food being served mixed with the somber looks and hushed replies.

A couple of young kids ran through the living room chasing a white bichon with their parents yelling after them.

"My sister's in here."

She took him into a small room that looked like a combination TV room and study. Wood shelves filled haphazardly with books and brochures. Financial documents all around. A leather couch and a wide-screen TV. Leslie Donovan sat on the couch. She had thick dark hair pulled back tightly and a pale complexion, and was dressed in a dark burgundy sweater and skirt.

"I appreciate you seeing me," Hauck said. "I'm sorry for your loss. I won't take up much of your time." He'd been in these situations many times and didn't want to impose.

The woman nodded a little blankly. She was pretty, with a small nose and high cheekbones, though the stress was apparent. "It's okay. Carlos said you were a Greenwich policeman?"

"I was in charge of the detective unit up there for six years. Now I work for a private security firm." Hauck sat down across from her and put his card on the coffee table.

She picked it up. "You're familiar with the Glassman murders that took place up there a month ago?"

"Of course we're familiar with it, Mr. Hauck. Everyone in the industry followed it. That was when Jim first started acting a little strangely."

"How do you mean?"

"He grew agitated. Withdrawn. He stopped sleeping. Got up at night. What is your connection to these murders, Mr. Hauck, if you don't mind telling me?"

"I was close friends with one of the family who was killed. I'm looking into whether the two incidents might be connected in any way. Two traders, two Wall Street firms collapsed. I just have a few questions."

"That poor family." Leslie Donovan sighed, shaking her head. "Terrible. But my husband took his own life, Mr. Hauck. Surely you know that. What do you mean, 'whether the two incidents might be connected'?"

Hauck removed a photo from an envelope. The photo Merrill had given him. Dani. "I was wondering if you know this person, Ms. Donovan. Or if anyone by the name Thibault had ever come up with your

husband. He's Belgian. Dieter Thibault, or
maybe Dani?"

Donovan's widow took the photo. "No. I
don't recognize him. I don't know the
name at all. Should I?"

"I don't know." Hauck shrugged, knowing it was a long shot. "He's someone who
had a connection to Marc Glassman that I
came in contact with. Is there any chance
his name might be in your husband's phone
log, or maybe somewhere in his records
or on his desk? Here, or at work?"

"If you believe there's some kind of connection between those murders and my
husband, why don't you just tell the police?" Donovan's widow asked. "Detective
Campbell of the local precinct has been
very helpful. I'm sure he'd see you."

"Already had the pleasure," Hauck said.
"But I didn't mention this man. I'm just not
at that stage. And I don't want to upset
you unnecessarily, until I know something
more. You said the Glassman murders
seemed to agitate your husband. Did he
discuss the incident with you in any way?
Was he unnaturally focused on it? Any
special importance to it you can recall?"

"Of course he was focused on it, Mr.

Hauck. They had similar jobs. The same kind of pressure. And now . . ." She wet her lips, shook her head. "With what's come out, those losses . . . It only seems more so." She took her thumb and forefinger and pressed them into her brow. Her sister sat down beside her on the couch and put her hand on Leslie Donovan's knee. She drew a deep breath and shook her head, not, it seemed, in response to anything.

"Did your husband seem afraid in any way?" Hauck asked her. "Recently. Did he ever give you the impression someone might be threatening him or out to get him?"

Donovan's widow stared at him. "You don't think those poor people were killed in a break-in, do you? Or Jimmy . . ."

Hauck looked back at her and shrugged. "I don't know."

"It's hard enough for me to think that Jim actually could have done these things they're accusing him of"—she pressed together her lips—"without having to think that maybe he was . . ." She didn't finish the phrase. "Just what is it you are trying to say? He wasn't sleeping. He would sometimes take calls late at night. Anyone who handles money knows what that is like. Of course, he showed a lot of stress. Of course, he wasn't right. Look at what's come out, Mr. Hauck. Just the other night . . ."

She covered her face with her hand. Not crying. Almost hiding. Her sister put her arm around her.

"Just the other night . . . Jim went downstairs. Took Remi out. At three A.M. I woke up when he came back up. He sat on the bed. He looked like he had seen a ghost. He started to tell me how he was afraid, what the losses he was suffering might mean to his career, to our family. I mean, everyone had losses. What he was hiding, I had no idea . . . He kept saying he'd seen the same car outside . . . I saw what he was going through. I wanted to help him in some way. I sat up with him for an hour. Yes, he seemed afraid. Yes, he was worried about things. But now he's dead. It's over. What difference does it make now, anyway?"

Hauck asked, "Do *you* think your husband killed himself, Ms. Donovan?" knowing it was more than he should have said.

Her sister looked up at him like *That's enough now. It's time.* Hauck collected the photo. He put it back in his sport coat. He stood up.

"Do I think he killed himself?" Donovan's widow shook her head. "I didn't think Jim was capable of *any* of the things they say he did. But take his own life? No. I can't believe that, Mr. Hauck. I don't think I ever will. He loved us far too much. If not me, then Zachy. His son was everything to him. So, no."

"Why do you think your husband had a key to the superintendent's office, Ms. Donovan? Seems to me he could have taken calls from here. It's private, no matter what time of night."

"I don't know." Leslie Donovan shook her head, tearing up. "I don't know."

Hauck figured he'd stayed long enough. "Thanks for your time. If you happen to look through his phone records, or any of his things, and come across that name— *Thibault*"—he pointed to his card—"you can reach me at that number."

He went to the door and was about to say "I'm sorry" again, when he turned back. "One more thing . . . Do you remember what kind of car it was?"

"Excuse me?" Leslie Donovan looked up, surprised.

"What kind of car your husband said he saw. Outside. That he thought might be following him."

"Some kind of SUV," Leslie Donovan replied. "I don't know. I didn't think it was important. Black, I think."

Hauck nodded. A black Suburban was the vehicle Evan Glassman had snapped a shot of outside his house.

"You know you're the second person to ask me that question today?" Donovan's widow looked up. "The make of the car."

"Who was the first?" Hauck asked. Maybe that's what Campbell had been hiding. That he knew something he didn't share.

"A woman," Leslie Donovan said. "She was up here earlier today. From Washington."

CHAPTER TWENTY-NINE

Hauck finally made it home at close to ten. He noticed Annie had let herself in, and it hit him then how he had promised to cook a meal for them tonight, her night off, curl up on the couch, and watch *24*.

Soon as he came through the door he knew he was in some trouble.

"Nice meal," Annie called out from the living room couch, her voice ringing with sarcasm.

Oh shit.

One glance at the kitchen told him she had done her best to resurrect what he was supposed to have put together: the flank steak that had been marinating in the fridge, along with one of her favorite weekday staples, spaghetti in oil and crushed black peppercorns. He saw that *24* was finishing up on the tube and Annie was in PJ bottoms and a T-shirt with a plate perched on her lap.

"Jeez, I'm sorry," he muttered, tossing his jacket over a chair. He came over and sat beside her. "Work."

"I called work," Annie said. "Brooke said you left early and went into the city."

"Right." Hauck cleared his throat contritely. "I left word. Would it make me out to be more or less of a heel if I told you how great everything smells?"

"More," Annie said, not letting up. "So don't try." She put her plate down on the old trunk that doubled as Hauck's coffee table. "You know, I take one night off a week, Ty, and it's a night Jared stays up at school, and it would be nice if I was able to maybe spend it with the guy I'm supposedly involved with. Especially when he makes the big hunter-gatherer gesture that he's going to cook."

"I know, I know," he said. "Truth is"—he tried to smile—"I never saw anyone so eager to get themselves poisoned."

"No humor, Ty, please. That's not the point."

"I know it's not the point." He squeezed her warmly on her knee, his hand staying there. "I went into the city to follow up on a lead. I guess I just got wrapped up."

"Ty, you've been wrapped up somewhere else since this woman was killed." Annie faced him. "I'm sorry about that, Ty, I really am. But I deserve some attention too. It's almost making me jealous. Like, is there anything you want to confess?"

Hauck shrugged and tried to smile. "Other than maybe taking you for granted from time to time." He saw the tightness in her jaw start to soften. She drew her knees up and pushed back her hair. It took a lot to get Annie mad, and he'd overachieved. Laughter was a lot more natural for her than anger. The ticking digital clock flashed on the screen and *24* went into next week's previews.

"Anyway, you missed a lights-out episode." She stood up and picked up her dish. "There's a plate for you in the micro-wave. A weak moment—don't ask me why. And don't even think of asking about what you missed because there's no way I'm going to divulge . . . Even with sex," she said, scrunching her nose playfully at him, climbing over him.

Hauck reached and caught her by the wrist and pulled her onto his lap. He squeezed her, hoping for a hint of forgive-ness. "Wouldn't even try," he said. "How-ever, I do have Dove bars in the freezer for dessert." He knew she would kill for those. "I *was* hoping that might work."

"Hmmm." Annie nodded, thinking for a second, then rolled off of him. "You're on dangerous turf there, mister . . . Maybe bring one upstairs when you're done. And remember, forgiveness is predicated on performance." She took her plate over to the sink and dumped it in. "Let's just say we can agree the dishes are yours tonight. And by the way, there's an envelope for you over there. It was under the door when I let myself in." She went to the stairs. "I'm heading up."

"Annie . . ."

She turned around on the landing in her baggy flannels and University of Michigan T-shirt.

"I'm sorry," Hauck said again. "I really am."

She continued up without saying anything but, to his delight, wiggled out of her top and tossed it back to the floor from the top of the stairs.

"Dove bar . . . ," she called teasingly.

"Got it." Hauck laughed and went around to the kitchen, weighing whether to follow her up before she'd even shut the door— *Right answer,* he thought—or surrender to his growling stomach and the plate she had put in the microwave. He picked food. He hit the reheat button on the microwave and opened the fridge, pulling out a beer. He heard Annie in the bathroom and sat at the counter, waiting for the meal to heat.

He hadn't been entirely forthcoming with her. And he was still holding back from being so right now. She was right; he had been elsewhere. He was sorry he'd let it all fall back on her, but he knew that if he was straight with her, it would only produce the lecture that maybe he should follow the advice of his boss right now and drop this thing for good.

While the meal warmed, Hauck reached out for the brown, taped-up legal envelope on the counter, which, he noticed immediately, had come from Vito. *Good man!* He slit it open and found a large ream of the phone records from Thibault he had asked for, along with a note on Vito's company letterhead: "Bill to follow."

Hauck chuckled.

He took a swig of beer. The microwave beeped. He went over and took out the plate and sat, flinching for a second from the heat, back at the counter. He cut into the steak, which was tender and flavorful, admiring how his own concoction of red wine, olive oil, soy sauce, and balsamic had come out to perfection, even if Annie had lit the grill.

Between bites, he leafed through the sheets.

He had homework to do. The stack was maybe two hundred pages thick. And he didn't have much to go on. The logs went all the way back to October like he'd requested—six months. He had mulled things over maybe a dozen times on the ride from the city. Should he just drop it? He knew he was treading on thin ice. Steve

Chrisafoulis was starting to get irritated. The detective in New York didn't exactly seem like his new BFF. And then there was Foley, his boss . . .

"How is it down there?" Annie called from the upstairs landing.

"Pretty good," Hauck yelled back. "Pasta's not bad, but this flank steak is a ten!"

"Oh, you're definitely pushing it, mister . . ."

"Up in a minute," he said.

He gulped down a few last bites and quickly flipped forward to late-February and March, just before April and her family were killed.

At first glance he didn't find any calls from Thibault to the dead trader. It was all pretty much just numbers and phone IDs he didn't recognize. He leafed forward a month, to April, just a couple of weeks ago, the weeks before James Donovan's death.

A number jumped out at him. 212-555-5719.

He put down his fork and knife and pushed away the plate. From a coffee mug near the wall phone where he kept things, he grabbed a yellow marker. He highlighted the number.

Then he leafed back through the stack of listings and locations. He searched for the same number. He found it several times, his pulse seeming to pick up each time. He noted the time of day of these calls.

One fifty-seven A.M.
Two fifteen A.M.
Three oh five.

Always in the middle of the night. Always to the same location. A location that just made that ice he was on even thinner.

He'd just been there today.

352 East Fifty-third Street. Donovan's apartment building. He dialed the number on his cell. A voice recording came on. Hispanic. "This is the super's office. No one is here to take your call . . ."

Hauck hung up. Something surged through his veins. Vindication.

That linked Dani Thibault to both dead traders.

CHAPTER THIRTY

The cheers from the crowd and the thwack of the ball on wooden sticks rang out on the Greenwich Academy field.

The Gators were playing the Lady Crusaders from St. Luke's in field hockey. It was a crisp May afternoon. Greenwich was ranked number one in the state. About a hundred people were on the field or in the stands, mostly parents and friends, shouting, *"Go, Green, go, Green!"* as a determined blond attacker in the home jersey sprinted down the sideline past the last St. Luke's defender. To rising cheers, she executed a spin and centered the ball directly in front of the visitor's goal. There was a heated scrum for control. A teammate wound up and whacked the ball into the open net.

"*Attaway, Jen!* Good goal, good goal!"

The team celebrated with a bunch of high fives.

Dani Thibault made his way across the top row of the bleachers. A man in a red Lands' End jacket and green bleached-out baseball cap stood up, clapping and yelling, "Way to go, Jen. Way to set Amy up!" Thibault waited until play resumed. He came over and took a seat behind him. St. Luke's sent the ball down to the Greenwich end.

He leaned over the man in the cap. "Your daughter, right?"

The man continued clapping, Thibault's voice seeming to take him by surprise. The man turned and recognized him from the meeting they had had in New York and also from the party circuit around town. "I didn't know you had a kid here."

"I don't. That's her who set up the goal, number fourteen, right? "

The man in the Lands' End jacket nodded, standing up. He was a fund manager

at one of the largest hedge funds in Greenwich. "Get it out of there, Jen! Dig it out!
Thataway!" He sat back down and said,
face forward, confused, "I thought we
decided I'd contact you if I wanted to talk
further."

"Oh, yes, right, on that other issue,"
Thibault said. "That situation is gone.
Someone grabbed it. Another time. She's
very good, your daughter." He leaned forward, elbows on knees. "North Carolina,
isn't it, next year?"

"Duke," the man in the red jacket said,
glancing along the bleachers, making sure
they were alone.

"That's right, Duke. And you've got two
more right behind her, don't you? Great
girls, I hear. All top students . . ."

"Listen." The man finally turned to him,
perturbed. "It's Dani, isn't it?"

"Yes, Dani." Thibault nodded.

Thibault knew the man's story better
than his own. He was a senior investment
manager at a troubled fund that had just
been bought by one of the large banks.
He'd bet huge on the spread between
mortgage rates and bonds, the evaporating spread, and now his positions were in

free fall. The last two years, multimillion-dollar bonuses had been paid in restricted stock. And to support his fancy lifestyle—the kids in the right school, the ski house in Vail, the twelve-thousand-square-foot castle under construction—Lands' End had been borrowing against it heavily. A little at a time, then more as the stock price went down. Never believing it was anything more than a blip. A blip that would reverse.

That blip was about to kill him now.

Thibault placed his hands squarely on the man's shoulders. "Actually, I thought we might discuss something else."

Soon he'd be getting margin calls. Calls, with all his cash pledged, that he couldn't meet. Then he'd talk about maybe unloading some property, property that was plummeting just as fast, that wouldn't sell. Who knew, in a month he might even lose his job. The sweats were definitely coming out at night. Thibault knew he was as good as dead, as dead as the banks. Just walking around. *Zombie.*

Piqued, the man said, "Listen, Dani, or whatever you go by, call me at the office if you have another deal. Not here. I'm watching my kid. You understand?"

Thibault had pitched him on a Dutch retailer that was for sale, a private equity thing. Just feeling him out. First they had met at the Field Club in Greenwich. Thibault had a nose for the smell of panic underneath his calm country-club veneer.

Zombie.

"I was just thinking about the future, that's all. Those big bonuses are a thing of the past now, aren't they, Ted? How much does it look like this year?'

"What are you now"—the man suddenly turned—"my fucking estate planner?"

"Yeah, Ted." Thibault leveled his gaze on Ted's eyes. "That's exactly what I am, my friend. I'm your ticket out, if you're smart. Your only ticket."

The whistle blew. Half time. The girls on the field headed to their locker rooms. The man shifted around, annoyed. But didn't walk away. "What are you talking about?"

"Maybe we can have a drink next week. About how you're going to get out of this mess. How you're going to finish that house. Fork up the hundred and fifty grand for the girls. Plus the place in Jupiter, right? You know what I mean?"

"I said we'd look at your proposal,"

the hedge fund manager said. "If that's gone, send me another. I'll run it by the committee."

"No, that's all changed, Ted. I'm no longer looking for a penny from *you*." Thibault's cool, purposeful smile seemed to make the man uneasy. "It's the other way around now. Enough to get you out of this mess. For good. Enough to sort out that life of yours that's underwater. Enjoy the game," Thibault said, looking past him to the field and patting him firmly on the shoulders. "I'm *your* banker now."

CHAPTER THIRTY-ONE

The connection he'd found between Dani Thibault and both dead traders weighed on Hauck the whole next day.

Taken separately, it all meant nothing. Only the loosest circumstantial connection that didn't prove a thing. Thibault lived in that world. He might well have known both Glassman and Donovan. It wasn't enough to take to Chrisafoulis or Foley.

Yet it was more than he could put aside.

Wednesday, he awoke clearheaded. And he knew what to do.

He called Steve Chrisafoulis at the station, Tom Foley's admonition still in his mind. Steve wasn't there. He chatted for a few seconds with Brenda, his old secretary. "Tell him to call me back," he asked her. "It's pretty important."

For the next few hours he did his best to focus on things at work. But he was distracted. He waited for Steve's return call. Thibault was connected. The two dead traders were connected. He knew it. But he just couldn't prove it—at least not on his own. Everyone was right. He had made his choices. He wasn't a cop anymore.

Now someone else had to run with the ball.

Around three, he realized he hadn't heard back from Steve. He tried him once more. He needed to get what he knew off his chest. This time, Brenda told him, "He had to run into the city. You have his cell, don't you?"

Hauck did. "Just tell him to give me a call on his way back."

When his phone shook a short time later he figured it was Steve finally calling him back, but it turned out to be Richard Snell from London. Hauck glanced at his watch, figuring the time there. "You're sure burning the candle a bit late . . ."

"I'm actually calling you from home," the Talon British director said. "That search you had me looking into, Thibault—"

"Listen, Richard," Hauck said, cutting him off, "I should've called. Tom Foley asked me to—"

"I know precisely what Tom asked," Snell said. "He called here as well. But if you've got a paper and pen, I think I can be of some help. Something came back."

Hauck grabbed a pen off his desk. "Go ahead."

"Before we were told to stop, we started looking into his banking connections over here. Thibault maintains a personal account in his own name at RBS. Most of what goes on seems on the up-and-up. He pays for a flat in Kensington. A housekeeper. Some monthly expenses. What did strike me as interesting, however, is that every month, like clockwork, there's a payment of three thousand euros wired from his account to another European bank."

"To the Netherlands?" Hauck asked. That was where Thibault was supposedly from.

"No, to an AstraBanca," the Brit replied. "In a town called Novi Pazar. In Serbia."

"Serbia!" Hauck pushed back in his seat. "Wired to whom?"

"We're not sure. A woman. The name on the account is a Maria Radisovic. Ring a bell?"

Hauck had never heard the name before. "No."

"I'm not surprised. We did a quick check. She's sixty-eight years old. Her husband, Evo, is dead. She's got a daughter, Ola. Receives a small monthly pension from an auto parts factory there."

Serbia.

It triggered Hauck's memory of Merrill Simons's mentioning a photograph she had found in Thibault's wallet. Two women, one older, in an unidentified European city. The other, she thought, was around Dani's age.

Hadn't Thibault claimed to have been part of a Dutch force stationed in Serbia during the war?

"My suggestion," Snell went on, "is to get me a set of prints. Or even better, a toothbrush or a drinking glass. His DNA. We'll find out who the bastard really is. But if you want my guess," the Brit said, "if we went and dug through the local birth records, it wouldn't surprise me to find out your Dani Thibault—whatever his real name is—isn't Dani Thibault at all, but most likely, in the end, Maria Radisovic's son."

CHAPTER THIRTY-TWO

What Snell had found coursed through Hauck. Thibault had claimed to be Dutch. Or Belgian. Now he had a tie-in to a woman in Serbia. He had lied about his past, his banking connections. Now he had a link to both dead traders. It was only getting deeper. Hauck knew it was gradually climbing over his head. He wasn't sure what to do.

Merrill should know this. The FBI should know this. He had given his word not to divulge anything. To his boss and to his client.

But it was also a potential embarrass-
ment if it ever got out that this was a guy
the firm was protecting.

He tried Foley at the New York office.
His secretary said he was in meetings and
wouldn't be free until after five. Hauck said
he was coming in and insisted on a couple
of minutes with him. This was always how
it began. Something small, an accident, a
confidential search he stumbled upon.
That grew. Four people were now dead.
Two large banks had failed. This was
larger than the firm's commitment to Reynolds Reid. Larger than something they
could simply put on hold.

It was building speed like an
avalanche—and he didn't even have the
charge to do anything about it.

Hauck grabbed his case and stuffed it
with all the files he had been compiling:
the photo of Thibault and Glassman, the
phone records Vito had pulled for him, the
connection between Thibault and Donovan. He told Brooke he was leaving for the
day. He went downstairs to the ground-
floor parking garage.

He found his Beemer in his private parking space and depressed the lock remote. He heard the familiar beep and opened the door. He threw his case on the passenger seat and went to climb in. He noticed something sitting on the windshield.

A book of some kind. He got back out and lifted it off.

The Idiot's Guide to Understanding Wall Street.

Hauck froze.

"Thought you'd like the touch." It was Shep Campbell's voice.

Hauck turned around and saw the NYPD detective leaning on a nearby car.

"You really learn anything in that book or do you just use it as a prop?" Hauck asked, lifting it off his car.

"Nice wheels," Campbell said, coming over. "But, hey, you deserve it, right?" A heavy-set black man remained leaning on the city detective's car. "Say hi to Detective Washburn." Campbell's chummy tone was starting to wear thin. Bringing in his partner. Making this visit official. What was going on?

"Hey." The large black dude waved. "Seen you on TV."

Hauck nodded. If they hadn't been two New York City cops, he'd have thought he was in for some kind of fight.

"Okay, I'm flattered." Hauck shut the door. "What brings you by, detectives? I'm afraid I'm in a bit of a rush."

Campbell came up to the other side of his car. "I took your advice. On the Donovan thing. I started looking at it in a different way."

"No charge," Hauck said.

"Talon." The detective bunched his lips. "You've been working there around, what, four months?"

"I feel like we've already been through this, Campbell. Check with personnel."

The auburn-haired detective cocked a finger at him and chuckled, like he was saying, *One for you, guy.* "They handle a lot of banks, I see. Tough time for banks, isn't it?"

"Listen, detective, I really don't have the time . . ." Hauck had no clue where this was going.

The detective smiled smugly. "This thing's been in your craw from the very beginning, hasn't it?"

"What thing?"

"These *murdered* traders. That's what *you* called it, isn't it? *Murder.* You were at the crime scene in Greenwich. Then the station right after. Called the new head of detectives a few times. That guy who took your place. What's his name, Chrisafoulis? Pumping him for details. Even harassed him at his kid's school. You had something going on with that first guy's wife?"

Hauck stared back, grabbing on to the door handle. To keep from slugging him. Only Steve knew about these things. Brenda said he'd been in the city. Where was Campbell going with this?

"Then you come into the city . . . All hopped up on this Donovan thing. Pushing me for info. Telling me how to do my job. Then, not an hour later, you're harassing his widow. *Tee-bo,* wasn't it?" He pronounced Dani's name like it was a Cajun nickname. "The guy you're trying to tie into all this. I checked him out myself." Looked at his partner and grinned. "Y'know, I'm finding myself in a whole new social circle these days."

"What do you want, Campbell?"

There was a click of heels against the pavement and a woman came out of the staircase and crossed over to her car. He waited for her to get inside and start the ignition.

"So, I'm trying to figure it out." Campbell smirked. "Your prints are all over this mess, aren't they, Mr. Private Executive? Mr. TV Star?"

"You check out the phone logs yet?"

Campbell shrugged.

"What about the security tapes in Donovan's building? I saw a camera. You look at them?"

"Maybe I did," Campbell said, smirking.

"So what'd you find?"

"What did we find?" Campbell glanced around to his partner, cockily scratching the back of his head. Then he dug into his inside jacket pocket like he was about to unholster a gun. To Hauck's relief, he came back out with just an evidence bag, something inside, and tossed it on the hood of Hauck's car, never taking his eyes off Hauck. "What we found was *this*."

Hauck picked it up and stared at what was inside. As he did, it became clear to him exactly what was going on. His lungs deflated like he'd been punched in the stomach.

It was a pen. A corporate pen. The lettering on it familiar.

The Talon Group.

"We found it on the floor, next to the super's desk," the detective said with a self-satisfied smile. A grin that seemed to suggest he enjoyed watching Hauck's worried reaction. "Could've fallen out of someone's pocket, I guess. Maybe during a spat. Never made the connection until you came in."

Hauck's eyes locked on the pen. He had several like them. Everyone did there.

"Just wondering"—Campbell blinked annoyingly—"how the hell you think that got there."

Hauck shook his head. "You're kidding, right?"

"*Kidding?*" Campbell clucked at his partner. "I'd like to think I was kidding, Mr. Hauck. Mister *Hero*. But y'know, you come around, pump us for information on the case, no longer on the job. Then whaddaya know . . . *whammo*. Look what pops up at the crime scene. A bit of a major-league clusterfuck, wouldn't you say?"

"It's not my pen."

"Well, I'm hoping that turns out to be the case." Campbell laughed. He turned back to his partner. "Don't you, Lee? *You sure?*"

"I'm sure," Hauck said. But he wasn't liking where his mind was going, bouncing back and forth, atoms careening through an accelerator, except in this case the atoms were saying, *What if that somehow did turn out to be my pen?* His prints on it. *And worse, why . . . ?* Of course, he had never been to the building before, never even heard of Donovan prior to the incident. But what was it doing there? What if he was being set up?

He looked at Campbell squarely and smiled. "And you're the one who said the other day it wasn't even a crime scene."

"Yeah, I did say that, didn't I? But y'know, you're starting to turn me around on that one. It's sure starting to resemble one now."

Hauck was thinking he could tell him what he would find in the phone log: Thibault's phone number. The proof was sitting right on his car seat. But this jerk

was the last person he was going to share
it with, until he could figure out just what
was going on.

"Just a Good Samaritan, huh?" The detective grinned, clearly cynical. "Just following up for an old friend . . ."

"A *dead* friend," Hauck said, glaring.

"I've seen her picture. Must've been
quite a friendship," the city detective
sniffed, glancing at his partner.

"I'm gonna head out now," Hauck said.
His fingers flexed and he felt his body heat
up. The thought crossed his mind that
slugging an NYPD detective with the case
he was making would not be the best of
moves. He tossed the evidence bag back
to Campbell. "Unless there's something
else . . ."

"Just keep in touch," the detective said,
and winked. "Until this baby comes back
from the lab. You know the drill."

"Yeah, I know the drill. And here . . ." He
tossed *The Idiot's Guide to Understanding Wall Street* over to Campbell's partner.
"Does that book have a chapter in there
that talks about collusion to defraud financial markets?"

"Not sure." The black detective caught it, surprised.

"Too bad. Tell your partner he might want to find one that does."

CHAPTER THIRTY-THREE

Outside the garage, Hauck pulled the Beemer into the first spot he could find—an old steak place on Steamboat. His collar was wet with sweat, and he knew he shouldn't run away with assumptions until he could think them through.

He had never met Donovan. Never been to his building before. Whoever killed him had had to sneak inside, gain access to the super's office. He had to have been caught on the security tape. Someone Donovan knew. Someone who also knew Hauck was trying to connect Thibault to these deaths. Talon. Merrill. He wasn't sure who to trust now. If he hadn't stuck his nose into this mess, widened Campbell's interest, no one would have ever attached any significance to that pen.

It was starting to concern him that the prints on it might actually be his.

Someone was trying to set him up.

Hauck realized his only options were crossing his boss and maybe getting himself fired—or ending up in jail.

He chose getting fired.

He dialed up Chrisafoulis on the detective's cell. This time, on the second ring, Steve picked up, sounding as if he was glad to hear from him. *"Ty!"*

"Listen, Steve, we've got to talk."

"I know we do, Ty. What the hell is going on? The city cops have been buzzing around all day. About you. They're saying they found something of yours at the Donovan crime scene . . ."

"It's not mine, Steve. But someone's going to a lot of work to make it look that way. Where are you?"

"Back at the office. Listen, you should come in."

"I'll meet you there." Hauck was about

to hang up, then hesitated. "Steve, I can trust you on this, right?"

"Of course you can trust me, Ty."

"I'll be right there."

It was only a couple of minutes' drive, a few blocks up the hill, to the Greenwich station house on the avenue. Hauck left his car in a visitor's spot in the lot and grabbed his briefcase. He realized his best option now was to clear himself of suspicion and just lay it out to Steve. Let the FBI or the SEC, or whatever agency handled this sort of thing, run with it.

And then hope he didn't find himself in a viper's nest at Talon.

He stepped inside the entrance on Mason, waving to the officer at the desk, who looked at him like, *Been seeing you a lot around here lately, lieutenant.* Chrisafoulis was waiting for him as Hauck headed for the stairs.

"Steve!" Hauck warmly squeezed the detective's shoulder. "I have to show you some things. Let's go find a place where we can talk."

"Ty, don't be upset," Chrisafoulis said, looking a bit nervous, "but Fitz wants to see you on this, *upstairs*."

Hauck felt whacked in the face. *"Fitz?"*

Vern Fitzpatrick was Greenwich's long-time chief of police. He'd hired Hauck, helped lift him back into the world after the year he'd dropped out. He'd been Hauck's mentor for most of the time he was there. Groomed him to take his job. But on his last case, Hauck had begun to doubt which side of the fence Vern was actually on. A drumbeat of concern started to pound inside him. He started to back out of the station.

"That's not going to work, Steve."

"Ty." Steve took his arm. "No one's accusing you of anything. The detectives from the NYPD went to Fitz and got him involved. You need friends now, buddy, not anyone doubting you. But you leave here"—the detective looked at him solidly—"that list of people starts to get smaller and smaller. You understand, don't you, Ty?"

He wasn't sure what to do. And it scared him. But Chrisafoulis was right. He had stumbled into something he could no longer outrun or outmaneuver. And where was he going to go anyway? He had to trust someone now.

"Alright." He nodded warily toward the stairs. "Lead the way."

CHAPTER THIRTY-FOUR

The chief's office had been relocated to the newly completed wing. Industrial carpeting, bright lights, modular workstations, computers on every desk. It looked more like *CSI: Miami* than the wear-worn wooden desks and fixtures from when Hauck had worked there.

Vern stood up at his desk in a plaid shirt and slacks. It had been six months since Hauck had seen him. "Ty."

"Nice digs, Vern," Hauck said, admiring the new paneling, the pictures of the chief with the governor, with Lee Trevino and Jack Nicklaus, with the state attorney

general. And his grandkids, one of whom
was serving in Iraq. A conference room
next door. Vern's hair was whiter, but his
smile was just as trusting and friendly.
Hauck had only seen him once since he
had left. "Going up in the world, huh, guy?"

"One could say the same about you."
He came around the desk and they shook
hands. "Until the present time, that is," he
said with a wise smile, motioning Hauck
over to a seating area by the large window.

"Yeah." Hauck smiled. "You might say
that, Vern."

"We miss you here, Ty," the chief said,
motioning for Hauck to sit down. "Steve's
doing a terrific job, but I don't have to tell
you that your imprint is all over the place
here."

"If I knew you were going to redo it like
this I wouldn't have left."

He laughed. He crossed his legs and
sank back in the couch. "So, how's the private sector treating you?"

"It's brought a few surprises."

Fitzpatrick nodded sagely. "You were
always a good man, Ty . . . But you always
did have a special talent for stepping knee-
deep in the shit bucket, didn't you, son?"

Hauck smiled in return. "Yeah, Vern, guess I always did."

"Well, hate to see that muck up the new career just as it's starting to bloom. Why don't you tell me what's going on."

Steve came over and leaned against the wall. Hauck took his old boss through the tale of how it had all begun: Hearing the news about Marc Glassman that morning. Seeing April's face. "She was a friend of mine, at a time before I moved up here, when I really needed one. I was part of a therapy group for a while. After Norah died. April helped me through. When I saw what happened . . ." Hauck took in a breath, blew it out, and smiled crookedly. "Well, you know me . . ."

"Yeah, I know you, Ty. I'm sorry. I wish we had made more progress on the Glassman thing. Still working it though."

"Around the same time," Hauck went on, "I was introduced to a woman through my job whose name I'd rather keep out of it for now. The assignment was confidential. It was a background search. She raised some doubts about a man she'd been seeing."

Vern chuckled. "I thought they had you

hobnobbing with congressmen and company heads over at that firm of yours. Didn't realize it was the same old shit, just with a fancier shingle on the door."

"It was a favor," Hauck said. "For my boss. The managing director there. Let's call the man Subject A."

"Subject A." Vern nodded. "Alright."

"As I looked into him, it became clear most of her doubts were valid. The guy just got dirtier and dirtier. At the same time"—Hauck opened his case and nodded to Steve—"I guess I started sticking my nose into the Glassman thing."

"Subject B. Can't say that went over well here, Ty. You left. You moved on to other things."

"She was a *friend,* Vern. During a rough patch of my life." Hauck wet his lips and thought about how to make it sound right. "Everyone had the thing labeled as a burglary. Doesn't matter now. What does matter is that in looking into this other subject, I came across something . . ."

Vern took off his wire-rims, folded them neatly, and put them in his breast pocket.

"Something that tied him back to the

other case," Hauck said. "To Marc Glassman."

Now Vern's eyes widened in interest.
"What?"

"A photo." Hauck reached into his case
and took it out of the file. He laid it on the
glass table. "That's them there. In conversation. A polo event at Conyers Farm. Last
summer."

Vern looked it over. "The two of them
talking . . ." He handed it to Steve with a
skeptical gaze. "You haven't been in the
private sector that long not to know that a
shot of two people talking in a public place
isn't exactly a slam dunk when it comes to
evidence. And for what? What is it you're
trying to say? Steve's been telling me
you've been pushing that this Glassman
thing wasn't a home break-in from the
start."

"And I turned out to be right, didn't I?
And no, it doesn't make much of a case
for anything—by itself. That's why when
the guy in New York suddenly died as well,
the other trader—"

"Subject C," Vern said, nodding pa-
tiently. "The suicide that's not a suicide."

"The second guy who died under other suspicious circumstances. Who was covering up massive losses. Not to mention who brought down a second Wall Street firm. I went in to try to see if there was any connection."

"That's what sticking your nose into an ongoing police investigation and harassing the victim's wife was all about?"

"There was no active investigation. And all I did was talk to her, Vern, with her consent. And yes, I can see how maybe I might've overstepped on some things. And how maybe it would be easy to think I'm a guy who just can't get used to life away from the force, or that a photo of two guys talking at a polo match doesn't mean shit—all of it—if it weren't for what I found."

The chief's smile suddenly got narrow and Vern's stare steadied on him. "You mean like a pen with your company logo on it found at the crime scene?"

"Come on, Vern, you really think I killed that guy? For what? So I could short Beeston Holloway in my 401(k)?" He turned to Steve. "What kind of vehicle did the Glassman kid claim to have seen at the end of the driveway that night?"

"A black Suburban. Unmarked."

"The same thing James Donovan's wife told me her husband spotted outside their apartment building two days before he died."

Vern wrinkled his brow. "Jeez, Ty, that's even weaker than the photo."

Hauck took out the rest of the file. He dropped Thibault's phone log in front of Vern on the table. He jabbed his finger at it. "How about I place three separate calls from that same person in that photograph to the very office where James Donovan hung himself? One, Vern, the night before he died. Are we getting warmer?"

Vern picked up the sheets and put on his glasses and scanned over the yellow highlights delineating Dani Thibault's phone calls to Donovan's apartment building.

"That enough to maybe make you re-think the home break-in theory?" Hauck pointed to the highlighting. "That's why they did it there. It wouldn't show up on a routine search of Donovan's phone records. The only reason it did turn up is I happened to be looking into the other case. C'mon, Vern, Steve, you don't have to know what a credit-default swap is to figure out two successful traders are dead, traders who lost billions and whose two firms are history now . . ."

Fitzpatrick nodded, seeming to glance in the direction of the adjoining conference room. "You said this was part of a confidential search. What does your firm think of what you stumbled on?"

Hauck shrugged. "This is where it starts to get a little sticky for me, Vern. I haven't told them."

"Haven't told them?" Vern put down the papers. "Some things don't seem to change, do they, son?"

"One of the firm's largest clients is Reynolds Reid. Apparently, they're seeking to pick up some of Wertheimer Grant's assets. Their retail broker division. My boss doesn't want to muck up the deal by bringing out possible revelations of fraud or a possible scandal. So they pushed me off the case."

"Some people might find it sticky that two New York City detectives are trying to tie you into a murder case, Ty."

"Someone's trying to set me up. I don't know whether that pen is mine or not. I don't know what they'll find on it. More to the point, what does it even matter? Do I have to prove myself to you? You think you're going to find my face on some security tape sneaking into the building? That's why I couldn't go to my firm. I can't trust them. Four people are dead, Vern. I don't know why they had to be killed, but while I'm out there having to prove my innocence two banks have collapsed. Am I the only person in the world who sees what may be going on?"

Fitzpatrick was silent. His gaze was fixed on the sheets. Hauck took back the evidence. He placed it back in the file. Stood up. He wrapped his briefcase around his shoulder and looked back at him.

"Am I, Vern?"

Suddenly the door to the adjoining room opened. A woman stepped out. In a navy pantsuit. Slim. Pretty. Round, gray eyes and short, dark hair.

Hauck's stomach almost hit the floor.

"No." She shook her head. "You're not the only one who sees it, Mr. Hauck."

Hauck looked back at Steve and Vern with a sinking feeling in his stomach that he had just been betrayed. "Who are you?"

The woman dropped a federal ID in

front of his face. Department of the Treasury.

"I'd like to see just what you have," the woman said. "And I promise, no one, at least no one with half a brain, thinks you had anything to do with those murders."

CHAPTER THIRTY-FIVE

My name is Naomi Blum, Mr. Hauck," the petite agent said. "I'm an investigator with the Treasury Department." She put away her ID. "And yes, I'm interested in how these deaths are connected too."

Hauck swung his gaze back to Vern. His first instinct was that the very people he thought were his friends had turned him in. And he'd laid it all out for them.

On a platter.

And a government investigator had been listening to every word.

"Ty, she came to *us,*" Fitz said. "She only

wants to hear what you found. No one turned you in."

"You're not under any investigation, Mr. Hauck." The Treasury agent met his gaze. "No one's thinking you had anything to do with either of these deaths. But if it's all right with Chief Fitzpatrick, I would like to speak with you alone, if possible." She motioned to the conference room. "*On* the record this time."

As a rule, Hauck trusted government agents about as much as car salesmen. He'd butted heads with enough over the years, last but not least on the David Sanger drive-by shooting last year. And he still hadn't figured out what side of the mess the FBI had come down on there.

But something about this agent seemed to put him at ease. He needed someone to run with what he'd found. And the last thing he needed after his run-in with the NYPD was to give anyone the sense that he had something to hide.

"Sure." He nodded. He looked at Vern and Steve with a grunt of disappointment. "Thanks. I'll decide later whether to buy you a beer or take a swing at you."

"I think I'd go for the beer," Naomi Blum

said with a smile. "They both went to bat
for you one hundred percent. They told
me there was zero probability you were
involved."

"Cheers," Hauck chortled, managing a
dry half smile.

He and Agent Blum went into the adjoining room. There was a large polished
table that would seat ten or twelve in front
of a picture window overlooking the courtyard between the new and old buildings.
Hauck took a seat at one side of the
table. Instead of sitting across from him,
Naomi pulled up the adjacent chair and
swung it around to face him.

She had bright, intelligent eyes.

"I guess it was you who spoke with
Leslie Donovan?" Hauck said to her.

She nodded. "And Detective Campbell
of the NYPD. Sharp as a tack, that man."
She rolled her eyes. He liked her even
more. "I'd like to record this, if it's okay.
Your call. Technically, you're not under any
official obligation to do so. Although we
both know I could have a judge's writ to
make it official in about a quarter of an
hour if you choose to decline."

"You had me at 'sharp as a tack,'" Hauck

said with a smile. "Go ahead. It would be good, however, if whatever I say could be kept clear of my current employers, only so I have a job to go back to when we finish up, if that's okay."

The agent took out a small digital recorder from her briefcase. "You seem to be eliminating that prospect rather well on your own," she said, matching his smile.

"Touché."

She flicked on the recorder. "Anyway, it's a deal," she said, adjusting the volume and placing it between them. "I'd like to go back over a few details of what you said in the other room, but first, it would be good to get a few things out on the table. You've never met either Mr. Glassman or Mr. Donovan, is that correct?"

"Never." Hauck shook his head.

"But you did have a connection to Mr. Glassman's wife? I think her name was April?"

"Yes," Hauck said. "I knew her several years ago, before I even moved up to Greenwich. It's what first made me look into her murder."

Naomi Blum turned off the recorder. "Do

you mind characterizing that relationship on the record?"

"I'm not sure what bearing it has on the case."

"It has the bearing that it will help eliminate any suspicion that your motives in looking into her death had any connection to her husband," she said.

"Okay." Hauck shrugged. "What the hell . . ." Agent Blum turned the machine back on. Hauck noticed that her fingers were slim and graceful and her nails brightly polished, a stylish brown to match a highlight in her hair. She restated the question.

"We were friends," Hauck answered. "We met as part of a support group for handling depression under the care of a Doctor Paul Rose in Manhattan." He shrugged awkwardly. "I had lost a daughter in an accident, and my marriage had fallen apart. I left the force. It was part of my union separation agreement. I stayed in the group for around four months. April—Ms. Glassman," Hauck corrected himself, "she helped me back onto my feet." The rest he felt he could leave out. "After I left, I never saw her again until years later, here in Greenwich.

On the street. And only one time. That was three years ago. But what happened to her"—he wet his lips—"I couldn't put that aside."

"Thanks," she said. "Picking up where we were before, you had never been to Mr. Donovan's place of residence, the place where he died, prior to the conversation you had with his wife, Leslie, in her apartment, after his death?"

"No, I had not."

"And you claim you have no idea how the pen found by the NYPD at the place of Mr. Donovan's apparent suicide, with the logo of the Talon Group, the company you work for, got there?"

He shook his head. "None."

"Even if, after testing, your fingerprints turn out to be on the pen?"

"Especially if my prints turn out to be on it," he said. "If that's the case, the pen could have come from a variety of sources. From a jacket. Directly from my desk. A business meeting . . ."

"Why would someone be interested in placing a pen that could be tied back to you at the scene where an unrelated person took his own life?"

"The obvious thought might be that someone was trying to set me up."

"Set you up?" The Treasury agent jotted on her pad. "For what purpose, Mr. Hauck?"

"My guess, since it would likely never be enough on its own to warrant any indictment, would be to distract me from linking the deaths of Mr. Glassman and Mr. Donovan."

"You said inside you were looking into a person's background on behalf of your firm? You referred to him as Subject A?"

"Confidentially, Agent Blum. I could get into a boatload of trouble if that got out."

"You're already in a sizable amount of trouble, Mr. Hauck. You've illegally obtained private phone records. You're being looked into by the NYPD. I don't know what your definition of a boatload is, but if I were you, I'd start to look at me as the person who's going to get you out."

He could have asked for an attorney. For a guarantee against further prosecution. But he decided there was no gain. He had done nothing wrong. Whoever was trying to steer him off, he had to trust someone, he realized. Agent Blum seemed capable and earnest. She might as well be the one.

"His name is Thibault," Hauck said. He spelled it out. "First name Dieter. He also goes by Dani."

"This Mr. Thibault is an American citizen?" Naomi Blum asked, making a note on her pad.

"Dutch. Or at least, that's what he claims. His passport is Dutch. He might also have a Belgian one as well. Of course, that's only the beginning." He shook his head and smiled.

"So what is it people might want to distract you from, Mr. Hauck? Take me through."

He did. Starting in his office with Merrill Simons. Then Thibault. The Conyers Farm photo—Thibault's connection to Glassman. Knowing he could get himself fired for what he was divulging, for going around Foley—and probably would. Finally Thibault's connection to Donovan, the phone calls to the super's office where the second trader died.

Agent Blum made notes. She could take it from here. She had the resources on the highest levels. Find out who Thibault was. Subpoena the security video in Donovan's building. Trace it back to Cat Rock Road.

The black SUVs. Find the guy with the red knotted hair and the tat. Maybe a hundred ways everything could be tied to Thibault. What his motives were. Where it all led from there.

April. Find who killed her.

Naomi listened, making occasional notes. She asked astute questions. Her sharp eyes deepened as the links to Thibault grew more clear. When he was done, around forty minutes later, she thanked him. Made copies of what he'd found. He felt a little deflated when it was over. After giving up everything he knew. He realized that for four weeks his juices had been running.

And he realized how much he had missed that. How good it felt again.

When she was arranging her notes, Hauck said, "I've given what I have to you. Now you owe me a couple."

Naomi Blum turned to him. "Okay."

"The first is, how did *you* get onto this? You visited Donovan's widow. That was a police matter, not Treasury. You weren't looking into either of these people. How did you know?"

The agent shrugged. "When two

high-level money managers die and both their firms fall apart due to their actions, it's my job to check it out."

"What do you think is happening?"

"I'm sorry, I'm afraid that's one I can't fully answer right now." The agent started to get up. "What's the second question? You said there were two."

Hauck placed his hand on her arm, stopping her. "I want to stay involved."

"Stay in?"

"I have a reason to keep looking into Thibault. Without attracting notice. There's also the chance my firm could even be involved. It won't hurt to have someone on the inside."

Naomi shook her head. "Look, Mr. Hauck—"

"Ms. Blum . . ." She sat back down. "These people think I'm onto something. As far as they know I'm only looking into this matter for a client. But that can be useful. Whatever they're hiding. You can chase down all the money wires, the fake passports, the overheard chatter, the e-mail trails. But I'm already involved."

"How about I think about it," the Treasury agent said. "It's not exactly the policy of the U.S. government to put private citizens at that kind of risk."

"I'll take the risk."

"I said I'll think about it," the agent said, standing up. "Look, Mr. Hauck, I know your background, and the United States of America owes you its full appreciation. But we have people who handle this sort of thing. Interagency people. The kind of money it takes to do what they're doing— it's the kind of money that takes on governments, Mr. Hauck, not suburban police departments. I know what you've already done, but to put it plainly," the pretty agent said, looking at him directly, "you have no idea the shit-storm of trouble staying in this could bring on."

Hauck stood up as well, opening the door for her. "I don't mind trouble."

CHAPTER THIRTY-SIX

There might have been a time, years back, Jack "Red" O'Toole reflected, riding the Metro-North train to Greenwich, that his soul was worth saving.

The teenage girl texting on her Black-Berry reminded him of someone from long ago. A girl he knew back in high school. Desiree Flynn. When he played line-backer at Haysville High in Kansas and the thought of stuffing the line and knock-ing heads for the blue and white of Kansas State was something he could reach out and touch. When maybe a job at a lathe at Great Plains Tool Company like his father had was a dream worth living for.

But that was before the sky grew dark and an F5 tornado crashed through town one May afternoon, leveling half of it, including the die plant.

Red O'Toole's parents too.

Before he left to go into the army and developed a deft touch with an M4. Before IEDs exploded in his ears or, amped on Dianabol, he chased a fleeing insurgent into a stone hut in Hilla and emptied his mag on six "unfriendlies" sitting there— who turned out to be a family at the dinner table and their ten-year-old son, who'd been chasing after a soccer ball.

That was when the army sent him home with a full discharge, and he came back to a town of rubble and zero prospects, bad as anything he had seen over there, and he spent all of six days there, Desiree off in Utah somewhere, before signing up for two years with Global Threat Management, making five times what he did for Uncle Sam.

And got a bona fide, free license to use his skills.

They played a game when they went out on a field trip, beyond the Green Zone. They called it Tin Can. Try to knock one off the fence with their M4s. Except the "can" was more likely an old man who popped his head up watering his plants or boys playing cards on a rooftop as their armored convoy sped by.

O'Toole kept looking at the girl across from him. She kept texting, as if she didn't even notice him.

Pop. Pop. Pop.

Like shooting a tin can off a fence in a dusty field.

The train slowed, approaching his destination. *"Greenwich,"* the conductor announced over the loudspeaker. *"Greenwich. Old Greenwich will be next."*

O'Toole stood up. He took one last look at the texting girl, who, he decided, didn't look like Desiree at all. He stood in the line of passengers waiting to disembark.

The door opened.

O'Toole crossed onto the platform. The exiting passengers funneled down into the station. O'Toole continued along the track.

The man he was looking for was reading a magazine, hair smoothed back, wearing wire-rim glasses, waiting on a bench on the northbound side.

O'Toole took a seat next to him. He glanced at his watch. "Right on time."

"If you can't trust Metro-North, who can you trust?" the man replied.

"Always a good question. I ask myself that a lot."

"Well, in your case," the man said, "I'm afraid you have to trust me." He closed what he was reading, the *Economist,* and removed an eight-by-eleven manila envelope from the pages. He slid it along the concrete bench to O'Toole.

"We have another job for you." O'Toole opened the envelope. "I want him to become disinterested in our affairs."

There was a series of photos inside. On top, a man he might characterize as rugged, handsome, opening the door to an office building. The next was a not-so-bad-looking chick with short, dark hair getting out of a Prius.

The third was a kid in an oversize hockey jersey. O'Toole noticed he clearly had something wrong with him.

Retard, he thought. *What did they call them? Down syndrome or something.*

He flipped back to the first photo. Hauck. An ex-cop. "You want him dead?"

"What I want is for him to be no longer engaged in our affairs." His contact took off his glasses and started to clean them. "What you do is your business. I always trust the judgment of my people on the ground."

O'Toole slipped the photos back inside the envelope. "Sounds reasonable."

His contact stood up.

"You know, I was thinking," O'Toole said. "See that guy over there?" A man on the other side of the platform, reading a newspaper, waiting for a train.

"The one in the suit?"

"If a twister hadn't leveled my town when I was a kid, that might've been me, waiting for that train. Coming home from work. Someone waiting for me with a beer. Maybe a kid. Who knows"—O'Toole raised his shades and grinned at him—"I might've even been like you."

"No." The man in the wire-rims rolled up his magazine and tapped O'Toole's knee. "You would never have been like me. Just make sure he's clear of our affairs. Whatever you decide, make it something he'll clearly understand."

"You know, we had a saying over there . . ." O'Toole squinted back at him. "'The unwanted, doing the unthinkable—for the ungrateful.'"

"Really." The man in the glasses smiled. He dropped another envelope on his lap. This time a fat one. "I think you'll find us grateful. As usual. Next train back's at five thirty-two."

He walked off, leaving O'Toole on the platform. He tapped the thick envelope against his knee and studied the man on the other side of the track.

Yeah, he thought, laughing to himself; his contact was right. That was never in the cards. He rubbed the back of his neck. Where his panther was. Shiva. The tattoo had kept him safe through five tours to the Sandbox. The tip of her long, bright claw reaching onto his neck.

If he had ever been worth saving, the statute of limitations had long run out. The pieces of his soul had scattered across the globe. Like an F5 blowing into town. Leveling most everything. Scattering the rest.

He reached back and reknotted his thick, red-brown hair.

CHAPTER THIRTY-SEVEN

The man in the Burberry raincoat turned up his collar against the drizzle as he stepped out of the office building onto Madison Avenue. He chatted for a second with a woman—maybe a coworker—who waved good-bye and headed north.

Thibault started walking the other way to the south.

Across the street, Hauck followed, several paces behind.

He had left the office early, telling Brooke he had some errands to attend to. He felt a little out of practice at what he was doing. He hadn't done this kind of thing in years.

On Fifty-fourth, Thibault stopped in front of a store window, seeming to admire a tie. Then he continued, taking a call on his cell. On Fifty-third Street he made a right, heading west. Hauck crossed after him, hunching into his jacket against the rain, twenty yards behind.

Tall, swarthy, with thick, black hair that came over his collar, Thibault cut a commanding presence. It wasn't hard to see why women might be drawn to him. Halfway down the block he veered into a recessed courtyard set between two larger buildings. It looked like a restaurant. He opened the glass doors and went inside.

The place was called Alto. Hauck had heard of it. Italian, fancy. The kind of place his boss, Foley, was always trying to drag him to. Annie would have been impressed.

He went up to the door, and through the glass, he saw Thibault remove his coat and hand it to a pretty hostess. It looked as if they were familiar with him there. He seemed to recognize someone at the bar and went straight up to him.

Hauck waited as Thibault greeted the man and took a seat, and then stepped in.

"Dining with us tonight?" The hostess, a twentysomething gal in a sexy black dress, smiled from behind a counter.

Hauck smiled back. "Just meeting a friend at the bar."

Thibault was seated at the far end of the crowded bar. His friend, who was Mediterranean looking, wore a nicely tailored sport jacket and open white shirt.

Hauck found a nook at the opposite end. The female bartender came up and he ordered a beer. Something Belgian. Palm. For the occasion. Through the maze of shifting bodies and faces, he watched them.

The two appeared to be friends. Even over the loud din, Hauck occasionally heard Thibault's deep-throated laugh. He'd gotten a drink—it looked like vodka—and he shifted the stool around and sat, his back to Hauck, chatting with his friend. They clinked glasses, Thibault patting him affectionately on the shoulder.

Hauck knew he was crossing the line. He had resolved not to accelerate the situation but to find out whatever he could, and at the same time, he knew this would send Foley off the deep end. But Thibault was

clearly concealing something, and whatever it was, Hauck felt certain it led back
to Glassman and Donovan. On his cell,
he snapped a photo of them through the
crowd. When the time came, maybe he'd
have something he could give to Naomi or
Chrisafoulis.

With a cherry on top.

Thibault signaled for another drink. When
he turned, there was a moment when it
was almost as if the man's eyes shifted
down the bar and, through the crowd of
faces, locked directly on Hauck. Their gazes
met momentarily.

Hauck took a sip and glanced away. A
shiver traveled down his spine. *Don't be
careless. Whatever you do.*

A moment later the hostess came up
and told them their table was ready.
Thibault threw out some bills, signaled for
the drinks to be sent directly. He let his
companion proceed first, with a pat to his
back, then followed as the hostess led
them both upstairs.

Hauck watched them disappear, then
slipped out of his spot at the bar and went
over to where Thibault had been sitting.
The female bartender tried to clear off his

space. Hauck reached for the empty glass.

"Mind if I take this?" He winked. "Souvenir."

The bartender hesitated at first, her eyes darting past Hauck, maybe to search out someone in charge, not sure.

Hauck put a fifty on the bar. "This ought to cover, right?"

Her eyes grew wide, and she started clearing off the remaining glasses and napkins, raking in the bill. She nodded. "Ought to cover it just fine."

CHAPTER THIRTY-EIGHT

Thomas Keaton, secretary of the treasury, to whom the Office of Terrorism and Financial Intelligence reported, was able to spare Naomi and Rob Whyte, her boss, just ten minutes. That was all. He had a meeting at the AG's office. Naomi and Rob literally rushed over to the main building, making some last-second copies, files in hand. She had shared what she knew with her boss, and he decided it was worth the call.

She was a little nervous. This was by far the most sensitive investigation of her career. She had looked into some of the notable hedge fund frauds and the possible dealings of an Iranian bank to dump dollars through the Middle East, trying to drive the currency down, but never anything like this. The stock market was down 30 percent since the beginning of March. Two of the world's largest investment banks had failed. Two more, Citi and Bank of America, had plummeted into single digits. Not to mention Freddie Mac and Fannie Mae, which were reeling.

And now she could pretty much prove that the deaths of two rogue traders, traders whose losses had sunk their banks, were, in fact, not unrelated incidents but connected.

The whole thing was one large domino effect, and she felt she knew exactly the point where it all started.

At this point, whatever "evidence" she had, at least from a prosecutorial point of view, was, at best, flimsy. No more than a weak connection between a shadowy individual and the traders who had suddenly died. Looking deeper would have to involve other agencies. The FBI, the SEC, the AG's office, maybe Interpol. They had to find out who Thibault really was. Who his contacts were. Whether there were any deeper involvements with the two dead traders. Whether money had changed hands. And most likely without taking him into custody. The cryptic message delivered to Marty al-Bashir that had sat on her desk without any apparent meaning now tolled in her brain like a warning bell.

The planes are in the air.

The secretary's office was at a corner of Treasury's vast limestone building overlooking the Washington Mall. Naomi had never even been to this part of the building before. Timeless portraits of past secretaries and historic figures lined the mahogany-paneled halls. Hamilton. Chase. Morgenthau. Baker.

"Don't be nervous," Rob said as they sat outside the suite waiting. "If you happen to be wrong on this, I can always land a job as a regional bank auditor in northern Montana."

Naomi nodded, adjusting her suit. "Hopefully, you'll need a secretary there."

The door opened and Keaton's secretary came out. "The secretary will see you now."

Whyte stood up. Let out a breath. "More like a snow blower."

They stepped into the large, window-lined office. Keaton, in a pinstripe suit and with a shock of white hair, came around to what seemed the mother of all conference tables, and just to add to the effect, the Washington Monument was clearly visible through the window. Naomi swallowed. *No pressure here.* The head of the Treasury had been at Justice, not to mention his highly regarded career as a Wall Street deal maker. Naomi had met him once briefly when he set up their task force and visited them across the street.

"Ms. Blum," he said, nodding cordially but not shaking her hand. "Rob. I asked Mitch Hastings to sit in, if that's alright with you?"

It wasn't meant as a question. Hastings was the no-nonsense chief counsel to the Treasury Department. She had seen him in the background at the hedge fund CEO and auto bailout congressional hearings.

"Of course." Whyte nodded. "Mitch . . ." The lawyer smiled back tightly and indifferently.

Naomi bit her bottom lip and took a breath. *Here goes . . .*

"I'm afraid I have to be at the AG's office in ten minutes." Keaton glanced at his watch and then at Whyte. "So I'll ask you to start right in."

"Mr. Secretary," Rob said, "Naomi's come up with a few things. Things we think you ought to be aware of."

The treasury secretary sat down directly across from her, nodding peremptorily. *"Alright."*

Two of the most influential figures in the government had their gazes directly on her.

"A few months back"—Naomi cleared her throat and removed a file from out of her bag—"a phone transcript landed on my desk. From the NSA. The text of a call between a well-known Bahraini financial figure, Hassan ibn Hassani, who is suspected of passing funds to certain organizations that appeared on the Terrorist Watch List, and an investment manager in London. A Saudi named Mashhur al-Bashir—Marty al-Bashir, as he's known in the trade. He's currently the chief investment officer of the Royal Saudi Partnership."

Thomas Keaton folded his hands in front of his face. "I'm familiar with his name."

"The transcript," Naomi said, her leg racing under the table, "referred to some kind of 'change in direction' for their strategy. If al-Bashir was to be involved I can only assume it meant a change in investment policy. Why a Bahraini financier would be discussing this with him, we don't know. But the conversation concluded with a bit of a concerning statement—'the planes are in the air.'"

The treasury secretary raised his eyes. His gaze shifted to Naomi's boss, Whyte. "This conversation was a couple of months back?"

Whyte nodded. "Yes, in March, sir."

"So clearly there were no 'planes.'" The treasury secretary exhaled. "At least in the most ominous sense, thank God."

Naomi cleared her throat. "I'm not so sure."

Keaton looked back at her. "Go on."

"February eighth was a Sunday," Naomi said, drawing their attention to the next exhibit. "Beginning the following Monday, February ninth, our analysts who track this sort of thing indicate the Royal Saudi Partnership began to systematically divest itself of its positions in U.S. stocks, starting

with its positions in the financial sector—
which, as you can imagine, were quite
sizable—and this had the effect of driving
these stocks down. I won't waste your time
on it here"—Naomi flipped over a page—
"but I can chart how the decline in these
stocks originated from this particular point
and how it weighed on the market as a
whole. What it started was a worldwide
sell-off in stocks."

"Helped along, I could add," Hastings,
the secretary's counsel, countered, "by a
wide array of factors."

"Yes, sir," Naomi said, "no doubt. That's
precisely what I came here to discuss."

She opened another file and got up,
placing hastily made copies in front of the
two Treasury figures. She explained that it
was nothing she could be 100 percent firm
on yet, just the most circumstantial links
between Thibault, as mapped out by the
person she had interviewed, Ty Hauck, and
the two traders who had suspiciously died.
Traders whose concealed losses were of
such a size they were the death knells of
Wertheimer Grant and Beeston Holloway,
dragging the rest of the financial markets to
the edge.

"And we all know where that has led," Naomi finished up.

"You're suggesting there's a possible criminal connection between these two investment managers' deaths?" Keaton drew in a hesitant breath, paging through Naomi's exhibits.

"I'm saying that's possible, sir," Naomi said.

"And that it's somehow tied back to this Mashhur al-Bashir. Through this figure Thibault? Why?"

"I'm just forwarding a theory, sir. One of our jobs is to put together possible unmaterialized threats and anticipate what might happen next."

"Yes, yes." Keaton rolled his hand, fast-forwarding. "Go on."

"Okay." Naomi took a breath. *Here goes . . .* "What if there were people on an organized basis, people of influence," she suggested, "who wanted to do our country systemic harm, using a new strategy, a 'change in direction,' as they referred to it." She steeled herself. "Not by flying a plane through our tallest buildings, like before, but by driving one, *figuratively,* sir, through the heart of our most vital national asset. The root of everything we stand for."

Keaton narrowed his eyes at her. Naomi had no idea if he was buying it.

"The economy, sir," she said. "The amount of economic wealth we have lost since the downturn, not to mention the unrest of our citizens, is impossible to measure. One could trace the start of the slide, I believe, to these two Wall Street investment houses going down."

The treasury secretary's face began to whiten, almost matching his hair. He nodded soberly, glancing at his chief counsel, and seemed to draw his words with care. "But who would possibly gain? We are in a global economy. Every stock exchange around the world is reeling from the decline. Oil is selling at less than half what it once was. It would be economic suicide."

Naomi shrugged, anticipating the question. "I don't know that yet."

"And you think there's a chance this Thibault person might be somehow at the heart of this scheme?"

"I'm saying it's possible, sir, yes."

Keaton leaned back in his seat. "What do we know about him?"

"His past is a bit vague, sir. He has a Dutch passport. It's entirely possible he holds multiple passports. This ex-detective I mentioned, Hauck, he's done some preliminary investigation through his firm and he seems to think he may, in fact, be Serbian."

"*Serbian?*" The secretary's eyes widened. He leafed through Naomi's exhibits. "Do we have the findings of this firm?"

"No, sir, I don't think we can go there, at least not right now. It seems someone has been trying to push Hauck off his investigation. And it's possible, I only say *possible,*" Naomi added, knowing she was rolling the dice here, "his own firm may be somehow complicit in this."

Keaton looked up. "Run that one by me again."

"It seems they represent other parties," Naomi said, "who might have a vested interest in this story not coming to light."

"*Other parties?*" Now the treasury secretary's gaze grew heated. "Other parties such as *whom,* Ms. Blum?"

"Such as Reynolds Reid, sir. I'm told

they're seeking to pick up some of Wertheimer Grant's operations . . ."

"Yes, we're involved in those negotia-
tions. For Christ's sake, what's the name
of this security firm?"

"The Talon Group," answered Naomi.

"Talon?" Keaton swallowed, concerned.
"You must be kidding. They're all over this
fucking town."

Keaton stared blankly back at her and
pushed back his chair. His eyes flicked to
his watch. He gritted his teeth.

Naomi glanced at Whyte, wondering if
he was asking himself the same thing—
whether they should both be making their
reservations to Missoula around now.

"This doesn't get out!" The head of the
Treasury looked at Hastings peremptorily.
"Not to the FBI, not to Justice. And for
God's sake, not to the press. Until we have
more. Agent Blum, you've done a credit-
able job on this. You can engage whatever
means necessary with respect to these
two traders' untimely deaths to find out
whatever you can on this Thibault figure."

"Thank you, sir."

"I'll authorize a probe by NSA. Maybe
there's been some direct contact between

him and this Marty figure, the Saudi fund manager. Or that Bahraini, Hassani . . ."

Naomi looked toward her boss, pleased. "I'm already on that, sir."

"And maybe this Hauck might prove useful. You say he's an ex-detective. How the hell did he ever get himself involved in this situation in the first place?"

"Marc Glassman's wife, who was killed along with her husband at their house in Greenwich . . ." Naomi shrugged. "Apparently, she was a friend of his. He was looking into her death on the side and became doubtful it was part of a burglary break-in. It was simply a coincidence that his security firm got him involved in probing into Thibault on a personal matter."

"A personal matter?" The treasury secretary pushed back his chair, standing up. "Well, it seems we're damn lucky if you ask me. Just following up on the death of a friend . . . What is the man, some kind of white knight?"

"I don't know, sir," Naomi said, suppressing a slight smile.

"Well, he's about to get his armor dinged a bit if this turns out to be true. Give me something to go on, Agent Blum. Find out who Thibault is. Just keep it, for now, under the radar. I don't want this out." He headed around to his desk. Naomi assembled her files to leave. "And Agent Blum . . ."

"Sir?" Naomi turned.

The treasury secretary smiled. "Good job."

"Thank you, sir."

A rush of relief mixed with exhilaration followed Naomi all the way back to her office. She almost felt lifted off her heels.

"Good job," Rob Whyte said, exhaling, as they crossed M Street to their building.

"Cancel that reservation then?" she replied playfully. "To northern Montana?"

He patted her on the shoulder. "Why don't we just see how it goes?"

When she got back to her office, Naomi stepped behind her desk. Files on various cases she was looking into were piled high. Thick, bound reports as high as the slit in the basement wall they called a half window.

Maybe she'd work her way up to a full window soon.

Her assistant, Talia, came in after her expectantly. "So how did it go?"

"Well"—Naomi blew out her cheeks in mock relief—"I'm still here!" Of course, she hadn't told Talia what her meeting had been about.

"This came for you while you were out." Talia dropped a FedEx carton on her desk.

The sender's address read Greenwich, Connecticut.

"Thanks."

Naomi waited for her to leave, then slit open the top of the heavily taped carton. She took out a large plastic bag, and sealed in it, protected carefully in bubble wrap, was a clear drinking glass, like a lowball glass.

There was a note attached. Naomi opened it.

Compliments of Dani Thibault, it was signed. Then underlined: *Go to town!*

Naomi smiled.

She knew exactly who it was from. This would get the ball rolling.

And underneath, the white knight had written, underlined again, *Have you thought it over yet?*

CHAPTER THIRTY-NINE

That Saturday night, at the Hamill rink in Greenwich, the twelve-and-under Trident-Allen Value Fund Bruins took it to the Commack, Long Island, Ducks by the score of six to one.

As the final buzzer sounded, Hauck stepped onto the ice and gave a handshake to the opposing coach as his players raised their sticks in the air and high-fived their opponents. Jared, whom Hauck had brought along, went onto the ice as well, going, "Good game, Kyle! Good game, Tony."

Some of them skated by, knocking

elbows with him, saying, "Thanks for getting us ready, dude!"

As they headed out, Hauck rallied the
kids around him for a couple of minutes.
"Solid game. Way to play defense, guys."
He clapped. "Okay, remember, we have
practice Wednesday at eight. No absen-
tees! Good game, everyone! And remember to collect your gear."

As the team filed off the ice, one or two
of the parents came over to say hi and con-
gratulate him on the game. While they did,
Jared grabbed a stick and took the chance
to shoot a few stray pucks into the side-
boards. Ted, the rink manager, got in the
Zamboni and started to smooth out the
ice. It was almost ten—theirs was the last
match of the night. Annie was at her café
until around eleven. Hauck had said he'd
drop Jared off, hang out at the bar, and
have dessert. Celebrate the win.

Within minutes, the place was virtually
empty. Elated kids piled into their parents'
cars. The Zamboni finished up on the ice.
Ted dimmed the lights.

Hauck noticed a guy in a black nylon
jacket he had never seen before just
watching from the other end of the rink.

"Hey, Ted, you got a minute!"

Hauck went over and chatted with the manager, whom he knew from when he was on the force, proposing the idea of a fund-raiser for an assistant coach of one of the other teams who had lost his job and was in need of a kidney transplant. Hauck thought maybe he could get the police and firemen to spar off in an exhibition.

"Jared," he yelled, "you mind going into the locker room and grabbing me the team bag?" The duffel held a bunch of practice pucks and rolls of tape, some extra equipment. Hauck had tossed his own gear in there after the skate-around.

Jared waved. "Sure, Ty."

"Sounds like a good idea," the manager said. "Lemme check the schedule and see what's free."

"That would be great, Ted."

"Solid game tonight," Ted called, parking the Zamboni.

Hauck tossed him a thumbs-up. "Yeah, guess they listen every once in a while!"

He made his way back across the ice. He grabbed his jacket from off the bench. He waited for Jared to come out with the bag. He'd been in there a long time.

Something wasn't feeling right to him.
Call it twenty years on the job, his antennae buzzing. He glanced to the far end of
the ice.

The man in the Windbreaker wasn't
there.

CHAPTER FORTY

Red O'Toole pulled the van into the crowded lot a little before nine thirty and waited outside the rink.

Sonny Merced hunched beside him in the passenger seat. They'd been together before, on the Glassman job. They'd served together back in the Sandbox. But Sonny's tale was just a bit different than his. He was an expert with a knife, could skin a cat with one, not to mention a man— and O'Toole had seen him. At Camp Victory, he'd been accused of rape three times. But getting female grunts to testify was another tale and each time they backed down. The third time, he got bounced home. Sonny was a liability the army didn't need. He kicked around with a couple of private security firms, came home, got a job digging pools in Michigan, no chance of a real job. Then he fell into drugs and had to support his habit.

O'Toole looked at what he did as a job, the only one he was qualified for. Sonny looked at it as a thrill.

The parking lot was filled. Some kind of game was obviously going on. A half hour ago, he had gone and stuck his head in the rink and saw the match still in progress. Parents cheering. The scoreboard ticking down. Now, he looked at his watch and nudged Sonny. "Mount up. It's showtime, man."

People finally started coming out of the rink. Parents starting up their cars, kids yelping, whooping it up, sticks held high. In a couple of minutes, the parking lot grew empty, except for a couple of cars.

They didn't see Hauck or the kid.

O'Toole told Sonny, "Go in and see what's going on."

Sonny zipped up his black nylon Windbreaker and crawled out of the van.

A few minutes passed. O'Toole put on the radio. He didn't entirely trust Sonny. The dude was reckless, a little crazed. It always got him into trouble. But O'Toole always knew how to calm him down.

Suddenly his throwaway cell phone rang. "What the hell is going on? I told you to check it out, not go for a goddamn skate."

"Relax," Sonny Merced said, "start the car. I'm doing it now."

CHAPTER FORTY-ONE

Jared!" Hauck shouted toward the locker room and waited for a reply.

None came.

The whole rink was dark now. Ted was somewhere in the back. The stranger who he'd seen standing at the opposite end of the rink was nowhere to be found. The antennae for trouble Hauck had built up over the years was buzzing like crazy.

"Jared!" he called out again. *Why wasn't he answering?*

Something was wrong.

He grabbed a stray stick off the glass and headed back to the locker room, his blood starting to race with trepidation. This was Annie's son. He turned the corner, accelerating into a run, and pushed through the swinging doors into the locker room, shouting, *"Jared?"*

"Ty!" His voice came back. Jared's voice. Scared.

He turned to the lockers and saw the man he had spotted lurking outside, his hand cupped over Jared's mouth, the boy's eyes wide as melons, fear in them. He was dragging Jared toward the bathroom area. The guy had a heavy stubble on his face, sideburns, and a thick mustache. He looked about fifty but he was probably twenty years younger. Wearing a black nylon jacket.

He had a knife held under Jared's chin.

Hauck froze.

"Hey, hero, get the fuck out of here!" The man glared at Hauck. With one arm he jerked Jared's head to the side. With the other, he deftly clenched the blade underneath Jared's jaw. "Do what I say, man, or I'll split him in two."

Jared, who didn't have it in him to hurt a flea, twisted vainly against the man's grasp, hyperventilating.

Tears flashed in his petrified eyes.

"Let the boy go," Hauck said. He squeezed the hockey stick two fisted and took a step toward them, fixing on the man's eyes. "Why are you here?"

"You know damn well why I'm here. Doesn't he, kid? Ask him why I'm here. Ask him what he's stuck his nose into." He dug the blade point into Jared's Adam's apple, causing the boy's eyes to bulge. "You and I, kid. We're walking out of here. You first." He motioned to Hauck. "One wrong move"—he twitched the sharp edge—"just one, Mr. Ex-Cop, and you can kiss your goofy little buddy here good-bye."

Jared freed his mouth momentarily. Gripped by fear, confusion, he uttered, "Why is he doing this, Ty?"

"Jared, I'm not going to let him hurt you," Hauck said. His blood pulsed with rage and intensity. "He's an innocent kid," he said to the man. "You can see he's not all together. Let him go. Take me. It's what you came here for anyway, isn't it?"

"*Ty . . .*" Jared's face was white, his breaths rapid and hard. "Don't let him hurt me, Ty. *Okay?*"

"He won't, Jared." The man knew who

he was. Which he realized was bad. This wasn't some random pervert. Hauck knew he was clearly here for him. He also realized there was no gain in killing the boy. If Hauck went at him, it would only incapacitate the blade.

"He's going to let you go." Hauck looked in Jared's cowering eyes, taking a step closer. Then he switched to the attacker. "And when he does, Jared"—Hauck flexed the stick—"I want you to run out of here, fast as you can. Don't go outside." It occurred to Hauck the man might not be alone. "Stay in the rink. I want you to find Ted and hide somewhere. Call 911."

Jared nodded fearfully. Hauck took another step. "You understand, don't you, son?"

He nodded again, petrified.

Hauck winked at him. "Good."

The man arched back the boy's neck, chortling, "Fuck I'm going to let him go . . ."

Hauck shifted his gaze solidly to the man. The knife gleamed. An army combat blade. He no longer felt nerves, just that he was the only thing between the boy's life and death, and he was glad it was him. He gave the man a purposeful smile.

"You know damn well I'm not gonna let
that boy out of my sight."

The assailant tensed his grip on the
blade.

"You came for me." Hauck nodded to
the man. "Have at it, asshole."

He lunged with the stick at his attacker's
head.

Hauck knew from twenty years on the
job what people in these situations do, no
matter what they've threatened, when a
SWAT team charges into a room. They
defend themselves. What the survival instinct orders them to do.

The man threw up his hands.

Stick high, Hauck swung it with all his
might across the assailant's shoulder, the
arm holding the knife. The man took a
step back, reflexively put out his arm, letting Jared go.

As the stick split in half across his arm.

The man cried out. Jared ran, screaming, out of the assailant's grasp. Hauck
took what was left of the stick and charged
him, knocking the guy backward and pinning the arm holding the knife against the
concrete locker-room wall.

He tried to squeeze the blade from the man's grip.

"*Jared, get out!* Do as I say. Get out of here!"

But the boy just stood there, paralyzed, as Hauck wrestled for the blade against the wall. The man was strong. Like Hauck suspected, no amateur. He kept squeezing the man's arm against the wall, trying to pry the knife free. "*Jared, go!*"

He spun, tried to ram the man in his belly with the butt of the stick, but the assailant pivoted and drove his knee into Hauck's groin, crushing the air out of him. The pain shot through him. He wrenched Hauck back, rolling him over a bench, against the edge of an open, metal locker door.

Hauck felt dazed, breathless, his belly on fire like he'd been speared.

The man came at him, flexing the blade in a way that said he knew exactly how to use it. Hauck scrambled to his feet, clinging to the jagged edge of the stick to defend himself.

The man grinned cockily. "Always have to play the hero, don't you, dude."

He swung, ripping through Hauck's

sweatshirt, scraping Hauck on the arm as Hauck tried to block the knife with the shaft of the stick.

Hauck cried out in pain.

He looked past him for a second. Jared was still standing there, paralyzed with fear. *"Jared, please!"*

The attacker dove at him again. This time Hauck flung out an open metal locker door, catching him flush. Skates, pads cascading all over them. Summoning every bit of his strength, Hauck slammed the open door against the man's hand—two, three times—trying to free the knife. Blood rushed into the guy's face as he tried to hold on.

Miraculously, the knife fell from his grasp and clattered to the floor.

Both their eyes darted to it.

With his free hand, the assailant took Hauck by the collar and drove him hard against the locker, the pain shooting up his spine. In the same motion, he lunged across the floor for the blade. Hauck dove on him, blood trickling from his mouth, his arm burning like it had been flayed by a slicing machine. They both fell across the wooden bench and onto the floor. The man spun Hauck on his back. Suddenly he picked up the splintered hockey stick and pinned it across Hauck's throat, venom in his eyes. Hauck's left arm was momentarily pinned behind the metal legs of the bench. Straining, the man realized his advantage and forced the stick into Hauck's larynx.

"Chew on this, fucker."

Hauck pushed back against it vainly, his arm finally freed, but it was too late.

The assailant was too strong, too adept, and he leaned on top of Hauck with all his leverage. Hauck started to gag. He couldn't push it back. His eyes flashed to Jared standing across the room, transfixed, squeezing a sliver of space for air, shouting to him, "Jared, please, run. Now!"

The boy took a step toward the door.

Hauck felt the oxygen and strength slowly seeping out of him. He strained, lungs bursting, pushing back with everything he had, twisting his torso to push the guy off. But he couldn't! He looked into the dark, wide pupils of the man's gloating eyes and realized, his breaths growing short and frantic, he might die here.

"Next time, be careful where you stick your nose . . ." The man grinned triumphantly.

Hauck's lungs were exploding. He looked helplessly at Jared one more time, unable to even beg him now. With the last of his strength, he reached, desperate for anything he could find, fingers grasping at his side—pads, towels, *nothing* . . .

A skate.

Suddenly he felt his hand come into contact with it. His fingers fumbled at the leather boot, the laces. He slid it along the floor, clutching on to the laces.

This could save his life.

That's when he heard someone scream. *"Get off him! Get off!"*

Jared coming over and beating on the man. What was he doing?

The boy's hands around the man's neck, trying to twist him back. *"Let him go!"*

Jared's blows were meaningless. The man flung his arm around, sending him flying into the wall of lockers.

It gave Hauck the instant he needed.

He squeezed on the boot and swung it upward, catching the startled attacker in the face just as he turned back, his eyes widening in surprise.

The grunt that came out of him was fearful, garbled; his hands rushed to his face.

Hauck spun him off. They both fell onto the floor, Hauck rolling on top of him. He heard a deep-rooted groan, more of a gurgling sound, and a crack, the weight of Hauck's body lodging the skate blade deep in his attacker's chest.

A matted slick of blood appeared.

Eyes glazing over, the man began to breathe heavily. Blood oozed from his jacket.

Hauck rolled off him, collapsing back in exhaustion against the row of lockers.

The man just looked at him, helpless, a pool of dark blood building up by his side.

"Who?" Hauck's throat was so tight and rasping he could barely speak. *"Who sent you?"*

The man just looked at him, taking short, croaking breaths. Denial in his eyes. Lips quivering. Until he stopped.

Jared ran up to Hauck. He pulled the traumatized boy against him, an arm around his shoulders, stroking his face. "It's going to be alright, son," he said, shielding Jared's view from the bloody sight of the man dying.

He repeated it, telling himself as well. "It's going to be okay."

CHAPTER FORTY-TWO

The Greenwich police arrived a few minutes later. The first officer, a ten-year vet, found Hauck sitting, bloodied, against a wall outside the locker room, with his arm around Jared. The cop stuck his head inside and came out white-faced. "My God . . ."

Maybe two minutes later, the medical team arrived. They checked out Jared—he was okay, thank God, other than a few marks on his neck where the blade had nicked him. Just in a state of shock. Hauck had called Annie. She was on her way now. One of the med techs took a look at

Hauck's arm. The knife wound hadn't gone too deep, but the flesh was torn pretty good. He'd need stitches.

Soon after that, the on-duty detectives arrived. Ed Sinclair and Sally Combes, doing the weekend graveyard shift. Followed a short while after by Steve Chrisafoulis, who'd been with his family coming out of the movies in White Plains. Shell-shocked, he looked at Hauck, relieved to find him okay. Hauck's arm was being dressed and he had lacerations all over his face and neck. Steve asked, eyes wide in disbelief, "Who won?"

"We did," Hauck said. "Six to one."

"Not funny, Ty." The head of detectives shook his head. "What the hell is it with you? Can't a guy just enjoy a relaxing Saturday night?"

Hauck shrugged. "If I can't, why should you?" The med tech applied a temporary bandage to his arm.

"How's the kid?" Steve looked over at Jared.

"A little shaken. Take a look inside. You'll understand why."

Steve nodded, scratching at his mustache. "You?"

Hauck exhaled, the kind of equivocation in his eye that said he was not exactly sure. He knew he'd come within an inch of losing his life. If he hadn't found that skate with his last breaths, if Jared hadn't distracted his assailant, Hauck was pretty sure it would have been him they'd be in there looking over. "Lucky to be alive."

"You don't exactly look it," Steve said. He put his arm on Hauck's shoulder and squeezed. "You know we can do this ourselves. Why don't you go outside and get some air? I'll have Ed and Sally take your statement in a while."

"No. I'm alright." He pulled himself up.

The tech finished up on his arm. "That ought to hold."

Hauck rolled down his sweatshirt. "Let's get it done."

Steve went in and asked Ed and Sally if he and Hauck could have a minute in the locker room alone. It was an unusual request, but they nodded, "Sure," given that only a few months ago, Hauck had been their boss.

Steve stopped and gazed soberly at the inert body, his eyes growing large at the sight of the skate still lodged in his chest, the pool of blood congealing next to him. He shook his head. *"Jesus, Ty . . ."*

"I know."

"These hockey dads are just gonna have to learn not to take things so damn seriously."

This time Hauck smiled and then told him how it had all happened. Chrisafoulis bent down over the body. He stretched on rubber gloves and turned it, gently, rummaging through the guy's pockets. "What do you think, was he after *you*?"

"He knew who I was." Hauck shrugged. "He knew I was an ex-cop. My gut says he was trying to prove a point with the boy. Trying to get to me by going after him."

"Get to you how?"

"I think you already know the answer to that one, lieutenant . . ."

The detective lifted a wallet out of the corpse's pants. "James Alan Merced. The address says Pismo Beach, California. There's an armed forces ID in here too. The guy's a vet. Camp Victory. Iraq."

He dug his finger deep inside the billfold and pulled something out. A small badge—a wreath of gold leaf overset with what looked like a World War I rifle.

Hauck shrugged. "What's that?"

"CIB badge," Steve said. "Means he saw hand-to-hand combat. You're a lucky dude."

"There's also a cell phone in the jacket pocket," Hauck said. "That should tell you something."

Chrisafoulis looked up at him reprovingly. Only the investigators were supposed to touch the body.

Hauck shrugged sheepishly. "Couldn't help myself. Old habits are tough to break."

Soon after, Annie rushed in, straight from the kitchen. She embraced her son tightly, her eyes wet with joyful tears. "Oh, baby, baby, what happened? Thank God you're okay."

"The man tried to hurt me, Mom." Jared squeezed her. "But Ty came in and saved me. They had a big fight. He told me to run, but I tried to help him, Mom."

"*I know, baby, I know,*" Annie said. "I heard. You're such a brave little man." She hugged him again and looked up at Hauck. "He's alright?"

"The med tech said just a little shock. Some small cuts on his neck."

"Ty got cut, Mom. He's hurt."

Annie draped her fingers across Jared's face and went over to Hauck. She put out her arms and gave him a strong, grateful hug, so tightly he could feel the worry and fear in her own accelerated heartbeat. He didn't resist. It felt good to be in someone's arms. Someone who loved him.

"They told me outside what happened. I don't know how to ever thank you enough. You know what Jared means to me. He—" She pressed her lips together tightly to hold back from crying. "You're hurt?"

"Just a cut. Enough to make me look a little sexy."

Annie said, "There's nothing you could ever do that will make you look any sexier to me. I owe you my son's life. Who'd want to hurt him, Ty? What kind of bastard would do something like this?"

"Someone who may have wanted to hurt me."

Her eyes flashed with anger. "I want to see him, Ty."

"No, you don't want to see him, Annie. I know how you feel . . ." He put his arm around her and wiped the tears off her face. "You have to take him away from here, Annie . . . Away from me. Anywhere. And you too. The two of you just can't be around me right now."

She looked at him, confused. "What do you mean?"

"Because it puts you in danger, Annie. Because whoever was behind this might try it again. Because someone wants to stop me and they'll hurt any part of me they can get to. Any part that makes me vulnerable."

"We're not running away from you right now, Ty."

"You're not running away. You're protecting him. Keep him up at school. Send him back to California to visit your folks. You know how I feel about him, Annie. But he just can't be around me right now."

The look of hurt that came on her face shone with fear and worry. She looked at him deeply. "What the hell have you gotten yourself into, Ty?"

"I don't know."

"We'll take you home," Annie said. "I know you need to give a statement, but I'm not going to let you be alone."

He shook his head. "No, you should be with your son."

"*Ty, please . . .* You were almost killed! You're hurt. That guy in there doesn't get to win by driving us away. *Please . . .*"

"You go on home," Hauck said. He put his hand gently on her cheek and walked her over to Jared. "They may need to talk to him again in the morning. I'll work that out."

Annie nodded, frustrated, not sure what she could do.

He knelt down and said so long to Jared. "You saved my life, guy! You are one brave little dude!"

The boy got up and hugged him, hard. Hauck realized he would have died himself if he had let anything happen to him. Even now, who knew how he was going to be able to process this? To Jared there was no evil in the world, only kindness. Hauck pulled the boy's face to his side and mussed his hair. "I'll see you soon, okay?"

Jared nodded, putting on a brave smile. "That was a good game, wasn't it, Ty?"

"Yeah, son, a really good game."

Annie left the rink with him. Hauck felt a weight of sadness pulling him down. He gave a detailed statement to the detectives, leaving out his suspicion on who might be behind this.

When he finished up, his blood was still pumping and he wasn't quite sure how to calm it. In his old job, he would've started the investigation. Looked into the cell phone. Run a criminal search on Merced.

But now there was really nothing for him to do but just go home.

Steve came up to him. "I can have someone follow you in your car, Ty. You want me to drive you home?"

"No. Thanks," he said. He shook Steve's hand. "I'm really okay."

"Sorry to say this, LT," the head of detectives said, calling Hauck by his old title, "but you don't look so okay."

A tight-fisted pressure had risen up inside him. An overheating boiler. About to explode. He realized just how close he had come to dying and what he would have been leaving behind. He had a sudden flash of feeling totally alone. He wasn't sure who to call or what to do.

Steve patted him on the shoulder. "Go home. I'm glad you're okay, Ty. I'll speak to you tomorrow."

Hauck took the detective's advice and went out to his car. The chill in the air felt good. The wind beating against his face. A light rain had begun to fall. He stepped around the corner and leaned against the concrete wall, his legs starting to weaken, what strength he still had starting to bleed way.

He lowered himself to the ground. He drew in a long, cooling breath of precious air. It felt good, cleansing, just to be alive. The wind from the sound on his face. The rain. The whoosh of the thruway off in the distance.

Grateful tears filled up Hauck's eyes.

He sniffed them back, took out his cell, and found a number on the speed dial. His heart racing, he waited for the line to pick up.

Jessie answered on the second ring. "Hey, Daddy-o, what's going on? It's a Saturday night . . ."

"Nothing's going on, hon." He blew out his cheeks. "I know it's a Saturday. I just wanted to hear your voice. What's going on with you?"

"A bunch of us are over at Kellie's and

we're watching a movie. *Ten Things I Hate About You.* Have you seen it, Dad?"

"No."

"You'd like it. It's not just a dumb teen flick. It's based on Shakespeare's *Taming of the Shrew.*"

"No kidding, babe . . ." He sat, tears starting to roll down his cheeks. He moved the phone away and pressed it tightly against his sweatshirt, imagining the horror if this had all had a different outcome. *What the hell have you gotten yourself into, Ty?* "That's great, hon."

Jessie paused. "Dad, are you okay?"

"Sure, honey, I'm okay. It's just . . . Go back to your friends. You have a fun night. I just wanted to say I love you. That's all."

"Dad, you're sounding a little strange. You're sure you're okay?"

"Everything's fine, hon." He wiped the tears off his cheeks. "Scout's honor."

"You never were a scout, Dad."

"Right," he said, chuckling. "Then how about, 'cross my heart and hope to die'!"

Jessie waited for a second. There was some high-pitched girl chatter in the background. "I love you too, Daddy."

He clicked off the line and continued to sit against the wall. His fists were coiled in anger—maybe in relief. He sucked a cooling breath into his chest. He felt ready to take them on. The man with the tattoo, the one who had killed April. He was still out there. Hauck was sure this one, at the rink, hadn't acted alone. He was going to get him; that he would bet his life on. For himself. For April.

He just had no idea who it was.

CHAPTER FORTY-THREE

You have to learn to relax more, Ty." April grinned, tapping his hand with her nail. "You seem like you're itching for a fight."

It had become a regular thing between them now. Lingering over a coffee up the block from the doctor's after their sessions. Before Hauck headed back to Queens and April to Connecticut. Occasionally, she stayed in town and went to dinner or a business function with Marc. Today they walked through Madison Square Park.

"I just feel like I'm going a little crazy,"

Hauck said. "Stir crazy," he pointed out with a smile.

"Glad you clarified that!" April said.

"It's just that it's time to get back to work. Figure out what's next."

Businessmen were sunning themselves at lunch. The cafés around the perimeter were busy. He got a soda and she got a chai at a local Asian market. They sat on a bench.

"See, I told you, you were just passing through . . ."

"You know, I sorta missed you," he said, taking a sip of Diet Coke. She hadn't been there for a couple of weeks. He missed their talks. He'd begun to think of her as a new friend, and his others, some choosing to rally behind Beth in the breakup, some just not a part of what he was going through, he no longer wanted to be around. "You guys were away?"

"No." She played with a string of brown pearls around her neck. "Just some things going on."

He stared at her, waiting to see if she was comfortable explaining.

"Nothing you want to know, Ty."

"Actually, I thought that's what this was all about. Marc . . . ?"

"No." She shook her head and smiled, as if with amusement. She cupped her hands around her tea and took a breath. "Okay. You asked for it. Agoraphobia. You know it?"

"Fear of going out?" Hauck said.

"Fear of going out. Fear of attachment. Fear of abandonment. Fear of fucking fear." She looked at him, hesitating, almost as if she was afraid she had disappointed him. "It's not that I'm fearful of the world. It's not like that with me. It's part of the depression thing. Sometimes it's like there's just this weight that pushes on me. I don't feel connected to anything. I have to force myself just to go out. Just to take my daughter to school."

"Tell me."

She pushed her long, sandy hair out of her eyes. "You're sure you're into this?"

He nodded. "Yeah."

She exhaled. "Okay. It goes back. I grew up in a small town in Virginia. Where I got my accent from, in case you hadn't noticed. Actually grew up riding a horse. Did competitions. My dad, who was a local lawyer, taught me how to shoot a shotgun before I knew how to braid my hair. I loved my dad," she said, eyes beaming. "He was like Atticus Finch to me, Ty. You know what I mean? Everyone in town looked up to him.

"My mom—maybe at one time she was a capable person, but by the time I remember she was simply a country-club drunk. Everything was always an effort for her. Parties. Why she couldn't make it to my riding events. Just getting dinner on the table. My dad, he was the glue that held everything together. Everything."

"I know what you mean," Hauck said, though his own dad, who worked for the Greenwich Department of Water for thirty years, was a million miles away from that.

"Do you?" April said. "When I was sixteen, I pulled my VW into the garage, grabbed my books from the passenger seat, and saw my father lying there . . ." Her jaw grew tight. "Sitting there against the wall, like he was wondering what shirt to wear, except there was this bright red pattern sprayed against the plaster behind his head. His shotgun was in his lap. Like he wanted me to find him there."

Hauck reached for her hand. "I'm sorry. You don't have to go back over—"

"You wanted to know, right? You wanted to know what makes me tick. Anyway, that's not it. That was a long time ago. Just backstory, as they say. Bank fraud," she said in response to Hauck's questioning eyes. "He'd been receiving kickbacks from a local bank where he was directing business. During the big S and L crisis. The thing was ripe with fraud and my father was a part of it." She chuckled bitterly. "Atticus Finch . . . I guess you can add fear of being let down to the list as well. Anyway, I ended up at UVA. I majored in art. Did a year of grad school at NYU. You ever hear of the Minimalist movement?"

He shook his head. "Can't say I have."

"Sol LeWitt. He did these amazing wall drawings. Richard Tuttle. That was my thing. I studied under Richard Dunn, who was the big cheese in that world. Sort of studied under him. More like I ended up perpetually under him. He was forty-two. I was twenty-three. I always was attracted to older guys. You getting the picture? Anyway, Richard"— April shook her head—"whatever scant trust or faith in myself had managed to make it through to that point, well, he took care of the rest. He was a pompous, spiteful bastard, but he had a long ponytail and everyone in the art world bowed down to him. I spent three years with him. I think he was screwing anyone who knew Rembrandt was Dutch."

"I thought he was Flemish." Hauck grinned.

"Well, then you'd have had nothing to worry about." April laughed. "And believe me, I think he was into that too. Finally I had to just leave the whole program. Dropped out. I stayed in a friend's apartment for about three months. Lost about twenty pounds. Not sure I ever went out. Read the Upanishads cover to cover. Got involved in a bunch of self-actualization things. I finally took a job selling ad space for this financial magazine. That's where I met this nice, sort of square, something-a-little-cute-about-him-somewhere guy who was into complex investment models and standard deviations from the mean"— she smiled—"but who I knew wouldn't let me down and seemed to think I was the most beautiful woman in the world."

"Marc?" Hauck said, smiling.

She nodded.

"Did he know Rembrandt wasn't Flemish?"

She chuckled. "I just didn't want to be hurt again." There was a shimmering in her wide, round eyes. "It wasn't like there was this great love. He's just the most stable man I ever met, and I didn't want to be let down."

"But you built a life."

"Yeah." She nodded brightly, happily. "We built a life. I have a beautiful little girl and a husband who gets up in the middle of the night like clockwork to check his overseas positions. We live in a fancy home. And go on nice vacations. I help out at Becca's school." She rotated her cup. "It's just . . . It's May. There are days it just comes and goes. I found my dad the first week of May. It's always a rough time." She shrugged and smiled. "See, for me, when you say 'happy,' I say that's just a piece of time I don't see my father's face in that garage."

Hauck looked at her across the bench. He squeezed her on the shoulder. "I won't let you down."

"No . . ." April smiled. "You wouldn't, would you?" She covered his hand. "That's why it's nice being with you. Like I said, you're just a guest at the old spa—not a resident."

"You don't have to be a resident either, April. Look at how you've helped me."

April glanced at her watch. Her eyes grew wide. "Good Lord, I have to go. Becca's got dance tonight. What kind of mother am I, going on so long with such a cute guy . . ." An idea seemed to hit her. "You know what we should do?"

"What?" he asked.

"We should take a picture. I have a camera here. You and I."

"A picture?"

She shrugged. "You never know, one day that might be all we have."

"That won't happen," Hauck said, "but sure . . ."

She dug into her purse, and as she did, it pushed her sleeve up, accidentally exposing her arm. April had always kept them covered.

Hauck's gaze went to it. A bit in shock—a bit in sadness too.

There were marks. Several short slashes up her arm. Most appeared to have long since healed, but one or two still looked fresh and bright. He suddenly realized why.

His eyes lifted to April's.

She smiled at him, as if her secret was now out. "So now you know . . ."

CHAPTER FORTY-FOUR

The phone that they removed from Sonny Merced's body led to a sister in California who hadn't spoken to him in months; a sometimes girlfriend who claimed she never wanted to see him again; a phone-in sex line; and a number that had been dialed just minutes before the attack, which led to a Michael Cassidy in Union, New Jersey. Who turned out to be a twelve-year-old kid, who, a week before, had lost his phone. Merced's address was a post office box, the account for which was two months delinquent.

Merced was an ex–army ranger with

the Eighty-second Airborne unit who had been drummed out of the service and had been an unindicted suspect in three rape investigations while over in the Middle East. He had an expired Michigan license and had been picked up twice in the past year on assault and drug possession charges. He had made a call to Cassidy's stolen line minutes before attacking Jared and the police had found no unclaimed car in the rink lot afterward.

Whatever Merced's motive, it was clear he wasn't acting alone.

Sunday, the local papers and news channels carried the story of the Iraq War vet who had assaulted a handicapped boy in the locker room of the Hamill rink the night before. The fight to the death of the ex-detective in town who had managed to intercede.

Monday, back at work, everyone seemed to know all the details. In the halls, catching coffee, they all were genuinely disbelieving and shocked, grateful Hauck was alright.

Basically, he tried to stay out of sight, at his desk doing paperwork, fielding a few calls. He asked Brooke to shield him from the press. But as the day went on, his

mind couldn't put aside the possible connection between the interests of his own
firm, people here, and the investigation
into Dani Thibault. Hauck had crossed the
line by continuing to look into him. Had
someone here tried to stop it by planting
that pen? Setting him up.

Around eleven, his cell phone rang.
When he checked the display, "United
States Government" came on the screen.

Naomi Blum.

"You got my gift?" Hauck answered
without saying hello.

"I got your gift. Thanks. And I'm about to
give you one in return. But first, I heard
what happened. Are you okay?"

"My arm feels like it's gone through a
chopper, but I'll mend. Make any progress
on the glass?"

"I want you to know," she said, "we're
starting an investigation into Thibault and
his connections. Thanks to you. One of
the ways is to follow up on the person who
attacked you. Assuming, of course, we're
not just dealing with some kind of sick
perv."

"I think we both know that's a pretty
safe bet. Besides, he knew who I was; he

called me an ex-cop. You still have lingering doubts on whether there's any connection between James Donovan's and
Marc Glassman's deaths?"

"I didn't have any after I met you," Naomi
Blum said. "I just put my career on the line."

There was something about her that
Hauck couldn't help but like. That was winning him over. She hadn't fallen for the
setup with the Talon pen. She thought
Campbell was a dipshit. She'd done her
homework on his background. And now
she had run with what he'd shared. Put
her career on the line. There was a lot of
heart and energy in that little body.

Not to mention a not-half-bad set of
bright, gray eyes. "You ready yet to tell me
what you think this is all about?"

"How's the boy?" she asked, dodging
him.

"A little rattled. But he's fine. He's back
at school. The local police have agreed to
beef up the security . . . How does it sit
with you that someone would try to get
me to back off by harming an innocent kid
like that?"

"I warned you, didn't I, what you could
expect for trouble." She paused a moment

and Hauck sensed some genuine concern. "Anyway, I'm glad you're both okay."

"So am I in or out?" Hauck asked. He figured he might as well throw all his cards on the table now.

Naomi chortled. "Didn't you just get yourself a pretty good lesson in what being 'in' means?"

"Yeah, and I thought I kinda passed. I can help. Seems to me it's a little late to pretend I'm on the sidelines."

She paused. Hauck thought he might have her. She finally said, "Haven't decided yet."

"Thanks. Why don't you let me know if there's anything short of getting myself killed that can aid you in the decision."

That made her laugh. "You were worried what it was going to be like for you back at work. Feeling any more comfortable?"

There was a knock at his door. Hauck wheeled around as it opened.

Tom Foley stepped in.

"How about I get back to you on that one." He clicked off the phone, surprised to see his boss. "Tom." He stood up. "C'mon in."

CHAPTER FORTY-FIVE

Hauck came around his desk. "I wasn't expecting you today."

"Everybody's buzzing about what happened." Foley was in a three-piece pinstripe suit and yellow tie. He came up to him. "Horrible thing." He shook his head. "Horrible to have to go through. I heard you were in, and I had some things I could get done up here today. How are you doing, Ty?" His boss's handshake was strong and concerned. He placed his arm around Hauck's shoulder. "There's no point saying just how glad we all are that you're okay."

"Thanks, Tom. It was a bit of a close call."

"I heard you were hurt." Foley released his grip and took a glance at his arm.

"Just a cut." Hauck waved it off. "Lucky."

"We're all lucky," he said. "Everyone in this organization knows what kind of person you are." He shook his head with empathy and gritted his teeth. "What kind of a sick fuck would even do something like that?"

Hauck had spent twenty years gauging reactions. People who had something to hide. Foley never once blinked. His outrage seemed genuine and concerned. But there was always something held a little in reserve. A measured quality in his tone Hauck could never quite figure out. He just shook his head in agreement. "I don't know, Tom."

Were they both playing the same game?

Hauck had defied his boss's warning about stepping up the investigation on Thibault. Did Foley know? Hauck hadn't been forthcoming about the New York police finding the Talon pen at James Donovan's suicide scene. Had Campbell spoken to him? Had someone planted it there?

Worse, Hauck had shared all he knew about Thibault with the U.S. government.

Things learned in the process of a confidential search. Technically, Talon's information. He saw his boss's steely gaze. The directness in his eyes. The twitch in his smile. Was he holding back?

"You know, as long as I'm up here, we should talk," Foley said, guiding Hauck back to his desk, dropping himself familiarly into the chair in front. He crossed his legs.

"Okay." Not sure what he meant, Hauck eased himself behind his desk.

"First, how's Annie's son?" Foley locked his hands behind his head and slumped back.

"Fine. Just a bit rattled." Foley had met Annie once or twice. Hauck had brought her along to a company dinner when the Greenwich office opened. He seemed to genuinely like her. Her easy laugh and natural charm seemed to cut through Foley's polished New England manners. "We thought it best to get him away from everything . . ."

Something made Hauck hold back the exact location.

"That's wise. I'd do the same. Maybe we can help with that."

"Thanks," Hauck said. "Annie doesn't want to attract any attention."

Foley grimaced, shaking his head. "Just thinking about someone trying to do that to a kid . . . You know what I mean, Ty?" He was looking right at Hauck, his tone somehow direct, suggestive.

Then, without waiting for an answer, he suddenly shifted. "You dropped that little matter we spoke on the other day as I asked? On that guy you'd come up with?"

"What guy, Tom?" Hauck tried to read the guy's eyes.

"You know, the one Merrill had us looking into." Foley snapped his finger. "What was his name . . . ?"

"Thibault."

"Yeah, *Thibault.*" Foley jabbed the air. "That's the one."

An uneasiness wormed its way through Hauck. Foley's measuring gaze seemed to bore right through him. Hauck wasn't sure how he should reply.

"You asked me to, Tom."

"Good." His boss winked and took off his glasses, blew on them to clean them. "Thattaboy . . ."

Suddenly Hauck had this exposed,

pulse-stopping feeling, like he was working undercover and his identity had just been blown. Like Foley was about to lay something on him, and at any moment everything could fall apart. He shuffled a couple of papers on his desk. "So how's that Reynolds Reid matter shaping up?"

"Sorry?" Foley put back on his glasses. His stare said he had no idea what Hauck was talking about.

"The Wertheimer thing they were looking to pick up. Why we were holding everything back. From Merrill."

"Right!" He smiled, clear eyed. "Moving along just fine, Ty, or so I'm told. In fact, the company and the government panel of overseers are meeting on it today. Some conflict-of-interest details, mostly in Europe, I hear. May have to divest that part. Should be brought to a head soon."

"Good."

"*Good?*" Foley looked at him a little funny. "For Talon, it's a frigging bonanza."

"I meant good that we can finally share what we have with Merrill," Hauck said.

"Got ya." Foley nodded. He gave Hauck a lingering look that ended up in a tight smile. "I'm glad you're okay, Ty. There's a couple of things I'd like to run by you . . ." He pushed himself up. "But that can wait for another day. Big doings out there today, in case you haven't heard."

"I haven't, Tom. What?"

"One of the top overseers of Freddie Mac blew his brains out in his study. Imagine, his own children found him when they were getting ready for school." He shook his head. "Only ratchets up all the worry that there's more shit to come. Citi. AIG. The whole world's crumbling, Ty. Shit, even my wife's starting to break a sweat. Asks me for the first time in twenty years about our stock portfolio. Tells me she and all her girlfriends haven't bought a pair of shoes in weeks. Not a single new spring outfit. Everyone bleeds in their own way. *Still . . ."* He headed toward the door and chuckled. "Doesn't mind hopping the company jet down to Naples. That's why we have to be one of the winners. Know what I mean?"

Hauck followed him to the door.

Foley turned. "You know, that old job, Ty, what you were doing before . . . That was sort of like splashing around in the kiddie pool, if you know what I mean. You get yourself wet, everyone has a good time. But try and work up a stroke."

Hauck nodded, not sure what he was agreeing to.

"But *here*"—his boss's smile was gone—"here, it's all kinda part of the big mosaic. One hand washes the government. The other some of the largest companies in the world. Everyone splashing around."

Hauck met his eyes. "Just what is it we're talking about, Tom?"

"The Wertheimer thing, of course!" Foley flashed an innocent smile. "That's what you meant, wasn't it, Ty?" He gave Hauck a gentle pat. "I'm glad you're okay. I really am. It's our job to keep tabs on what's going on. With our key employees. In all our clients' firms. Even at Treasury. *Comprende?*"

Hauck stared.

"Dumbass effing traders . . . Who knew what hell they wrought, huh?" He cocked both hands at him like two loaded pistols. "In case you don't know it, son, you're swimming in the grown-up pool now."

CHAPTER FORTY-SIX

News of the impending collapse of the American banking system was met with a grin of amusement and even pride by Dani Thibault, who watched it in his midtown Manhattan office.

Pacific-West, the largest bank in California, had just failed.

His pride stemmed from the fact that behind the scenes, he had helped put it all in motion. And he was amused because with all the world's eyes focused on the causes—the housing bubble, CDOs, credit-default swaps, overleverage, regulators looking the other way—no one had any idea what was really happening.

The treasury secretary was appearing before Congress, stammering like a first-year loan officer trying to explain a risky loan.

The Dow had just hit a six-year low.

Yes, the system had already been weakened, the banks leveraging up their balance sheets with tiers of worthless assets and debt. Sure, the two desperate traders he had lured with the promise of millions, millions they would no longer be able to receive from their firms, had simply been the final, artfully conceived nudge of the rotted carcass off the ledge.

Ultimately, Thibault knew, there was some larger purpose to the small but profitable role he played in this. His was just to put the plan in motion. The whole system, already foundering, was just waiting for the right flick of an invisible finger to send it off the edge. And he had found them! Borrowed up to their dicks against their own company's tumbling stock. A margin call away from extinction. Yet still controlling billions of their company's assets. Traders who with one push of the button could sway the fortunes of a large bank.

And who had put it all in play? A simple hog farmer's son. Who had shoveled shit out of the pens until he was seventeen. Yes, he definitely took some pride in that. And at the same time he had carried his deception right into the bed of one of the most wealthy and desirable women in the world. He had used her to reach his ends, like he had used everyone and everything he had encountered along the way.

Now he was known in the most elite circles. The press referred to him as an "international financier." It was just like that royal Belgian slut had done for him. Only better! Merrill had opened more doors for him than the head of a multinational corporation. Soon, he'd be moving on anyway. He had gotten about all he could out of her. And there were younger, fresher fields for him to sow.

Dani put his feet up on his desk. He couldn't help but admire how it all had worked since, on the run, his path had crossed with that faggot Belgian banker in a bar in Lyon. How he'd driven out into the country on the pretense of finding a secluded spot to fuck him. Stopped the car along a lake, then smashed his head with a rock, with the guy's pants down and his dick out and ready. Threw the body into a leechy pond. Driven in his own car back to his town in Belgium, copied his birth documents, falsified his history. Applied for a job at RezionsBank.

A new man.

Thibault watched as some hayseed congressmen who didn't even know how to add raked the treasury secretary over the coals over monetary policy. Trying to assure the world it would hold together.

He laughed. They had no idea the disaster that lay ahead.

Thibault's cell phone chimed, his private one. The one he used for only this purpose. He took it out, noticed the scrambled number from Dubai that was completely secure.

Dani answered. "I'm just watching the proceedings now. Have you checked out the markets? The Dow is down over seven hundred points . . ." He leaned back, looking over the view of Manhattan with satisfaction. He'd done so well, his employers might well double what they had paid him.

"Yes, an excellent job, my friend," the caller acknowledged in heavily accented English. "You can be assured we won't forget." The man was one of the most powerful people on the planet. His backers controlled those who influenced the purse strings of billions. Behind the shadowy curtain that divided the highest levels of finance and those who had their own agenda to bring that same world down, his influence was unequaled. "But now there is something important that you should know."

"And what is that?" Dani Thibault asked, barely noticing the shift in tone.

"You are presently under investigation, Dani. By the United States government. The Department of the Treasury."

"What?" Thibault sat up. What he was saying was impossible, of course, a joke. But he also knew the caller was not the kind to trifle with idle rumor or speculation. He turned down the TV. "Just what are you talking about?"

"They know your name," the caller said. "They know you had dealings with both deceased traders."

"That's impossible!" Dani jumped to his feet. In that instant, he retraced every contact he had made on all his assignments. There was just no chance. Who would have connected him? He had covered every trail perfectly. He had left no link to himself. *"How?"* he asked, stammering in disbelief. "How could anyone possibly know that?"

"How doesn't matter, Dani. What *does* is that you must become invisible to the world. And now."

"You're sure of this?" A tremor of concern pounded in his chest. "This information is one hundred percent reliable?"

"More reliable than even you, my friend," the caller said, his tone unmistakable. "I warned you your prick was your Achilles heel. Apparently, the connection was revealed through your girlfriend."

"Merrill?" Thibault almost choked. How could Merrill know? She had never even met Glassman or Donovan. Their names had never surfaced. All the bitch cared about was passing herself off as ten years younger than she was or going to her silly garden club gatherings in Greenwich and Palm Beach. She was too busy combing Saks with her personal shoppers for Prada shoes. *How could Merrill know shit?*

"You know how this has to be handled now, Dani?"

Thibault realized the man on the other end of the line was not someone to be fucked with. He had the network to do anything. He would already be dead if that was the man's wish. "Yes, you're right," he acknowledged—what else could he do? "It's time to disappear."

"I can have one of my associates pick you up. I've already taken the precaution of having a jet at Teterboro that can take you out of the country, no questions asked."

"To where?" Suddenly the concern beating in Thibault's chest became full-out panic. It occurred to him that *he* was the one go-between among all the connected parties. *He* had recruited Glassman and Donovan. He had paid them. The funds, however well hidden, originated from his accounts, where, through the maze of partnerships, counterparties, and countries, it would simply appear to be an investment in one of Thibault's many deals. *Out of the country?* Thibault swallowed nervously.

There was no way he would ever make it through the Lincoln Tunnel alive.

"A stretch here in Dubai might do you

some good about now, don't you think, Dani? No worry over extradition. And I assure you, we have our own pleasures here too."

"Yes," Thibault said, his mind flashing forward. "I think so . . ."

They arranged for a car to pick him up at five that afternoon. At Dani's apartment on Central Park South. In three hours. Dani knew he was one dead Serb if he ever got in that car.

As soon as he hung up, he ran over to his safe, hidden behind a false shelf in the bookcase. Fingers barely cooperating, he feverishly spun the lock open and reached for the thick folder of documents he kept inside for just this purpose. Passports. Each with an identity and destination he had worked out. He leafed through the stack and chose the one he wanted. And into the altered bottom of his alligator Hermès briefcase he stuffed several wads of cash, each more than ten thousand dollars in dollars and euros.

Most of what he had stored away was perfectly safe in various banks in Geneva and the Cayman Islands. The rest he would leave where it was, in his accounts in

London and New York, so as not to attract attention.

He had rehearsed this moment well.

There was an alternate exit from Dani's office building. It led straight to the Grand Central subway station. He had chosen the location for just such a situation as this. If the government was investigating him, they might be watching him as well.

He called Air France himself and made a first-class reservation on the seven thirty flight to Paris in the name on the new passport he had chosen.

Three hours. Dani's blood grew heated. As he thought of how he had somehow been exposed, it irked him more. Merrill. *How?* Dani Thibault was dead. He had reinvented himself before. Now it was time to do it again.

He just wished, in the time he had left, he could give that bitch one last lesson she would never forget.

CHAPTER FORTY-SEVEN

Over the past few days Hauck had done his best to put what happened at the rink behind him.

He put the finishing touches on a deal he'd been working on with the town of Milford police department. He gave a second deposition to the police, who were digging into James Merced's contacts over the past weeks. He talked with Annie. She told him Jared was doing much better. That she might send him back to California to visit his grandparents until things settled down. He was still trying to figure out just how Tom Foley and Talon all fit in.

Wednesday he was coming out of a meeting when his cell phone chimed. He noticed the caller. The United States Government. He went into his office and shut the door and plopped in the chair behind his desk. "So—you made a decision yet?"

"On what?" Naomi Blum answered, acting coy.

Hauck leaned back, knowing his gift of Thibault's prints and DNA was a game changer. "On whether I'm in or out."

"In. Do you have lunch plans?" the agent asked totally out of the blue.

"I was just gonna have a sandwich at my desk."

"Then how 'bout you have one with me?"

"Where are you?" Hauck spun around, looking out the window at the harbor and waterfront estates of Glenhaven, as if somehow she was watching him.

"In a car. Across the street from your office." Her voice grew in excitement. "We know who Thibault is, Ty."

"I'll be right down."

* * *

They bagged the sandwich and drove to the Boxcar Cantina, a Mexican place. He figured it was the most inconspicuous place they could find.

A few tables were filled with moms in yoga outfits and office types in casual business attire. He waved to the owner, Regina, who directed them over to a booth. Naomi was in a stylish brown pantsuit, her short, dark hair curled around her ears. And shades. She had a couple of freckles on her cheeks. Wide, gray eyes. Seemingly not an ounce of body fat on her. She wore a simple chain around her neck with some sort of pendant hidden under her top, which looked to Hauck like a military dog tag. There was something about her, her directness, her brains, that he couldn't help but find attractive.

The waitress came up. Naomi ordered the tortilla soup and an iced tea, Hauck a chicken enchilada and a Diet Coke. When the waitress left he leaned back against the wooden booth. "So what do you have?"

"The prints you supplied us with came back. They were flagged by Interpol." Naomi took out a file folder and placed two photos on the table. "You were right." Her eyes twinkled. "He's Serbian."

The large black and white photos were police mug shots. Thibault, maybe ten years younger, his wavy, dark hair sheared close, military style. His meaty face more gaunt, hungry looking. A dark intensity in his brooding eyes.

The name underneath the photo wasn't Thibault but Franko Kostavic.

And there was a number underneath that: K43750. A prisoner number. And a date, August 23, 1999.

"Kostavic?" Hauck said, studying the photo. The likeness was unmistakable. "These are mug shots?"

"NATO." Naomi nodded. "You see the date? He was a major in the Serbian Army during the Kosovo War. He was part of what they called the Scorpion Brigade. Apparently, Thibault—*Kostavic*," Naomi corrected herself, "was taken into custody after the war trying to make his way through the Italian border."

"Make his way from what?"

Naomi put another paper in front of him. A report. "The Scorpions were a secret paramilitary offshoot of the Serb army that operated freely during the war and was responsible for some of the most brutal genocidal atrocities."

"Atrocities?" Hauck looked at the report. Thibault had boasted of how he had seen action in the war. Since he'd claimed to be Dutch, they had all assumed he was part of the NATO contingent there. Richard Snell had done the search, but his name was nowhere to be found. Now Hauck knew why. The scent of Dani Thibault's secret past had just grown decidedly more rancid.

"Yes." Naomi nodded.

Their drinks came and she passed over a new series of photos. What Hauck was looking at was completely stomach turning. A long maze of dead bodies strewn together in a deep ravine. Dozens. More than dozens. There was also a photocopied report from the UN War Crimes Commission.

"Franko Kostavic was being held by the new Serbian government in connection with his role in events that took place on the night of August fourth, in the village of Donje Velke in Kosovo. Sixty-seven townspeople, mostly women and children, were massacred in a Serbian raid."

Hauck felt the moisture dry up in his mouth. He fixed on the grisly photos. Bullet-riddled bodies in nightclothes and traditional native garb, lying in a seemingly endless line at the bottom of a gorge. Old men and women. Kids. Painful as it was, it was hard to remove his eyes from them. It was one of the saddest things he had ever seen.

"Donje Velke is in the Drenica valley," Naomi explained, "a region that was home to much of the Kosovan resistance. On August fourth, Serbian forces came in after midnight. The Scorpion Brigade was an unmonitored military arm. Its commanders were said to take their orders directly from Milosevic himself. It was filled with violent thugs and common criminals and led by zealots who committed the most brutal acts in the name of ethnic cleansing. From what I've learned, the village, mostly ethnic Albanians, was rousted up in the night from sleep. The men who came in went door to door. Some were in uniforms, others wore civilian clothes. They concentrated on women and children. Some were raped and then lined up against the walls of their own homes and shot in the head, right where they stood. The rest were marched up the trail to the gorge and flung in. Machine-gunned. The troops forced the remaining townspeople to fill the ravine with dirt. Lye was spread over it. Because the village was isolated, for years it was just a rumor that anything like that even took place. As you know, there were many such atrocities. The townspeople claimed they always feared the men would come back. After the war, NATO got involved, the UN War Crimes Commission. Witnesses finally spoke up."

Hauck raised his eyes from the terrible photos. His blood was boiling. *"Thibault?"*

Naomi nodded. "Never proven, of course. He was never brought to trial. It was his unit, the sixth regiment, that was proven to have been involved. According to the UN affidavits, he had boasted about leading the raid, along with several others. Some of the witnesses talked about a man who led the raid who matches up. He was being held in connection with it. In the aftermath of the war, with emotions still mixed on both sides and graft running high, he escaped from the local prison in Split where he was being held. That was 1999."

Naomi collected the photos. "Not a big fish," she said with a shrug, "one of hundreds. According to the Council on War Crimes at the Hague, he was never seen since."

"Until he was seen here, in the United States," Hauck said, "under someone else's name."

"I checked with Interpol." Naomi nodded. "Dieter Thibault was a Dutch national who was born in Rotterdam in 1964. He went to the University of Rotterdam and emigrated to Belgium, where he worked as an account manager for the Nazions-Bank in Anderlecht, outside of Brussels. In 2000, he disappeared while on a business trip to France and was never found."

Hauck recalled the file he had given to Naomi and the information he had gotten from Snell.

"Yet not long after, not that anyone would have checked, there was a Dieter Thibault employed by the RezionsBank in Brussels. Then at the KronenBank in Lichtenstein, where he was a senior investment manager . . ."

Hauck leafed through the file. A hard lump the size of a rock stuck in his throat.

Thibault was scum. He had likely over-seen the killing of dozens of innocent vic-tims. There was no telling how the real Dieter Thibault had disappeared. Hauck looked up and met Naomi's level eyes. In them, he saw the same glint he knew was in his eyes. This had far eclipsed two dead traders. Far eclipsed April.

This was a guy they had to bring down.

CHAPTER FORTY-EIGHT

Their food arrived, but neither of them felt particularly hungry.

"He told Merrill he had been in the Kosovo War," Hauck said. "He claimed he was Belgian and Dutch. We thought to look only among the NATO forces."

Naomi nodded. "And he's been hiding under the radar ever since. Ten years. Right in plain sight. Building a new life. Not so prominent a case that anyone was really looking for him. Christ, he was right there in the European gossip columns, clubbing around with cousins of Princess Beatrix of Belgium. But Donje Velke was just one of many such incidents in that war. He was never even a priority on the UN's list. Bigger fish to fry. It would have gone on indefinitely if—"

"If Merrill Simons hadn't come to us to look into him," Hauck said, finishing her thought.

Naomi nodded with a smile. "Or until some midlevel magistrate in the Hague who happened to have a fetish for the party-hopping friends of the Belgian royals finally made it to the bottom of his open files. And even then, he barely looks the same and operates under a new ID."

A surge of anger started to burn in Hauck's chest. Merrill Simons's instincts had been right from the start. Dani was never who he claimed, not the freewheeling financier, not the attentive boyfriend. But how for a second could even she have suspected this? A wave of sadness for her came over him.

"So now you have a reason to pick him up," Hauck said. He dropped the UN report back in front of her. "I assume there's a valid Interpol warrant outstanding against him?"

"There is," Naomi said. She leaned

forward and looked him firmly in the eye. "But I think you can understand how the people I work for aren't altogether keen on cleaning up the files for some bureaucratic war-crimes commission in the Hague with all that's going on. What's pressing *today*"—she tapped her nail against Dani's photo—"is to find out what Thibault's role was in the deaths of Marc Glassman and James Donovan and, even more important, where that might lead. Later, we can always hand him off to the UN to answer for what he's done."

"So then pick him up." Hauck shrugged. "You have sufficient cause. There's nothing stopping you now."

"Yes, there is." Naomi looked at him directly. "Just one thing . . ."

Suddenly Hauck started to wonder why they were even meeting. Why she was sharing all this with him.

"Thibault's missing."

"Missing!"

Naomi nodded. "He's gone underground. We were keeping tabs on him—loosely, until we could fill in the details. He went into work in his office two days ago. According to the agents tracking him, they haven't seen him since."

"Someone doesn't just completely disappear!"

"That's exactly what he did. He never came back out. According to his secretary, he told her he had a sudden trip that had come up and he'd be back in a few days. So far, he hasn't called in. We executed a warrant and impounded his computer. We found a wall safe in his office, cleaned out. We think he may have kept alternate passports in there."

"He knew you were onto him," Hauck said, putting it all together. "He fled."

"The agents who were watching him claim there's no way they could have been made. If he fled, it wasn't under his own name. I don't know if he got tipped off, but there's no record of Thibault leaving the country. There is, however"—Naomi reached inside her case and pushed across a series of new black and white photos— *"this."*

The photos showed a bearded man in a black leather jacket with a baseball cap drawn over his eyes passing through an airport security station. "It's at Newark international. Last Tuesday night. The same day he went missing. It could be him. We've interviewed various gate agents and they seem to recall someone similar boarding an Air France flight for Paris."

Hauck stared closely at the photo. He felt a fist clench in his gut. "It *is* him."

"How can you be sure?"

"That's the same satchel he had with him the night I followed him to the restaurant and got his DNA." He passed the photos back across to Naomi with a shrug. "That's him."

"Look, until we know for sure what the hell is going on, all of this—Thibault, Kostavic, whatever he may have done—is not to be shared, you understand?" She tapped her nail and it brushed against his hand. "Especially when it comes to other investigative arms of the government. Or Merrill Simons, for that matter. That's clear, right?"

Hauck met her round, gray eyes. "It's clear."

He had known for a time this would lead somewhere. When he first had doubts about Talon. When he pressed Naomi to let him remain involved. Maybe that day when he first saw April Glassman's face on that screen.

"You believe Thibault recruited these traders, don't you? To go off the reservation, so to speak. To drive their firms under."

"It all fits." The Treasury agent's eyes shone with the same intensity. "Both of them were used to earning millions; both were bonused largely in their own company stock, stock against which they had borrowed heavily to cover their lifestyles and that was now underwater. Both had margin calls against them just a few days away."

"So where's the money trail?" Hauck asked. "If Thibault bribed them, it had to be for something big."

"It was something big." She grinned. "Depending, of course, on your definition of big." She reached back inside her case and this time came back with a photocopied, handwritten note. The stationery letterhead read *James Donovan*. She slipped it across the table to Hauck. "Leslie Donovan came to me. A couple of days after you went to see her. She didn't know what to do with this. She had no idea what it meant, only that her husband was seemingly into something she couldn't explain. She said you had asked her if she honestly thought he had taken his own life . . ."

Hauck read it. The note was written in an awkward, harried script.

Les, my love, I've asked Bill to give you this in the event anything should happen to me and I'm not there. Not being with you and Zach is the most painful thing I can ever imagine. Not seeing him grow into the person I know he will become. Not being there to take care of you. Listen—I've managed to put away some money. Money that can help take care of you, in the event I'm not around. It's in an account that no one knows about at the Caribe Sun Trust on Grand Cayman Island. The account number is 4345672209. The account is in both of our names. You may remember, I had you sign something once. The pin code is Zachy. (Corny, I know!) Your signature is on file.

Whatever you do, this is money that must not be explained and cannot, <u>cannot</u> be brought back to this country.

I can't go into it other than to say it's all a measure of my love for you. I'm hoping this is a letter you will never have to read, but if you do, don't tell anyone. I'm not proud, but it's to protect you when I'm not there.

The letter went on to talk about his love and it was signed *Jim*.

Hauck put it down. "So what's your definition of big?"

Naomi pushed him another photocopy. This time, it was a bank statement, from the Caribe Sun Trust.

Hauck scanned down the list of deposits until he hit the bottom. It showed over eight million dollars in the account.

Hauck whistled. "Works for me . . ."

"It was probably only a down payment," Naomi said. "This is a guy who was teetering on the edge financially. A guy with a six-thousand-a-month apartment in New York and two vacation homes who had leveraged himself heavily against his company stock, which in the near term had no prospect of ever coming back. A guy whose future earnings flow was up in the air. Why would I not be surprised to find a similar account somewhere when we dig into Marc Glassman?"

Hauck nodded. He would definitely believe it. "But you think there was a full-out conspiracy here. There's more?"

Naomi looked at him. "Yeah, there's more. But now we're getting into things that someone like me shouldn't be telling someone like you. You understand?"

He nodded. "I understand."

She told him about the call intercepted from Hassan ibn Hassani to Marty al-Bashir in London. The sudden shift of one of the largest investment funds in the world, which started the plunge of the financial markets the very next day, building on the mortgage debacle, fears of Fannie and Freddie failing, the world creeping to the edge.

Glassman and Donovan just gave it the final, invisible nudge.

"Someone was paying them off. Someone used them to start the slide in motion. You want to hazard a guess, when we fully dig into Thibault's accounts, where the flow of all that money originated from?"

It *was* huge. If this was an organized,

plotted attack, it was terrorism. *Poor April,*
he thought . . . How could she have known
the forces behind what happened? Her
family never had a chance.

"So why me?" Hauck asked finally.

"My people don't want an interagency
thing on this until we know more. If any of
this leaks, it's the sort of thing that would
only create more chaos in the markets.
Plus"—the agent's gaze softened and for
the first time she didn't try to hold back
her smile—"you seemed to desperately
want in."

Hauck smiled back. "I suppose I did,
didn't I? Look, my 401(k)'s in the shitter as
much as the next guy's, Agent Blum, but
for me, this isn't about the markets. It's
not about what happened to Wertheimer
Grant. These people did what they did. But
innocent people were killed to hide what
they knew. One of them was a friend."

"I understand." The Treasury agent nodded.

"That said"—he shrugged—"I have been
known to stumble into a well-concealed
conspiracy every once in a while . . ."

She nodded, pleased. "So I've heard."

"The first thing is to locate Thibault—
Kostavic," Hauck said, correcting himself.
He looked at her.

"I have my people tracing him out of
Paris."

"Any luck so far?"

"Not yet." She shook her head. "It's a
big world."

"It is . . ." Hauck's mind flashed back
to something he remembered from weeks
before. "Luckily for you, I think I know
where he is."

CHAPTER FORTY-NINE

The easy part was grabbing a few days from the office.

He was owed that much. Foley had even suggested it. Not to mention he had just brought in a fat new account.

The hard part was squaring what he was about to do with Annie.

Not telling her the truth behind what he had let himself be drawn into. The reason her son had been attacked. About where he was about to go. And why.

He'd wanted in all along, hadn't he? If he was honest.

From the start.

Hauck sat on the deck in the dark with a beer, looking over the sound. He followed the flickering lights of planes descending into LaGuardia across the water. He put his moccasins up on the railing.

It was one of those shifting lines in the sand where you had to make a call. What side you came down on. Who you fought for.

Who you let down.

April deserved that much, didn't she? He thought back to the last time he had seen her and remembered her beaming face. *This is Evan, Ty* . . .

Then the wind suddenly shifted and the line was gone all over again. He knew why he was doing it. Why he was putting it all at risk. His job. Everything he had grown comfortable with.

Annie.

He knew why, and if he was honest with himself he could say it now.

It wasn't all buried in the past.

It was his last time there—at the group. Dr. Rose had given him the okay to leave. His obligation to the department was complete. For weeks, he'd been

feeling restless, boxed in. Ready to get on with it again. He'd grown to accept that there were simply things that had happened. Events out of his control. An unguarded moment where fate had intervened.

"I put my résumé out to a few places," he told the doctor after the last session. "One in a town outside of Boston, where my sister lives. One in PA. I even sent one up to Greenwich."

Dr. Rose seemed pleased. "In the group you said you still blame yourself a little. For what happened . . ."

Hauck shook his hand and smiled. "I guess I'll always blame myself a little; I just figure I can do it with a paycheck coming in."

It bothered him that April hadn't been there. They had grown close over these weeks. Their talks . . . He would miss her. And he wondered: when they saw each other again, in a different place and time, would it ever be the same? Life would interfere. It always seemed to. He wished he could tell her they would always be friends.

He took the subway home, picked up

something to eat at the Italian deli down the block. Went upstairs.

Around eight, he was watching a game when his cell phone rang.

April. Her voice sounded a little fuzzy. "Ty . . ."

"Gee, you skipped out on me," he said, pretending to be hurt, not fully realizing it then. "I wanted to say goodbye."

"I didn't talk to Becca's school," she said, woozily. "I'm sorry, Ty. They won't know on Monday . . ."

Her words were garbled, her thoughts random and unclear. Alarm sprang up in him. His mind immediately flashed to her wrists. "Know what? April, are you alright?"

"Yes, I'm alright, Ty, I told you, didn't I . . . you were just passing through . . ."

He bolted up. "April, listen to me, what have you done? You're not sounding right. Have you taken something?"

"Just to make me sleep, Ty . . . I really need to sleep. I'm sorry I wasn't there for you . . ."

"Where's Marc?" His blood rushed

with alarm. "Where's your husband, April? Where's Becca?"

"He's away, Ty . . . Always away. In Hong Kong. Becca's with her friend . . ." Her voice started trailing off.

"Where are you, April? Where are you now?"

"At our place. In the city. I'm sorry, Ty; you know that, don't you? I so wanted to be there for you . . . I . . ."

He knew the address. On East Sixty-fourth. He had dropped her off there once after one of their talks. "You keep it together, April! I'm coming. You hear me, April? I need you to stay awake. You hang on. I'll be right there!"

On his landline he dialed 911. Reported a possible suicide in progress. Gave the address. Her name. On his cell he tried to keep her on the line. Alert. Her voice kept growing woozy. It sounded bad.

He ran downstairs and into his Bronco, talking to her all the time. He had an old rotating top hat from his department days and threw it on top.

Lights flashing, he sped down the

Van Wyck, to the LIE, to Queens Boulevard and the Queensboro Bridge. He kept pushing her to hang on, to stay awake. He felt like he was losing her.

At some point, April's voice fell off.

"April!" He veered off the bridge onto Sixtieth, his heart racing at a hundred miles an hour. A minute later he was there.

An EMT van and a police car with a flashing light were pulled up in front. Hauck screeched to a stop behind them. He talked his way up, flashing his old police ID at one of the cops. When he got there, they already had her on a gurney with an IV in her veins and were giving her oxygen. Her eyes were rolled back, her pupils small. He kneeled down and took her by the hand and squeezed. "I'm here, April. I'm here . . ."

A glimmer of life flashed back into her eyes.

She murmured, "Ty . . . I'm sorry, Ty. I'm sorry I wasn't there for you. Your big day . . . I just didn't want to feel so alone. Not anymore."

"You're not alone, April." They said they had to take her now. Her pulse was

weak and they'd already called the hospital. He held her hand as they wheeled
her out to the elevator. "Not anymore."

He stayed in the ICU while she slept
until dawn. The doctors said she would
recover. But if they'd been fifteen minutes later . . . She'd taken seven Sones-
tas along with some muscle relaxers.

When she finally opened her eyes he
was there.

She turned her face and smiled fog-
gily at him. "It would be you, wouldn't
it, Ty . . ."

"I told you, didn't I, I wasn't just passing through."

"No, maybe you're not." Her pupils
shined with a sparkle of green back in
them. Then she looked away. "I'm a terrible mother, Ty. Marc wants more. I
just—"

"No." He moved closer. "You're not a
terrible mother. Any more than I was a
terrible dad. I called him. I found his number on your cell. He's on his way back."

She shut her eyes, tears making their
way down her cheeks, shaking her
head. "I'm so ashamed . . ."

"No, no, don't . . . ," Hauck said. He

winked. "You remember what they say about crazy . . ."

She nodded with her hands over her face. A tear fell onto the sheet. "I know." She looked at him. "I wish . . ." He knew what she wanted to say. What maybe they both were thinking. I wish it were you. Why couldn't it be you? And in a way maybe he was feeling it too. Things just hadn't worked that way.

She smiled, sniffing back her tears. "What did you say? When you called him . . . Who you were."

"I just said I was a friend."

She smiled, looking back up, monitors beeping her vitals, IV pumping life back into her blood. She seemed to draw some comfort from the word. "You are, Ty." She nodded. "You are."

They spoke once or twice after she was released and on her way to getting better.

Then they didn't see each other again for four years.

See, you were wrong. Hauck smiled, staring out at the sound. *You were always wrong. I wasn't just passing through.*

He took hold of his cell and scrolled to the familiar number he was searching for. He pushed Send and waited for the call to connect.

Annie answered on the third ring. *"Hey."*

"Hey yourself," he said. "Busy?"

"Swamped. Manuel's out sick. I'm holding my end down and doubling on desserts too. Can't really talk now. Everything okay?"

"Yeah." He stood up, leaned against the railing. The plane he had been following had disappeared. "I just wanted to let you know," he said, "something's come up. I'm going to be away for a while."

PART III

The international airport at Belgrade in Serbia looked like any other modern European terminal—sweeping curves of glass and digital flight boards. Hauck barely dozed on the flight over, his anticipation running wild.

He had told the people at Talon that he needed a couple of days off, and that ran into Memorial Day weekend. So he kept what he was doing to himself. All he told Annie was that he wouldn't be around for a few days. And she only asked back, a little helplessly, *What are you getting involved in, Ty?*

Thibault had fled through Paris. Hauck felt pretty certain that if Thibault needed to disappear, if he needed to blend into a backdrop where the outside world would never find him, he knew where he would be.

Richard Snell had traced wire transfers every month from Thibault's RBS account in the UK to a local branch of AstraBanca in a town called Novi Pazar in southern Serbia. The recipient's name was Maria Radisovic. That had to be Thibault's family back home, Hauck figured, a sister or his mother. It seemed right that no one would judge him where he had grown up in Serbia for what he had done in the war. He would have family to protect him. He could blend back into his roots.

On the flight over, Naomi mapped out how tricky and sensitive this all was. He couldn't help but notice how cute she looked out of work clothes, in slim-fitting jeans, a white T-shirt, and a loose lavender sweater. She explained that even if they were able to locate Thibault, the last people the government wanted to get involved were the Serbian police or their security arm, the BIA. First, there was no acting extradition treaty between the two countries. There was some Serbian basketball player who had assaulted a fellow student while in college in the U.S. The legal battle to get him back to stand trial had gone on for years. And if it got wrapped up in the fight to bring back someone who had been part of atrocities in the Kosovo War, the story would be in headlines all over the world. The Serbian government would never back down. The press there would go crazy if they let a suspected war criminal be ushered back to the U.S. for a lesser crime. Naomi's team would lose whatever leverage they had against him.

The plan, as she mapped it out, was first to simply see if they could locate him. The next step would be determined then. They might try to bargain with him. Use the threat of turning him over to the Serbian government to be prosecuted for war crimes as leverage.

Then there was always the next option, which Naomi didn't seem inclined to talk about. This was a U.S. government action. The stakes were high. This was looked at as a Homeland Security issue. Thibault was a vital person of interest. There were professionals who could be brought in—to interrogate him or to whisk him surreptitiously out of the country.

But the first step was to see if he was even there.

Upon landing, they passed through immigration on a diplomatic visa. They registered their firearms. Hauck was surprised and impressed that Naomi even carried one. They got their bags and rented a mid-size Ford diesel. They got directions to the central highway south, the E75; plugged their hotel, the Vrbak in Novi Pazar, into the GPS; and drove past the industrial areas that ringed the city, into the flat Balkan countryside, which became picturesque green hills and small, rustic villages for the three-hour drive.

Hauck took the wheel, excitement fending off the jet lag. He prayed his instincts were right and that he hadn't dragged both of them on a senseless wild-goose chase. But Naomi (and her superiors) agreed it was worth the bet. They got to know each other a little along the way. "Hauck" and "Agent Blum" turned into "Ty" and "Naomi." She told him how she had first gotten involved in working for the Treasury. How she had started out studying music at Princeton.

"Music theory," she said, noticing his surprise, but brushed past it so as not to bore him. "Sort of academic stuff."

She told him how her brother had enlisted out of college after 9/11 and then had the training accident that had cost him his legs. She told him how she felt compelled to follow in his steps. How she had ended up in the investigative corps, worked the Nisoor Square and Tabitha shooting incidents, which ended up as army whitewashes. Fighting off sleep, she shared the story of how one of the convoys she had been riding in had been ambushed, a small child by the side of the road struck by shrapnel from the IED. How with small-arms fire raging all around, she had crawled over and had to bag the kid with a makeshift ventilator while the medics attended to their own. She told him how fire was whizzing back and forth pretty heavily, how she didn't know if she was going to be hit. "I just blew and blew into the kid's chest, everything going on around me, until reinforcements finally came, and then I stopped, sitting there on the dusty road, his blood all over me. I realized he had died.

"His name was Ahmed. He had this Michael Jackson T-shirt on." Naomi shrugged. "I'm not sure why I'm telling you this."

"You did what you could," Hauck replied, watching her gaze drift out the window. "What you did was brave. You can't ask for more."

"No." She shook her head. "I'm not into any more whitewashes, Ty; you understand that. You can always do more." Then, switching subjects, she said, "What do you think, we have maybe another two hours?"

Sixty kilometers south, they crossed back west, onto more local roads, cutting through steeper, mountainous valleys and through centuries-old hillside towns. The roofs were always red and clung to the slopes, the churches old and stone with Serbian Orthodox markings, and old men in caps towed goats or cattle out of the way of young people scooting by on mopeds. The local signs were generally in Serbian, but Hauck always recognized a "taverna" by its signs for Jemel beer, Pepsi, and Jugopetrol.

It was around three in the afternoon when they finally made it to the outskirts of Novi Pazar. It was a larger commercial center of red roofs and white stucco houses clustered in the pit of a green, sloping valley. Spring flowers were just starting to bloom. The city was built on both sides of the narrow Raska River. Hauck got off and followed the GPS through narrow boulevards crowded with modern stores and Western brands to the city center. They were staying at the Vrbak, a drab four-story hotel, built in a style somewhere between quaint and industrial, that was probably the best in town. It straddled both sides of the flowing river.

It was late afternoon by the time they reached the hotel and settled into adjoining rooms on the fourth floor. Too late to do anything. Hauck asked if she wanted to meet later for dinner.

Naomi wasn't sure if she was up to it. "I may just hang and make some calls, if that's okay."

"Sure, that's fine."

He went inside. Hauck's room was sixties modern and spartan, a minimalist style. It had a flat teak platform bed and a down bedspread with a matching teak desk and chair. Drab local art hung on the walls.

He went to the window and opened the curtains. The red roofs of the town sprawled out, and in the distance there were green, rolling hills. Everything was quaint and friendly, but fifteen years ago, in this town set near the Kosovar border, the tensions between the Serbs and Muslims would have been running high.

Every family might have had a Dani Thibault in it. And would do whatever they could to protect him.

He looked out at the hills in the gray, dissolving light. He felt wired, too wound up to rest. Maybe he'd go for a run, try to locate the AstraBanca, which was near the city center. Or find the address they had for Maria Radisovic.

His blood rushed with anticipation, like the river running below.

He felt something, something in himself he recognized, like a familiar face. Something he hadn't felt in months.

Alive.

CHAPTER FIFTY-ONE

The next day Hauck was having breakfast around seven in the dining room overlooking the river when Naomi came in, in a tight tank and black running leggings, sweaty from a run.

"Hey." Hauck pushed out a chair for her. "I knocked on your door."

"Morning," Naomi said, taking a seat. "I was up. Went out for an early run."

"You sleep okay?"

"A little restless," she admitted. She shook out her short ponytail. "I was up in the night doing some work." She took out a city map from a fanny pack and unfolded it. "I checked out Market Street. Where the AstraBanca branch is. Then I was wired. I figured what the hell. I kept on going to Zinak Street." Maria Radisovic's street.

"Small apartment house. Interior courtyard. Butcher across the street."

Naomi widened her eyes.

Hauck grinned. "I did the same route last night. Pretty good distance." He nodded admiringly. "Four miles."

"Usually get in six," Naomi snapped defensively, as if trying not to be outdone.

Hauck couldn't help but notice that she looked pretty tight in her heather-gray T-back Under Armour top. On her right shoulder he spotted a small tattoo. A sword with a lightning bolt running through it. Underneath, the initial "J."

The logo of her brother's unit—the Special Forces Airborne.

Music theory . . . Hauck laughed to himself. *No telling how tough this gal is.*

"C'mon, have something to eat," he said, prodding her. "It's going to be a long day. My tab."

"Accepted." Naomi smiled. She dropped an orange file on the tablecloth.

A waitress came up and Naomi ordered

a yogurt and some cereal. "I printed out some e-mails I received during the night. You want to hear?"

Hauck nodded. "Of course."

"I have people trying to trace the history of the money going in and out of Thibault's bank accounts. The payments to James Donovan's Cayman Islands account came from something called the VRV Development Trust. It was a payment for a real estate sale on a property Donovan had bought just thirty days before on the island of Antigua. Three weeks later he flipped it—to VRV—for five times the price."

"Not a bad rate of return," Hauck mused cynically.

"I guess. VRV turns out to be a shell company based out of the Bahamas. It was set up about a year ago. The principals are all a bunch of local functionaries, lawyers, local officials, designed to shield what it does. Block anyone checking into who controls the funds."

Hauck had had some experience with this kind of hocus-pocus while trying to track money flows in the Grand Central bombing case.

"But the Antiguan government is

cooperating. There's a new banking trans-
parency around the world." She pulled
another page out. A corporate document.
VRV letterhead. "This is one of the articles
of incorporation. It's a power of attorney.
Granted to an Edwin Cahill, Esq., a lawyer
there. Check out the grantee . . ."

Hauck took the document. The signature was scratchy at the bottom. But it
clearly read *Dieter Thibault.* "So that's how
he paid him. Donovan."

Naomi's eyes shone in confirmation. "I
suspect we'll find a similar pattern when
we dig into the affairs of Marc Glassman.
But right now we don't have the time."

"So how do we find out where the eight
mil originated from?"

"Here's a start." She placed another
photocopy out on the tablecloth. "According to the Caribe Sun Trust, it came by
way of wire from the Bank of Nova Scotia
in Canada. A firm named Crescent Bay
Partners. Crescent Bay is a real estate
holding company, investing in plush resort properties—you know, these partial-
ownership franchises. It has properties in
Mexico, Costa Rica, all throughout the
Caribbean. Legitimate properties. Just

the kind of thing Dani Thibault looked to put together.

"On the surface, it looks like a standard real estate investment—except at five times the price. Its financing is pretty murky. It seems to come from a variety of sources, some rich Europeans, also some investment funds out of the Middle East. The funds in question seem to have been filtered through the KronenBank in Lichtenstein."

Hauck raised his eyes. "KronenBank. Didn't Thibault work there for a stint?"

"He did," Naomi said, nodding, "and this is where it starts to get good. You remember I told you about the Bahraini businessman that investment manager in London was overheard talking to? Hassani?"

Hauck nodded. "Yeah."

"Well, he has his own investment portfolio as well. A private partnership out of Dubai. It's a large source of funding to private equity groups—here in the U.S. and in London. Ascot Capital."

Naomi slid a fastened document across the table to Hauck. He put down his coffee. It was photocopies of a marketing brochure for Ascot. The first pages listed

Hassan ibn Hassani among the many company directors. Others were recognizable names from finance and business, even an ex–U.S. president.

On a separate page, listed among the many companies Ascot maintained investments in, was Crescent Bay Partners.

Naomi's face seemed to glow with pride. "I can't quite prove Donovan's specific eight million came from there, but it ties Thibault to Hassani and thereby to al-Bashir in London. We're onto something here, Ty . . ." She tapped her finger on the pamphlet. "We tie what went in to what went out, we have a plot that leads straight to a conspiracy. One way is to pierce this transfer of funds all the way back through Lichtenstein."

Hauck let out a breath. "Which would take time."

"*And* having to show cause," she added skeptically, "when we don't know anything right now. And that gets the rest of the whole frigging world involved. Not to mention the bankers in Dubai and Lichtenstein would just say our issue is with those back in Canada or the U.S., not them.

"The other option . . ." She met Hauck's

gaze. "The other option is to see what we find with Thibault. He knows where the money came from. Who orchestrated the funds. You ready?" Naomi's eyes gleamed in anticipation.

Hauck got up. "Let's just hope he's here."

CHAPTER FIFTY-TWO

They decided the best approach was to stake out the address they had for the only person in Novi Pazar with a name that matched that of the AstraBanca account holder.

An "M. Radisovic" was located on Zinak Street, a winding road on the outskirts of town. The embassy in Belgrade had cooperated without Naomi's divulging too much and found that the address matched the one on record with the bank. They didn't have a clue what Maria Radisovic looked like. They didn't even know for sure if she was, in fact, related to Thibault. Had her husband died and she reverted back to her family name? Had she remarried?

The location was a drab five-story apartment building with an interior courtyard centered around a nonworking stone fountain. An iron front gate was open. Novi Pazar was a small town and security didn't seem the main concern. It was a damp May morning. People rode by on bikes on their way to work; old men in drab clothes and tweed caps gabbed on the street; teenage boys went by in Nikes and American sports jerseys. Teenage girls were going to school in jeans and sweatshirts like girls in any American town.

Hauck and Naomi went up and looked at the tenant board. A buzzer with a handwritten card next to it had an "M. Radisovic" on the fourth floor.

"Ready?" Hauck asked with a wink of support.

Naomi nodded back. "Let's go."

They went inside and climbed the wide staircase to the fourth floor. The paint was chipped, the stairs asphalt and worn. There was a tiny elevator. They found Maria Radisovic's apartment near the staircase at the end of the hall. They heard a dog barking.

A noise came from above them. Two people, a man talking loudly in Serbian, his teenage daughter chattering right back at him. They came down the stairs and passed Hauck and Naomi on the staircase, greeting them with a quick *"Dobro jutro"* as they passed. *Good morning.* Naomi waved back politely.

They agreed Naomi would take the first shift. A woman there would attract less attention. She took a seat on the stairs, hidden from view but still in sight of Maria Radisovic's apartment. It was just after eight A.M. They had each other's cell numbers already programmed into their phones.

"I'll be right outside," Hauck said. "Call at the first sign."

"Talk soon." Naomi winked. She took out a tourist guidebook to act as cover. "At least I hope so."

Hauck headed back down the stairs and perched himself near a tobacconist's shop across the street. He called back upstairs to check the connection. It was fine. He settled in. No telling how long it would take. While the high-tech wheels churned ceaselessly back home, all there was to do here was wait.

An hour passed. No one came out. Who knew if M. Radisovic was even related to Thibault? If Thibault was even there? He found a *USA Today* at a newsstand and read through. Twice. Around 9:20, he called upstairs. "Anything happening?"

"Nothing," Naomi replied, disappointed. "Just people coming down the stairs, staring at me. I think I'm starting to look suspicious. *Wait a minute*," she suddenly said in a hushed whisper. "The door just opened . . ."

Hauck held on—Naomi covering the phone—as maybe thirty seconds passed. Finally she came back on. "A woman just left. Definitely not Thibault's mother. Too young. Around forty. She has dark hair. She's wearing a red nylon parka and a white beret. She should be coming out any second . . ."

Hauck stepped around the corner, hiding himself from view. He saw the woman come through the gate, start to walk along the sidewalk. "I have her."

"Wait for me," Naomi said, excited. "I'll come down."

"No, you stay there," Hauck said. "There might be someone else inside. I'll stay

with her. I'll let you know if it leads anywhere."

"Whatever you do, don't make contact
with anyone if I'm not there," Naomi warned
him with an edge of concern.

"Don't worry. Bye."

The woman in the red jacket headed
down the street. Hauck rolled up the newspaper and followed from the other side. At
the corner she turned and headed toward
the city center. It led down a hill and onto a
commercial boulevard. Pilic Street. Hauck
stayed about twenty yards behind.

The woman stopped at a corner where
a small queue of pedestrians was huddled
up and checked her cell phone. After a
minute or two a streetcar came, the old
electric kind, wide doors in both the front
and rear. The woman climbed on in front.
She put out some kind of a card. The driver
clipped it. A few others boarded through
the rear door. Hauck stepped on with them.

An old conductor, with white hair and a
rumpled navy-blue uniform, made his way
back, people flashing their transit cards.
Hauck didn't have one and didn't want to
attract any attention. He squeezed through
a couple of commuters and opened his

paper. He caught the eye of a young boy, maybe eight, who seemed to have noticed. Most everyone else was in the standard early-morning commuter daze. He kept sight of the woman, who had taken a seat up front. He settled back and glanced at his paper. The bus wound its way through town. People got on and off, and at some point the boy and his mother got up, and the kid cast a knowing grin at him.

Hauck winked back at him, as if this would be their buried secret forever.

It took around ten minutes for the bus to weave its way to the other end of town. It was a more upscale neighborhood. It reminded Hauck of where they had come off the main road. Finally he saw the woman in red stand up to get off. The bus stopped. At the back of the bus Hauck stepped off onto the street. The woman jumped off at the front and started to walk.

Hauck fell into step behind her.

A short way ahead she crossed the street and Hauck watched her go into a small shop. A cosmetics store. He came up and saw her wave hello and chat with one or two of the people in there. Not customers, but salespeople. She took off her jacket and placed her bag on a shelf underneath a counter.

It was clear the woman worked there. She wasn't leading him to anyone now. *Damn.*

That was when his cell phone sounded. Naomi. "Any luck?" she asked.

"No." He sighed, dejected. "I got dragged clear across the city on a dead end."

"Well, things are better back here." Her voice held excitement in it. "Get back! I think we've got her, Ty!"

CHAPTER FIFTY-THREE

A woman whom Naomi pegged as around seventy, in a gray skirt and blue Shetland sweater, had come out of the apartment just before ten, locking the front door behind her.

Maria Radisovic.

Naomi followed her down the stairs and onto the street. Her first stop was a butcher store down the block, where she spent several minutes. Then a liquor store across the street, where she came out with a package. Then she picked up two newspapers from a stand. One a *USA Today*. Bundles in hand, she headed back up the block and stopped at the tobacconist.

By that time Hauck had flagged a taxi and in minutes made it back across the street from the apartment house. As he jumped out, Naomi waved him over.

"I think it's her," she said, pointing to the gray-haired woman visible through the tobacco shop window. "She picked up some meat at the butcher, some booze, and now she's in the tobacco shop. She's shopping for *something . . .*"

"Let's hope it's not just Sunday dinner," Hauck said.

They remained across the street and watched. Four or five minutes later, they spotted the woman emerging. Naomi tapped Hauck on the elbow. *"That's her."*

Hauck could see she did have a possible resemblance to Thibault. She had the same dark features, the heavy jaw; her hair still was thick and probably once black. But a lot of people bore those features here.

Clutching her packages, the woman headed back up the block toward her building. A wave of disappointment traveled through Hauck. She seemed to be going back in. In itself, that didn't mean much, other than now they'd have to wait all day, maybe into the night, maybe even until tomorrow, to see if Thibault happened to show up.

But to his excitement, she continued past the front gate.

The woman glanced around once, then turned into a narrow alley behind the building with her supplies.

Hauck said, "Stay here." He waited for a car to pass. "I'll go see."

He crossed after her, following her down the narrow alleyway. Around the back of the building, the small road opened up.

A car parking lot.

Maria Radisovic was depositing her parcels into the rear of a small blue Opel. Then, taking a last look around, as if she felt Hauck watching, she got in.

The instincts that had guided Hauck all these years suddenly kicked in. Blood pumping, he ran back out of the alley and signaled Naomi over to their Ford, parked on the side of the street.

"Get in!" he shouted, throwing the driver's door open.

Naomi hopped in beside him as he turned on the engine. "What?"

"We're in business!"

CHAPTER FIFTY-FOUR

Maria Radisovic's blue Opel pulled out of the small alleyway and turned left on Zinak Street, heading out of town.

Hauck waited until the car disappeared around a bend, then pulled out after her. He felt confident that the woman, supplies in tow, was leading them somewhere promising.

About a mile ahead, tracking the river, the road widened and the commercial shops and apartment dwellings gave way to warehouses, gas stations, even a local power facility. Hauck followed, keeping a couple of hundred yards behind.

A road sign read SEBECEVO, 8 KM.

A couple of miles beyond town, the road they were on started to wind and climb. It narrowed, cutting through the dark hills surrounding the valley Novi Pazar was situated in. Traffic was sparse. Radisovic chugged along at a modest pace. Hauck had to work at it to remain so far behind. Every once in a while a commercial truck zoomed past them.

Neither he nor Naomi had much to say. They both seemed to feel the same anticipation that Maria was going to lead them to something. As the road climbed, the little Opel slowed and Hauck had to keep his diesel in second gear to remain an appropriate distance behind.

SEBECEVO, 3 KM.

As the road crested and started to descend into a wide valley, the Opel's turn signal began to flash. It was remote terrain. Hauck glanced at Naomi.

They had arrived somewhere.

An unpaved road came into view, marked only by a telephone pole with a sign, SISTENA R, the river. The car ahead made a right turn. It slowed and chugged along the dirt road, and coming upon it, Hauck drove by, glancing at Maria Radisovic bouncing along the rutted terrain. "I don't want her to spot us turning."

About a quarter of a mile down the main road he turned onto the shoulder. He spun back around and stopped before the turn-off. They could no longer see Maria Radisovic's car.

"This is it." He eyed Naomi expectantly. "Last chance to pull out."

She shook her head. Anticipation shone in her eyes. "Let's see what she's up to."

They turned down the gravelly road. It cut through a fallow field and wound through a dense thatch of woods, steadily rising. Hauck's pulse seemed to bump along in the same rhythm as the car.

They passed a tree-shaded cottage, barely more than a hut, with a few farm animals in pens. A dog ran out at them, barking.

No sign of Maria's Opel.

Around a bend, the road cleared the woods and led them into a wide valley. Hills rose up in front of them. Hauck could see a couple of houses dotting the hillside ahead.

"I'm pulling off for a second," he said. "I

can't take the chance she'll spot us following her."

He slowed onto the side of the dirt road and threw the car into park. Hauck reached into the back and took out a pair of binoculars from his canvas bag. Focusing, he made a wide sweep of the hills. About a mile ahead, he spotted the Opel climbing a steep ridge and, following its path and the valley beyond, came upon the outline of a dwelling, the brightness of a red tiled roof.

Naomi asked, "What do you see?"

The Opel drove down the road and came to a stop in front of the white, red-roofed farmhouse.

"I think I see pay dirt," Hauck replied.

They drove past the ridge and left the car hidden behind a cluster of trees where it wouldn't be spotted. Hauck grabbed the bag and took the binocs, some bottled water, a Nikon camera, and his Sig 9 mm, just in case.

"You're sure you're up for this?" he asked Naomi one last time, a little playfulness behind it. "Desk detail is over."

She tied her hair in a ponytail and zipped

her Windbreaker. "Let me know if I go too fast for you," she answered.

They decided to climb the adjoining ridge and look over the house Maria Radisovic had driven up to. Naomi strapped on her government-issue Colt.

"You even recall how to use that thing?" Hauck asked with a teasing grin.

"I think I can still conjure up the image," Naomi said, locking in the magazine and brushing past him.

The terrain up the hill was steep, with tall grasses that led to a drier brush as they climbed above the trees. The sun had come out and made the climb hot. And steep. Hauck felt a little out of breath. His leg throbbed a bit, still stiff from the bullet in the thigh he'd taken eighteen months ago.

Naomi, leading the way, never even slowed.

They finally made it to the top. They kneeled down on a rock and looked over the ridge Maria Radisovic had driven up to.

"Look!" Hauck pointed to a stucco farmhouse. Some animal pens built along a sloping hillside, maybe for sheep or oxen, but no sign of any livestock around. An earthen well dug along the side of the house.

White smoke rose from the chimney.

"Someone's there."

A black Audi was parked along the side of the house in back, almost hidden from view.

The cargo hatch open, Maria Radisovic's Opel was pulled up in front.

Hauck peered through the binoculars. She had unpacked the car and gone inside. He guessed he was gazing at an abandoned farm. Maybe in the family or something they had rented. He muttered to Naomi, "What would you be thinking about why an elderly women needs to bring stuff way out in the sticks like this? Food. Booze. Tobacco."

"I'd be thinking maybe it's for someone she wants to hide," Naomi said, watching over the ridge.

They had to wait a few minutes. Fifteen or twenty. The sun made it hot up there, and they opened up some water.

Finally, the front door of the farmhouse opened back up.

Maria came out first. She was followed by a figure Hauck recognized instantly. He zoomed in with the binoculars. The man was dressed in a blue plaid shirt, rumpled pants, and leather work boots. He was heavyset and broad shouldered. He looked like any anonymous worker from the town.

Except that Hauck saw his face.

"And I'd be thinking you're right," he said, rolling over and passing the binoculars to Naomi. "Agent Blum, say hi to Dani Thibault." He grinned triumphantly.

CHAPTER FIFTY-FIVE

Inside the farmhouse, Dani Thibault was going crazy.

He'd been cooped up at the old family farm for a week, unable to communicate with anyone, nervous to even show his face in town, even though he'd hadn't been there for fifteen years. He was virtually in prison, yet he knew he had to remain there, at least for a while, until things calmed down.

He went out for a smoke and looked around the foggy valley. It was a perfect hiding spot. He was in one of the most remote mountain regions in Europe, and having driven through the EU from Paris under an identity no one could trace, there was no way anyone would have tracked him here. He was sure he had gotten out before anyone would have known he was missing. He had communicated only through a private e-mail address with his mother. Franko Kostavic had disappeared fifteen years ago. And if it did somehow come out, if some old-timer recognized his face and put it together, in his family's old village, surrounded by friends who felt the same way, he would be celebrated as a hero for what he'd done in the war, not turned in.

But it wasn't the police or the U.S. government he was primarily worried about. No . . .

On his way there, in Germany, he had stopped and e-mailed the man who had recruited him at a designated cyber address. Thibault wrote that the trail of money he had received and recordings he had made of their communications were in the secure possession of a lawyer in Switzerland with instructions to share it with the U.S. government should Thibault not be around to call in and instruct him not to every six months. A simple plan, he had to admit, but a safe one. All he wanted was his freedom in return for what he had done. His silence was guaranteed.

Ultimately, Thibault knew, there were places he could go where no one would ever find him and new aliases he could adopt. Just like he had done before. He possessed all the funds he would ever need. He knew how to sniff out people, vulnerable people. The instinct came to him like the scent of a hare to a hound.

His only regret was that he couldn't get even with Merrill. To make her pay for her betrayal. That was driving him nuts. She was a horny little bitch and his only amusement now was the knowledge that he had let free urges from deep inside her she would not so easily satisfy with someone else.

Unfortunately, the thought of her brought his own physical urges to the surface. Up there, what prospects could there be? Filthy barmaids or mountainous old farmer's wives. He was used to having the most desirable women in the world. Maybe he would go into Novi Pazar. No one knew him there. There were places he could go. Women found him instantly attractive. He knew he radiated something mysterious to them, a side he had played up his whole life. Using women had never been a difficult thing for him.

The stupid old Bahraini had said it. It was his dick that would get him into trouble.

Yes, he was going crazy there. *So be it,* Thibault thought. He stared up at the hills. It was like he felt someone watching him, but he knew that was impossible. They'd held in secrets for centuries.

He stamped out his cigarette. His was just one more.

CHAPTER FIFTY-SIX

They watched Thibault for another day from the same hillside, perched high on the ridge. Naomi snapped several photos. Thibault. His car. Its plates. She sent them immediately back to Washington.

They deliberated about what to do.

Thibault never strayed far from the cottage. Once or twice he came out for a smoke or to bring in wood from a shack, as the nights were still cool. Once he took a short walk along a nearby brook. The next day, Maria Radisovic came back around noon. This time Hauck and Naomi were there ahead of her. She brought along a suitcase that seemed stuffed with clothes, and Thibault came out of the farmhouse and took it in for her. He puffed on a cigar and stamped it into the ground. Before going in, he gazed around the secluded valley—almost directly at the spot where he and Naomi were located, making Hauck duck back. It was almost as if Thibault had sensed someone was watching him.

Then he went back inside.

The options they faced were complicated. They could arrest Thibault themselves, but that would mean bringing in the Serbian police. Anything else would be unlawful. Which no one wanted. That would only create a public legal battle over extradition. Without a formal treaty and with local lawyers dragging it out, a thing like that could go on forever. And once the government became aware Thibault was actually Kostavic, who knew how that would play out? They might lose whatever negotiating leverage they had.

The next best option was something more clandestine. Bring in professionals. Call in a team that could subdue Thibault, disable him, and sneak him out of the country across the border with Romania or even Macedonia. Back into U.S. hands. The new international antiterrorist accords gave them broad powers. But apprehending a Serb in his home country, doing a covert abduction in a friendly state—that would never fly. That wasn't exactly part of the current U.S. presidential administration's foreign policy theme.

They had found him. But time was running out and they felt their viable options slowly drifting away.

"What's the goal here?" Hauck asked atop the ridge, swigging water as the day grew hot and long.

He had come to a decision on his own.

"Apprehend him," Naomi said. "Find out what he knows."

"You can always apprehend him. We know what car he's driving, what name he's traveling under. You can always petition the local government to hand him over. Whatever the case, he'll be facing serious charges here. And you'll know where he is."

Naomi stared at him quizzically. "So where are you heading, Ty?"

"You want to find out where this leads, right? What's important is discovering what's behind those murders?"

She nodded, going along.

"What we need to do is get inside that farmhouse."

He turned and focused back on the house, not elaborating further. He could see Naomi weighing what he'd said in her mind. She wasn't a field agent. She worked behind a desk. Her job was to fit together the threads of financial conspiracy and assess the threat. In the army, she'd been an investigator. Going in there, on the fly, without the backing of her bosses in DC, like some kind of operative—that definitely wasn't the way careers were made in Washington. She'd be crossing a huge line.

Some time later, after Hauck figured she'd stowed the idea away as a bad one, she turned. "How do we do that?" she asked.

Hauck grinned. He'd been waiting for her to reply, "Over *my dead body*!"

"Thibault's used to being a public person. He's going to have to leave that farmhouse sometime."

She sat back against the ledge and nodded, not so much in agreement as in coming to grips with the idea. Finally she replied, without turning, "Anyway, if anyone's going in that farmhouse, it's going to be *me*. I know what I'm looking for."

He waited a moment. "You ever done anything like that before?"

She looked at him without answering.

"I'm just saying, this isn't exactly music theory at Princeton, Naomi."

"Any more than it's handing out traffic tickets in Greenwich." Her glare suggested there wouldn't be much negotiating on this.

"Okay." Hauck turned back to the binoculars, suppressing a smile.

Naomi said, "I thought this was just about your friend. The one who was murdered. You don't have to do this either. We found Thibault."

"What can I tell you?" Hauck said. "I'm learning to multitask."

Now she was the one hiding her smile.

They watched a little longer. Hauck's cell phone began to vibrate. It was Steve Chrisafoulis, he noticed, relieved it wasn't Annie.

"Steve."

"Where am I catching you?" the detective asked. The reception made it sound as if he was a block away.

"Just doing a bit of house-hunting,"

Hauck said, rolling a few yards down the rise. He'd have liked to hear the guy's reaction if he divulged he was on a hilltop in frigging Serbia.

"House-hunting . . . ? We got something interesting back on James Merced. You remember your skating partner?"

"Yeah, Steve, I recall. I'm listening."

"Turns out he came back stateside after receiving a get-out-of-jail card from Iraq. Seemed he had a few social problems with the enlisted women over there. Harassment. Assault. Attempted rape . . . They gave him a less-than-honorable discharge."

"You don't have to try hard to convince me, Steve."

"When he got home, he knocked around a bit in California and Michigan, digging pools. Then he tried to hook on as a private contractor with a security outfit back in Iraq. Global Threat Management. You familiar with that company, Ty?"

"Yeah, I'm familiar."

"That's part of your outfit, isn't it, Ty? Talon?"

Hauck felt a tremor tighten in his chest. "It is."

"Apparently they shipped his ass right

back out, soon as they found out about his record. I spoke with the employment director there. Still, quite a little coincidence, don't you think? You and he, tied to the same firm . . ."

"You think that's why he was trying to kill me, Steve?"

Hauck thanked him, and Steve said he'd keep him posted. They signed off. House-hunting . . . *If he only knew . . .*

Hauck crawled back up to the ridge.

"What was that?" Naomi asked.

"Real estate thing," he said. She stared back at him. "Nothing . . ." He retook the binoculars. But it wasn't *nothing*. It was the second time in a month he had doubts about his own firm, thought they might somehow be involved.

The sun was out. It was hot on this hilltop in Serbia. His brow was sweating. So why did he have the disturbing feeling that he was walking on thin ice?

"You know, I never handed out traffic tickets," he said, focusing back on Thibault's farmhouse. "Least not in Greenwich."

"That's okay," Naomi said. "I've never done anything like this before."

* * *

They waited until almost dark. For a while, in the late afternoon, Thibault came out and walked around, smoking. He leaned against the wooden fence of the animal pen, staring up at the hills.

He had to have a plan.

Then he went back inside.

At the onset of dark, about seven, they went back down the hill. They'd come to a decision.

In the car, Hauck turned onto the main road and headed back toward town.

A gray delivery van pulled out on the road behind them, the driver waiting before they'd gone around a bend to turn on its lights. There were two men in the front who'd been sitting for most of the day. One had short, dark hair, long sideburns, and a heavy mustache.

"To je u njima," he said in Serbian. *That's them.*

CHAPTER FIFTY-SEVEN

Look!"

It was the next day, Friday, in the late afternoon. Naomi pointed toward the farmhouse. They'd been watching it all day. The sun was just beginning to set and they were about to pack it up and head back into town.

Hauck took the glasses from her and zoomed in.

Thibault stepped outside. He was wearing a black leather jacket and tossed a duffel bag in the backseat of the Audi. He was heading somewhere. He locked the front door.

Hauck put down the binoculars and looked at Naomi. This was their chance.

They had talked it over for most of the day. They had already passed back the license number of the rented Audi, and they knew for certain what identity Thibault was traveling under. What name he used to rent the car. They'd decided that if he left, one of them would take their car and follow.

The other would go inside.

That would be her.

"You better get moving." Naomi stood up and strapped on a pouch that held a Nikon digital SLR, a special computer flash drive, a pen flashlight.

Her gun.

Thibault got into the Audi and started it up.

"*Nervous?*" Hauck asked. She was a desk agent, not a field agent. What she was putting herself into was definitely crossing that line.

"No," she answered without hesitating. Then, blowing air through her cheeks, she shrugged. "Maybe a little."

"Me too. Be careful going in not to trip any wires or safeguards he may have set up. Take a mental picture of how everything looks as soon as you get in. And make sure you leave everything just as you found it."

"You think you can manage to tail the guy without blowing your cover?" she asked, a little peeved. "But hey," she betrayed a smile. "Thanks."

Thibault backed the Audi around and started to make his way down the winding road.

Hauck said, "I better go. Whenever I get to where he's going, I'll check in with you." He squeezed her on the arm. "You be careful in there, okay?"

"You too, Ty. No heroics. Remember, I'm responsible for you."

With a last wink, Hauck headed down the steep embankment to where they had left the car. Thibault had a bit of a head start, but Hauck knew what he was driving and figured traffic would be light. He finally made it down to the road, hopped into the driver's seat of their Ford, and did a U-ey in a clearing on the deserted road, starting after the Audi with his headlights off. As he passed through the woods heading back to the road to Novi Pazar, he finally caught sight of it.

Thibault had pulled up for a moment at

the turnoff. He stopped too. Then the Audi turned left on the road toward town.

Hauck slowed, and when he got to the intersection, he put on his lights. The Audi was a minute or so ahead of him. But it was starting to get dark and they were the only ones on the road. As they climbed up over the pass, he saw the Audi's taillights in the distance.

Heading to Novi Pazar.

It took about fifteen minutes to reach the outskirts of town. Hauck narrowed the distance as the main road fed into the town and traffic picked up. At a circle, he let a slower fuel truck and a minivan sneak in between them to conceal his pursuit. At an intersection, Thibault accelerated through a light that was about to change and Hauck had to zip around the truck so as not to lose him, then fell a few car lengths back.

He was pretty sure he hadn't been spotted. The Audi wove through the main thoroughfare, turned down a side street near the river, and pulled to a stop, parking on the sidewalk. Hauck slowed, passing by, and eyed a brightly lit bar with a frosted glass façade and a sign with old-fashioned

American lettering that said O'FLYNN'S CHICAGO-STYLE BAR, like some garish American sports bar. Probably the local hangout. Through his rearview mirror, Hauck saw Thibault climb out, flick the automatic lock of the car, and go inside.

Hauck continued on the narrow side street and squeezed into a spot in front of a brick building that had a yogurt billboard in Serbian with a photo of Ana Ivanovic, the pretty tennis player, on the side of it. He locked the car and stepped around the side to the main street. He pulled his cap down over his brow. In front, a man and woman came out, almost bumping into him, speaking loudly in Serbian. *"Izvinite,"* Hauck grunted under his breath. *Excuse me.* He peered inside the frosted windows. A Heineken beer sign. Inside, the bar was dark. And crowded. The din that escaped was loud.

There was always the chance he was walking into a trap. *No heroics . . .*

He went around the side. There was a small deck overlooking the river. Six or seven tables on it, mostly young people drinking, eating, under beer umbrellas. Hauck followed a waitress through a rear door. A wave of noise hit him at the entrance.

He made his way inside.

The main bar was raucous and packed with people. Women crowded the wooden bar surrounded by local types. Everyone was smoking. Some looked like businessmen; others hunched over tables, drinking beer, smoking, gesturing at the large TV screen above. A soccer game was on that a lot of people seemed to be watching. When the ball went down one side, the bar seemed to erupt in cheers. The women were laughing, chattering, looking like secretaries out on the make. The local beer, Jemel, was flowing.

Hauck made his way up to the end of the bar and lost himself in a crowd. Just like in New York, he recalled. He looked around for Thibault, searching for his face through the haze of smoke and patrons.

He finally found him sitting alone at a table near the far end of the bar, sipping a beer.

Thibault was looking directly at him.

CHAPTER FIFTY-EIGHT

Naomi wound her way down to the farmhouse. She waited a few minutes to make certain Thibault wasn't coming back. It had become dark, and the path down was treacherous with sliding rocks and false steps, even with her flashlight, causing her to stumble and almost fall several times along the way.

Thank God Ty was following Thibault.

As she watched the house her blood started to race. The dark silence of the unfamiliar valley and realizing just what she was about to get herself into gave her one of the deepest feelings of loneliness and isolation she had ever felt. She begged her heart to calm down. There was no one there, nothing to be afraid of. She kept telling herself that this was the right thing to do. Still, her heart wouldn't quite respond. A thought passed through her that would have made her laugh if she wasn't so afraid: *What've you gotten yourself involved in, Naomi?*

She wasn't a desk agent anymore.

When she was certain Thibault wasn't returning, she darted across the mountain road, careful to avoid leaving imprints from her sneakers in the gravel. She moved over to the arched, wood-planked front door. The latch was locked. *Shit.* She poked her light through a crack in the shuttered window. She couldn't see much. The lights inside were dimmed.

She hurried around the side. It was a stone and stucco cottage, could have been built a hundred years ago. The brush that crept up to the side of the house was sparse. Cautiously, she peered in through a cracked shutter. She could see an open kitchen with a large stone hearth. She tried the door off the kitchen. The iron latch

didn't budge either. *Damn.* She continued
on around back.

She knew she had the time, the time to
sort it all out and be careful, but her heart
was thumping and she wanted to get this
over with, and she didn't want to take the
chance that someone, *anyone,* might show
up at the house. She peered into what
looked like a bedroom window. She knew if
she had to she could break the pane of
glass. They knew where Thibault was. They
knew what car he was driving, what name
he was traveling under. They could always
find him. Busting the window would blow
their secrecy. But what was important was
finding out what he knew.

She checked the shuttered windows
along the back and, to her elation, saw
that one of them was cracked.

She slid her fingers underneath the sill
and jerked upward. To her relief, the window lifted. She wiggled a space just wide
enough for her body to slip through and
climbed inside. She was right; it was a bedroom. In fact, it seemed to be the one
Thibault was using. His clothes were
strewn haphazardly about a chair; the open

suitcase she had seen Maria Radisovic bring in was on the floor. The bed was mussed.

She was in.

In the front room she spotted a breakfast table in a nook outside the kitchen that Thibault seemed to be using as his work space. There was a small TV that was hooked up to a satellite. There was a laptop set up on the table. Some books, papers stacked around. Naomi sat down and inserted a download flash drive in the USB port and tried to log on. Not surprisingly, the prompt came up for a password.

Damn.

Thibault had to have records. Records of who he communicated with. His financial interactions. The money flow. She was certain she'd find all that inside. The thought passed through her that maybe she ought to just take it. That it didn't matter anymore, this cat-and-mouse. What was important was to track the trail to someone higher. Where this conspiracy led.

She tried to bypass the security but it proved to be futile. Pulse racing, she turned her attention to the papers scattered all over the table. She rifled through the files, mostly financial papers—partnership agreements, corporate documents, deal brochures. She had no idea if these were legitimate or part of Thibault's illicit doings. But he'd brought them with him, so she assumed they must have some value. She laid them out on the table and snapped pictures of the cover pages, focusing on the corporate logos. There was a stack of business cards bound together by a rubber band. Naomi unfastened them and began to leaf through.

Most seemed like legitimate contacts from around the world. Thibault's network. JP Morgan, Citi, Reynolds Reid. She even came upon James Donovan's card and those of other securities traders from different firms, which made her wonder if they might have been more potential victims. She laid them all out on the table, snapping digital shots. She came across one that made her heart come to a stop.

The black, embossed logo of Ascot Capital.

Ascot was the investment partnership in Dubai that was linked to Crescent Bay in Toronto, the company that bought Donovan's house.

The name on the card was Hassan ibn Hassani.

Her pulse rocketed. Hassani was the contact overheard on the phone with Marty al-Bashir in London. That had started the whole thing rolling.

The planes are in the air.

Thibault knew him. Hassani. Ascot was also a link in the chain of funds that went to pay off James Donovan. Not enough to prove a thing, to seek an indictment. But enough to hand over to the FBI and Interpol. Enough to widen the investigation. Everything was knitting together.

Naomi snapped away.

She wasn't making any distinctions. Everything there could be important. She shot receipts, plane tickets. Even what looked like a ski-lift ticket. From Gstaad, the posh resort in Switzerland. Naomi took a look at the date: 06/26. The summer before. Maybe just a memento. It cost forty euros.

She snapped it anyway.

With haste, she threw the pack of cards back together, reattaching the rubber band. She checked her watch. Fifteen minutes. She felt comfortable that she had more time. She turned back to the computer and saw the download flash drive had connected and tried to enable the password-busting program to do its work. No way she was going to leave it behind.

That was when she saw a light flash outside and heard a vehicle coming up the road.

Naomi's blood froze. *Oh, shit.*

Someone was here.

CHAPTER FIFTY-NINE

The lights were from a car coming up to the house. The sound of the tires on the gravel knifed through Naomi like a heart attack.

Could Thibault somehow be coming back?

Where the hell was Ty?

The thought that Thibault might have somehow ambushed him and had now come back for her sent her heart into a frenzy. Her throat suddenly got very dry and her blood was pumping at what felt like ten times its normal rate. She checked the table one last time. Everything seemed in order. She hastily threw the camera in her pack and headed back into the bedroom.

She pressed against the wall and took out her gun.

She heard the car door slam. Footsteps coming up the walk. Then a loud knock on the door. And a woman's voice. Which came as a slight relief to her.

"Franko? Franko?"

It was Maria Radisovic. Thibault's mother. Naomi wasn't sure what to do. Stay in the house? Leave?

Then suddenly she realized she had left her flash drive connected to Thibault's laptop.

Oh, God . . . If Thibault ever saw it, they were completely blown. She made a move to run out and retrieve it, but the door handle started rattling, scaring her.

"Franko?"

Naomi ducked back in.

Suddenly she heard a key in the lock at the front door. The door was pushed open. Naomi squeezed herself against the wall.

The woman stepped into the house. It was Maria. Naomi recognized her instantly from the day before. She was in a light-brown parka against the chill and a cloth hat pulled over her hair, and she was carrying what Naomi took to be a bag of groceries.

"Franko?" she called out one last time. Then she started muttering loudly in Serbian, no doubt upset not to have found him there.

Then Naomi saw she wasn't alone. She had a dog with her. It looked like a shepherd. Her heart started to pound. She was trapped there now. The woman had gone into the kitchen and was placing the groceries into the fridge. Maria pulled out her cell phone and punched in a number. Whoever she was calling didn't answer. Naomi was sure it was Thibault. Maria flicked it off in disgust.

The dog started exploring around the house, going from room to room, as if it was familiar with the place.

It was only a matter of time before it alighted on her.

Naomi pulled back the action on her Colt. She wasn't sure what to do. She'd never used it, not like this. Only firing at a faceless, remote enemy in Iraq. Not an old woman.

She felt a chill and realized she had left the bedroom window wide open. There was a draft that went around the entire house. Maria would find her way back there.

Shit.

"Katja, Katja?" The woman was calling the dog. Her voice started to get closer. "Katja . . ."

Naomi backed inside the room and hurried over to the window. This was one time she was lucky she was small. She lifted her front leg through and adroitly climbed out. Then she leaped to the side and started to lower it gently. Not quite all the way.

She heard the dog come into the room.

Then, shortly after, Maria. "Katja . . ." A loud sigh. She seemed to look around petulantly, angry at the mess. Naomi backed away, hugging the house. The woman came to the window. Naomi heard her grunt. She pressed herself against the side of the house and tensed her finger on the trigger guard, her heart beating wildly. *What would she do? Please, please*—she gripped the gun—*don't stick your head out . . .*

Muttering, the woman tried to jam the window shut. She seemed to get it most of the way. Naomi's pulse started to relax.

She didn't want to back away into the darkness, just in case she was seen. In case the dog might notice. She just stood there, frozen. Her heart beating at a steady pace. For what seemed like an hour.

At some point she heard the front door open again. The woman called the dog into the car. The car engine started up.

Naomi shut her eyes in relief.

As the car drove away, she went back and tried the window. It opened again. *Thank God.*

Why hadn't her phone rung?

Where the hell was Ty?

CHAPTER SIXTY

Hauck turned away from Thibault, glancing at the overhead TV, the European soccer match. He ducked back into a huddle of rowdy beer drinkers, who erupted in whoops and cheers every time the attack went down the field their way. He signaled to the bartender and pointed toward a local beer.

Every once in a while he glanced through the bodies to where the Serbian was sitting. Thibault had ordered a meal. He consumed it quickly, what looked like a plate of sausage and sauerkraut, and it seemed whatever attention he may have directed toward Hauck had now been transferred to his dinner. Hauck checked his watch. By now, Naomi was likely done. He ought to check in. He could always pick Thibault up from across the street. He lost himself again inside the crowd of drunken fans.

A minute or two later, he saw Thibault glance at his cell and motion for a check. A young waitress came up and the Serb threw some bills on a tray, chatting flirtatiously; she seemed no older than a college student. Then he took his leather jacket from the chair and headed out through the crowd. He came within a few bodies of Hauck, who turned, taking a swig of his beer. In the frosted mirror he saw that Thibault never looked his way.

Hauck breathed easier. He must've been imagining it.

He waited about thirty seconds, threw a few bills on the counter for the beer, then wandered back to the rear and out the rear entrance. He waited a few seconds and made his way around to the front. There were a couple of locals there huddled around, smoking, conversing loudly. Hauck glanced along the street and saw

Thibault's black Audi still parked on the sidewalk.

But Thibault was nowhere to be seen.

Hauck tucked his cap down over his eyes and thought about calling Naomi. There was an alley off to the far side of the bar that seemed to lead down toward a perch over the river. Losing sight of Thibault made him nervous. Maybe he had crossed the street. Maybe he had gone to meet someone. Hauck looked around and didn't see him. He stepped around the side to the alley and looked down there.

No one.

Then something with the force of a bus collided with the back of his head.

Hauck went down. His brain grew all fuzzy. His eyes glazed over and the next thing he knew he was on his knees. He knew something was deadly wrong, then a second later he felt another rattling blow to the back of his ribs.

The air went out of him. His face hit the ground.

"Who the fuck are you?" a heavily accented voice demanded. *In English.* Which, through his haze, worried Hauck even more. There was a knee dug into his back and the attacker dragged him up by the collar. "I know you. I've seen you somewhere before. *Who are you?* You're not from around here."

To Hauck, the words had the feel of a distant echo, slamming around in his dulled head. Not to mention the pain radiating in his ribs. He pushed himself up off the ground, trying to clear himself, knowing that how he replied and what happened next might mean his life.

How had Thibault found him? How had he been made?

The Serb reared back and kicked him again, this time in the stomach. Hauck doubled over and fell again, the air shooting out of his lungs. Thibault flung him against the brick wall.

"Who are you?" he shouted again. He patted Hauck down before Hauck could fully regain his senses. He found the Sig tucked into Hauck's waist. The Serb removed it, chuckling a derisive laugh, then pulled back the bolt and thrust the barrel against Hauck's head. "I don't forget a face. I know I've seen you. *Where?* Who sent

you? You've got three seconds to fill me in, or I spill your brains all over this alley."

"I'm an investigator," Hauck said, ribs exploding, more of a gasp.

"An investigator? For *whom*?"

Hauck took a look behind him. He saw no one in sight. Thibault had spoken to him directly in English. Not even a pretense that he was from around here. He now realized his mistake had been made back in New York. At the restaurant he had followed Thibault to. That was where he had first been spotted. Not here.

And he knew he'd better say something that would buy him some time. And fast. "From back in the States." He sucked in a breath. "I'm looking into the death of Marc Glassman."

"American?" Thibault turned him around and looked directly into Hauck's face, more of a sneer. "How did you find me?" He pushed the barrel of the gun into Hauck's head. "There's no cavalry here in Serbia, Mr. Investigator. *How did you know I was here?"*

Hauck knew he had to come up with something. Thibault was an ex-Scorpion.

Trained at this. If he had shown no qualms about shooting dozens of innocent towns-people in a ditch, surely he'd have none about pulling the trigger here, with his survival at risk.

"Bank records," Hauck gasped, straining for breath. He looked the Serb in the eyes. "You sent money here."

The answer seemed to shock him. Hauck stared, weak-kneed, into the Serb's glowering eyes. "Bank records, huh?" He sent another hard blow into Hauck's ribs. Hauck gasped, air rushing out of him, his ribs seeming to cave in.

Thibault yanked him up again by the collar and forced him farther down the alley, away from the street. He flung Hauck over a railing above the river as Hauck desperately tried to catch his breath. He could hear the whoosh of the water rushing below. Thibault took him by the back of his head and cocked the gun against it. Hauck's insides froze. He looked down. There was some kind of mill close by, and a waterfall. A drop of maybe thirty feet. Hauck realized the roar of the current would conceal the sound of any blast.

He knew he couldn't fight him. He was

defenseless, still reeling from the blows. Any resistance would only earn him a blast from his own gun.

Thibault forced him farther over the edge. *"Who sent you, Mr. Investigator?* Who else knows I'm here?"

"No one," Hauck said, the spray from the rushing water splashing onto his face.

"Don't lie. I smell lies, the way I smelled you. Are you ready to take a swim? You may make it through the current, but I wouldn't recommend it with a bullet to the back of the head."

A winch of fear began to tighten in Hauck's gut. He knew he had only seconds, and whatever he said, it better be the right thing. It better buy him some time.

"Franko Kostavic," Hauck yelled, shutting his eyes as he waited for the hammer of darkness to bludgeon his brain.

It never came.

A few seconds passed. Thibault jerked him back up. He turned him around, pressing the gun sharply into Hauck's ribs. His eyes smoldered with determination and anger. "How do you know that name?"

"I traced it. I took your DNA. I followed you in New York. To a restaurant. Alto."

Hauck thought, *What does it matter now if it buys me a few seconds?* "That's where you saw me before."

As it sank in, Thibault smiled. His face had a certain submission and resignation in it. He dug the gun in deeper into Hauck's gut. "Then you know this is like a walk in the park for me; isn't that what you Americans say? A slam dunk. Tell me why you're here. Tell me what it is that has brought you all the way to Serbia. What it is you are about to die for."

A final fear rose up in Hauck. But not for him. For Naomi—whom he had left helpless. He prayed he hadn't put her in danger. Two other faces came into his mind. It was strange, he thought, who came to mind.

Jessie. A feeling of such terrible sadness. *Would she even ever know?*

And April. The glint on her proud face. *See, I was there for you,* he thought.

I kept my promise.

"I'm here to make you pay for what you've done," Hauck said, looking back at him. Over Thibault's shoulder, he saw two people come into the alley. He looked in his assailant's eyes and smiled.

"In another life, perhaps," the Serb said, raising the gun. "But in this one, your job's done."

"Not just yet," Hauck said.

CHAPTER SIXTY-ONE

The two men approaching from down the alley stepped closer. Unsteady, bantering loudly in Serbian, they were probably drunk. Maybe they had come down there to take a piss. Or puke into the river.

Hauck didn't care. They were the cavalry to him.

Thibault glanced around when it was clear there would be witnesses to what he was about to do. Annoyance crossed his face. They came to a stop about ten feet away when they came across Thibault, who looked to them like he was roughing up a drunken customer.

One of them was short and squat, barrel-chested. In an open striped shirt and a black leather jacket. The other was taller, in a kind of soccer sweatshirt. A shaved head and long sideburns and a rough, Slavic face.

"Hey, what are you doing?" the shorter one muttered in Serbian, gesturing at Thibault in an animated way.

Thibault shouted something back, which Hauck took to be the equivalent of "Get the fuck away," flashing the gun in his face.

The two men's eyes widened. Hauck harnessed his strength. Maybe as they went away he could spin Thibault around.

But instead of fleeing, the two men simply raised their hands in a defensive manner, their drunkenness making them seem more annoyed than afraid, still not leaving.

Thibault pressed the gun sharply into Hauck's ribs. "Don't think I wouldn't do it . . ."

At the end of the alley, another man and a woman poked their heads in to see what all the commotion was about.

Suddenly, there were witnesses. A small crowd.

The two Serbians were shouting at Thibault and waving their arms at him, cursing. Even with the gun, Thibault was no longer in control. He didn't know what to do. If he shot Hauck, he'd have to do the same to several others. Or leave witnesses. There was no way to escape. And the last thing he needed now was to be on the run from the local police; avoiding that was even more important than killing Hauck.

Hauck realized these people were saving his life. Seizing the moment, in full sight of everyone, he pushed Thibault aside. He met the Serb's gaze with a victorious grin.

"Go on, get out of here," the tall one with the sideburns said. In English now. "This is not how we treat visitors in Serbia. This man is clearly drunk. We know what to do with his kind here."

They thought they were saving some poor tourist from a mugging.

Hauck nodded at the man with gratitude, then glanced back at Thibault, who, he could see, was flashing through his options. Should he kill him? And then, how many? What he was interested in was survival.

Enraged, but helpless to do anything about it, he let Hauck pull away.

Relieved, Hauck stepped down the alleyway, quickening his stride and praying Thibault wouldn't reconsider and put a bullet in his back.

A small crowd had built up at the head of the alley, sensing the altercation. He looked back. Thibault was seething, but the two men were cursing at him brazenly. Taking it out on him like they were from the local chamber of commerce.

Whatever. Hauck let out a grateful breath. For the moment, they had saved his life.

His thoughts flashed to Naomi. She must have been going crazy, wondering where he was. He ran out of the alley, dashed down the street to where he had left the car, jumped in, and pulled out of the side street. He didn't like leaving Thibault. The man had been behind April's death. At least three others. Not to mention the poor guy in France whose identity he had taken.

But if Naomi had found something, they could turn him over to the Serbian police now.

He took off down the street, looking

back to see Thibault coming out, still trying to get free of his tormentors, shouting after him. He had to get back first. He took his cell phone out and called Naomi.

"Where the hell are you?" she answered, obviously waiting, picking up after the first ring.

"On my way to you. Get back to where we keep the car. I'll meet you there."

"You wouldn't believe what happened," she blurted in relief. She told him about Thibault's mother and how she had come to the house.

"Yeah, I've been up to my arms in a bit of a hot sink as well," Hauck said. "With her son."

CHAPTER SIXTY-TWO

Hauck raced back through town to Thibault's farmhouse to pick up Naomi. A flickering reel of questions bombarded him.

Who were the two men who had just intervened and saved him? Just a couple of drunken locals? One had addressed him in English. Had Hauck said something first? Whoever they were, their timing was impeccable, and they had surely saved his ass.

And what had Naomi found? Had she linked Thibault higher up the chain? Part of Hauck ached at leaving the bastard who had orchestrated the murder of four people free. Not to mention what he had done in Bosnia. Thibault might well be coming after him. He could be getting in his car right now.

Mostly, he realized just how lucky he was to simply be alive.

He made the twenty-minute trip to Sebecevo in under fifteen. He found the turnoff and drove his Ford down the bumpy, deserted road, through the wooded glade that was completely dark this time of night, past the steep incline up to Thibault's farm. He dimmed his lights, just in case the Serb was following him. He found the thicket of trees where they had been hiding their car.

Naomi stepped out of the darkness.

He breathed in, relieved.

She opened the passenger door and hopped in. Her face was taut and nearly white with worry, but seeing Hauck, being in the car, her color began to return.

"You okay?" he asked. He reached out and squeezed her arm.

"Yeah." She nodded. "You?"

"Yeah," he said, exhaling, *"now."*

Something inside made him almost want to reach over and give her a hug—they had both been through hell—and, in his hesitation, he could see Naomi felt the same way.

Instead, he just asked, "Did you find something?"

She looked back, eyes wide. "Yeah. Enough to tie him to Hassani."

"Then we better get out of here." Hauck threw the car back in gear. "Thibault made me. You don't want to know the details. I'll tell you about it on the way. I was lucky to even get away. The point is, he knows we're onto him."

"Then I have to go back in," Naomi said, putting her hand on his arm to stop him. "I have to take his computer."

Hauck shook his head. "No way. He could be on our tail right now. No time."

He flipped a U-turn, careful not to drive off the embankment, and headed back toward the main road, lights dimmed, praying they wouldn't run headfirst into Thibault, who might have been heading back to the house.

"Give me the gun," Hauck said.

"*What?*" Naomi hesitated, as if this was another veiled slight.

"I don't want to argue." His tone was charged with urgency. "Please, just give me the gun."

Naomi stared, for a second angry, then took it out of her belt and placed it in the cup holder between them. Hauck took it, checking the bolt while he drove. He placed it next to him on the driver's seat. He proceeded down the rocky road with caution, fearful Thibault might turn in at any time. To his relief, they made it back to the turnoff to Novi Pazar without any sight of him.

Hauck swung a left back toward town. He was starting to feel better now.

For the first time in an hour his heart rate came back to something approximating its normal pace. "I'm glad you're okay," he said. He looked at her and gave her a teasing wink. "I hear these old ladies around here can be pretty tough."

"I got what *I* went in for," Naomi said. "*You're* the one who seemed to have the trouble." Then, seeing he wasn't amused, she asked, "What happened?"

"Thibault recognized me from New York." Keeping an eye out for Thibault's Audi, Hauck took her through how the Serb seemed to catch sight of him in the bar, how he had waited outside, suckered Hauck in the alley.

Then everything after.

Naomi's eyes widened in horror. There was also a measure of concern in them.

"My God, are you alright?"

"Yeah, I guess I'm alright." In truth, his adrenaline had stopped and now Hauck's ribs were aching and the back of his head felt like one big, throbbing knot.

"You're lucky to be alive."

Hauck breathed in and focused on the road as it climbed the pass. "I know."

For a while, they drove on in silence. Naomi seemed stunned by his tale, how close he had come to death.

Finally she said, "I found a business card with an e-mail address for Hassani among Thibault's things. I don't know what's behind these killings, but it's clear Thibault was just the point man who carried them out. They were part of a larger plan. I'm gonna call in when we get back. I'm certain now they'll issue a warrant through the right channels to pick up Thibault. He may have more in his computer. We know the name he's using for himself and what car he's driving. He can't get far . . .

"More than that," Naomi, said, looking at him, "I'm just glad that you're okay."

He looked back at her and saw something in her eyes. "Me too."

They sped back to the outskirts of Novi Pazar. Maybe Thibault was already on the run. He could have gone back to his mother's, Hauck surmised. He could have exchanged their cars. If so, they already had the license plate number of Maria Radisovic's Opel. He wouldn't get far. The guy was in a real bind now. He had to decide whether to stand trial in the U.S. for the murders of four people or waive extradition and be put on trial for war crimes here.

As they neared the city, Hauck noticed lights flashing up ahead. A bevy of police cars to the side of the road.

Hauck slowed as they approached. "What's that?"

"Probably some drunk driver," Naomi said. "You saw firsthand, these people here hit it pretty hard."

"Yeah, they do."

He tried to make out what was going

on. A car had spun into a ditch. Half the police cars of Novi Pazar seemed to have been called in. A gray-clad uniformed policeman was on the road, waving traffic through. Hauck wished he could just lower the window and flash his credentials, like back home, ask what was going on.

Naomi said, "Looks bad."

As they inched closer, Hauck caught a glimpse of the color of the disabled car, which was pitched forward. *Black.* Then he saw the make.

Audi.

He turned to meet Naomi's frozen gaze.

It was Thibault's car.

He slowed to a virtual stop. Hauck made out the figure of a man slumped over the wheel.

The thick head of black hair. The black leather jacket.

It was Thibault. *No doubt.*

Naomi uttered, "Oh, my God . . ."

There seemed to be no visible damage to the car, but a blotch of blood oozed from the side of the lifeless Serb's head.

This didn't have the feel of any automobile accident.

As they passed, Hauck saw that two

words had been scrawled on the Audi's
rear windshield. In large, bold letters that
looked like smeared blood. Thibault's blood,
Hauck realized. Normally he wouldn't have
been able to make out anything written in
Serbian, but these two words needed no
translation.

DONJE VELKE, the letters read.

The Bosnian town where the massacre
Thibault had been accused of overseeing
had taken place.

CHAPTER SIXTY-THREE

They drove on past Thibault's car in silence. Naomi was ashen faced, numb. Even Hauck felt a hole in the pit of his stomach.

Thibault had been executed for what he had done.

Who was responsible? Who had pegged Thibault for Kostavic? What flashed through Hauck's mind was the scene back at the river, the two drunks who had seemingly wandered up at the right time. They had spoken to him in English. As if they knew.

Donje Velke.

"Who the hell *were* those people?"

Hauck pulled the car over to the side of the road. He racked his mind to recall exactly how everything had taken place.

"Retribution? The BIA?" Naomi thought out loud. The Serbian secret police.

"I don't know. They seemed to be drunk. But one of them spoke to me in English. Like he had an idea who I was. But why would Serbs have done this? What happened in Donje Velke took place in Bosnia. To ethnic Albanians. And Kostavic has been "dead" around here for fifteen years. How the hell would anyone have figured out who he was? We only stumbled on it by accident. Thibault kept pushing me: 'Who sent you?' He was definitely scared of someone . . ."

"Hassani?" Naomi said.

"Maybe." Hauck nodded. "Covering his tracks."

"If it was Hassani, we'd better get the hell out of here. *Now*."

"No." Hauck shook his head. "I don't think we're in any danger. If that was so, they definitely had the chance to eliminate us both. They didn't seem to have much of a problem sending me on my way."

"I'm not talking about *us*, Ty," Naomi

said. "If Hassani was behind these hits—
Glassman and Donovan, now this—
Thibault's gone. But there's someone else
who was involved. Someone who's now
become our only link. Who put this whole
thing in motion."

"That guy in London." Hauck looked at
her. "'The planes are in the air.'"

Naomi nodded. "Marty al-Bashir. If Hassani knows we're onto him, no way he's
going to let him live."

Hauck nodded. Without this al-Bashir,
who was at the heart of all that had happened, there was nothing they could prove.
The conspiracy ended here. With Thibault.

"I need to make some calls," Naomi
said. "I have to set a few things up."

"You want to go to London?"

"Someone's trying to wreak havoc on
the U.S. economy. Al-Bashir is the only
link we have now."

The flicker of flashing green and red police lights lit up the rearview mirror. Hauck
put the car back in gear.

"You're lucky," he said, pulling back onto
the road. "I just happen to be free."

Naomi looked out the window with a
worried smile. *"Whew."*

CHAPTER SIXTY-FOUR

The young girl trembled a bit, clearly scared.

Hassan ibn Hassani looked her over. She was only fourteen. Often they lied. But this one was truly a goddess. Her breasts were fully formed and he saw them quiver expectantly under her robe. Her hair was thick and soft as sable. Her eyes were dark, perfectly almond. Her lips were small yet full. There was a deepness to her that delighted him. Afraid, and yet intrigued by his attention.

And she had never been touched before.

"Exquisite." Hassani smiled, signaling to the woman who had brought her that he was truly satisfied. There were twenty thousand euros for her in an envelope on the way out. *Twenty thousand euros.* For a fraction of that, he could fuck the most beautiful women in the world. Models, beauty pageant contestants, aspiring Bollywood starlets. But this one was a jewel. Unspoiled. He couldn't take his eyes off her.

"What's your name?"

"Sera," the girl replied tremulously.

Sera. She had come from one of his villages back in the kingdom. A village that his family, sheiks for over two hundred years, still controlled. Her father had gotten into some trouble, built up a world of debts. A trifle to Hassani, who was willing to wipe the slate clean in an instant.

For such a price.

"Are you afraid?" he asked. He sat back in the gilded antique chair at his desk, a Louis XVI. He reached out and touched her hand. Electricity surged through him.

She flinched.

"Don't be," he said, letting his fingers fall from her hand and brush against her thigh. He imagined the heave of her delicious breasts underneath, the tautness of her nipples. "You are doing your father a great service. There, you would have nothing. And he would have been ruined. Here, you will have everything you need."

Here, Hassani thought with pride, was his home on one of the many private islands that had been reclaimed from the sand in Dubai. More of a palace than a home. Modeled after a Venetian palazzo on the Grand Canal. Like a Canaletto painting, of which he possessed two.

Desire and anticipation surged through him. Yes, he lived a complicated life. He had contacts all over the world. He had sold arms. Secrets. He had enabled those who had caused many deaths. In the prophet's name.

And yet he had also been a great friend to those in need—in the West. He had arranged financing for their most troubled banks. He was a conduit to the greatest wealth in the world, which these companies now needed. He was welcome in boardrooms across the globe. In government houses.

It was necessary to tread in both worlds in these times. To serve several masters. To keep a sense of balance.

And one of his many masters was the desire that rose up in his loins as he imagined the soft purr she would emit as he entered her before any others.

The way Hassani looked at it, he had sent many men on the path to countless virgins in paradise.

He was simply hedging his bet, as always.

He would take his here.

As he admired her, Hassani's cell phone rang. His attention was so complete, he barely heard it. He looked at the display, disappointed that it was a call he had to take. "I'm sorry." He sighed sadly. "I'll need you to wait outside."

He took the call, imagining the thought of running his hands underneath her robe. Hearing her cry out for the first time. Having her many times, until he dumped her back in her remote village, where she would be looked at as a whore.

"Hello," Hassani said, lifting the phone and staring across the bay at the majestic Dubai skyline.

"Just letting you know," the caller said in code, "that that matter of an old debt has been finally taken care of. But I fear there's another issue. The two bondholders have left."

"Left?"

"Another interested party, perhaps. Perhaps in London . . ."

"London," Hassani said sadly. That would be a shame. He loved that lad like a son.

"See if they make contact," the Bahraini said. "If they do, let me know."

Maybe the time had come to close up the loose ends.

It was a complicated time. You had to see things many ways. It was written in the book: destruction first before renewal.

His entertainment would have to wait.

Hassani looked at his watch. A Breguet masterpiece. One of a kind. This little problem had to be shared. With the next level. There were others involved. It was six P.M.—morning in New York. He should just be catching him at his desk.

He pressed the speed dial and waited.

"Hanni," his contact said when he picked up, six thousand miles across the globe.

Peter Simons. The CEO of Reynolds Reid.

PART IV

CHAPTER SIXTY-FIVE

They arrived at Heathrow midday Saturday.

This time Naomi had alerted a contact with Scotland Yard that she wanted to speak with a Saudi residing in London about his involvement in a case she was working on. The official asked if she needed any support while she was there and she said she would advise. She also registered her firearm with the authorities. The last people she wanted to piss off were the British government. They weren't in Serbia anymore.

She and Hauck booked rooms in a

boutique hotel in Kensington called Number 29, a reconverted row of town houses that Naomi had stayed in before. On the way, they had their taxi pass by Marty al-Bashir's home—a stately town house on Chesterfield Mews in Mayfair amid a quiet row of Georgian homes.

"There's number sixty there," the driver said, pointing out a three-story white façade with a roof terrace and coffered red door.

"Not exactly shabby," Hauck remarked as they passed. It looked as impressive as any on the street.

"Ought not to be," Naomi said. "This guy runs the largest investment fund in the world."

Leaving, they had to wind through the maze of one-way streets of charming, tree-lined homes, embassies, and hotels to get back to Knightsbridge, the main thoroughfare back to the hotel. They checked in. Naomi went upstairs to shower and call her boss. Hauck turned on the news and unpacked his Dopp kit and went into the bathroom to shave. He thought about calling Annie. He'd left only a single message on her machine from Novi Pazar to tell her he was okay. He checked the time and thought maybe she'd still be sleeping. Friday nights were always late ones at the café. He knew he had withheld quite a bit from her. About April, and why he was even here. There were things he'd have to answer to when he got back. He knew he was avoiding it.

The BBC news report talked about the fear of the world banking collapse. While they were in Serbia, Fannie Mae and Freddie Mac had gone under. The Fed would have to step in to bail them out. The insurance giant AIG was also said to be reeling. Not to mention JP Morgan and Reynolds Reid. All were selling for a fraction of what they had two months before.

The mood was darkening.

Around two, he and Naomi met back in the lobby for a coffee. Naomi told him what she knew about al-Bashir. "He's young. Smart. Western. Very media friendly. He's got an MBA from the University of Chicago. Did stints at Reynolds and Blackstone. You may have seen him on CNBC."

"I don't watch CNBC," Hauck said.

"Stick around. This afternoon may have a positive effect on you."

Hauck smiled, took a sip of his black coffee. "Do you know what you're going to do?"

Naomi nodded. "I talked to my boss. We're prepared to offer him a deal. We're going to take him in."

"You think he's really going to bite? People who live in homes like that usually don't cave in to the government without a fight."

"My guess is it'll beat where his *next* home might end up being." She put down her coffee and slung her case over her shoulder. "*Ready?*"

They took another cab back to Mayfair. Chesterfield Mews was a couple of blocks from Hyde Park. They got out a block away and waited on the street, keeping an eye on the posh white Georgian. Hauck looked around. It didn't appear anyone else was watching the house. They agreed that if they didn't see any signs of activity they would knock on the door.

It was important to catch al-Bashir off guard away from the office.

A short time later the front door opened. Naomi nudged Hauck to look. Two young boys stepped out onto the limestone land-ing. They had dark, Middle Eastern fea-tures and were maybe around seven and five. The older one had on a striped Man-chester United soccer jersey. The younger one was in a David Beckham T-shirt and sneakers. They could have been kids from anywhere. Following after them was an at-tractive thirtysomething woman in jeans, a baseball cap, and a hooded cashmere sweater. An expensive purse was slung over her shoulder.

She waited at the red door, holding it open. Soon after, a man came out dressed in khakis, a red knit shirt, and leather driv-ing moccasins. He had short, dark hair and wore wire-rim glasses. He held a soccer ball in one arm and the lead of a King Charles spaniel with the other.

He looked like any dad taking his wife and kids out on a Saturday-afternoon stroll.

Naomi nodded. "That's him."

CHAPTER SIXTY-SIX

The al-Bashirs walked a couple of blocks toward Park Lane. It looked like they were heading into the park. The dog pulled the dad along and the kids went ahead, the older one tossing the soccer ball.

Hauck and Naomi fell in behind them.

The mom taking her kids' hands, they crossed Park Lane, which was bustling with traffic, and headed into Hyde Park, London's largest. It was a beautiful weekend afternoon. The park was packed. Couples strolling or on blankets. Street musicians playing. Young couples with strollers. Kids kicking soccer balls around. Lots of dogs.

Al-Bashir and his family walked along the path. The older boy started to play keep-away with the soccer ball; the younger one whined. Their mom kept after them, urging them not to bother the pedestrians and take their game onto a field. Marty al-Bashir let the dog wander onto the grass, sniffing some others.

Hauck and Naomi followed about fifty yards behind.

At some point al-Bashir's cell phone rang, and he handed the spaniel off to his wife. The call took only a couple of minutes.

When he hung up, Naomi said to Hauck, "Let's go."

They went up to him just as he was about to rejoin his wife. "Marty al-Bashir?"

Surprised, he looked at Naomi. "Yes."

She took out her ID. "My name is Naomi Blum. I'm a federal agent with the U.S. Department of the Treasury. Would you mind if we talked?"

"Talked? *Here?*" He glanced at his wife, looking both confused and a little irritated. "It's a Saturday, Ms. Blum. I'm with my family. Why don't you call my office and—"

"It'll only take a few minutes," Naomi said.

"I'm sorry about the interruption. But I think it will be worth your while."

Hauck heard a bit of a tremor in her voice and knew Naomi had to be nervous. This was a big fish, and how she finessed the situation would mean everything.

"It concerns a friend of yours," she said. "Hassan ibn Hassani."

The annoyance in Marty al-Bashir's expression suddenly shifted to concern.

"I can come Monday with an agent from the Exchequer, if you like. But I don't see how that's preferable . . ."

One of the kids called out, "Dad, c'mon, see if you can score . . ."

"I'll just be a minute." He waved back. "Start without me."

His wife came over, a bit concerned. "Marty, is everything alright?"

"Of course everything's alright. These people just need to ask me a few questions. I'll be right along."

They moved down the path to a small grove of cherry trees, the Wellington Arch behind them. "Alright." He turned back, not hiding his annoyance. "You've got five minutes, Ms. Blum. What is it that couldn't wait until Monday?"

"This is Ty Hauck," she said. "He's a partner in a security firm in Greenwich, Connecticut."

Al-Bashir nodded dismissively, not offering his hand. *"Okay . . ."*

When it became clear that that was about as formal a greeting as they were going to get, Naomi said, "You know Mr. Hassani, do you not?"

"I don't know. I may. The name is familiar. What does it matter anyway?"

"To refresh your memory, Mr. Hassani is a native Bahraini who is a principal in a number of businesses. Among them a United Arab Emirates firm named Ascot Capital Partners. I believe you have some experience with them at your firm."

"Yes, yes, I know the firm." Al-Bashir rolled his hand impatiently, shifting his gaze back and forth from Hauck to Naomi, trying to read what was in their eyes. He glanced at his watch. "So what? Can't this wait?"

"You should be used to this kind of interruption to your weekends, Mr. al-Bashir." Naomi met his eyes. "It was on a Sunday, the eighth of February; you took a call from Mr. Hassani. From Dubai. The subject matter was all very vague, of course.

Investment strategies, the worrisome market . . ." She opened her satchel. "I happen to have a transcript of that conversation if it will help."

"I don't need a transcript," he snapped. "I still don't see the point. Mr. Hassani and I shared a business conversation. A private conversation, to be exact. How in the world are you in possession of—"

"Mr. Hassani is a person of interest for several matters related to U.S. national security," Naomi said, cutting him off and squinting at him. "And as such, unfortunately, Mr. al-Bashir, so are you."

The Saudi's eyes grew narrow. He took off his glasses. "I don't understand . . ."

She stared at him unflinchingly. Hauck was impressed. "Did you know Mr. Hassani was a figure who had attracted the attention of the United States government, Mr. al-Bashir?"

"No." The Saudi shifted on his feet. "I did not. He is also a person who has helped facilitate a six-billion mezzanine financing tier from the king of Bahrain for one of your largest banks."

"Mr. Hassani has also brokered sales of

weapons from Chechnya that have found their way to the Taliban in Pakistan. He has siphoned money for the Islamic American Cultural Foundation, a sham organization that has set up madrassas that train terrorists all over the world, some right here in Britain, and is on the terrorist watch list."

"Terrorist!" The Saudi blinked nervously. "I've done nothing wrong."

Al-Bashir's wife moved closer. "Marty, is everything alright?"

"Yes, everything's alright, Sheera," he snapped, his mood shifting. "Stay with the boys. I'll be there soon."

Naomi said, "Getting back to that conversation, Mr. al-Bashir, directly after it, you altered the investment strategy of your firm, did you not?"

"What do you mean I altered our investment strategy?"

"The very next day, Monday, February ninth, your fund began liquidating most of your financial interests in the United States markets. In fact, across the globe. Just to be clear, you'd call those interests *sizable,* would you not, sir?"

"Yes, of course, they're sizable. We're a significant fund. But whether or not you say it was a result of any conversation—"

"In fact, you began shorting the stock of many of the largest financial entities in the market. Citicorp, Goldman, Bank of America, AIG . . ."

"I'm not sure of the exact date."

"Lehman Brothers, Beeston . . . ," Naomi went on, her eyes locked on his shifting gaze. "Wertheimer Grant."

The Saudi's complexion grew pale.

"If you don't mind me asking, was Mr. Hassani some kind of partner in your firm, Mr. al-Bashir? Or one of the lead investors?"

"You seem to know very well who the partners are in my firm, Ms. Blum," the Saudi reacted with irritation.

"Just to be clear, sir, it's *Agent* Blum." She stared at him and continued. "But he *was* someone from whom you took investment advice?"

"No, I wouldn't say that. We were just two people discussing their views."

"Yet you immediately altered course after that conversation. *Why?*"

"I think this has gone far enough, Agent Blum. I suggest this may be something you would want to take up with our attorneys, if you're alleging there is something I've done wrong. Whatever it is you are trying to prove, it's not for this location or this time. I think your five minutes are up."

"I'm pretty sure this is something you would definitely *not* want me to run by your attorneys, Mr. al-Bashir. Do the names Marc Glassman and James Donovan mean anything to you?"

The Saudi blinked, now seeing where the conversation was leading. "I believe they were those two financial traders who died suddenly in the U.S. One was a home break-in. The other a suicide . . ."

"That's correct, Mr. al-Bashir," Naomi said, "except for one thing. There was no suicide. Mr. Hauck here has proved that. Both were murdered."

"I didn't know that," the Saudi said. He glanced uneasily at Hauck, concerned about where this was going.

Naomi pressed on. "That sudden shift in strategy certainly changed the price of a lot of stocks, didn't it, Mr. al-Bashir?"

He shrugged. "Anyone could see the financials were ready for a tumble. We were simply early on that one."

"Yes, they did tumble, didn't they, sir? Royal Saudi is one of the largest players in the market. Its support or withdrawal can move an entire sector, can it not? As it did."

"I think the verdict is already in on that one, Agent Blum. But I still don't know where you're going—"

"Where I'm *going,* Mr. al-Bashir"—Naomi's gray eyes fastened on him—"where the U.S. government is going, is that shortly after that shift in strategy, after their firms' stocks had already been cut by more than two-thirds in the past year, Mr. Glassman and Mr. Donovan were both murdered. After their deaths it was discovered each secretly had lost billions in trading and concealed those results from their firms, making their companies' balance sheets all the more fragile. These were considered the last straws, so to speak, in driving these firms into insolvency, *correct*?"

Al-Bashir nodded blankly.

"Dragging down the rest of the market, wouldn't you say? Like a chain of dominoes."

"Along with several other causes," al-Bashir replied. "You *have* heard the words 'subprime mortgage mess' at Treasury, haven't you? Or 'credit-default swaps'? Or maybe, 'reckless'?"

"Yes, they've come up. What if I could make the case, Mr. al-Bashir, that both Mr. Glassman and Mr. Donovan had been receiving substantial outside payments to commit such actions? And that those payments could be tied directly to Mr. Hassani? And, through another of his associates, tied to their murders as well?"

Al-Bashir's face knotted tighter. He put his glasses back on, his face pale. "I'm going to walk away now, Agent Blum. I think I've had enough of this."

"Before you do," Naomi said, "two more quick things. One, does the name Dani Thibault ring a bell with you?"

The Saudi blinked. Hauck kept his gaze on him, measuring his reaction.

Clearly, it did.

"And the second . . ." Naomi squinted. "If you don't mind answering, sir, just what did it mean, the parting phrase of your conversation with Mr. Hassani: 'The planes are in the air'?"

CHAPTER SIXTY-SEVEN

All at once, the defiance in Marty al-Bashir's face seemed to drain. The Saudi blinked, removed his glasses again. Trying to gather his composure. *"What?"*

Naomi had sucked him along like an expert prosecutor. Like a barracuda, Hauck thought with admiration, fixed on her prey. Hauck had seen this moment many times. The most hardened deniers begin to crack. Seemingly calm outside, but inside their brains revved frantically, trying to decide what to do. He couldn't have done it better himself.

"I think you heard me, Mr. al-Bashir."

Naomi continued to gaze at him, knowing she had set him back. "What did it mean when Mr. Hassani said to you, 'The planes are in the air'?"

"It meant nothing." The Saudi cleared his throat and glared at her. He was an investment manager, hardly used to having to defend himself this way. "It was simply a phrase. A business conversation between two professionals. Mr. Hassani is a well-known figure. He has facilitated a mezzanine financing tier for Reynolds Reid with the Bahraini royal family, for God's sake."

"Then it shouldn't be an issue to you if I share the transcript of that phone conversation with your employers, the Saudi royal family," Naomi said, sensing the kill.

"*Look . . .*" The young investment manager shook his head, seeing the arc of his life falling apart.

"Your career is over, Mr. al-Bashir. You conspired with a person who has known terrorist ties to defraud the already shaky world financial markets. You've made billions of dollars illegally. Investment managers were lured to commit financial fraud against their banks and take those firms over the edge. At best, it's a conspiracy to manipulate the markets. At worst, it's an act of terrorism, adjudicable under Homeland Security laws. Regardless, Mr. al-Bashir, when do you think is the next time we can expect to see your face on CNBC?

"Not to mention," Naomi continued to look at him without letting him respond, "that as a result of this, four innocent people have been murdered."

Al-Bashir's color drained. He glanced toward his wife, who now was looking at him with concern, then took a few steps farther along the path, away from his family. He spoke back in a hushed tone, almost a whisper, but with a measure of desperation in it. "What is it you want from me, Agent Blum?"

"I want to know what was behind that phone call, Mr. al-Bashir, and how it ties into a plot to recruit Marc Glassman and James Donovan in an effort to destabilize the United States economy. The United States government wants to know."

"I had nothing to do with any of that. All I did was merely shift our portfolio."

"Oh, I think you *did* have something very much to do with that, Mr. al-Bashir. I think you had something to do with it the minute you bedded down with individuals like this. But unfortunately"—Naomi shrugged and inhaled a breath—"that's not even your biggest problem right now."

He cleared his throat and adjusted his glasses. "What are you talking about?"

Naomi glanced over at the Saudi's wife, now huddled with her boys, clearly worried about what was going on. "You have a lovely family, Mr. al-Bashir. I'm sure, like any husband and father, you would do whatever you could to keep them from harm."

The Saudi's gaze darkened. "What are you talking about?"

"Dani Thibault was murdered yesterday. He was shot, execution style. In Serbia. In a remote village we had traced him to. Thibault had recruited Glassman and Donovan with a series of payments that we can tie to Mr. Hassani. We believe his death was ordered by Mr. Hassani, to cover it up."

Al-Bashir's cheeks twitched. He swallowed and did his best to sound bold. "I still don't know what that has to do with me, Agent Blum."

"Well, it's this: All the players in this plot,

Mr. al-Bashir, are dead. Glassman, Donovan, now Thibault. All but one, Mr. al-
Bashir . . . ," Naomi said, staring at him.
"*You.* Puts a whole new meaning to the
word, 'reckless,' doesn't it, sir?"

"*Listen,*" the Saudi said, sweat on his
brow, "I sold stocks, that's all. That's the
extent of what I did. I adjusted our positions, as any money manager might do.
That happens as a matter of course many
times in a year. There's not a jury in the
world that would convict me of anything
illegal. There's nothing, nothing at all, to
connect me to any of these horrible crimes."

Hauck finally intervened. "This has nothing at all to do with any jury, Mr. al-Bashir.
This woman is trying to save your life. Your
family's life. Don't you understand?"

The Saudi glared back at him, about to
challenge him. But the fight seemed to go
out of him.

Naomi took his arm. "If I wanted to have
you arrested, we'd already be having this
conversation in a cell, Mr. al-Bashir. You
have no way out. You've put yourself and
your family at great risk. But what you *don't*
want," she said, her tone softening, "is for

there to be no way out and for you to end up dead."

A cast of recognition settled over the Saudi investment manager's face. He grew sullen. He ran his hand through his hair and glanced, seemingly out of answers, toward his wife and kids.

"What if I just walk away? Do nothing?"

"Then *I'll* do nothing." Naomi shrugged. "Other than maybe make sure that the transcript of that conversation I referred to gets in the hands of your employers. They may not feel the same way, I suspect, when it comes to how their investments are being handled. We'll also let it be known that we had this conversation. About Mr. Hassani. Considering what just happened to Mr. Thibault, are you really willing to take that chance?"

The Saudi wiped his mouth. He released a long, deflating breath as the full measure of his predicament seemed to fall on him.

"I'm giving you a way out, Mr. al-Bashir. In our protective custody. For your cooperation. You can hold on to the majority of your assets. Those that were rightfully earned. But what we want to know, sir, is what was the extent of this plot? Who was involved? Where does it lead?"

He shook his head. "I need time."

"You have no time, sir. Go back home. Talk it over. I've arranged a car from Scotland Yard to be stationed outside your house. I'm sorry for all this, sir, but the time to answer is now."

CHAPTER SIXTY-EIGHT

Behind the closed doors of their study, Sheera looked at her husband, aghast.

He had told her everything. How his roots with Hassani went back many years. To when he was a young student. Not even in the U.S. At the university in Riyadh. How they had singled him out. Educated him. Groomed him. For a purpose. For one day.

How his sensibilities had been so different back then.

"How could you possibly have gotten in with people like this?" His wife tearfully shook her head.

"I never thought about them for twenty years," al-Bashir said. "It was before I went to the U.S. Before I met you. As time passed, I thought they had forgotten the debts. I thought life had let me be free of them."

"These types of debts are never forgotten. Life will never let you be free of them." Sheera sat forlornly on the couch. She looked at him, something angry and judgmental in her eyes. "You should have refused, Marty. You should have gone to the police."

"They would have killed me, Sheera, if I didn't comply."

"And they will kill you now that you have."

He wanted to go over and sit next to her, his wife for all these years, the most treasured thing in his life. But he was sure she would just pull away. This had drawn a line between them. Maybe forever. "I'm so sorry. We'll get to keep much of what we have. I know what it is to give this up."

"To give this up?" She lifted her eyes and regarded him as if she was horrified. "You think for one second this is what I care about giving up? *This house?* Your fancy position? The things it has brought

us?" From out in the hall, they heard the sounds of their boys playing. "It's *them*. Amir and Ghassan. It's *their* lives that matter to me. Will they now be targets? Will we live in fear the rest of our lives? Wherever we are . . . These are debts that don't get forgiven, Marty."

He glanced, empty of all hope, out the window. There was an unmarked car parked across the quiet street. "I'll call Arthur," he said, closing the drape. Their lawyer. "He can arrange some kind of deal."

"It's not about lawyers, Marty. Not this time." She picked up one of Amir's Transformer robots from the floor. She smiled and looked up at him. Resigned. Even forgiving. Tears flooding Sheera's eyes, she held out the toy. "I think we made our choices long ago."

Marty al-Bashir nodded. Tears in his eyes too. Tears of shame. Of fading hope for them. "We did, didn't we, Sheera."

CHAPTER SIXTY-NINE

Annie Fletcher picked out the set of spare keys to Ty's house from where she knew he always left them, along the side of the house behind some flower tubs in a fake rock. She went up the stairs and let herself in.

The alarm signal beeped. She pressed in the code, 70794.

His daughter Jessie's birthday.

Annie knew he wouldn't mind. She'd let herself in many times before. The place looked clean and smelled fresh. It was a Saturday, and Elena, his cleaning lady,

would have been in the day before. She
was trying to find her gold hoop earrings, which were missing. She seemed to
remember last leaving them on his night
table when she'd stayed over a few nights
before.

Before there suddenly seemed to be a
widening gulf between them.

Maybe it had first begun with the attack
on Jared. Ty had said maybe it was best if
they kept apart for a while, for her safety,
but Annie somehow felt that was Ty being
Ty, maybe not wanting to face the truth,
being noble. Or maybe, if she was honest,
it had started some time well before. Maybe
it went back to when they woke up in bed
that Monday to the newscast of that family
who was killed in town.

I knew her, he had said.

It was like something had changed in
him since then.

She'd never pried. She'd never asked
how. Or why. Never pushed him. That
wasn't her style. The last thing Annie would
ever want was for someone to say that she
was clingy. After all, they'd both agreed to
keep things light.

From around town, he had told her. That was enough for her. He didn't have to share everything with her. Though she may, in truth, have hoped that he would. She held a lot of things in herself—she'd left her own son out west until she could make a place for him here—and the truth was, while maybe she had fallen in love with Ty, just a bit, they weren't exactly engaged.

He'd been away for four days, and she'd barely heard from him in that time. He said it was best that she didn't know where he was going. But she had a clue. She had asked him, *What are you getting involved in, Ty?*

She had wanted to say, *Okay, you don't have to justify it with me,* but in her heart, she worried. Worried something had happened. Somewhere. She worried he was getting himself into something over his head. He did that.

She worried something might have come between them. Something she couldn't fight. Or even understand.

She went into the kitchen. Unable to help herself—*what was it?*—she put away a few dishes that Elena had left on the counter to

dry. She almost tripped over a pair of running shoes. Then she went upstairs.

In the bedroom, she went over to the
night table on the side of the bed she usually slept on, looking for her hoops. *Damn.*
There was nothing on top. Where she
thought they might be. Just a picture of
Jessie and his boat, which Ty had just gotten out of dry dock—the *Merrily.*

She opened the drawer.

Nothing again. She sighed in disappointment. She had been sure they were
there.

The room gave off an eerie feeling; it
looked just like it had the last time she'd
been there, a couple of nights before he'd
left. They hadn't made love that night.
She'd felt something, distant, growing, separating them. And now he was gone.

Maybe it was just a stupid feeling.
C'mon, Annie, what are you, ten?

It suddenly hit her that she should check
on his dresser. There was a messy pile of
photos, credit card receipts. Mail. Bills.
Whatever came in, that's where Ty threw
it! If she didn't want to intrude on his space,
she would have organized it a hundred
times.

In an ashtray, along with some loose change, were her gold hoops.

Hooray!

Annie wrapped them in a tissue and put them in her jacket. She was about to leave when something on the dresser caught her eye.

A voice inside her said to leave it alone. *It's Ty's. Snooping's not allowed.* Another little voice urged her to take a look.

It was a photo. Left under the ashtray. Annie picked it up.

Her heart sank at what she saw.

Not so much because of who it was—it was a long time ago, and somehow, inside, she'd always had her suspicions.

As much as it was their relationship drifting away.

Her trust.

The photo was of Ty, smiling, a look on his face she had never seen when he was with her. On a bench. In a park. Other people around.

And next to him someone she recognized. Her head on his shoulder. Her hands wrapped around his arm. It didn't make Annie jealous.

As much as it just hurt.

The woman's face had been burned into her mind since the first day she saw it. On the TV. It was the one who had been killed. At that house.

April Glassman.

CHAPTER SEVENTY

The car that came to take al-Bashir and his family into custody arrived at just before nine the next morning.

Overnight, Naomi had been on the phone with her team back in DC. The plan was to get him to a safe house in the country, where he would be debriefed by Naomi and representatives from the British government, then flown out of the country. They needed to do this quickly and without notice, before Hassani or anyone else could intervene.

Hauck and Naomi arrived at the house in Mayfair a half hour early. An unmarked car from Scotland Yard was stationed across the square, having watched over al-Bashir's house during the night. Otherwise, the street was empty. Like any quiet Sunday morning. Robins chirped in the trees. One or two families stepped out, dressed up, on their way to church.

The fewer people involved, the better.

Naomi flashed her ID by the two policemen in the car. Then she went up the stairs and knocked on the red paneled door. Hauck stayed on the steps, watching the square. A few houses down, a mother was dragging her cranky, whining son into the family BMW 330i for what seemed like a Sunday outing.

Sheera al-Bashir answered the door. She was dressed in a black blazer and designer jeans. It was hard, Hauck thought, not to feel sadness for her and her family. They had done nothing wrong. She could have been any modern, attractive young mom, dragged into a whirlwind in just a day. Now everything was about to change for them. Until Hassani was in custody—and maybe even well beyond that—they would always have to live in fear that people would find them.

Naomi smiled at her as best she could and glanced at her watch. "The car should be here anytime. Are you ready?"

"Shortly," Sheera al-Bashir replied. She didn't have any makeup on and her eyes looked drawn from a very difficult night. She managed a reluctant smile. "We're just packing up a few of the boys' toys."

Naomi nodded. "Sure."

Fifteen minutes. Naomi came over and sat next to Hauck, smiling, partly philosophically, acknowledging that there were no winners in this kind of thing, and partly with a glimmer of satisfaction that they would finally be able to get to the truth. People plotting against the United States. And who was behind the murders of Marc Glassman and James Donovan?

"You did *good*." Hauck winked, proud.

"Thanks." She exhaled nervously, as if there was some small detail she hadn't checked. Or double-checked. But there wasn't.

"Quite the three days, huh?" He grinned. "Be sure and let me know when you're planning your next vacation."

"I'll do that," Naomi said, with a smirk.

"The south of France would be nice. If there's ever anything going on there . . ."

She glanced at her watch again. "Maybe I should check in with my contact at the Exchequer . . ."

"Relax," Hauck said with a squeeze of her arm.

Then she pointed up the block. "There it is."

A black Mercedes SUV with darkened windows had come into the mew from the direction of Knightsbridge. It drove around the square and pulled to a stop in front of the house.

Naomi was relieved.

The driver's window rolled down. One of the police guards stepped out of the car and checked the driver's ID. He nodded in confirmation up at Naomi.

She sucked in a breath. "Let's get this done." She went up and knocked on the door again. This time a housekeeper answered. "The car's here."

A short time later the door opened back up and Sheera came back out, a tote bag over her shoulder, clasping the hands of her two young sons. The little one was still in his pj's and obviously had been crying, forced to leave his home. He clutched a stuffed bear. A few suitcases were dragged out to the doorstep. A second agent jumped out of the Mercedes. He looked up and down the street, then quickly went up the stairs, taking the bags, and loaded them into the back of the SUV.

"Don't forget the ski bag," Sheera said, pointing back inside. "It has some things for the kids in it."

The agent nodded agreeably. "We should have room, ma'am."

Seconds later, Marty al-Bashir came out onto the steps. He was dressed in an open plaid shirt, blazer, khakis. A bulletproof vest he had been given the night before. The second agent put himself in the line of fire. Al-Bashir's demeanor was sullen and resigned. Yesterday, he had been running the largest investment fund in the world. Today, his fate was in the state's hands. A computer case was slung over his shoulder. He stepped up to Naomi. "Can you tell us where we're going?"

"You should hurry," she said. The agent stowed the last case in the trunk. Al-Bashir followed him down. "Everything will be made clear on the way."

Before he got in, he looked at Naomi with a final, deflated smile. "You called it 'jihad,'" he said. "It was never about terrorism. You'll see. This was much larger than terrorism."

Naomi pushed him into the car. "You better get on."

He climbed into the backseat next to his wife. The accompanying agent shut the door, waved officiously to the policemen. He hopped in front, and then, without a siren, as if it were just a normal limo on its way to the airport, the Mercedes circled the mew and drove off through the grid of one-way streets back out to the main road.

It was done.

As it drove away, Hauck caught sight of the face of their youngest boy through the rear window, turning back a final time, grabbing one last look at his home.

Naomi exhaled. "That wasn't exactly easy." She nudged Hauck and they headed back down the street to their cab.

"Never is."

His role was over now. She and the Feds

would take it from here. He'd probably head back to the States that afternoon. He had a life to resume and a lot of things to explain.

Naomi's cell phone rang. She checked out the display, saying to Hauck, "My contact at the Exchequer . . ."

She listened, then stopped, her face suddenly turning ashen. She looked back at Hauck, the blood rushing out of her face.

"What's wrong?"

Naomi's jaw fell open. "She said the government's Range Rover is close by. It'll be here in three minutes."

Hauck's heart stopped. He ran into the street, straining to find the black Mercedes moving away up the block.

He caught only the rear taillights as it disappeared around the corner.

CHAPTER SEVENTY-ONE

That wasn't them! That wasn't them!"

Naomi sprinted over to the detectives from Scotland Yard. "It wasn't them. *The car was bogus.* Did anyone get a look at the plates?"

The two policemen looked at them, completely stunned. Then they jumped in their car, one with his cell phone out, the other spinning it around, siren beeping, and took off after the Mercedes.

Naomi started in after.

"No." Hauck grabbed her by the arm. He remembered the maze of one-way streets that led out to Park Lane. The SUV could be on any of them. "Come with me!" He pulled her in the other direction. *"This way!"*

He took off in the opposite direction, Naomi running a stride behind. Toward Hyde Park, out of the quiet mews. How could this have happened? Everything had been tightly controlled. Only insiders knew. It was like with Thibault all over again. He just knew they had to get to that car before it disappeared into traffic. Or they'd never see the al-Bashir family again.

They shot around the corner. It led to a short residential row of Georgians that intersected Chesterfield on the diagonal. Mayfair Terrace. Hauck stopped, frantically tried to reconstruct the labyrinth of streets and squares and how they led back onto the main road. He realized he had only minutes. He pointed toward a street. *"Down here!"*

They ran down it, his pulse on overdrive, as if his own daughter was in that car.

Naomi took out her gun. She kept up stride for stride. They got to the end of the street. It led to two more streets, each splitting off in a different direction. Hauck had no idea where they led. He scanned both ways, trying to calculate where the Mercedes would have to intersect back with Park Lane.

Naomi looked in both directions, white with fear. "We can't lose them, Ty!"

"Down here!" He chose left and prayed. The street was like a replica of Chesterfield Mews. More expensive homes. There was a fancy, small hotel across the street. Ahead of them a family stepped out on the sidewalk with a stroller. *"Federal agents,"* Naomi yelled, almost barreling into them as they ran by.

At the corner they both stopped, looked around in frustration. "Are you sure?"

"No," he said. He scanned around frantically for some sign of the car. *"I'm not sure!"*

He didn't see it! He knew they had only about a minute to find the car, maybe seconds, and then it would disappear into traffic. There could be dozens of black Mercedes SUVs around the city.

Without a read on the plates, they could be anywhere.

His heart was pounding.

His gaze turned to a small street that cut off on a diagonal in the direction of Park Lane, a church on the corner. His instincts said go. The bell was tolling. People milled around in front. Past them, Hauck could see that it seemed to connect with a larger street up ahead. He spotted traffic, people crossing by.

Naomi took off ahead of him. *"Up here!"*

This was going to be their one and only chance. He took off, praying what they saw up ahead was Park Lane. Praying even harder the Mercedes hadn't gotten there first. He recalled how they had to weave around through the grid to get out of there earlier. Sweat was coming through his clothes, soaking him.

He caught up to Naomi as they neared the end. They both came to a stop, huffing. The lane fed into the main thoroughfare. *Thank God.* The Mercedes would have to have come through here. It had to wind around. That's what they had done the day before. But there could have been many ways out of the mews.

"This is it!"

They got to the corner, praying they

weren't too late. Feverishly, they looked around in every direction.

Naomi shook her head in frustration. "I don't see it! *Damn it,* where is it, Ty?"

Then, about a block ahead, he caught sight of the front grille of a black vehicle, about to turn, pulled up at a light.

It was his only option. He ran toward it.

The car turned onto Park Lane. A Mercedes SUV.

His heart sprang with hope. *"There it is!"*

He sprinted after it, praying it was the same vehicle. Naomi kept up a couple of lengths behind.

There was no sight of the Scotland Yard car. They ran into the middle of the busy street, dodging through traffic. A cabbie stopped and angrily blew his horn at Hauck.

The distance between them and the black Mercedes began to narrow. *Please, be it,* Hauck begged.

Park Lane was a bustling thoroughfare. Six lanes. People everywhere. Obstructing them.

Hyde Park was to their right. Up ahead, the Mercedes pulled up at an intersection.

Onto Piccadilly. It had its signal on, about to turn. Piccadilly was a long, traffic-free straightaway.

This was their only chance.

Holding up his palms, knifing in between oncoming cars, Hauck ran across the street. His lungs were bursting now as he pursued as fast as he could.

Naomi stayed right with him. "Get there before it turns, Ty . . ."

Hauck ran through the middle of the crowded street, searching for a policeman but not seeing one. A car pulled out from behind the Mercedes's lane and now they had a clear shot.

Thirty yards ahead.

Twenty. The vehicle in front of the Mercedes made its turn.

The Mercedes lurched. *They were out of time.*

Hauck heard Naomi's voice shout from behind. *"Get out of the way!"* She stopped and kneeled into a shooting position. She had a clear shot, no pedestrians in front of them.

She extended her gun.

She squeezed off three quick shots, aiming for the Mercedes's tires.

Two skidded off the asphalt; the third clanged uselessly into the underbelly of the vehicle.

None of them seemed to find its mark.

"Shit!"

Suddenly people everywhere began to scream.

The Mercedes's tires screeched and the vehicle jerked into a sharp turn. It forced its way through the onrushing traffic. Hauck chased it in the oncoming lane, ten yards behind.

Five.

Damn it—it was turning. Naomi's shots hadn't struck home.

In his one last chance, just as the vehicle jolted forward, he dove.

He felt his hands scratch against the driver's-side rear window, then make contact with the door. He clung desperately to hold on to the metal handle. He squeezed, trying to open it, his only hope.

The sonovabitch was locked.

The SUV sped up on Piccadilly, starting to pull away.

Hauck held on, one hand on the handle, his other groping for the luggage rack above. His feet dangled against the pavement as he was dragged along. He caught a view of the startled family inside— Marty, his wife—suddenly realizing what was happening to them. Screaming at the driver. Somehow Hauck had to pry the door open.

He had to stop this car.

The vehicle picked up speed and wove between lanes in an effort to shake him off. If he could just get his other hand on the luggage rack, he could stay on. Some- one would have to see them. A policeman. See what was going on.

Stop them.

His heart bursting through his chest, he lunged with both hands for the rack. The Mercedes lurched to the side with a jerk. He tried to pull himself up, every muscle in his body straining. *Hold it, Ty . . . Now, just a second more . . .*

The SUV jerked to the right. His fingers slid off. *No . . .*

He hit the road, screaming inside.

The Mercedes accelerated sharply along the straightaway, no traffic to obstruct it now.

Helpless, Hauck watched it drive away,

prone. He sank his head against his arm, mashing his fist into the road.

The frightened face of al-Bashir's youngest son looked back through the darkened window as it sped away.

CHAPTER SEVENTY-TWO

Empty, dejected, Hauck found his way back to Naomi, who was waiting, ashen faced, at the corner of the park.

He shook his head. "I'm sorry." He wiped off his clothes and looked at his hands, which were imprinted with deep, red marks from his attempt to hold on to the car.

Her eyes glistened with tears of blame and disbelief, and she gritted her teeth. "We lost them, Ty."

"Not entirely. I got the plates. HZ-36PAB. We can track them." London had the most advanced network of street surveillance cameras in the world. That gave a ray of hope. One might pick them up.

Suddenly, they heard the clamor of sirens wailing everywhere. Police vans screeched to a halt around them. Uniformed security personnel ran up, weapons drawn.

"Here's trouble," Hauck said.

They both put up their hands, Naomi flashing her ID, identifying herself as a U.S. government agent.

"Get down on your knees!" a security agent in riot gear shouted in her face, thrusting a submachine gun at them. "Put your hands in the air!"

"We're United States government agents," Naomi declared, getting down, holding up her ID. Hauck did the same. Police were screaming at them like they were terrorists and he understood. Lights flashed everywhere. On the sidewalks, a ring of bystanders had formed. "We were chasing a suspect who kidnapped a government witness—"

"Put up your hands!"

It took a full ten minutes and two phone calls to the authorities before they finally let them go.

Naomi pulled out her cell and frantically called her contact at MI5. He said a full alert for the black Mercedes was already under way. Ten minutes too late, she read him the plate number.

Then she called her boss at Treasury. It was four in the morning back in DC. He seemed to be waiting. She desperately pushed back her hair and, pacing, gave him the bad news. Hauck could almost hear him barking through the phone. He could feel Naomi's bitter frustration.

"How the hell could anyone have known, Rob? *How?*"

Finally, she said she'd keep him informed. They clicked off, and for a second, all Naomi could do was just stand there numbly, the hopelessness of the situation becoming clear. Al-Bashir was gone. He had been their last real lead. Without him they had nothing—nothing to tie in Hassani. All the elation of what minutes before had seemed a successful completion to their mission had now turned into anguish and self-reproach.

"Maybe the cameras will pick them up," Hauck said, putting his arm around her shoulders, trying to comfort her.

She spun out of his grasp, slapping her palm with force against a nearby light post. Staring out at the police lights, the gathered crowd, the long straightaway that led away from the park, she shook her head in rage. *"They're gone, Ty . . ."*

CHAPTER SEVENTY-THREE

By the time they made it back to al-Bashir's town house, a throng of police and investigative officials were already on the scene.

The housekeeper let them in.

Over half an hour had passed. There had been no report of any sightings of the Mercedes. That wasn't a good sign. Hauck knew whoever had taken them would have had a plan. They would have known the security cam situation better than anyone. Even if the vehicle turned up, the more time elapsed, the less it boded well for the al-Bashirs.

Naomi did her best to hold it together and oversee the scene. But inside, Hauck saw, she was dying. She was on the phone back to DC, to British security. They had set up a coordinated local command—traffic police, Scotland Yard. The counterterrorism unit, SO15. Every passing minute throbbed with tension. It only made their likely fate more clear.

At some point, the grim finality setting in, Naomi stepped outside. She was a desk agent, not a field supervisor; this was her big case, and the pressure of losing the al-Bashirs, seeing them whisked away in front of their eyes, even being party to it, was a hard one to take. Even for a seasoned agent.

Hauck gave her a few moments alone, then went out after her. He found her on the landing, staring blankly at the square, her eyes moist and her fists clenched. She tapped them against the limestone railing in frustration.

"They were my responsibility, Ty."

He went up and put his hand on her shoulder. "No, it was al-Bashir who was responsible for whatever happened to him, not you. He was a dead man the minute he got into bed with these people. You did everything you could."

"I keep seeing that kid," she said, her teeth clenched. "It's like that one in Iraq all over again. Looking back at us through the rear window. You saw it too, didn't you?"

"Yeah," Hauck said. He pulled her toward him and she sank against his chest. "I saw it."

"He was mine to protect, Ty. That kid didn't do anything wrong. They were mine."

Tears dampened his shirt. He squeezed her close. Hauck, whose own dreams were haunted by many such faces and scenes, did his best to make her feel it was okay. He remembered how she had told him about the boy with the open chest in Iraq, who she tried so hard to breathe life back into after the ambush. He stroked the back of her hair.

"I'm sorry." She sniffed back guilty tears. "I know this isn't exactly out of the procedure manual. I've been in combat, for chrissakes . . ."

"Don't worry about the manual," Hauck said, letting her stay. "It's in my manual. It's okay."

Finally, Naomi pulled back and looked up at him, nodding.

"You're still in charge." He winked. "With me."

She smiled a bit and cleared her throat. "Thanks." She turned back to the house and wiped away the tears. "There's got to be something here . . . Al-Bashir took his computer. But he had to leave something behind." She seemed to say it more out of a need to believe it than out of any actual hope. She sucked in a deep breath. "I have to *do* something, Ty."

"I know."

They went back inside. The lavish house was decorated as if money was no object. Beautiful moldings. Ornate rugs. Polished antique tables. Each room bore the mark of the family that had just disappeared. Naomi kept checking her watch, calling central command, hoping they'd hear some word.

It was like the SUV had just disappeared.

More in desperation than anything, they both started searching throughout the house. The dining room on the second floor, with a view of the park. There was a modern media room. A huge Sony screen built into the walnut bookshelves. Reminders of the family were everywhere—photos, clothing they had elected not to take, the kids' games and toys.

While Hauck spoke with one of the inspectors, Naomi found the investment manager's study. The large cherry desk was piled high with fund brochures, old copies of the *Financial Times* and *Forbes*. Reams of annual reports and analysts' opinions. Naomi was able to access his desktop computer. The password was simple. *Sheera.* Mostly, what was there was all personal. Gmail messaging and various investment sites. She reconstructed a history of al-Bashir's most recent Google searches. Wine buying, travel sites. All perfectly legit. Naomi pushed away from the desk in frustration.

Whatever al-Bashir had that might have incriminated Hassani was lost on his laptop.

It had been an hour now. No word. She searched the drawers for some kind of flash drive, anything he might have downloaded that could've been left behind.

Nothing. Her heart beat with the realization that now there was not much hope.

Desperate, she leafed randomly through the piles of papers stacked about.

Again, nothing.

Nothing related to Thibault or Hassani or Ascot. Nothing on Donovan or Glassman. Or on any matter connected to al-Bashir's involvement in the case.

She wheeled back from the desk, riddled with anger. She'd felt so close to making a case against Hassani—*al-Bashir had basically admitted it*! Now, how would she make him answer for what he'd done? Six people were dead. Now you could add to the list the al-Bashirs. Never before had she wanted to prove something as badly as she wanted to implicate Hassani. She felt the same sense of drive and intensity as when she'd seen her brother in the hospital after he lost both his legs and she enlisted herself the very next day.

Find something, Naomi. Find something! It's here . . .

Within hours, British government agents would be plowing through every inch of this room. Every sliver of RAM on his computers. She got up and walked around. *It's here. I feel it.* Her blood was hot with blame. This was her case. She had felt the whole thing from the start. Now she had screwed up. She didn't want to lose it. *Not now.*

She spotted a kid's Transformer on the carpet. Sadly, Naomi picked it up. She held the toy in her hand, her mind flashing through a hundred scenarios. Out of answers, she sank back on al-Bashir's couch.

She put the toy on the glass coffee table.

Something met her eye.

It hit home immediately, a spark of hope, recognition, firing up inside. *Can't be.*

She reached forward. There was a stack of art and coffee table books on the glass tabletop. One was from the New Tate Museum. Another was on the Gauguin and Picasso exhibition from a couple of years ago. Naomi had seen it in DC.

But it was the third book, underneath, that, like some kind of superconducting magnet, held her stare.

Yes, it can.

Naomi removed it from the pile. It was a travel book, about a destination the al-Bashirs might have once visited.

The thing was, she had seen the very same destination just two days before.

On the ski-lift ticket at Dani Thibault's farmhouse. In Serbia.

She fixed on the cover. A snowcapped mountain rising from a valley bathed in amber light. It couldn't be a coincidence. At this stage, there were no coincidences. Her heart started to beat like crazy. She had found it. She had found the link that bound them together.

Gstaad.

CHAPTER SEVENTY-FOUR

Naomi motioned Hauck inside with a con-cealed wave, closing the door behind him. She showed him what she had found.

"Two days ago," she explained. Her voice was hushed yet driven with renewed emo-tion. "In Thibault's farmhouse. I didn't think it meant anything. Just one of the things I found searching through his possessions. A ski-lift ticket." Naomi's eyes twinkled. *"To Gstaad."*

"Okay." Hauck nodded, picking up the book and staring at the cover.

"It's a ski resort," Naomi said. "In Swit-zerland."

"I know it's a ski resort," Hauck replied.

"Sorry. Just check out what's inside."

He leafed through the glossy pages. It was filled with scenic photos of ski runs, the snow-covered mountains in winter, and in summer, the picturesque village. He found a bookmark inside. On the high-lighted page, one side had a description of one of the resort's most treacherous runs, the Chute; the other had a shot of beautiful people in expensive ski clothes sunning themselves on a deck at lunch. At a fash-ionable restaurant, high on the mountain.

Christina's.

In the margin, someone had scrawled some words. Maybe al-Bashir. Hauck tried to make it out.

"It says, 'The Gstaad Gang,'" said Naomi, who already had.

"The Gstaad Gang?"

"Something took place there." Naomi's eyes were bright. "This isn't just some tourist book. Thibault and al-Bashir, both there. It can't just be a coincidence. What do you want to bet Hassani's been to Gstaad too?"

Hauck looked at the book. He felt it too. The throbbing in his chest. "What we have to find out is when al-Bashir might have been there and see if Hassani was there at the same time."

"We can do better than that," Naomi said. "Lift tickets have dates on them."

"If we happened to have it," Hauck agreed.

"We do. It's in my camera." She lit up in a grin. "I photographed everything there."

Her face now shone with renewed purpose. If they could connect everyone there at the same time, they might have a reason to go at Hassani. He'd be a slippery one to latch on to, maybe protected by the Bahraini or Emirates government, but this was the best they had.

"We can track his movements through immigration," Naomi said. "Through credit card records."

She was right. No way this was just a coincidence. Something *had* happened there. Between Thibault and al-Bashir. And maybe Hassani. He stared at the hand-scrawled margin note. Underlined. A surge of optimism coursed through Hauck as well.

The Gstaad Gang.

"Who knew about this?" he asked Naomi.

"I'm talking about the arrangements around al-Bashir."

She shrugged. "Gavin Toller of MI5. Linda Maxwell, my counterpart at the office of the Exchequer." Britain's treasury department. "Obviously, it was passed along to the police."

"Who else?" Hauck asked, his gaze fixed on her. He meant back home.

"Rob Whyte, my boss. I'm sure he ran it up the line. Just what are you saying, Ty?"

"I don't know what I'm saying. Except that someone knew Thibault was Kostavic and in Novi Pazar, which was something we fell upon only by accident. Now al-Bashir . . . I have a suggestion, Naomi. Actually, it's not so much a suggestion as it is something that would be really, really smart and might end up keeping us alive."

"What's that?" Naomi asked, her look darkening.

"Until we find out where this goes"— Hauck held the Gstaad book in his hand— "don't call this in."

PART V

PART V

Hassan ibn Hassani passed through customs at JFK and found the private limo driver waiting for him in the terminal.

His private security man followed a step behind.

The driver took Hassani's expensive Hermès carry-on, exchanging the usual pleasantries about the trip with him. Hassani had used the man before. He led them quickly to the custom BMW 750i, which was permitted to wait for him at the curb, the security man hopping in front. They drove into the city.

As the car navigated the bumper-to-bumper traffic along the Van Wyck Expressway, Hassani got on the phone. He was here, principally, as a representative of the Bahraini royal family's interests, for the annual meeting and the preceding board meeting of Reynolds Reid. A year ago the sultan had made a six-billion-dollar mezzanine investment in the ailing firm, which converted, if needed, to almost 7 percent of the company. That was eighteen points ago on the stock. The sultan's six billion was now worth less than half that.

But Hassani knew that was about to change.

It would change because Reynolds Reid was clearly going to be one of the survivors in the world financial collapse. Not simply a survivor but a clear winner. When the world calmed, it would be more powerful than ever. And now, with a place at the table, who would be better set to represent their country's vested interests?

One just had to have patience, Hassani knew. As well as take the long view.

This was a twenty-first-century kind of jihad.

Apart from Reynolds, Hassani also had

other affairs to attend to in the States. He had legitimate business interests there and in Canada. And various other matters not so transparent. There were Islamic cultural organizations, religious freedom groups that funneled money from back home into mosques and Islamic communities in upstate New York.

That reflected the other side of his causes as well.

He found his mind wandering and he stroked his goatee, his thoughts flashing back to Sera, his new treasure back in Dubai. How sad he was to have to leave her behind. But he had to focus on other things here.

The car went through the tunnel into Manhattan and then wound its way up Park Avenue to the Waldorf Astoria, where Hassani had the six-room Roosevelt Suite, which was sometimes home to visiting heads of state. He told the driver and the security man to wait while he was shown around his quarters, quickly showered and changed, put on his Brioni pinstripe suit, custom-made Turnbull and Asser shirt, and a yellow Alan Flusser tie. In half an hour he was back downstairs, totally refreshed.

He decided he would walk and told the driver he could pick him up again in two hours' time. He was heading to 457 Park, on Fifty-fourth Street. The tall glass headquarters of Reynolds Reid, only five blocks away.

It was a beautiful day and Hassani felt safe enough to enjoy the summer weather in New York. Street vendors were out on the avenue, selling kabobs and pretzels to office workers who sat sunning themselves outside their buildings. His security man kept up a couple of paces behind.

On Fifty-fourth, he recognized the familiar stone and glass tower with the iconic intersecting "RR" wrapped in a lion's tail. He almost felt an owner's pride.

Crossing the street, he passed through the large glass doors and walked up to the marble desk in the reception center. He announced himself to the guard, who printed off a VIP security badge and directed him to a private elevator bank that served the executive offices on the forty-second and forty-third floors. As the elevator whooshed them high above Manhattan, he knew there was much to talk about.

The largest bank in California had gone

belly-up this week. In Spain, the leading real estate developer was underwater. The walls were tumbling, one by one, with even more speed than they had imagined. Mighty Lehman Brothers and Citi—their stocks were now the lowest they had even been. Everything was in play, if you had access to an unlimited supply of capital. The carnage was only beginning. Only those who had the long view, who had the required patience to accept the pain, with the promise of future reward, future domination, would be there to pick up the pieces in this new world.

The elevator opened on forty-three. Hassani and his security man stepped out. A pretty, nicely dressed secretary was there to greet him. Hassani admired her and wondered if something might be arranged later on. (Though the thought did also cross his mind that she might be just a tad old for him.)

The woman smiled and said, "Mr. Simons is waiting for you now."

She led him along a row of important-looking offices, executives who wouldn't even be there now, earning their large bonuses, Hassani mused, were it not for the timely investment of his own king. She led him into a spacious conference room. Hassani motioned to his man to wait outside.

"Make yourself at home," Peter Simons's secretary said. "Mr. Simons will be with you shortly."

"Thank you." Hassani smiled.

The room had a large rosewood table that might have seated as many as forty, and a sprawling, wall-to-wall vista of midtown Manhattan. In one corner there was a Giacometti bronze on a pedestal. Hassani had acquired such tastes himself, having studied at the Sorbonne. A six-foot-wide video presentation screen boasted the familiar logos of all the iconic brands that Reynolds Reid had acquired, ready for the upcoming board meeting. A set of antique silver tea and coffee pots sat on the credenza.

As Hassani admired the view, a private door to one side opened. Peter Simons stepped in.

Simons was tall, lanky, raw boned, slightly graying. He was fifty-six, but with his still light-brown hair and fit, trained body, he looked much younger. He came over and hugged Hassani with open arms. *"Hanni!"*

"Peter." The two embraced, kissing each other on each cheek in the Middle Eastern fashion. "It's very good to see you again, my friend."

Simons patted the Bahraini warmly on the back. "I'm glad you could be here."

There was much to talk about before their meeting, but first the Reynolds Reid CEO leaned close to Hassani's ear and said, his voice no louder than a whisper, *"One thing . . .* That little matter in London, which so concerned us . . . It's been taken care of, I presume?"

"Completely taken care of, my friend." Hassani gave a pat to the CEO's back. "Let us get on to other things."

CHAPTER SEVENTY-SIX

Hauck flew back to New York on Sunday. Eight A.M. Monday, he was back at his desk.

The plane ride back was the first time he'd been able to think about what Steve Chrisafoulis had shared with him, the connection between Talon and Sonny Merced, the man who'd attacked Jared at the rink. He recalled how Foley had tried to put the brakes on his investigation into Thibault, citing the firm's "other" interests with Reynolds Reid.

It also worried him how someone was always one step ahead of them in Serbia and London. Only a handful of people in the world knew about Thibault. Or al-Bashir's connection to Hassani.

Was it possible he and Naomi were being played?

Around ten, one of the partners transferred in a call from Tom Foley. "Glad you're back," his boss said with seeming enthusiasm. "Ready to go forward?"

"Totally ready," Hauck said, looking to deflect any questions on where he had been.

"Good. I want you in on a lunch meeting Skip Haley is holding up there around noon on Landmark Communication . . ."

Landmark owned television stations and was looking to make an Internet acquisition. Hauck told him he'd sit in.

Naomi had remained an extra day in the UK, to check with some contacts there and see if they could pin Hassani in Switzerland on the date of the supposed meeting in Gstaad.

They knew the date in question, June 26, a year ago, from Thibault's lift ticket. If they could pin Hassani there, coupled with the flow of funds from Ascot through Thibault to James Donovan's account in the Caymans, that might be enough to re-start their investigation. Something had brought both al-Bashir and Thibault to the Swiss resort. Hauck began to wonder could there have been others? Others they didn't know about. Something al-Bashir had said before he stepped into the car: *It was never about terrorism . . . This was much larger than terrorism.*

A thought occurred to him. He took out his BlackBerry and searched through the contact files for a name from years before, when he worked for the Department of In-formation at the NYPD.

Marcus Hird was a criminal inspector from Kantonspolizei in Zurich. They had gotten to know each other at a conference they both attended in DC and later, Hauck had done a favor for him, actually for his cousin who had moved to Greenwich to work for UBS; the cousin's son had been caught with some beers behind the wheel. Hauck had gotten the boy off with a sus-pended license and probation.

Hauck located the number. It was four P.M. over there. The overseas call went through and connected with the usual short beeps.

"*Bitte,* Hird," the inspector answered officiously.

"Marcus," Hauck said. "It's Ty Hauck. From Greenwich. In the States."

"*Ty!*" the Swiss inspector exclaimed, switching to almost perfect English. "It's been a long time."

"It has," Hauck agreed. They exchanged a few pleasantries about work; Hird's cousin, who was now back home; and the man's son, who was now a student at the local polytechnic college. Hauck then got to why he was calling: "Marcus, there may be something you can do for me."

"Always happy to assist the local police there in any way I can," the Swiss detective said politely.

"I'm afraid I'm not exactly with the local police any longer," Hauck admitted. He explained what he was doing now, then why he had called, keeping the reason vague. "Do you ski?"

"Sure. I'm Swiss, Ty. I grew up in a village near Davos. In younger days I was quite the racer."

"Good. I need some information from another of your resorts. From Gstaad."

"Gesh-*staad,*" the Swiss said, drawing

out the German pronunciation. "Beautiful place there. What is it you need?"

"I want you to look at only the five-star hotels there for me. Just the very top echelon."

"Understood," the Swiss said. "The Grand Hotel Park. The Grand Hotel Bellevue. The Gstaad Palace. Do you need a booking, Ty? If so, I recommend you call the Ministry of Tourism, not me."

Hauck laughed politely. "No, not a booking, Marcus, sorry. I'm going to give you a date. On or around June twenty-sixth of last year. I'm also going to give you a series of names . . ."

"The twenty-sixth of June, only the top hotels . . . Go ahead. What is it you're looking for, Ty?"

"I'd rather not go into it, if that's okay. It's part of a private investigation. You understand."

"I understand perfectly," the inspector said without argument. "You may have heard, we Swiss are used to matters of privacy. So tell me, what it is that you need?"

"The hotel guest lists for those days," Hauck said. "All of them, if you can."

CHAPTER SEVENTY-SEVEN

Naomi flew back to Washington that Monday afternoon and went straight to her office across from the Treasury.

She threw herself behind her desk, which was submerged under piles of memos and security reports that had stacked up in her absence. So far there was still no word on the Mercedes. She tried to convince herself over and over that it was al-Bashir, not *her,* like Ty had said, who had put his family in danger. But still, she couldn't shake the sting of feeling responsible. The boy's panicked face, peering out the back window, had haunted her all the way home. She sank back wearily in her chair under the weight of never having lost anyone before.

She logged on to her computer and scanned for a message from her contact at the Swiss Federal Office of Police's financial crimes division. With Thibault and al-Bashir gone, there was only one course left—to try to prove Hassani was in Gstaad at the same time as the others. That some kind of conspiracy had been hatched there.

Then there was the added worry of just how to proceed. Ty's concern was real. Someone always seemed one step ahead of them. There were only a handful of people on the inside who knew, and she had grown to understand, as Ty said, this was no longer something she could go on managing in the usual way.

She was scanning through her e-mails and calls, sipping a latte to fight the jet lag, when her boss, Rob Whyte, appeared with a knock at the door.

"Talia said you were back."

Naomi straightened up, surprised. She cleared her throat. "Just got in now."

"I'm sorry," Whyte said, coming in, "about

what happened, Naomi." He pulled out a chair across from her desk. "Still no word?"

She shook her head. "I think we've got to proceed as if they're gone."

Her boss nodded. "You realize, Naomi, there'll have to be a review of this. How it all went down."

"I understand."

"I know how it must make you feel. You had him."

"Thanks," she said, growing suspicious that he was buttering her up for something.

Whyte sat. His tie was loosened, and for the first time Naomi felt something unspoken and distant between them, a stiffness in his eyes. Was it what had happened in London or something more? She had always trusted him completely. Why not? Rob had been JAG. An ambitious lawyer. Passionate about the good they were doing. One day he would go on to bigger things. It gave her a queasy feeling holding important information back from him. But Hassani had recruited al-Bashir. He had seduced Glassman and Donovan. Something had gone awry. And this was what she felt she had to do right now.

Her boss rocked back in the chair. "So where do we stand?"

"Back at square one. Al-Bashir was the only one who could fully implicate Hassani. Now that he's gone, I'm going to have to try to retrace some of the movement of cash between Thibault and Hassani's firms. It's possible there were other people in play. I'll try to see if we can find a fit."

Whyte nodded, his fingers folded in front of his face. "That thing in Serbia, Naomi, what you did was crossing the line. It could get our department in a lot of trouble."

Naomi shrugged. "I did what I felt I had to do, Rob."

"I know, I know. It's just that, when Justice finds out . . . They're already bent out of shape we didn't bring them in on taking al-Bashir into custody. They're calling us a bunch of amateurs."

"I don't care what they're calling us. There was no time."

He nodded. "Listen . . . there's something else. Hassani is in the States."

"The States?" Naomi put down her coffee and fixed her gaze directly on him.

"Uh-huh. He's here for the Reynolds Reid annual meeting. You know he helped arrange that preferred financing for the Bahraini royal family . . ."

Naomi's blood began to surge. "Then we can pick him up, Rob. We can question him. He's here!"

"Question him on what, if you don't mind me asking? On some perfectly legal flow of funds that, at worst, might tie him to Dieter Thibault? Which he would clearly insist he knew nothing about. You haven't established a single direct contact between him and Thibault. Only that phone conversation with al-Bashir. He'll deny it meant anything, just as al-Bashir did. What's there to use as leverage against him? Two co-conspirators, both dead? This is a big fish, Naomi . . ."

She looked back at him, suddenly feeling something different, a weakening in her boss's will. A loss of nerves? His career path suddenly in jeopardy, would he take on the very institutions he might one day look to for a deal?

Or maybe it was worse . . .

"That auditor's position up in Montana," Naomi said, smiling cautiously, "you're thinking that may not be such a joke . . ."

Whyte got up. He smiled only enough

to let her know he wasn't amused. "Come back to me with something firm. Facts, Naomi—not conspiracies. You're a god-damn Treasury agent, not Jack Bauer on *24*."

In his gaze Naomi suddenly saw that everything was now in play. *Her* future as well. That auditor's position up north, it might not be Rob's next posting.

She might get there first.

"I'm working on something, Rob . . ."

CHAPTER SEVENTY-EIGHT

That first night back, Annie came over. Mondays, Hauck generally cooked. Then they'd hang out on the couch and watch a game or rent a movie. Monday was Annie's only night off and the last thing she needed was to spend it at a restaurant.

That Monday, Hauck felt a little nervous how things would go.

He knew he hadn't been completely honest with her. About what had been taking up his attention as of late. Where he had been in the past week and why. It was time to come clean. As she came up the stairs, in a pair of torn white jeans and a cute orange tee, she waved brightly, but he could tell in her reserved smile that something was a little wrong.

"Hey, stranger." He gave her a hug and a kiss on the cheek.

"Glad you're back," she said, hugging him back.

Tonight, Hauck was doing lamb burgers on the grill, with caramelized onions in balsamic and topped with Danish bleu.

"Sounds awfully good," she said. "Spoil me."

They opened some wine and sat on the deck overlooking the sound, feet up on the railing. A nice breeze came off the water. She didn't ask about the trip. It was like she was waiting for him to volunteer it. They chatted about the restaurant. How it was time to get his boat in the water. He asked about Jared. She said he was doing okay. The conversation felt like the weight of a two-ton truck pressed across his back. They both felt it. There was something distant between them tonight.

How could there not be?

Hauck stood up. "Maybe I should go fire up the grill . . ."

"Listen, Ty—"

"Me first." He sat back down. "I've actually got something to say. About where I was. What it is I've been up to lately. I haven't been entirely honest with you, Annie, and—"

"I know what you've been up to, Ty . . ."

He stopped, looked at her. Annie's eyes were round and totally nonjudgmental. Still, her gaze made him feel a bit ashamed.

She said, "I let myself in here while you were away." She put her wine down and faced him. "I wasn't snooping. I'd left my earrings the last time I was here and I went upstairs to look for them. I found them, on your dresser. Elena must've put them there . . . I also found something else."

Hauck swallowed. The breath he inhaled almost hurt him; he knew what it was.

"I found that picture, Ty. It was right there. I think you know the one I'm talking about. That gal who was killed . . . What was her name, April?"

"April." He nodded a little guiltily.

"And you." Her eyes stayed solidly on him. Not accusingly; more like she was hurt. "Who was she, Ty? I'm not jealous. Well, maybe a little . . . But you've been different since the very day that happened, and you withheld it from me. I think I deserve to hear the truth."

"She was just a friend, Annie," Hauck said. "I promise, that's all. That photo was taken a long time ago."

"I know it was a long time ago, Ty. So *why . . .* Why did you have to hide it all from me? Why couldn't you just tell me? Whatever your connection to her. You knew her—and not just from around town."

He nodded, releasing a contrite blast of air from his cheeks. "There's a period in my life, Annie, I've never gone into much. With anyone. Not just you. After Norah was killed. As things started to fall apart with Beth . . ."

He told her about how he walked out of his job at the NYPD. The dark period that followed. The guilt he bore. About not being able to find a reason to even get up in the morning. "One night I just sat in my car in front of the store I was heading to when it happened. I was so angry . . . I took a rock and hurled it through the window. The cops came . . . If I wasn't a cop, I would have spent the night in jail. Maybe it was depression." He shrugged. "Maybe it was just blame. I had a lot of it. I didn't know how to talk about it then. Clearly, I'm not exactly a whiz now . . . April just helped me back, that's all. We met in a depression group. We started to meet, afterward, for coffee. I needed someone then. I don't know how I would have made it on my own. I don't even think about that period now, but when I saw she was killed . . ."

Annie stared at him. "You've been following up on her death, haven't you? All this time. You don't think I saw it in your face? You don't think I felt that something had changed? That maybe I had done something—"

"You haven't done anything, Annie."

All of a sudden her expression changed and her hand covered her mouth. "Oh my God! That's what the attack on Jared was all about, wasn't it? It was meant for you—to pressure you off the case. Did you keep that from me too? Did they try to hurt my son because of you?"

He nodded, flattening his lips. "Yeah, I think so, Annie."

"*Oh, Ty . . .*" Her eyes glistened. "How could you possibly keep something like that from me?" She stared, tears about to flow, as if she was looking into a face she had seen a million times but that had now changed. "What have you gotten into, Ty? You have a new life for yourself. You have *me.* What hold does she have on you? What is it that's dragging you back there, Ty?"

"I'm not dragged back anywhere, Annie . . ."

"Yes, you are." She nodded. *"You are . . .* This woman's dead, Ty. *I'm here.* Why are you willing to throw it all away? Why can't you love me like that?"

"I do love you, Annie," he said. "I do."

"No." She shook her head with tears in her eyes. "Not like that."

He wanted to reach out and take her in. He wanted to tell her there was more to it. More than he was saying. But what hurt him was that she was right. They had only made one commitment to each other. Dealing in the truth. Honesty. She deserved that one thing.

And he had withheld it from her.

"I won't even ask you where you've been." She tried to smile bravely. "I mean, it's not my business. You're a good man, Ty. I know that, and I know you'd do anything for me. And for Jared. You've already proven that. You treat him like a son. But he's not; I know that. And I'm not your wife either."

"I was in Serbia, Annie. And London." He swallowed. "I was with an agent from the Treasury Department, and we were tracking someone who may have been responsible for her death."

"Serbia?" Annie shook her head, wiping away a tear. "London. Well, at least it wasn't anywhere exciting or glamorous, right?"

"We weren't exactly on a Butterfield and Robinson bike tour, Annie."

That made her smile. "I'm sure. Was it dangerous?"

He looked at her, not really wanting to say. Not now. "I guess."

"You guess . . ." She sniffed a little cynically and shook her head. "So did you catch him? The person who did this thing."

"No. He's dead. Annie, listen . . ." He took hold of her hand and squeezed it in his own. "I'm sorry. I'm sorry I held things from you. I'm sorry to have hurt you in any way. That's the last thing I wanted to do. Or that you deserve."

"You're damn right it's the last thing I

deserve. But I can't make you love me either, can I? And I deserve *that* too. I don't need the roses or the Valentine's Day hearts or some big commitment. But I deserve to be loved, don't I?"

"I do love you, Annie . . ."

"No." She shook her head. "I meant like her."

She smiled at him one more time, then glanced at her watch. "I guess firing up the grill doesn't exactly seem like the thing to do right now."

He looked at her and tried to smile back. "No, I guess not."

"I hope you find 'em, Ty."

"Who?"

"The one you're looking for."

Hauck didn't know if she was talking about April's murderer or maybe someone else.

She got up. "You know, it's not like me to leave with something corny like this . . ." There was a wistful twinkle in her clear blue eyes. "But I guess I was always hoping, inside, when you went to someplace like London, it might have been with me."

She brushed past him and he reached for her arm.

She stood there for a second in his grasp.

"Regarding April, I haven't told you everything. There's one more thing . . ."

"I'm sorry, Ty." Annie pulled free. "But I don't want to know."

CHAPTER SEVENTY-NINE

The e-mail flashed on Naomi's laptop when she logged on at six the next morning. It was a short, three-line response, and she stared at it in her oversize Princeton tee. She read it twice, just to make sure.

It changed everything.

She waited as long as she could, showered, her heart racing. Then she punched in the number on her speed dial. "Ty . . ."

"Hey." He sounded groggy.

"I figured you'd be jet lagged. You okay?"

"I'm okay," he said. He cleared his throat. "Didn't sleep much. I've been up since three. Just something personal. What's going on?"

"I got something back from Bern." Her voice shook with excitement. She told him about the response. From the assistant consul general at the embassy there. "A private jet, registered to a Dubai aviation company, landed in Geneva at seven twenty-one A.M. June twenty-fifth. Hassani passed through immigration there half an hour later. That's the day before Thibault's lift ticket was dated, Ty."

"Geneva's not Gstaad, Naomi."

"Geneva's the closest airport to Gstaad for someone clearing immigration. It's only a two-hour drive away. I checked. Hassani was there, Ty!"

She had tried desperately to fit it all together ever since she had received the reply. It was clear now something important had taken place there. A conspiracy mapped out, put in motion months later by the largest stock fund in the world dumping U.S. securities. Two investment managers secretly paid off to conceal massive losses at their teetering banks, then killed, setting in motion a terrible slide in the already reeling financial sector. Stocks sent plummeting. Banks going under.

The walls tumbling down.

Now she had to get her people involved. Hassani was in New York. This might be their only chance to get him. The FBI, the Justice Department . . . What she had to do now was figure out who she could trust.

"Who have you told about this, Naomi?"

"No one," she replied. "Just you. But I can't keep it that way any longer. Hassani's in New York. He's there for the Reynolds Reid annual meeting. I'm not certain for just how long. I know Geneva's not Gstaad, but we can prove he was in the area at the same time as Thibault and al-Bashir. We have the transcript of him on the phone setting the plan in motion. The flow of cash from one of his firms to pay off James Donovan. The three of them were behind a plot to take down the economy of the United States, Ty. Marty al-Bashir basically admitted that much."

"What are you going to do?"

"I don't know. I'm going to jog on it first. There's a lot at stake. Not to mention my career if I blow this up. I was thinking . . ." Something al-Bashir had said had occurred to her. About how it wasn't terrorism but something much, much larger. "What if there were more than three? What if there were others involved? Who were there. What if this Gstaad Gang had a few more paying members?"

"I've thought that too," Hauck said back. "And I'm already on it, Naomi."

CHAPTER EIGHTY

He was getting ready to leave when his cell rang. Steve Chrisafoulis.

"I want you to see something, Ty," the Greenwich detective said. "Are you near a computer?"

"Can be," Hauck said back, throwing his car keys on the counter and heading to his desk.

"We had an ID come back. One of Sonny Merced's buddies in Iraq. They knew each other in the Hundred-and-first over there. I told you we were checking that out. He also worked as an armed security consultant with GTM, the security firm that told Merced to get lost. Talon's firm."

"Yeah." Hauck turned on his computer. "I remember, Steve."

He logged on to his e-mail account. He saw the message flashing. He clicked it open and then the attachment.

A photo came on the screen.

A man in fatigues, leaning on an armored vehicle. From his GTM days. Muscular, ripped. In a gray army T-shirt, brandishing an M4 rifle. His hair short, wiry, pulled back in a stubby ponytail.

Jack "Red" O'Toole.

"I'm on it, Steve . . ."

"He did two yearlong stints with GTM after his military tours of duty were over. I spoke to his field boss. Known as a real cowboy over there. Quick on the trigger. I think it's our guy, Ty. I asked who his main clients were over there. Just on a whim. You're never gonna believe what he came back with."

"I'm listening, Steve . . ."

Hauck stared intensely at the photo. The muscular physique. The short pony-tail. The connection to Merced.

But it was something else that made Hauck's blood come to a boil.

It was what was on his neck. A kind of tattoo. A claw, it looked like, maybe a lion or a panther. Just as the photos Evan Glassman had snapped from the second-floor window had shown.

The person who had killed his family.

Jack "Red" O'Toole.

"Nice work, Steve."

CHAPTER EIGHTY-ONE

She did jog on it.

Close to five miles. On the path along the Potomac. Until the answer came to her. Stopping, hands on hips, breathing heavily, she knew she'd be taking a huge risk. To go out of channels this way.

Yet it was something she had to do. To let this situation pass, to possibly lose Hassani, was not an option now. Eight innocent people had died. Not to mention the global economic collapse that he had precipitated. Or the fact that al-Bashir's son's face still resonated in her.

Corny as it was, she found herself staring at the Lincoln Memorial.

This was her job.

She took out her cell and put in the call. She had only been with him privately that one time. She requested ten minutes—alone. That morning, if possible. And to keep the call confidential.

Ninety minutes later Naomi walked into the office of the treasury secretary of the United States.

She had gone through the list of anyone she could talk to, anyone who could take action, someone she could trust. Thomas Keaton was the one name that came to mind.

His secretary walked her in, opening the large, paneled doors just as she had once before, revealing the spacious room, the polished mahogany desk and gleaming conference table. The bright seal of the United States staring up at her from the carpet. The unobstructed view of the Washington Monument.

I hope you know what you're doing, Naomi . . .

From his desk, Thomas Keaton stood up. He motioned for her to take a seat in a large leather chair that suddenly seemed way too big for her.

"Agent Blum," he said. "You asked for a private meeting. You realize how unorthodox this is . . ."

Naomi sat down, her heart pounding like a jackhammer. "I realize that, sir."

"I assume by private, you didn't mean Mitch." Mitch Hastings, the department's chief counsel, was seated on the couch nearby.

"No, of course," Naomi said. She nodded to the lawyer. "How are you, sir?"

Hastings gave her a tight smile, adjusting his glasses.

She removed a large file from her satchel and placed it on her lap. "I'm sure you both have important matters to attend to. I won't take up much time."

The secretary sat back down. "If by 'important matters' you mean the world markets being in free fall, California's largest bank having collapsed, the world wondering which iconic investment house is going to go under next, the president's going on the air today to tell the public to have faith in the markets . . . yes"—he glanced at Hastings—"the day *is* a bit full. The last time you were here you made some pretty lurid innuendos. I asked you to come back with proof. Have you found that proof, Agent Blum?"

"Yes, sir." Naomi nodded. "I think I have. I'm sorry, but I didn't feel comfortable taking this through normal channels. When I was here last I mentioned a Saudi investment manager named Mashhur al-Bashir, who I suspected had precipitated a global sell-off in stocks as part of a plot to destabilize the U.S. economy. I think you're aware that two days ago we attempted to take him into custody?"

"I *am* aware of that, Agent Blum." The treasury secretary's face soured. "This al-Bashir was a respected figure in the financial world. To date, it's just been reported he and his family are somehow missing. I instructed you to keep this under the radar, not create a public incident. What the hell happened on that?"

"I don't know. I'm sorry." Naomi shifted uncomfortably. "But before it occurred, Mr. al-Bashir confirmed to me he had, in fact, been part of a conspiracy just as I mapped out, along with Hassan ibn Hassani. As you may recall, the original evidence of this surfaced from a transcript of a monitored phone conversation between Mr. Hassani and al-Bashir, which I was trying to tie to the two traders whose deaths sent Wertheimer Grant and Beeston Holloway into insolvency through an intermediary, Dieter Thibault."

The treasury secretary leaned forward. "And were you able to make that connection, Agent Blum?"

Naomi opened her file. "I've been able to show a trail of money between Thibault and one of Mr. Hassani's corporate entities, a real estate development firm in Dubai, Ascot Capital, that was used to advance a significant amount of money to James Donovan of Beeston Holloway, who we are now pretty certain did not kill himself, but in fact was murdered, sir."

Keaton's gaze grew somber. "I'm still waiting for you to take this somewhere, Agent Blum."

"Yes, sir. I'm fairly certain Mr. Hassani, Mr. al-Bashir, and Thibault developed this plot to collapse the financial markets in June of last year. We found evidence that all three men were in Gstaad, Switzerland, on the same day, June twenty-sixth."

"Gstaad?"

"Hassani's private jet landed at the Geneva airport the day before. Geneva is the closest international airport, at which he would have had to land. He took off to London two days later. I believe they discussed this at a restaurant there named Christina's, on the mountain. I'm in the process of trying to nail down their whereabouts, the hotels they might have stayed at as well as the restaurant where this meeting took place."

"Proving they were there at the same time doesn't exactly tie them to this plot, does it, agent?"

"No, you're right." Naomi nodded. "It doesn't. What does is that Dieter Thibault was actually the assumed identity for an ex-Serbian-paramilitary officer who was implicated in a mass murder in Bosnia during the war. He's been directly linked to the murders of Glassman and Donovan. Tying him to Hassani through the money that went to bribe Donovan, and then tying Hassani to al-Bashir through the monitored transcript and the sell-off of global stocks, is enough in my eyes to warrant a full investigation, Mr. Secretary. But it gets more urgent. That's not in itself why I'm here."

Thomas Keaton motioned for her to continue.

Naomi took a deep breath. "Hassani is currently in the United States. He's attending a board meeting at Reynolds Reid tied to their annual meeting. It's clear he orchestrated a major international conspiracy that resulted in the collapse of U.S. banks—and contributed to a worldwide panic that cost billions in lost net worth and personal hardships."

Hastings cut in from the couch. "Hassani and al-Bashir didn't bring down these banks, Agent Blum. Are you forgetting a few minor issues such as the subprime mortgage collapse, the housing meltdown, CDOs, the rating agencies' lack of governance . . . ?"

"No, sir, you're right, but they clearly hastened it. It's just as much of an attack against the United States as if they flew a plane directly into the Capitol dome.

"Not to mention," Naomi said, looking back at Keaton, "at least eight innocent people presumably killed between here and the UK."

Keaton's face grew stonelike.

"I can't put everything together. I can't put together why this was done or ultimately who benefited from what took place. There may even be others involved I haven't identified yet. But there was a plot, sir, make no mistake. A plot to destabilize the U.S. economy by taking advantage of weaknesses in the financial system. Hassani should be detained—today. He should be made to provide answers about his activities in this plot. If he was carrying a bomb you would have no problem picking up the phone to the FBI immediately. This is no less a bomb, and it caused more damage than any device they could have detonated. I wish I didn't have to come to you on this, sir."

"And the reason," Keaton asked, "you're not proceeding through normal channels is . . . ?"

"You mentioned London, Mr. Secretary. You know what happened there. Somehow someone beat us to both Thibault and al-Bashir before we could take them in. Two days earlier, Thibault had been killed in Serbia. It was made to look like a retribution killing for his offenses in the war.

But no one knew about that, sir. And no one knew he was back in his home village.

"I don't know who it is," she continued. "Hassani, I assume, covering his tracks. But only a handful of people knew we had placed Thibault and Hassani together. In light of this I couldn't take the chance of what I had on Hassani finding its way into the wrong hands. I felt I had to go directly to you with this, sir. I hope you understand."

Thomas Keaton's jaw grew taut and he glanced toward Mitch Hastings with a sobering stare. The lawyer eyed him back with an equally concerned expression.

"Very serious stuff," he said, turning back to Naomi. "You were absolutely right to bring this to me, Agent Blum."

CHAPTER EIGHTY-TWO

Peter Simons was skimming the *Wall Street Journal* in the back of his company Maybach, making his way down the FDR. He had an eight thirty breakfast with the head of the New York Fed in the Washington Room at their headquarters on Liberty Street. Along with the chiefs of Goldman, Citi, and Blackstone, some of the most powerful people in finance. The government had to craft a response to the deepening Wall Street crisis, a plan for how to hold the system together. And who better to consult with than the very people most responsible for pushing it over the edge?

The historic meeting room on the Fed's thirteenth floor was three stories tall and completely windowless. In the most symbolic sense, to lock in whatever was discussed within its hallowed walls.

You didn't have to be a genius, Peter Simons knew, to have seen it all coming. The geniuses were all responsible for creating the mess. For years, the world had been lulled to sleep by the toxic double dose of credit and debt. The banks, the rating bureaus, the governance agencies tasked with keeping it all together. Even the insurance giants who devised the logarithmic schemes to offset all the risk, like AIG. The system was corroded, rotted from the core. And, as most failed to understand, completely rigged. Deregulation had allowed the banks to lever their capital up at forty to one. Rating agencies were collecting fees from the very firms they were assigned to vet. Complex derivatives and credit-default swaps no one understood drove trading volumes. The mortgage market had melted down to dross. The whole rotted mess spiraled upward in an unimpeded arc, throwing off record profits for everyone. Until it stopped.

Until it simply didn't anymore. Until the winds changed. No, you didn't have to be a genius, Simons knew. Certainly he wasn't. You just had to be willing to do something about it. To make sure not to be blown away by the gale.

And Simons had never been one to be pushed aside by a little shift in the winds. His father had been a middling merchant outside of Philadelphia, and from the beginning, Simons had dreams that he was destined for higher things. He had run track in high school, still held the record for the four hundred at his school. Now the stadium was named after him. At Yale, he had been invited into Skull and Bones. The day he had been asked into the exclusive club was one of the proudest of his life. It had made his ascent to the top of Wall Street almost a self-fulfilling plan. Opened doors to the right contacts. There was always a hand above him guiding his way. No one worked harder. No one sold his ass off like he had. He knew he wasn't one of the "geniuses." And he surely had no pedigree that was going to pave his way.

First, he became head of the trading floor

at Reynolds, when it was a quiet, retail-based institution. Then he was put in charge of the bond department, riding the wave of growth in the nineties. He built the firm from a quiet old-line brokerage house into the new model of leading investment banks in the world. He rode the crest of the subprime rally all the way to the top. But the signs became clear—when everyone else started piling on, he wasn't about to let it take him down as well. That was the difference between him and many of his peers. Even the people who, in fifteen minutes, were about to sit around the same table with him and thrash over how to right the ship in this storm.

In school, Simons had studied the Austrian economist Joseph Schumpeter, and it had formed his view that the system was made anew by every generation. Capitalism wasn't static. It was constantly remaking itself, like a living organism. Innovation cleansed the system. Behemoths rose and fall. Creative destruction. Nature did it, in evolution, in great forests ravaged by fire. Schumpeter called it being carried away by the "gale."

The idea had first occurred to him a year

ago over drinks with Hassani in Dubai, after the Bahraini had helped facilitate a needed investment by the royal family. How, if they could just influence events, tip the scale, you might say, in their favor, despite the coming downturn, everyone could win. It was all inevitable anyway. Nature was going to take its course. Simons had the network of like-minded people. People to make it happen on a global scale. Hassani would just need to implement the plan. Put it all in motion. Give it the proper impetus. That was where al-Bashir fit in. A man with obligations to Hassani of a different sort. The perfect fit to start the chain unraveling. Send the banks' stocks plummeting. Bring the short sellers out. Then the rogue traders. That was Hassani's idea.

And he had found the perfect piece of scum to make it happen.

What a lark that that scum had ended up seducing his ex-wife.

Simons knew, in the end, he was only speeding up the inevitable. Reynolds Reid would be poised to pick up the pieces. Some of his competitors would be blown away; that was bound to happen. Surely he would suffer losses. Personally. As well as the firm. In the short term.

But in the end, he would be one of the winners. The innovative player. The one who alters circumstance to fit design. They would be made stronger by the gale.

After breakfast he had a board meeting. At that meeting they would ratify the acquisition of Pacific-West, California's largest bank, which had just been taken over by the Fed. They had picked up coveted pieces of Wertheimer. And ArcCo, the country's largest mortgage company. They would announce it at the annual meeting this afternoon.

What they would never announce was just how it all came to be.

Simons's car pulled up at the Fed on Liberty Street. His driver, Carl, leaned back around. "Shall I let you off here, Mr. Simons?"

"Great, Carl. Stay close to the phone. I should be back down in ninety minutes. We have to be back up at the office by ten."

"You got it, sir."

Simons stepped out onto the street.

There was only one thing that gave him pause.

His friend.

At his core, Hassani was still too much of an ideologue for him. He still carried this crazy belief in jihad. People who believed too strongly in anything always made Simons a little nervous. It made him smile that despite the lavish meals and the warm hugs of friendship, the Bahraini probably shared the same doubts about him as well.

You never knew how that would fall.

Heading through the gilded door, Peter Simons reminded himself he'd have to do something about that.

CHAPTER EIGHTY-THREE

Naomi was at Reagan International, waiting for the government jet to take her to New York. She had finally found a moment to look over what Ty had sent.

She was on her way up to connect with Anthony Bruni, a senior agent in charge of the FBI Financial terrorism task force. Together, they would take Hassani into custody later that day.

Keaton had given the word. It was delicate. There were many entanglements between the U.S. and Bahrain over matters of national security. The king might well be enraged. Hassani might even claim diplomatic immunity. As the jet rolled out, Naomi quickly scanned through Ty's attachment. The e-mail it had arrived in said, *Proof Hassani was there. And check out who else.*

Excitedly, Naomi clicked back and forth between the three hotel guest lists. Her blood whipped like a squall running through her veins. Thibault. Al-Bashir. *Hassani.* All highlighted in Ty's document. She felt vindicated.

They'd all been there.

Just as she had laid it all out weeks before. Only this made the case against him a hundred times stronger. Not to mention her job security. Naomi took out her Black-Berry and was about to place a call back to Ty when the "who else" he was referring to hit her like a lacrosse stick to the face.

Peter Simons.

Peter Simons was head of one of the largest investment banks in the world.

Naomi's stomach almost climbed up her throat. *Simons was there.* She tried to wrap her brain around what this meant. It made it a whole new thing.

It was no longer about jihad or some terrorist plot to cripple the West; this was a deep-rooted conspiracy, one that sprang up not from overseas *but from within.* Naomi tried to grasp it. How did anyone profit from this kind of thing? What did Reynolds Reid have to gain?

A military officer came through a door. He nodded at Naomi. "Agent Blum, your aircraft's on the tarmac now."

"I'll be there in a second," Naomi said, her body breaking out in an exhilarated sweat.

Could there be others?

Excitedly, Naomi scrolled up and down the three lists, shifting between hotels, the two nights.

Other names began to pop out. Important names.

Marshall Shipman. Shipman was chief of Orpheus, a large hedge fund. She felt her hands tremble. *Stephen Cain.* Cain ran a boutique private equity group. A mini-Blackstone. *Vladimir Tursanov.* A huge Russian financier.

Hassani. Al-Bashir.

The Gstaad Gang.

She took out a pad and feverishly scratched the names on it as she read on. It left her feeling queasy and uncertain, like she was facing the unclimbable walls of some deep well she was at the bottom of.

She realized she was opening a Pandora's box of something that was way beyond her control. Like al-Bashir had said on the landing before he was driven away. *This was much larger than simply terrorism.*

She punched in Ty's number on her BlackBerry.

"You see what I found?" he answered on the first ring. *"Simons."*

"Simons is only the tip of the iceberg, Ty. It was a plot—a plot to take down the markets. Not some terrorist thing. Well-orchestrated, by some of the most influential people in the investment world. *From within.*" Her mouth was dry. "I don't know what we stumbled into."

"Is it possible this was just a part of other meetings that were scheduled around it? *Legitimate* meetings?" Hauck asked.

"*No.* Nothing like this. Nothing this big. It would be public. I would know about it." She had to hold her head to keep it from spinning.

"Naomi, who have you shared this with?" Hauck pressed. His voice was laced with urgency. "Who approved the arrest? Who else knows?"

"I went directly to Thomas Keaton. I . . ." As soon as his name fell off her lips her heart slowed to a stop. "Oh my God, Ty . . ."

She hadn't seen it before, but now she did. It was all there. Not behind some curtain. But in plain day. Hassani. Al-Bashir. Tursanov.

Simons.

She had to hold her stomach from lurching up inside her. Even a blind person could see. If they knew what they were looking for.

"Naomi, what—"

"Ty, I need you to meet me in New York. I'm about to board a government jet. We're taking Hassani into custody. Today, after the Reynolds Reid meeting. But Hassani's only the front man for this . . ." She put her fingers to the front of her head as if she was trying to keep it from exploding. "Oh, God, what have I done, Ty?"

CHAPTER EIGHTY-FOUR

Red O'Toole leaned against the car and stared out at the New York landmark.

He had been told to come here and wait. That this was a final job for him. An important one. Then he could collect his last pay and disappear. He had sensed a tone of desperation in his contact's voice. He knew that sign—like in the field when a position had become too hot to hold. Taking on fire. He'd been in several of those, and this one had that feel. You always had to have a way out. A line of retreat.

He was mapping his now.

He knew he'd done more bad stuff in

his time than he cared to admit or remember. He figured one or two more added to the list wouldn't mean shit when it came to an accounting of these things. It's not like he'd set out to do them. If his dad, a devout man, was still alive, he'd have said, *Johnny, don't do anything you can't repent for. That's the one rule.*

O'Toole smiled and wondered if there was enough repentance left in the world for what he'd been forced to do.

He knew Merced had been ID'd. His name was now all over the news. They knew his background. In Iraq. At Global Threat Management. Sonny had always been careless. And a little desperate. O'Toole realized it wouldn't be much of a stretch for them to find a connection back to him.

After this last job, he needed to disappear.

Behind his shades, he watched taxis and limos pull up. His cell phone rang. He knew who it was. He didn't even have to look. He took it out of his pocket and flipped it open. "I'm here."

"Are we secure?" the caller asked, meaning the line. The caller never lost the chance to dot his "I's" and cross his "T's"; he was not a little paranoid. Guess a man like him had to be. An important man.

O'Toole assured him that it was.

"Matters have gotten a little out of hand," the man began. "I need you to settle a past-due account for me. We've set it all up. We've got a way in for you. But it's tricky . . ."

He took the target's name and looked at the location. It *was* tricky. Getting in. Cameras all around. Lots of people. A public venue. Not to mention bodyguards.

"Call it in to me when you're done," his contact said on the line.

"When I'm done," O'Toole mused, "I intend to be long gone."

"Before you go, there are one or two last details that need to be settled. One you already know. It'll be almost a sort of reunion for you. The other, call it your retirement party."

He gave O'Toole the names. He'd seen them before. A fist of anger ground inside him. He lowered his shades.

"That one I do for free."

CHAPTER EIGHTY-FIVE

Two large black Suburbans pulled up in front of the Waldorf on Fiftieth and Park Avenue. The doorman attempted to wave them along, but the driver in the lead vehicle rolled down his window, flashing his ID. The doorman's expression changed and he motioned for them to double-park right in front.

A team of government agents jumped out. Hauck saw a stocky, dark-complexioned man in a tan suit, followed by Naomi, in a brown pantsuit, close behind. Three more agents exited the second SUV, wearing earphones.

He recognized them all as FBI.

He went up to Naomi and her demeanor brightened when she saw him. "I'm glad you're here. This is Senior Agent in Charge Anthony Bruni." She introduced him to the agent in the tan suit. "He's with the Financial Crimes Task Force in New York. This is Ty Hauck. He's worked with me on much of this case. More like I've worked with him."

Hauck shook hands in front of the entrance to the hotel.

"I know who you are." Bruni nodded respectfully. "I followed what you did on the Grand Central bombing case and that mess up in Hartford. Glad to have you aboard."

Hauck nodded back appreciatively, as if surprised his exploits had made their radar.

Bruni grinned. "Hey, FBI agents watch CNN too."

He stationed two of his men at the cars and one in the lobby; the other two went with them in FBI Windbreakers as they entered the posh hotel. "This could go several ways," Bruni explained. "And it won't be quiet. One thing I know: the ruling family back in Bahrain is going to throw a fit. We have a representative of the State Department meeting us back at FBI offices." He smirked. "You might also think about shorting Reynolds Reid stock before the end of the day. This isn't going to go well on the Street, either."

The group entered the crowded lobby and went up to the front desk. The hotel manager, in a black suit, came out to meet them. "I'm Special Agent Bruni," the FBI man said. "We spoke on the phone."

The manager, a tall fortysomething man with a receding hairline, appeared understandably anxious that a procedure of this magnitude was taking place at his hotel. "I checked. Mr. Hassani is still in his room," he said. "He arrived about forty minutes ago and hasn't come back out. I'm hoping you can exit through the side entrance on Fiftieth and keep this as discreet as you can."

"We'll do everything we can," Bruni assured him. He radioed to the drivers to wait around the block. Then he turned to Naomi. "Ready, Agent Blum? It's your show."

The determination was clear on Naomi's face. Not only was this the biggest arrest of her career, but she had traced this since it was no more than two seemingly unrelated deaths of Wall Street traders. They'd tied them to a cryptic call from Hassani and followed the chain of money to Serbia and London, murders blocking them every step of the way. Now they were back to Hassani.

"One hundred percent," Naomi said, inhaling a deep breath and casting a tight smile at Hauck.

"Then let's go."

Hauck, Naomi, Bruni, the hotel manager, and the two accompanying agents went over to the elevators across the red carpeted lobby. When it came, the manager politely asked a couple about to step in if they could wait for the next one. They climbed in. The elevator whisked them to the twelfth floor, where Hassani was staying. On the private floor, there was a concierge seated behind a desk.

"Chris, is Mr. Hassani still in his room?" the manager asked.

"Yes, sir." The concierge nodded, checking. "He went in about forty minutes ago. There's only been one other person on the floor, another guest, who went in and out shortly after."

In and out.

Naomi's gaze shot to Hauck. He saw in it the same sense of alarm that was buzzing through him.

This couldn't happen again.

Naomi started to run. With her leading the way, they went quickly down the long hall of rooms and turned the corner to the suite at the end.

The wooden double door read 1201.

Naomi knocked. *"Mr. Hassani!* This is Agent Naomi Blum of the United States Department of the Treasury. We need you to open the door."

There was no answer.

She knocked again, this time with more force. "Mr. Hassani. This is the United States Treasury Department. Please open the door."

They waited again. Nothing came back. Hauck could feel the nerves rising in Naomi's blood.

The same feeling was going on in his.

Bruni stepped in. "Mr. Hassani, this is the last time we are going to ask you. This is the FBI. We need you to open the door. We have a federally executed warrant for you to come with us on matters of national security. If we don't hear a response, we'll be forced to make our own way in."

They waited a few more seconds. No sound emanated from the suite. Bruni nodded to the hotel manager, who stepped between them, wearing a concerned look, and slipped an electronic key into the lock. The green light flashed with a click. He turned the handle and opened the door, then backed away.

Bruni and the two agents behind him drew their arms. "Mr. Hassani, we are coming in . . ."

The door struck something hard.

With an anxious look, Bruni put his shoulder against it and forced it open. It took just a second for it to become clear something was deadly wrong.

A heavyset, Middle Eastern–looking bodyguard in a dark suit was on his back on an expensive-looking Oriental rug.

Two dark circles of blood spread on the man's white shirt.

Hauck's own blood scame to a stop.

Naomi muttered, "Oh, *no, no, no, no* . . . ," and, rushing inside, shouted, *"Mr. Hassani?"*

The entrance opened to a spacious and

modern living area. There was a wall bar,
a set of curtained windows overlooking
Park Avenue. Next to it was a large dining
room and a kitchen.

"Mr. Hassani!" she called out again.
Now everyone had their weapons drawn.

The team of agents spread, the cry of
"Clear! Clear!" echoing through the multi-
room suite.

Hauck went ahead of Naomi and found
what looked like the master bedroom. He
carefully stepped into the room, his Sig in
front of him, but when he saw what was
there he lowered the weapon.

when did he get in back

"He's in here."

A man reclined on the bed, in his sixties
maybe, wearing a white terry bathrobe,
gray bearded, reading glasses on his forehead, composed, a newspaper spread on
his chest as if he were napping.

A bright red hole dotted the center of
his forehead.

Naomi and the other agents rushed in.
She stopped, as if some invisible force
had halted her motion, and she gazed, deflated, at the bed. Her fists clenched and
she pressed her lips tightly, her eyes glass-
ing over in anger and dismay.

A look of understanding spread across her face.

"Simons?" Hauck asked.

"No." She shook her head. "It's larger than Simons." She took her gaze off Hassani and turned back to Hauck. "I know what's happening, Ty."

He nodded back. "So do I."

CHAPTER EIGHTY-SIX

Peter Simons was pleased.

The annual meeting had been a home run. He had stood up in front of two thousand concerned shareholders in the Grand Ballroom at the Pierre and mapped out—simulcast on a giant screen above him and across the globe—how Reynolds Reid was in position to emerge as one of the victors in these challenging times.

Yes, he had acknowledged, the stock price had taken a hit. The entire financial sector had.

Yes, there were billion-dollar write-downs

that would have to be taken. The government had proposed a possible rescue plan for the troubled banks. It was conceivable the firm might participate in it, he told the shareholders.

Participate?

Simons had to hold himself back from laughing out loud. It was the biggest bonanza in the company's history. And he had been sitting at the table where it was conceived, Simons reflected with glee, but, of course, he could not divulge this.

Still, the firm was solid, he declared. It was not in line to be one of the casualties, he said with commitment. It had shifted out of its subprime positions long before many of its competitors, like Wertheimer or Citi or Merrill. Its balance sheet was fundamentally strong.

In addition, he announced, the troubled times had worked in the company's favor. The board had just approved their offer to acquire one of the largest mortgage companies that had recently failed. It had added prized pieces of Wertheimer too, which the firm had long coveted. It had just put in an offer to buy a 20 percent stake in AVO, a Dutch bank, which would strengthen its position in Europe. It had recently shored up new and substantial lines of capital in the Middle East.

Of course, he said, the firm had taken hits. But they were in a strong position to weather the storm. Not to simply weather it, he declared, but to emerge stronger and better positioned from it.

The packed ballroom responded with a standing ovation.

Now, hours later, back in his office on the forty-third floor, Simons caught the reactions on CNBC and Fox Business. The commentators were saying how Reynolds seemed uniquely positioned to take advantage of the crisis. Even if they needed government funds, it would only serve to strengthen the company's reserves. Wertheimer and Beeston were history. Merrill and Lehman seemed ready to join them there.

The stock price had jumped almost 20 percent in an hour.

Satisfied, Simons reclined back at his desk and took out a cigar. He had done what he had to do. What he needed to do. The landscape around him had to be cleansed. Yes, there would be a year, maybe two, of turmoil. Of uncertainty. Yes, their own results would be slow to come back. Job loses. Contraction. Those were all just statistics. All simply debris, he mused, swept away by the gale forces of change.

But when the winds finally calmed, who would be there to profit on the rebound? Who, made flush with endless government funds, strengthened by their tight relationship to the Fed, would emerge the winner in this new world? The administrator of the TARP fund was an ex-Reynolds man. The head of the New York Fed had been their head of fixed income for years. It was like Skull and Bones all over again. *You don't leave things to the government to sort out,* Simons thought, chuckling with pride.

We are the fucking government.

The seeds were planted well.

Harold Molinari, Simons's CFO, called saying he wanted to share the Street's reaction. Simons buzzed for him to come on down. Later, there was a partners' dinner at Cipriani. Yes, it would be a long road back. A difficult climb. But Peter Simons had done what he had to do to win.

He had not let them down.

His office door opened. Simons spun

expansively, expecting to greet his gloating CFO. "Hal!"

Instead he was staring into the panicked face of his secretary, who was followed by two men he did not know.

One was in a tan suit, and he came up to Simons's desk and dropped a badge in front of his face.

A heavy weight plummeted inside Simons. Over the years, he'd become very familiar with the look of someone who was holding your balls in his mouth and was about to chew. He had that look down to a science.

He was staring at that same expression now.

"Mr. Simons," the man in the suit said, smiling victoriously, "my name is Senior Agent Anthony Bruni, and I'm from the FBI."

CHAPTER EIGHTY-SEVEN

They took the Amtrak Metroliner back to DC.

The government jet had already returned; they had assumed Naomi would be in New York for a while as part of Hassani's interrogation.

But now Naomi realized the less anyone knew about their whereabouts, the better. Outside the hotel suite, Hauck had run the photo Steve Chrisafoulis had sent him earlier by the desk concierge on the twelfth floor. Jack "Red" O'Toole. The man immediately pointed to him as the "other guest" on the floor who had come by just after Hassani had gone in. They looked into who had made the booking: A phony name. A stolen Amex card. But now at least they knew. They knew who was doing the killing. Who had killed April. And the picture began to come clear just for whom. Hauck showed Naomi something else, something that Marcus Hird in Switzerland had sent back today. Naomi's mood grew somber. This changed everything again. Hauck had never seen her look as nervous and unsure of what to do.

On the train, she and Hauck sat in two facing seats in the business car. They rode in silence for much of the way, stations flashing by. Newark. Metropark. Trenton. It was clear Naomi was gearing up for what she had to do. She joked fatalistically to him about some frozen lake up in northern Montana—how that might not even be an option by the end of the day. She took a call from Bruni, who now had Simons in hand. He arranged for them to be met by some of his colleagues when they arrived at Union Station in DC.

Sometimes you just step into something,

Hauck knew, watching her steeling herself for the task that had to be done. Something larger than yourself. Something that just needs to be seen through. It may not be what you set out for at the beginning. It's not exactly your plan. It's more like your fate—or where fate guides you. Those with the part of them inside that does not look away. Back down. You look around for someone else to carry the ball. To run with it.

And it's just you.

And it can cost you, Hauck knew, dearly. His whole career seemed to be a lesson in that. It had cost him a brother. If he had only looked away . . . It had cost him his friend and closest protégé on the job. It might now cost him Annie. *Why can't you love me like that?* Chasing the ghost of a dead friend.

He looked away and felt the train rattling on the tracks. *If only that's what it was . . .*

But you see it through. Certain of them were like that. You follow it all the way to the end. Regardless of who it swallows up or to what frozen lake it leads. When Naomi looked up and the two of them caught each other's eyes, it was as if they were both thinking the same thing. Both recognized the look.

They smiled.

"I need something to eat," he said. "Want anything?"

Naomi shook her head. "No, thanks."

He got up. "I'll be right back."

The train was shuttling swiftly between Philadelphia and Wilmington. Hauck headed back up the aisle. A group of four businesspeople were crowded around a table, laptops out. In the next row, a man in a military cap appeared to be dozing, his brim pulled down.

Hauck flung open the door and crossed into the next car.

He found a snack bar two cars ahead and ordered a roast beef sandwich and a coffee for himself, and in spite of what she'd said, a turkey sandwich and a bottle of water for Naomi. She probably hadn't had a bite to eat all day.

The clerk gave Hauck one of those cardboard trays. He made his way back up to his car, the motion of the train making it all hard to carry. He slid open the heavy outside door to his car, holding it open with his foot. Made his way back up the aisle. He saw Naomi still sitting at the far end of the car. A female college student had a *People* magazine on her lap. A black woman was knitting. The businesspeople were still recounting their meeting. He passed the guy dozing in the cap. He noticed the lettering in gold embroidery on the back, and a warning bell suddenly went off in him

101st Airborne.

Hauck glanced down, noticing the thick braid of hair knotted into a short ponytail that peeked through the back of the cap.

Everything stopped.

He immediately flashed to the photos Evan had snapped of the two men who had killed his family.

One had a short ponytail.

Some kind of tattoo on his neck.

His body suddenly tingling, he flashed to the photo he had seen today.

He started forward again, catching Naomi's eye. As he passed, the man in the military cap seemed to stir, shifting to the side. Hauck looked down with a quick glance. The man was wearing a gray T-shirt under a nylon jacket.

What he saw sent a tremor down his spine.

That same tattoo. On his neck.

It looked like a panther's claw.

CHAPTER EIGHTY-EIGHT

Hauck's body went rigid with determination.

It was him. O'Toole. It had to be. Even before Hauck sat back down his mind fast-forwarded through what he had to do. Anger roiled in him. It was a crowded car. The train still had an hour to go. There could be no mistake. Thibault. Al-Bashir. Hassani. Dead.

They were after them now.

There was no way they would make it to DC.

He sat back down, his stomach tensing, this time on the opposite side, next to

Naomi. His heart raced with the inevitability of two speeding trains about to collide. He put the tray between them. Naomi looked up, unsuspecting. She smiled, looking over what he had brought her. "Thanks."

Hauck looked back up the aisle. The man was solid, shoulders hunched, arms folded, hugging his chest. His face was hidden underneath the hat's brim.

Hauck wanted to leap up and kill him.

But he also knew O'Toole was aware of him too. The guy was a professional. Army trained. He clearly had no hesitation about what he had to do. He had killed a kid, for Christ's sake. Murdered an entire family.

Hauck knew the guy was measuring him too.

Hauck leaned close to Naomi and squeezed her knee, trying not to give a sign that anything was wrong. "You remember that nice couple who picked up our Saudi friend in London?" he whispered under his breath.

Naomi looked back. Seeing his steady gaze. Sensing something wrong.

She nodded slowly, her pupils widening, meeting his.

"I don't want you to show a reaction,"

Hauck said, tightening the pressure on her knee, "but those very same people are here for us now."

She blinked. Her gaze displayed the slightest tremor of fear. She leaned back and nodded, this time with a beat of alarm. "What are we going to do?"

Hauck glanced back toward at the man, who seemed to shift their way. "I don't know."

He felt underneath his jacket for his gun. He quietly unsnapped the holster. The car was crowded with unsuspecting people. Maybe the only thing to do was to seize the fact that he knew. Rush O'Toole. He had killed April, her family. His heart starting to throb, he had to hold himself back. His only ally was the element of surprise.

Suddenly the train began to slow. An announcement blasted through the tinny speakers. *"Wilmington. This is Wilmington, Delaware. Next stop, Baltimore . . ."*

The man in the army cap stirred, grasping his satchel. He looked up and made it appear as if he was getting ready to leave. Briefly, his gaze darted their way. Didn't make eye contact. Just made sure they were still there. He stood up. Departing passengers began to fill the aisles.

Suddenly it became clear. This was how O'Toole was going to do it. As he went by, exiting the train. Then he could bolt onto the platform.

"Wilmington. Wilmington Station . . . ," the call came through again.

Hauck tried not to show a reaction, but the sweat had built up under his shirt. Any way out of their seats was blocked now by the lineup of passengers. The man fiddled with his bag. Hauck saw him put something underneath his jacket. People left, carrying bags, suitcases.

They were blocked in.

He leaned close to Naomi and whispered with urgency, "Take out your gun. It's happening now."

Hidden by the departing passengers, Hauck reached under his jacket and took out his Sig. He transferred it to under his seat, hidden in the palm of his hand.

The train slowed. It entered the open station. Hauck kept his gaze riveted on O'Toole. The train came to a stop. The doors hissed open. People began to step off onto the platform.

O'Toole was about six passengers in front of them. Advancing. What if it wasn't him? What if he was someone else? He couldn't just start shooting. Four people between them now. Hauck saw him reach inside his jacket.

Three.

There was no more time.

O'Toole was turning toward them now. Hauck put his palm on Naomi's back and pushed her to the floor. *"Stay down!"*

He jumped up, leveling his Sig at the approaching assailant. *"O'Toole!"*

The killer looked at him, a glint of recognition in his eyes. He went for whatever he had under his jacket, then he ducked behind a passenger.

Hauck couldn't shoot. He shouted, *"Everyone get down!"*

There was a scream. A black woman directly in the line of Hauck's aim spotted his weapon. Then everything descended into chaos. The line of passengers shifted as if they were one, people crouching, diving into the rows, covering their heads.

O'Toole stared directly at him now. Hauck spotted the Glock 9 equipped with a silencer. O'Toole was startled by Hauck's sudden response. He grabbed one of the businesswomen in a gray suit and pulled her across his body. She was terrified, shrieking.

There was no way Hauck could shoot.

O'Toole didn't have the same qualms. He raised his Glock and squeezed off two rounds in Hauck's direction, bullets thudding into the seat cushions where Naomi had been sitting, his captive's jerking movements altering his aim.

Hauck ducked down.

Everyone was screaming in panic. Running for the exits.

O'Toole stepped backward, forcing the terrified woman with him, using her as a shield. He spit off two more muffled shots as Hauck dove out of the line of fire.

"Shut the fuck up!" he screamed, twisting her by the hair. There was a flash and another silenced round clanged off the luggage rack.

Everything was at close quarters and happening fast. Hauck knew that if O'Toole simply rushed forward using the woman as a screen, he wouldn't be able to fire back. He had nothing to protect them.

But instead, he went backward, firing as

he did. Two more bullets slammed into the wall of the train, one grazing Hauck's arm. It stung like fire.

He winced.

Naomi had made it up and had her gun leveled at O'Toole. The man kept the woman in front of him and began to back his way through the aisle to the rear of the car, trying to get to the far exit. He reeled off one more shot, and it ricocheted off the wall, hitting a bystander, who groaned. The man sat upright in his seat, his shoulder spewing blood.

Someone shouted, *"Oh, God!"*

Finally O'Toole threw the woman to the side and ran to the rear as people darted out of the way into the seats.

Hauck went after him.

Naomi pushed her way toward the front entrance, shouting, *"I'm a government agent!* Everyone out of the way. *Get down!"*

O'Toole had made his way to the back of the car, turning once to fire. Hauck ducked under a seat and drew a line on him. At that very moment a black train conductor rushed out of the next car, holding a radio, shouting, *"What the hell's going on?"*

Hauck stood up in horror and raised his gun. *"No!"*

O'Toole shot the man twice in the chest, the heavyset conductor dropping down to his knees, grasping a railing to hold himself up.

O'Toole ran out onto the platform.

Hauck pushed the few remaining people out of the aisle and rushed up to where the conductor was clinging to the railing. His large eyes glassed over. He was breathing heavily. A young Latino woman jumped out of a seat. "I'm a nurse."

"Call 911!" Hauck said. It didn't look as if the guy would make it. He had rolled onto his back. A bubble of blood came out with each labored breath. "Tell 'em there are two people down. Call for EMTs."

She nodded, grasping her cell phone.

He jumped out of the train onto the platform. Two bullets clanged off the side of the train, whizzing past his head. He saw O'Toole running down the platform at the end of the long track. Everyone on the platform had hit the deck.

He started after him, looking behind him for Naomi.

He saw her. She had her back pressed

against the side of the train, her gun at her side. She had a fixed, glassy look in her eyes and she seemed to stare right through him.

Then she glanced at her shoulder and muttered, *"Ty . . ."*

CHAPTER EIGHTY-NINE

Hauck froze, focused on Naomi, as O'Toole made his getaway.

"No, no, no, *no!*"

He rushed back to her. Naomi pulled herself a little unsteadily off the side of the train, the stunned look in her eyes trying to become a bit more firm. "O'Toole's escaping . . . We're not letting him get away, Ty. *C'mon, let's go!*"

Then her legs buckled again and she fell back against the side of the train.

Hauck looked at her, his heart exploding. "You're hit!"

Her left arm hung limp. There was a hole

in her suit jacket right below her collarbone. She shook her head, pulled herself off the train. "I'm not letting him get away . . ."

"No." Hauck restrained her by the other arm. *"You can't!"* Blood had started to seep out from her jacket. He wasn't sure how bad it was. She was showing a bit of disorientation. He spun and took a quick glance down the tracks and saw O'Toole heading for the end of the open platform. "You stay here. *Someone help her!"* he shouted. "She's a federal agent. You get the police to come after me. You hear what I'm saying, Naomi? Get them to come after me!"

"No." She grabbed her gun with both hands, her shoulder hanging loosely.

"You're staying, Naomi. Do you understand? Help her," he said to a man in a business suit exiting the train. "I'll be back. You wait for the EMTs. *Don't let her leave.*"

He didn't wait for her answer. He took off along the track after O'Toole. He was maybe fifty yards ahead and had made his way to the far end of the platform. Beyond the station it looked like just open terrain. As he ran, O'Toole loaded a new mag into his gun.

Hauck raised his Sig and squeezed off two rounds at the fleeing man. Way out of range. They both kicked harmlessly off the asphalt platform.

O'Toole got to the end, hurdled a metal railing, and jumped onto the southbound tracks.

Hauck headed after him. The man who had killed April. He wanted to grind him into pulp with his own hands. But O'Toole was younger, fit, and didn't have a leg that still carried metal from two gunshots from a little more than a year ago. Hauck followed him to the railing and hurtled over it himself, continuing on.

There was blood escaping from a wound on his own arm. A gash was visible under his torn jacket. Hauck didn't even feel it.

O'Toole still had about fifty yards on him.

There was a train at rest on the northbound tracks. It looked like an empty commuter train, maybe a local heading up from Philadelphia. Dense woods bordered the southbound tracks. O'Toole could maybe hide out in them for a while. But he could also be trapped with nowhere to go. Across the northbound side there was a wire fence that ran six feet high. On the other side was the train station's parking lot. If O'Toole could somehow get across, he could force his way into a car. That seemed to be his best way out. It appeared he was trying to find his way through the parked train. Or under it.

Hauck made up some ground behind him.

His heart raced tremulously about Naomi. He didn't know how bad her wound was. He hated to leave her there. But she was right—there was no way he could let this man get away. Not now.

This was the end of the line.

O'Toole turned back and fired off a couple shots at him, meant more to keep Hauck at bay than to stop him. At this distance, his silencer wasn't exactly helping his aim. Hauck knew that sooner or later the police had to arrive. All he had to do was keep O'Toole contained until they got here. Not let him escape. This had been his goal since the day he first heard April's name on the news. Thibault. Hassani. Serbia. London. That had only been his way of finding her killer.

That had been his vow.

Around a hundred yards ahead, Hauck

spotted a small trestle railway bridge span-
ning the four tracks. O'Toole seemed to be
heading directly for it. If he could make it
across the tracks he might manage to leap
the fence, jump into the lot, and force his
way into a car.

That was his best way out of here.

Hauck quickened his pace. As O'Toole
made it to the bridge, Hauck stopped, took
aim, and squeezed off two rounds at him.
The first kicked off the tracks, clanging into
the trestle. The second managed to find its
mark, striking him in the leg. He pulled up
with a hop, spun around, and fired three
wild shots back at Hauck, all dinging off
the side of the resting train.

Favoring his leg, O'Toole started to climb
the bridge. He made it up to the crossing
platform as Hauck, ducking out from behind the train, reached the stairs. He started
to go up himself, heart pounding, not knowing if O'Toole might suddenly appear above
him and fire down at him or lie in wait at the
top of the platform.

He glanced back toward the station.
Where the hell were the police?

In the distance, sirens began to wail.
Halfway up the metal steps Hauck spotted

flashing lights arriving at the station. He sent off three shots into the air to draw their attention. In the heat of it he no longer knew how many he had used. O'Toole was heading to the other side of the tracks. There wasn't time to wait for anyone to respond. Hauck hugged the railing, gun drawn, and started up the stairs.

O'Toole would have seen the same thing. Hauck searched for him through the trestles. No sight. Which didn't give him the best of feelings. As he cautiously made his way up to the platform, he positioned himself behind a metal stanchion. Three muffled shots came back at him, all clanging loudly off the iron rails. Hauck pinned himself against them.

The last shot felt like a flame against Hauck's gun hand.

The Sig flew out of his grasp.

It fell over the side of the railing onto the tracks. *He was unarmed*.

He now had about a second to make a decision, a decision that might mean his life: whether to jump and run for it. O'Toole was a trained shot, an ex-Ranger. It would leave Hauck in the open, even if he managed to make it to the gun. Or to stay. He heard a train's horn blare loudly in the distance. His eyes fixed on the gun on the tracks. He realized he had nowhere to go.

"Step out," O'Toole said to him.

Hauck remained glued against the stanchion. He caught a glimpse of the police back at the station starting to come his way.

"Step out here, *now*," he heard O'Toole say.

Hauck's only hope now seemed to be to stall for time.

Warily, he stepped up the last step to the platform and came out from behind the post.

O'Toole was standing there, teeth clenched, the damning tattoo peeking out from his jacket collar. Hauck had to hold himself back from charging at him like a bull and hurling both of them off the bridge.

"The police are here," Hauck said. "You're done. We know who it is you work for. Strike yourself a deal. Turn yourself in as a witness." He looked into the man's desperate, raw-boned face, glancing toward the station. "There's no gain in killing me."

"Other than that's what I was sent to do." The man's dark eyes carried a resignation Hauck had seen before. It was the narrowing realization that there was nothing left to lose. "And I don't let down."

To the north, Hauck heard the train horn again, this time getting closer. His gaze turned and he saw the first reflected light of an advancing train.

A gust kicked up and O'Toole's army cap blew off his head. He reached after it, but it fell beyond his grasp and went over the side. He smiled, sort of a futile, hopeless acknowledgment, and looked back at Hauck. "You know, I didn't set out for it to be like this."

"No one does."

The police were still a long way off on the other side of the tracks. O'Toole took a step back on the platform, his only chance.

He said, "I served my country." His gun was trained on Hauck's chest. "But you probably know that, don't you? I was a goddamn kid out of Oklahoma and they taught me how to use a gun and a knife. And I did it well. I don't back down."

Hauck met his eyes with equal intensity. "Nor do I."

"*Why?*" O'Toole winced from the wound in his leg. "What's *your* stake in this anyway? You're not even a cop anymore. The girl I know—but you, why do you even fucking care?"

"You killed someone . . ."

"I killed a lot of people." O'Toole chortled.

A siren blared from the parking lot as cop cars streamed in. Now O'Toole's only way out was to go through Hauck to the woods. "Sorry, man." He pointed the weapon at his chest. Hauck stiffened. "You're just one more."

He never heard a shot.

All he saw was O'Toole's legs begin to buckle and reach for his back.

The first shot slammed in between his shoulder blades, straightening him. The second hit him in the thigh, making him stagger backward. His foot caught only air and he slipped through an opening in the railing, lunged to right himself, his hand grasping the platform just as he was about to fall over the edge.

O'Toole's gun toppled over the side.

Hauck looked down. He saw Naomi, on the tracks, her arms still steady and extended, her gun raised.

He reached down for O'Toole.

"Lift me up," the man said. He was about to fall and was clinging to the railing.

The front lights of the oncoming train were approaching fast.

Hauck wrapped his hands around the man's wrists and pulled against his weight.

"Come on," O'Toole urged him. Hauck gazed into the struggling man's eyes.

And then he stopped.

O'Toole just seemed to hang like a sack of wheat, trying to climb Hauck's arm. His gaze flashed to the advancing train and he said, "I can bring people down. I know things you would want to know."

"I already know what you know," Hauck said. "You asked me why. And I said you killed someone . . ." He felt the rumble of the oncoming train. O'Toole's face started to grow panicked, and he grasped Hauck's arm more forcefully.

"I told you I killed a lot of people . . ."

"I heard you"—Hauck looked in his eyes—"but I only care about one."

He dangled O'Toole over the tracks as the trestles started to rattle. "You shot her in the closet, with her daughter, back in Connecticut . . ."

"I was paid to do that. To make it look like a break-in."

"Her name was April, you sonovabitch. And this is a promise I made to her."

O'Toole's face froze. His gaze shot to the train that was almost upon him. A sheen of understanding lit his eyes.

Hauck let him go.

He fell, a dead weight, bouncing onto the lead car of the train. There was a thud and the body simply fell off to the side and disappeared, dragged under the wheels as the Metroliner rumbled by.

Hauck watched, the bridge trestles shaking, and bowed his head. He didn't feel anger or satisfaction, just resolution. *It was a promise I made to her.* He heard the massive train's brakes hiss and watched it come to an abbreviated stop.

When he looked up again, Naomi was staring at him.

"I'm sorry," he said. Hauck stood with her off to the side while the EMTs lifted O'Toole's body. He pressed a damp cloth against the burn on his own arm. Naomi had her shoulder immobilized under her jacket in a makeshift splint, but she'd declined any further treatment. "I couldn't hold him," he said. "He slipped out of my grasp . . ."

"We could have used his testimony," Naomi said.

Hauck shrugged. "We don't need it."

"What was it he said to you up there?"

"That it wasn't always like this. That he served his country." Hauck picked up O'Toole's hat, from the 101st Airborne, from the track. "He asked why I was here. What was in all this for me."

"And what did you answer?" Naomi asked. She looked up at him in the same direct way she had after O'Toole had slipped to the tracks.

"That I was in it for a friend," Hauck said. He eyed her wound. "You ought to get that shoulder looked at. Take it from a pro."

She shrugged. "The bullet's gone clean through. Makes me seem tougher. Anyway, the day's not over. We still have some work left to do."

"Yeah, I guess we do." He grinned. "Any chance we can go the rest of the way by car?"

Naomi smiled, looking at him, and started to head back along the tracks in the direction of the station.

"Hey," Hauck called after her, "one more thing . . ."

Naomi turned, a hand over her eyes, squinting against the sun.

"I have a daughter." He tossed O'Toole's hat back on the tracks and caught up to her. "I bet right now she'd like to put her arms around you and thank you for a helluva shot. As would I."

Naomi smiled. She turned and headed back along the tracks. "Told you I knew how to use this thing."

CHAPTER NINETY

Only moments before, Thomas Keaton had stood behind the president on the White House lawn, outlining the details of the administration's aggressive plan to brace the deteriorating economy.

His government car had just dropped him off at the guarded gate off Fifteenth Street behind the Treasury building, and he hurried through the marble three-story lobby where Alexander Hamilton, Salmon Chase, and Henry Morgenthau had all walked, followed by Mitch Hastings, his chief counsel, a group of House members expecting him upstairs.

Naomi stepped up. "Secretary Keaton . . ."

The Treasury head appeared caught by surprise. His gaze flashed to her arm, loosely hanging in a sling under her suit jacket. She stood, looking up at him, with a quiet but resolute stare that seemed to disarm him. "*Agent Blum . . .* I heard you were . . ."

"Heard I was *what,* sir, *detained*?"

"I heard you were *injured,*" he said, showing surprise. "But I'm relieved to see you're okay. Come, walk me up to my office. I've just come from the president. I was told about Hassani. Dismal news . . . I'd like to hear your report."

"This is Ty Hauck," Naomi said. "I think you know his name."

From against the wall, Hauck, his sport jacket ripped at the arm, came up to them. He stared into the shifting eyes of the white-haired government man who had come from years on Wall Street, where he had had a distinguished and lucrative career.

"Mr. Hauck." Thomas Keaton extended his hand. "It's great to finally meet you. You know Mitch Hastings. I've heard we owe you quite a debt of gratitude for what you've already done on this matter." Hauck took his hand and stared into his eyes. The man seemed to flinch. "Walk with me. I'd like to hear what you both have to say."

"I'm sorry, sir," Naomi said to him. "I was hoping we might spare you that and have that conversation here."

The ruddy-complexioned, dark-suited Treasury man looked perplexed. *"Spare me?"* He glanced at Hastings.

"I'm afraid the secretary has an important meeting scheduled. There are House members who have carved out time from their schedules waiting for him there—"

"Which is why," Naomi said, cutting him off, "it might be better if you heard what we had to say down here."

An intransigence dug its way into Keaton's jaw. Clearly, he wasn't keen on being dictated to by an investigator. And one from his own staff. *"Alright . . ."* He stepped over to an isolated spot in the corner as people rushed by. "I'm listening, Agent Blum. Go on."

Naomi cleared her throat. "You said you heard that Mr. Hassani was killed? Before we were able to pick him up."

"I did. As I said, *tragic.* I also heard there was a lead on his killer."

"There is a lead," Naomi said. "But I don't know if it would trouble you or not to know he's dead too."

"Trouble me . . ." The treasury secretary narrowed his eyes sharply, the steely gaze of rank bearing down on her.

"It always bothered me," Naomi said, "how Hassani always seemed to have a step on us. When it came to apprehending Thibault in Serbia. What we had learned about his past, things no one else could know. What happened in London . . . I shared my feeling that there was no one I felt I could trust. I came to you directly with what I knew." She stared solidly into her boss's eyes. "You must've thought I was one helluva fool, Mr. Secretary. And maybe I was."

"Agent Blum . . ." Keaton was growing impatient. "I'm not sure where you're going with all this, but I remind you, despite all your good efforts, the arc of where your career is headed is still very much in play here."

"My career . . ." Naomi nodded thoughtfully. "My career isn't where I would be

thinking right now, sir. I was thinking more of yours. Al-Bashir told us it was so much larger than terrorism—larger than anything I could imagine. And it took me a while to put it all together. To even have the will to think it . . ."

"I'm very interested to hear where your mind is going," Keaton said with a glance at Hastings, his dismissive tone beating down on her.

She said, "The past two presidential administrations have stripped most regulatory control out of the system. Am I right? Banks acting as investment houses, dealing in complex financial products even an MBA wouldn't understand. Leveraged with debt at forty to one. The rating agencies all looking the other way . . . We had the whole teetering house of cards, the worldwide economy, all holding together just as long as the system continued to grow. As long as one last house could be sold, one last mortgage approved, right?"

The secretary looked at her.

"And then it didn't," Naomi said.

"I'm not sure I need the lesson in current events, Agent Blum." Keaton glanced at his watch. "Mitch, maybe you could—"

"Stay," Naomi said, looking at Hastings. "I think you'll find this interesting too. Suddenly China stopped rushing in to buy up our debt. Russia issued half a trillion dollars of notes built on future petro-rubles and the price of oil halved. The housing market dropped off a cliff. All you had to do was take a step back and see it—a train wreck about to take place. The real question wasn't whether you could prevent it. It was *who*, in the end, would be saved? Separating the winners from the losers. Sort of a Darwinian thing, no? Except it wasn't. You just rigged the deck.

"You put together the largest trove of stopgap funding the world had ever seen— almost a trillion dollars—and sold it as a bailout. A giant injection of liquidity to keep the economy in gear. When all it did was prop up the banks. Some were rescued; some were left to be swallowed up by the tsunami. Who decided? The ones that made the wrong bet—Wertheimer, Beeston, Lehman—they're gone. While others got the brass ring. All you had to do was tip the balance just a little bit, if you could see it from high enough. To be one of the winners. Am I making any sense, sir?"

"And who exactly would those *winners* be, Agent Blum," the treasury secretary huffed at her, "as seen from your lofty heights?"

Naomi realized the next years of her life would be dictated by what she was about to say. "Why don't we start with the Gstaad Gang? Or, even better, sir, Reynolds Reid."

The space around them in the vast lobby became suddenly quiet. Her voice echoed off the marble walls.

"I saw the names." Naomi stared into his eyes. "Stephen Cain. Vladimir Tursanov. Al-Bashir. Hassani. *Simons.* The head of the largest investment bank in the world. All of them who were there. I suddenly realized they all had one thing in common. How could I have missed it? One thing: they were *all* Reynolds Reid."

Thomas Keaton blinked.

"Isn't that right, sir? All trained, grew rich, cut their teeth, at Reynolds Reid. And then it hit me." She shook her head. "How could I have been so blind? It hit me that *you* should know that better than anyone, sir.

"Because *you* were Reynolds Reid too. You were a managing director there. You knew all these people. Not to mention Kessler of the New York Fed, and Carl McKnight, in charge of dispersing the bank relief fund . . . All of you were Reynolds Reid."

Keaton's jaw went slack and his eyes reflected the worry of someone about to take a great fall.

"We *are* the government, isn't that right, sir? We *are* the Fed. That old bromide about GM . . . Now it's 'What's good for Wall Street is good for government.' Because you're all embedded. You're everywhere. *We* are the reason some banks are saved and others are left to fail. Maybe you weren't all involved, but it's clear: a nod from you, and no one was standing in the way."

"It's no crime, Agent Blum"—the treasury secretary's gaze became granite—"that the firm has a long-standing tradition of service."

"*Service?* It's not service, Mr. Secretary. It's the gradual takeover of the government by a bunch of insiders whose power and money are used to buy elections, weaken regulations, so their firms can one day profit at the expense of all these blind, unwitting shareholders, who we used to call simply taxpayers. It's an oligarchy. Same as any little banana republic. Except just an extra couple of zeros at the end.

"The Gstaad Gang . . ." Naomi smiled. "We checked the hotel records. We found the names. Every one of them. Al-Bashir. Tursanov. Hassani. *Simons.* All but one, sir . . . Maybe that's because he didn't stay at any of the hotels. Maybe because he didn't even remain in town overnight . . ."

"And who was that?" Thomas Keaton glared, his gaze that of a cat about to spring.

"Why, *you,* Mr. Secretary." Naomi looked back at him. "You were the last one who was there."

She glanced toward Hauck, and he finally opened the envelope he'd been holding under his arm.

In it were the security photos Marcus Hird had e-mailed to him yesterday. Photos taken at the base of the Gstaad main ski lift. Showing all the members of the group. Arriving separately. Shipman. Cain. Tursanov. Simons. Al-Bashir and Hassani. All heading up the lift to the restaurant, where no one would ever spot them. The time and date clearly displayed at the bottom. *June*

26. Last year. Almost eight months before
the call from Hassani to al-Bashir that had
started it all. Before Marc and April Glassman were killed. Before the world began
to fall apart.

Hauck laid a final photo on the top of the
pile.

The treasury secretary's head flinched.

"*You,* Secretary Keaton." The fissure in
Keaton's forty-year career cracked open
in his gaze, the practiced solidity of his im-
penetrable veneer breaking. "*You* were the
one who set it all in motion. The bank rescue plan. That's exactly what it was meant
to do. Insure the survivors, so they could
pick over the spoils. You had the power—"

"*Power.*" Keaton's voice echoed suddenly across the lobby. "What would you
possibly know about power, Agent Blum,
in your little office where everything has to
fit into your black and white vision of the
world? Power was once the by-product of
violence. Coups, militias. Oily little bribes.
Secret envelopes stuffed with hundred-
dollar bills, offshore accounts . . .

"But now power, *real* power, Agent
Blum"—Keaton's eyes bore down on her—
"lies in policy. In recognizing that whatever

keeps the system afloat is what's good for everybody. If Wall Street's interests fail, we all fail! Do you understand? That's what we do, Agent Blum—Reynolds Reid. We keep the machine going. Regulators, academics, legislation, they're just the buildup in the cogs that slows it down. Someone had to keep it going. Someone has to manage the risk. It was out of control. It would have broken for all of us. Just simply think of it as maintenance, Agent Blum, if that concept works. For a while, it just had to be shut down."

"Four innocent people are dead," Hauck said, staring into his eyes. "Four others are missing. Kids. Not to mention millions who have seen their savings collapse or lost their jobs."

"We saved the world," the treasury secretary said, offering no apology. "We kept it from collapsing. I had nothing to do with those murders. This O'Toole person, or whoever did those terrible things, I've never even met him or spoken with him."

"You're right, you haven't." Hauck nodded, agreeing. His gaze shifted to Hastings. "But your chief counsel has."

Mitch Hastings's eyes grew wide.

"When you worked at the Council of the Economic Forum, before Treasury. Jack O'Toole was assigned to your security detail while in Iraq. Not once but twice. Isn't that right, Mr. Hastings?"

The chief counsel loudly cleared his throat, adjusting his wire-rim frames. "I can't recall . . ."

"Do you think when we requisition your cell phone records, and they show you have made calls into the same areas where we know O'Toole to have been, you'll be able to recall?" Hauck removed something from his pocket. O'Toole's phone. "Maybe to *this* cell phone. Is there any chance the record of calls at the Waldorf, where Hassani was killed today, will show one from a location that you can be traced back to?

"Don't be so surprised," Hauck said to Keaton. "You may have only tipped your pal Hassani off about whatever Agent Blum here brought to you, but your loyal counsel here, Mr. Hastings, he's got real blood on his hands."

Keaton took his arm. "Don't say a word, Mitch. I have forty years in public and private service, Agent Blum. Whether I was in Gstaad or not, whether Mitch may have been overzealous on some matters in protecting some of our interests, we'll see where all that goes. But for you, I assure you, this investigation is through."

"That may be true, sir," Naomi said. "But I'm afraid there's another one just beginning."

Three men in tan and brown suits came up from behind them in the lobby. Part of Anthony Bruni's financial terrorism team.

"Sir, my name is Ralph Wells. I'm a senior regional director of the FBI, and I have here, pending notification of the president of the United States, a court order to search your personal records, computers, and cell phone for information related to a criminal conspiracy of investment bankers to defraud the United States government."

"What?" The treasury secretary became apoplectic. He grabbed the document, his jaw going slack. He took a step back and sank against the marble wall.

"And in terms of *this* investigation, sir," Naomi said, staring at him, "it's also possible Peter Simons might have some interesting things to add about you too."

Hauck's eyes met hers. There was no longer determination on Naomi's face but a sheen of triumph in her eyes. The face of al-Bashir's son reflected there. The triumph that comes after a bloody battle. Where it's hard to tell who has won and who has lost.

Except this time they both knew.

PART VI

CHAPTER NINETY-ONE

The resignations of Thomas Keaton and his chief counsel sent shock waves around the world. It was reported they were being held under house arrest, pending a Justice Department investigation into their actions in a conspiracy to defraud the financial markets in which eleven people, including some important figures in the world of finance, had died or were missing.

In New York, the related arrest of Peter Simons, Stephen Cain, and Marshall Shipman on charges of fraud and conspiracy to defraud only made the rumors wilder. The markets plunged 20 percent the next day and were held back from a total free fall only when the Fed announced at midday that it was pumping half a trillion dollars of new liquidity into the ailing economy.

Still, parts of the story were leaking out. Murdered Wall Street traders. An enigmatic Serbian playboy whose past was tied to a bloody massacre in the Bosnian War. A shadowy Middle Eastern financier murdered in his suite at the Waldorf. A wild shoot-out on an Amtrak train. The involvement of the CEO of one of the largest firms on Wall Street, leading all the way to the treasury secretary of the United States.

The president promised a swift and thorough investigation. "The financial markets must be above suspicion," he declared from the White House lawn. "Its lifeblood is confidence, and confidence will be restored."

In the meantime, the Department of the Treasury was to be run by Allen Schaper, currently head of the SEC—a corporate lawyer, an economist, a friend of the president.

And himself a former banker at Reynolds Reid.

Eleven people were either dead or pre-

sumed dead. Three Wall Street investment banks had gone under, their assets
absorbed. Across the globe, millions of
people had lost jobs, countless pensions
destroyed, life savings halved. Millions of
homes foreclosed on, industries set in crisis, bailed out; the deficit soared. On
CNBC, Tim Schegel, the noted financial
reporter, remarked, "Whatever their crimes,
those participants in what is now known as
the Gstaad Gang only hastened, in their
activities, what was sure to come." The es-
timated loss in investor capital related to
the economic meltdown was said to be
over four trillion dollars.

Across the pond, in London, a related
investigation into the unsolved disappear-
ance of Saudi national Mashhur al-Bashir
and his family was under way.

Their bodies would never be discovered.

Back in DC, Hauck and Naomi gave two
days of testimony to officials at the Justice
Department.

By Friday, Hauck was back at his desk.

Tom Foley was the first one there to con-
gratulate him. Hauck thought it the better

part of valor not to divulge how sure he was, until right up to the end, that his boss was the intermediary to Red O'Toole. Since word had come out, the phones at Talon were ringing off the hook. A new era of compliance and security and regulation was being promised and the business was coming to them. Foley promised that the firm would indeed be showing its appreciation, reflected in his bonus at year end. He came by later to take Hauck out for drinks.

But by that time Hauck had already gone.

He took the drive out to Dublin Hill Road. To Merrill Simons's house. At this point it no longer mattered whether Foley gave the okay.

She deserved to hear it firsthand. Dani's fate. Who he was. What he had been involved in. How her instincts had been right. And how Peter had been involved.

She was in the garden in a pair of white capris and a wide hat, planting begonias. She sat with Hauck on a chaise under an awning and stayed silent for a while after he told her, brooding on the story that might never fully be revealed.

"Two real bastards," she finally said,

shaking her head with a bit of a derisive laugh. "I surely can pick 'em, can't I?"

Then it seemed to overwhelm her and she took her sunglasses off and wiped away a tear.

"Next time," Hauck said, shrugging, "maybe you should give Match.com a try." Merrill laughed. He squeezed her arm.

"Thank you for what you did. I think I may owe your firm some money."

"Why don't we just call it a wash?" He winked and got up. "Let's just see if we can get Uncle Sam to cover the bill."

CHAPTER NINETY-TWO

A few days later

He sat in the BMW looking out at the pleas-ant white ranch on the quiet cul-de-sac in Darien.

It was the kind of tree-lined residential street any kid would be happy to grow up on. SUVs, on their way to baseball prac-tice and dance rehearsals, backed out of the driveways. A yellow school bus pulled up at the corner and several kids jumped off with one or two friendly shoves and high fives, then scattered on their way. A UPS truck parked at the curb and the driver waved to the homeowner as he de-livered his package.

A kid would be lucky, Hauck thought as he focused on the clean white house, a plastic soccer goal set up on the lawn, *to grow up in such a place.*

A few minutes passed and a silver Volvo wagon came down the block. It made a sweeping turn into the driveway Hauck had pulled up across from. The white electric garage door went up. The wagon parked outside. A gangly black Labradoodle jumped out and happily pranced around the lawn, followed by a boy, around eight, his mop of sandy hair reminding Hauck so much of his mom's. An oversize A-Rod jersey on. He had a knapsack slung over his shoulder and before he ran inside after the dog, he gave a soccer ball on the lawn a pretty fair wallop and sent it flying over the plastic goal, over the chain-link fence into the neighboring yard.

The boy put his hands to his face like he'd screwed up, but the older man, Marc's father, merely came up and put his arm around his grandson and drew him to his chest.

"You see that shot, Grandpa?"

"Seemed like a goal to me." His

grandfather made a face as if impressed. "That's how I used to kick 'em back in the day." He mussed the kid's hair. "Around the Civil War."

The kid smiled guiltily. "Sorry."

Watching from his car, Hauck felt his eyes well up with tears. The older man said to the boy, "You go inside. You've got homework to do. I'll go over to the Kendells' and retrieve it."

The boy yelled, "Thanks, Grandpa," and ran into the garage.

Hauck stepped out of the car. The older man came down the driveway toward him. Hauck was about to go up to him. He had practiced in his mind what he would say, how he would handle it. But he felt something, a sudden caution, rooting his feet. A memory rushed into his mind and it made him stop.

April took him outside the dry cleaner's to the street. "There's someone I want you to meet . . ."

She took him over to the Mercedes, the soft freckles on her cheeks seeming to beam, and looked at the boy sitting in the rear car seat.

"His name is Evan . . . Evan Ty Glassman."

Hauck stared at the child and before he could wave hi, before he could even speak, he knew. He knew what it was April had brought him out to see and with a glisten in her eye, what she was trying to say. A wave of emotion hit him head-on.

"He's your gift to me, Ty . . . To all of us. Something I can never repay."

"You don't have to repay me for anything, April . . ."

He looked at her. Then back to the boy. There were parts of who he was inside he felt he owed to her. There were parts of her he felt as close to, even after all these years, as if they were part of his own skin.

"The only reason we have him is because of you. Because of what you did. Every once in a while I just look at him and it takes me back. We both made it through, didn't we?"

He looked at her, his heart expansive. "Yeah, we did."

She opened the door and the four-year-old finally looked up. "Hi, Mommy."

"Evan, I want you to meet a friend of mine. Lieutenant Hauck. He's a policeman here in town. The top cop, I hear."

"In my own mind, at least," Hauck said, chuckling. He winked at the young boy. "Hey, guy."

Evan smiled.

He saw what he'd once found so special about his mother in the softness of Evan's green eyes and his light brown hair.

"He's beautiful," Hauck said. "Thank you."

"No, thank you, Ty." Her eyes grew shiny. "I don't know what to say . . ."

He put his hand on April's cheek and let it rest, their eyes meeting, really meeting, for the first time in years. Since she had turned and saw him across from her in her hospital bed. A moment that seemed so far away now. "You promise me, Ty, that you'll keep an eye on him. If anything ever happens to me."

Proud—proud of her as well—he nodded. "Of course. I promise."

I'll do whatever it takes.

* * *

Marc's dad came toward him as he wound around the fence to retrieve the ball. Maybe he saw Hauck staring. Maybe he noticed the look that was on his face, that made him appear lost.

"Looking for someone?" the older man came up and said.

I did it for him, April. For the boy. How much Hauck wanted to tell him. How much he felt in his heart like he was about to burst. But not now. One day he would find a way in. He'd offer to take him to a game, introduce himself as an old friend of his mom's. Tell him a story. But not now. He fought back tears.

I did it for him, April.

"No, not lost." Hauck smiled. "Just passing through."

Two weeks later

Agent Blum . . . Mr. Hauck . . ."

The heavyset government lawyer sat across from Naomi and him in his law offices on K Street in Washington, DC.

"As you know," he said as he turned on a small digital recorder, "we're here as part of the special prosecutor's charge on this case to take additional depositions from you both on the matter we will call, for now, *The United States Government versus the Gstaad Gang.* Specifically referring to Messrs. Keaton, Hastings, and Simons, and any actions they might have participated in against the United States . . ."

Hauck glanced over at Naomi. She was dressed in a slim black pantsuit, a light blue top, a U.S. flag pinned on her lapel. Her hair was down to her shoulders. Her arm was out of the sling. He hadn't seen her since their separate depositions right after Keaton's arrest.

Despite the official proceedings, he couldn't help but admire her. She looked great.

Naomi nodded smartly to the lawyer but shot a glance toward Hauck.

He caught her smile.

"This office will be interested in any and all matters related to the events, no matter how small or how seemingly unimportant. I guess we might as well start at the beginning." The lawyer turned to Hauck, pushing the microphone his way. "I think it was this past March sixth when you first became involved in this case?"

Hauck looked back at him and shrugged. "This'll take a bit of time."

"We have as long as it takes, Mr. Hauck," the lawyer said. "I hope you don't have anything more pressing . . ."

"No, nothing more pressing."

"You, Agent Blum?'

"No, nothing," she replied, that familiar twinkle in her eye.

Hauck winked at her and started in. "Okay, then, here goes . . ."

He took the lawyer through the first time he heard of April Glassman's death. That morning with Annie. Leaving a few choice details out. His first efforts to follow it up, then Merrill Simons, Thibault. Donovan. Even Campbell, the New York cop. After a couple of hours they were only up to Naomi's arrival on the scene.

At noon, the lawyer looked at his watch and asked if they'd like to break for lunch.

That left Hauck and Naomi alone for the first time.

"So how goes it?" he asked. They packed up their cases, got up, paused at the conference room door.

"*Swamped.* Totally swamped. I got a promotion. My boss is moving on. I've been put in charge of my department now."

"Mazel tov!" he said. He held the door for her. "Deserved."

"Maybe you'll want a job yourself one day." She smiled. "You've shown a real knack for this kind of work. I happen to have a nice basement office for you. The heat knocks a bit, and I'm afraid there's no view. If you're interested, I can see what I can do."

"Thanks," Hauck said, grinning, "but I've already done my time with the government. Anyway, I'm gonna stick it out for a while at Talon. See what comes up . . . By the way, you're looking great," he said, totally out of the blue.

"Thanks." She blushed and put on her sunglasses. "Amazing what not getting shot at can do for you."

"The arm's doing well?"

"Well enough," Naomi said. "Yours?"

He raised his elbow. "Good as new."

They headed out to the elevator bank. He pressed the button. "So you want to get some lunch?" he asked. "We have an hour."

"Do you think that's entirely professional? I mean, this is supposed to only be about what happened on the case."

Hauck couldn't take his eyes off her. "To me this is one hundred percent about what happened on the case."

The elevator came. She stepped inside. "Good. I know a fish place we can walk to from here."

He followed her in and pressed the button for the lobby. Leaned with his back against the railing. It was a small office building, and they were alone.

She said, "You know, much of this may never come to light. The government wants a thorough job. But they also want to move forward, I'm told . . . Some things might never come out."

Hauck shrugged. "That's okay. My résumé's already long enough."

Naomi smiled. "Mine too."

Suddenly the elevator jerked and came to an abrupt stop. Between floors. The lights flickered out.

Naomi said, *"Oh, shit."*

"Generator must be down," Hauck said. He pushed the buttons for several floors, but nothing happened. "Hope you're not the type who gets all nervous in the dark."

She shot back, "I'm the one who had to hide in Thibault's closet, remember? You're the one who couldn't even follow the guy in a car. Anyway, have you ever known me to get flustered?"

He was about to chuckle, *Yeah, I can think of just a couple of times,* but Naomi pushed past him and started pressing

buttons at random. *"Hello! Hello . . ."* One
was the red alarm. Seconds later, someone from the building came on. "The
generator's down," the scratchy voice
replied. "There's a camera on the console.
You guys okay in there?"

Hauck felt Naomi next to him. "Yeah,
we're okay."

"This might take a few minutes. Fifteen, maybe more . . . We'll try to get the
auxiliary power back up. Make yourself
at home."

"Fifteen minutes?" Naomi groaned.

"Or more," Hauck said.

She sighed. "That's half our break."

"Damn." Hauck called back to the voice,
"Don't hurry."

She looked at him.

"You have a great tattoo on your back,"
he said. "I'd like to see it again some time."

"Some time . . . ?" Even in the dark
Naomi saw where he was heading. She
shook her head. "No chance."

"Fifteen minutes, it's an eternity . . ."

"Zero," she said again, the tiniest crack
in her defiance. "You're wasting your time."

He could feel the flutter of her heart
going crazy against him. The scent of her

perfume was driving him wild. He lifted her sunglasses.

"I have a better one on my butt," she said. "The opening of Glass's 'Music in the Shape of a Square' . . . Very seminal piece."

A crackle came out of the speaker, something sharp and barely decipherable. Hauck took off his jacket and draped it over a button, covering the lens.

"Now, this is totally unprofessional," Naomi said. Actually it was more of a sigh. "I'm head of the department now."

He pulled her close to him. Even in the dark he saw the smile light up her eyes.

"So write me up, Agent Blum," Hauck replied.

Acknowledgments

A warm thanks to so many people who played a hand in the writing of this book.

To Roy and Robin Grossman for the discussion of things financial and myriad other aspects of the story and book as well. To Janusz Kryszynski, head of the U.N.-Kosovo Peace Mission, Tasha Alexander, Nicholas Gross, and Andrew Peterson for assistance on some of the many diverse settings and other details that bring a book to life.

To Mark Schwarzman, Liz Scoponich,

and Brooke Martinez, and other early readers of the draft. I appreciate you all!

Several books and articles also figured into the formation of the story and the background of the financial meltdown. *House of Cards* by William D. Cohan, "The Quiet Coup" by Simon Johnson in the *Atlantic Monthly,* "The Big Takeover" by Matt Taibi in *Rolling Stone,* "The Omen" by James B. Stewart in *The New Yorker, The End* by Michael Lewis, "The Worst Is Not Behind Us" by Nouriel Roubni in *Forbes,* as well as various postings by Frank Rich and Naomi Klein. And *Big Boy Rules* by Steve Farineau on the wild life of security personnel stationed in Iraq.

My usual thanks to David Highfill, Liate Stehlik, Lynn Grady, Pam Jaffee, Gabe Robinson, and my whole team at William Morrow, and that goes all the way to the top! Very few writers ever get to feel the belief and partnership you've given me.

And to Simon Lipskar of Writers House, a partner in the book in every way.

And of course, to my wife, Lynn, whose healing touch always keeps me whole, and my three kids, all making their way successfully in life and of whom I am very proud.

And, oh yeah, my mom, Leslie Pomerantz, my biggest fan, who never thinks I mention that enough. *See!*